THE

BELIEF

IN

Angels

THE
BELIEF
IN
Angels

J. DYLAN YATES

SheWritesPress

Published 2014
Printed in the United States of America
ISBN: 978-1-938314-64-3
Library of Congress Control Number: 2013957198

For information, address:
She Writes Press
1563 Solano Ave #546
Berkeley, CA 94707

This book is dedicated to my grandparents.

All of them, whoever they are.

"When I am dead, and over me bright April
Shakes out her rain drenched hair . . ."

—*Sara Teasdale*

"Fiction reveals truth that reality obscures."

—*Ralph Waldo Emerson*

"Love alone is capable of uniting living beings in such a way as
to complete and fulfill them, for it alone takes them
and joins them by what is deepest in themselves."

—*Teilhard de Chardin*

"Last night I dreamt Moses and I were rowing underwater.
We could breathe and talk to one another.
We rowed past schools of fish
and sea anemones and Moses named them for me."

—*Jules Finn*

Author's Note

THIS STORY IS ABOUT surviving truth. It's about surviving our connection to truth. Truth is so much stranger than fiction that, for it to be believed, you sometimes have to tell the truth selectively. Truth is gray, and there are two hundred and fifty-six shades of gray, although the human eye can only detect thirty-two.

Also, truth has a curve—a bell curve. Somewhere along that curve is my truth, and somewhere else along that curve is another's. The truth does bend. This makes truth frightening.

And so it is that we live in a curved world and struggle to get to one point of truth, which is really nothing but a personal approximation.

Consider the theory of relativity. The shortest distance between two points in a curved world is a curve. We are all curving toward one another to find our truths together—into infinity. It is in this way that our search for truth drives our connections and, ultimately, our survival.

This story has several versions of endings. There are as many as there are dreams and nightmares in the universe. Each version depends on where along the bend of truth each of us is. All we can see is our own truth and maybe a bit further ahead and a bit further behind. The past that sits behind the bend is truth, although it's not within our sight lines anymore. That is belief.

Belief has substance and matter. It has to, or the entire curve would disintegrate.

Physics proves that the part ahead, the part of the truth that you can't see, doesn't end with one truth. We curve truth toward another point. That is hope.

Maybe we all live in fractured prisms like kaleidoscopes, in encased and private worlds, yearning for light but tumbling in shadows. When we hold our worlds to the light and turn them, one truth is revealed. Turn it again, and the first disappears but another manifests.

Ultimately we connect and survive, even in death.

We do this consciously and unconsciously.

We do this infinitely and unbound.

It is in this way that truth sets us free.

—San Diego, California, November 2013

Part 1 | Unraveling

One

WITHENSEA, MASSACHUSETTS

SOMETIMES IN ORDER to tell a story well, so it's truly understood, you have to tell it out of order. My story tells like this. It unravels . . . and ravels up again.

My name is Julianne, but everybody calls me Jules. I was named after my Great-Uncle Jules on my father's side. That's what my father, Howard, told me. My mother, Wendy, told me I'm named after a dead racehorse trainer.

It's hard to know what to believe.

For now, I live here in Withensea, a seacoast town north of Cape Cod, an island that thrives on summer tourism. In two weeks I will leave for college and never come back.

Many people I went to school with will stay, however. A kind of Withensea tradition. They'll move down the road with their high school sweethearts, who'll become their spouses, and settle close to the homes they were raised in.

Sometimes a place can be as much a part of you as the people you grew up with. I won't miss most of the people here, but I'll miss this place. The ocean, for me, holds the power to turn a moment mystical. Accompanying my memories of childhood there are always ocean sounds—sometimes faint, sometimes louder, the waves crashing and beating their own score. When I picture the breathtaking beauty of our cliff, the ocean, it almost masks the memories of the things that were not picturesque. I've spent eighteen years soaking up every beautiful part of Withensea, hoping to crowd out the memories of the painful parts of my life—of guns, of violence, and of loss. A kind of glass-housed chaos, tolerated by the community in order to feed the starving brains bred in small towns.

My life, so far, has also been an existence filled with secrets. Two kinds of secrets. First: the kind that need lies to keep them hidden. Second: the kind our brains create to cope with sorrow.

Still, perspective offers me solace enough to not measure my own sorrow against another. What I understand now about survival is that something in you dies. You don't become a survivor intact. Survival's cost is always loss. This is my mourning book.

What follows is a collection of memories I've saved. I've learned memories are lost more often than objects. I will keep whole parts intact in my telling, where I feel it's important. In a way, I think it will keep me intact to tell the truth of it this way. It's my evidence—a way of documenting to keep the truth in my sight line. There are parts of my life I've been absent from. These I will tell from where I am now along the bend of truth. I will call these parts belief.

It's all left me with this weird love for the moments after something good happens. I call it *delayed joy*. I hear an achingly beautiful song, and when it's over I enjoy the immediate moment, the quiet, more than I did the sounds of the song playing. I taste a buttery lick of Butter Crunch ice cream, and after the flavor is gone I savor the loss of the deliciousness in my mouth.

It's like I'm wired backwards inside my head.

—

Withensea harbors a scrabble of townies who live in salt-beaten homes scattered among swanky summer estates. Winters on this island are brutal to homes, cars, skin—anything exposed to the elements. But in the spring, after the last of the gray-brown clumps of snow have melted, and before the tourists hit town, everything enjoys a fresh coat of paint and not much more. Rather than shoulder the emotional and physical cost and energy of upkeep, all things considered non-essential are left to deteriorate or grow wild. Deferred maintenance is a practice applied to most everything in the town, including the people.

My brothers, David and Moses, and I are kind of like the town. We started out sturdy, with a semblance of familial structure to support us and a new coat every September when we started school. But, eventually, with neglect, we were left as straggly as those other non-essential elements.

In the long run, this may turn out to have been a blessing.

From the turn of the century until about twenty years ago, Withensea was gorgeous. It used to be a summer vacation destination for Rose Kennedy's family. But the Kennedy family seems to have forgotten about their ancestral home, which sits, in its dilapidated glory, across from a seawall by the ocean, close to where I live.

Townies call the people who come to live in the estates along the beach "*the summer people*" and have a general disdain for those who can't or don't have to brave the winter by our ocean. The ones who can, the ones who stay, manage to eke out a living working a year-round business, make their money off summer tourists, or travel inland toward Boston—sometimes by ferry—to find work.

Many of them take a nine-month detour to the bottom of a bottle. Alcoholism in this mostly Irish/Italian Catholic town is more a winter industry than an embarrassment.

When I was six, my father— a short, Irish, orange-haired, pink, and doughy-faced man—owned a bar called the Little Corporal. It did a booming business in the summer months, and the winter industry provided enough support to warrant staying open year-round.

From outside, in the summer months, the Little Corporal's vivid green doors separated long, tall panels of clear glass windows through which you could see several pool tables. The glass panels continued on the south side of the building, turning two sides of the bar into a pool table terrarium. The tables floated, lily pad-green felted over a gray concrete pond. In winter, all the windows were covered in cheap, shamrock green-painted plywood to protect the glass.

The building squatted at the intersection of a small interstate highway and the boulevard that flows into Withensea's one main avenue. The boulevard flows in the other direction onto a land bridge that grips it to the mainland, tight as a choke hold. This intersection is the only way to enter or exit Withensea without a boat. All the cars slow to a crawl to navigate the sharply curved, signage-laden rotary, which spits them out again in either direction, going in or coming out.

In the summertime, pedestrians paraded from the surrounding parking lots down the wide sidewalk with their whiny, strollered babies and cotton-candied children, headed for the public beaches or Aragon, the amusement park anchoring the southern tip of the town. The day trippers and the townies who worked the other bars, restaurants, and amusement park arcades, all pushed in or passed by the wide doors and terrarium windows of the Little Corporal.

In the winter, people parked their cars right on the snowy sidewalks that wound around the Little Corporal to avoid the icy winds that whipped up over the seawall and across the avenue.

Inside the bar, a long expanse of intricately carved dark oak ran the length of the back of the room; an ornate gold-leaf mirror hung on the wall behind it. Above the mirror, a late-eighteenth-century, crudely-carved, wooden ship figure-head thrust herself from the wall, her peacock-blue robe draped under the curve of her bare breasts. Serene and anachronistic in the space, she gazed with detachment out beyond the walls of the bar, beyond the cars, beyond the imprisoned stroller babies and the laddered heights of the roller coaster to the sea.

To the landlocked fishermen, the career drunks in their thiamine-deficient stupors, solitary and stranded on the stools at closing, she was a familiar meditation. For me, she served as promise of another, better, life out there, beyond Withensea. A beginning to a life that had, thus far, been mostly about endings.

Two

THE LITTLE CORPORAL

"I'M PLAYING THE winner!" I shout to my brothers over the song on the old jukebox.

It's "Wild Thing," and David has pitched ten nickels in the old jukebox to play it over and over. Every time it gets to the part where they sing "groovy," he yells it out and wiggles his butt. They're ignoring me. David's got Moses doing it now, too.

While my father and Grandfather Samuel have an *important* talk in the office behind the bar, I sit on a barstool in the Little Corporal drinking a Shirley Temple I made. It's mixed the same way I always do it, with ginger ale, orange juice, a bit of grenadine, and four maraschino cherries. I know tons of drinks by heart, and I can make any drink out of the *mixerology* book behind the bar. My father showed me. I mix Rob Roys for my brothers while they play pool.

It's eight in the morning on a Saturday, and school starts in a week. It's one of the last big weekends of the season. Early this morning, my father packed us in the car.

Last night my father gave us all horsey rides to bed and read us fairy tales, but afterwards he and my mother screamed at each other again.

"Crooks go to jail!" I heard my mother scream.

"Idiots go to jail!" my father shouted back, and my mother agreed. But he got even angrier when she did.

"Don't you lay a hand on me, you fucking coward. You fucking bully."

I got scared the police might come again. When they fight like that, my stomach hurts.

The wind came out, so I listened to the bell buoy noises until I fell asleep. They sound kind of like St. Joseph's bells except it's not the same song every time. I like that the song's always different. When the wind's not out, I count the seconds between the light beams that slide across my wall. They shine from the lighthouse in the ocean and come after ten seconds if I count slow.

"Your mother's asleep and you kids make too much noise," my father said to us this morning. "If you behave yourselves, you can come down to the bar and play pool all day."

We all screeched like monkeys.

"Behave!" my father bellowed, and we calmed right down.

"You all need to be good today. Your grandfather is meeting me down at the bar for a talk. A really important talk."

I figured it must be, because my grandfather never drives out to Withensea.

"*Meshugeners* drive the Boston Freeway," he always says.

That means crazy.

The bar doesn't open for an hour, so me and my brothers have the place to ourselves. My brothers pretend to play a fair game of pool, but David's on a run, socking the balls in with regular *pock-pocks* and saying weird things to himself. Pool games with David are never fair. He's the only one tall enough to hold the pool stick level with the balls. Moses is almost four, but he can barely see over the edge of the table without standing on his toes.

"Winner. Winner!" David shouts every time he sinks another one.

We can all hear my father's voice slam through the door; we can hear it over the music, angry like a fist.

"They're gonna kill me if I don't give them the money. Do you understand, old man?"

I stare up at the huge wooden woman with the naked breasts hanging above the bar.

I know you listen. If I don't tell anyone, maybe you'll tell me what to do? You're the most beautiful lady in the world. I think your eyes are much prettier than the statue of the Virgin Mary at St. Joseph's.

The Virgin Mary's just a statue. Even Father Donald ignores her. He prays to the naked Jesus.

My grandfather's talking, but he's too quiet to hear. He doesn't want us to hear what they're talking about. He thinks we're all still babies.

If I tell about the fights and the police he'll take us with him to Boston for sure. But if they find out I told . . .

I know what my father wants. He wants more money. It's always the same.

My grandfather is a tailor who owns a few shops in Boston. My father thinks my grandfather is made of money.

———

My grandfather smells like butterscotch and lemons. My grandmother smells like chicken. They live in an apartment in Boston, and we visit them once a month. My mother drives us, although she hates to go. She screams at us practically the entire way.

"Shut up and sit back in your seats. If I have to pull this car over you're going to get a smack. For Christ's sake, whatever you do, don't throw up in the fucking car or I'll kill you!"

My mother zigzags in and out of the traffic lanes on the freeway; she doesn't use the silver signal stick, but she yells at my father when he doesn't do it. We like to kneel on the back seats and stick out our tongues at the people who honk at us. We watch to see if anyone crashes when she cuts them off because once she made two cars crash in the same day. She kept driving both times.

When she isn't screaming, my mother sings along to the radio songs, except she doesn't get the words right. She makes up her own words, which never make sense.

My mother barely talks to my grandparents once we're there. She's always real mad at them, although once I asked and she wouldn't tell me why. She goes because my grandfather gives her money after dinner. I like to go. I love my grandparents and they love us. I wish we could live with them.

It's the same dinner every time. Chopped liver with lettuce and egg on rye bread, matzoh ball soup with chicken and rice. I get the *poopick*. Grandma says it's the chicken's belly button, but I know it's something else because all the grown-ups laugh when they say it. We always have the same dessert, too. Fruit cocktail from a can.

The money to buy the bar, to pay for everything, comes from my grandfather. My father spends most of the money my grandfather gives him on things my mother gets mad about.

Scotch, horseraces, and poker games.

My grandfather doesn't spend much money on himself, though. He never goes on airplanes like my parents. He sews all the clothing he and my grandmother wear. He lives in a Jewish neighborhood in Boston in an apartment. It has a scary monster made of cement on the roof. It watches us when we go in. He has a *doessowtoe* he parks on his street, but he doesn't drive it much anymore except on Sunday.

My mother says he has lots of money. She says he's a millionaire. I think she makes this part up, because my grandparents never buy new stuff for the apartment. They replace the plastic coverings on everything when they turn yellow. My grandfather says they never buy new stuff at all because almost everything can be used forever if it's man-made, except the TV tubes in his old Zenith.

Our grandmother's name is Yetta. She never says anything in English because English isn't easy for her. She speaks Yiddish and Russian, and my mother translates for us kids. When Yetta doesn't want any of us to understand what she's saying, she speaks Polish to my grandfather.

——

After I finish my Shirley Temple I watch Moses and David play another game. Moses bites his lip and concentrates hard on David's shots.

One of these days, when he can lift the stick high enough to practice, I bet he's gonna wipe David's butt. David hardly talks to anyone, and when he does it's like he's sure no one cares what he says because he repeats himself or speaks nonsense. He's nine now, and he's got *hyperaction*.

I know he's the one who broke the crystal plate the other day. Moses would of told when they said we were all gonna be in trouble if someone didn't tell who did it. David let us all get the horsewhip. He didn't even care. I wish he'd show he's mad or do something when Dad hits Mom, but he pretends he can't hear it.

I pull my glass to the edge of the bar and lower myself off the stool. I stretch up to lift the glass off the edge when one of the Little Corporal's green doors flies open and bangs against the wall. The noise makes me drop the glass.

"Where the fuck's the ginger-haired midget?" a huge man with a weather-puckered face yells at me. He stands in the door making fists.

"Ah . . . I-I think he's outside t-t-talking with my grandfather." I try not to wince at the angry roughness of his words.

Sometimes when you don't act afraid of them they calm down.

He throws me a dirty look. I frown at the broken pieces of glass scattered on the waxed wooden floor. It's all mixed up with the leftover ice cubes, and it sparkles in the light that floods in from the sidewalk.

You can blame it on the man.

I glance over to the other side of the bar. My brothers have stopped playing. Moses and David stand frozen, pool cues braced against their chests like fishing spears.

"Who's tending bar?" The man growls and stomps over to me. He's standing right in front of me now.

Turpentine and poop.

I decide not to tell him the bar is still closed.

Breathe. Say it like Mary Poppins. Breathe.

"I can make a hundred different drinks."

The man smiles a nasty thin line of lip, and I can see he's missing teeth between the brown, beany ones he's got left.

"You wanna be a barmaid? You wanna job? I'm the one who owns this joint now." He shouts this loud enough for the people passing by on the sidewalk to hear.

My father comes out of his office and shouts back at the man. "Shut up, Pratt. These're my kids you're screaming at. If you wanna have a civilized conversation, come back in the office. If you wanna act like an animal, go do it where there aren't any youngsters around."

"I don't give a shit who's listening. This is my bar now," the man, Pratt, shouts back.

"You're an asshole. I can pay you what I owe. I'm not giving you the bar."

I step behind the bar and duck. Then I peek over the edge where the sink and the silver mixing glasses are.

"What? Who do you think you're dealing with? I'm not some pansy you can two-bit hustle. I won last night. You owe me, you fucking bastard, and if you don't pay up I'll fucking . . ." He stops when the door to the office swings open.

Both men stop shouting and scowl over at my grandfather, who ignores them and marches over to where my brothers are. He drags them back into the office. He's looking around, but can't see me peeking over the edge of the bar, and I'm afraid to run out.

"You'll fucking what? Don't be an asshole, Pratt. I'll pay you what I owe, but I'm keeping the bar."

My grandfather closes the door to the office with my brothers inside. He doesn't know I'm out here. He must think I'm outside playing. My hands start to shake so bad I make the glasses on the bar counter rattle. I duck down so they don't see me, but I can't help peeking my head over the edge again. I want to see what's going to happen next.

"I don't want your money. I want the bar. You shouldn't have put it up if you didn't have the 50K. You're gonna give me the keys or I'm gonna blow your fucking head off."

I watch as he reaches into his coat, pulls out a gun, and aims at my father.

"Put that fucking thing away." My father takes a few steps away and puts his hands out in front of him. Like his hands could stop bullets.

Holding my breath, my body goes numb and my stomach goes hollow.

I don't know why, but I start to sing: "Raindrops on roses and whiskers on . . ."

Two things happen.

One: both men stop shouting and turn to see me behind the bar. Two: the gun goes off.

I think it must've scared the man when I started to sing because he swung the gun away from my father's head and toward me, then pulled the trigger.

The bullet hits the mirror behind the bar, followed by a thousand crashes of glass. The next second my neck is stinging like someone stabbed me. I put my hand up to touch it. Something warm and sticky is oozing on my skin and down across my chest. I glance down. My blouse, which is powder blue, turns a deep, magenta-purple.

My father stands in front of me. "Oh Christ! You shot my kid! You shot her! Somebody call an ambulance!"

The man, Pratt, is standing next to him.

"Oh Fuck No! Oh Sweet Jesus!" he repeats over and over.

I can barely hear them. I see their mouths moving, but the sound is muffled like they've got pillows over their mouths or something. Everything around their heads looks swimmy and my eyes narrow down to just them. Like a camera's eye, only all blurry like on *Star Trek* when they use the transporter.

I'm feeling awfully dizzy.

The only thing I see is the wooden woman. I'm lying on the floor behind the bar right under her. She turns her head and stares right at me and says,

Think of me as an angel. Everything will be all right. You are loved and I'll always be with you.

———

I wake up in an ambulance, my father lying on a bench on the other side of the truck.

"Is—is my father dead?" I ask the ambulance guy, who sits on my bench and wraps up my arm where he stuck a needle in. "Did he get shot too?"

The ambulance guy smiles down at me. "Nobody got shot, hon. Your dad passed out is all. I guess he don't like the sight of blood much."

"I didn't get shot?"

"Nope. You got a piece of glass cuttin' your neck, though. We're taking you in so's the doc can take a peek at you."

"Am I gonna die?"

"Nope. A few stitches is what you'll need. You're gonna be fine."

I wonder how long my father will be asleep and if he'll be mad at me when he wakes up.

The ambulance guy sticks a plastic cup on my face and tells me it will help me breathe easier. It smells like new Barbies.

"Did you clean her up?" my father asks from his bench across from me.

I look over at him. He has his head turned away from me.

"Hi Dad."

"Is she wrapped up?"

The ambulance guy winks at me and says, "We have a bandage on her wound, Mr. Finn. How's your dizzy?"

My father turns his head to me. He smiles. I figure he's not mad at me.

"It wasn't a bullet, Dad. Just glass."

He smiles a weak smile at me, frowns at my neck and down at my arm where the needle is. He makes a long sigh, "Oooooohhhhh."

"You doin' all right, Mr. Finn? Don't you be passin' out on us again."

"I don't think I'm gonna pass out. I think I'm gonna be sick."

"Here you go." The ambulance guy hands him a plastic bowl. He holds it on his stomach until we get to the hospital.

———

At the hospital they take me to a chilly room and give me stitches, which hurt a lot. They put a big bandage on my neck. They wrap up the piece of glass that got stuck in my neck in a wad of gauze and give it to me as a souvenir.

While the doctor stitches me up my father sits in a chair across the room. He won't look at the stitches 'cause they make him sick to his stomach. When the doctor asks me what happened, my father tells him that someone threw a rock at the mirror behind the bar and that's how it got broken and hurt me. I guess he doesn't want to tell the truth about the gun.

The nurse asks if I'm hungry and brings me a bowl of Sugar Pops, which is neat because we never get good cereal at our house. My mother only lets us eat Wheaties. She says the other stuff rots your teeth.

"Okay, time to go home," my father says as the doctor leaves, pushing through the double doors of my hospital room. He seems better and doesn't look the same sick greenish color he looked in the ambulance.

"Can you bring her another blouse?" he asks the nurse.

I try to wolf down the Sugar Pops.

She gives him a glare and says, "I'm sorry, we don't store clothing here. If you like we can send her home in a gown?"

"Whatever."

The nurse grabs a peach-colored thingy. Way big for me. She pins and ties it so I can walk around in it. She gives me my bloody blouse in a paper bag that says Children's Hospital. I didn't know they took me to a hospital just for children. No wonder they had the Sugar Pops.

When I jump in the car my father tells me I shouldn't have been hiding behind the bar and it serves me right I got cut. I'm mad he doesn't see he could've gotten killed from a gun. I probably saved his life better than Mighty Mouse.

"Are you gonna lose the bar?" I ask.

"None of your business. It's not polite to eavesdrop on other people's conversations."

"You were swearing. Everybody could hear you," I say, not meaning to be sassy.

He raises his fist and I flinch over against the door.

"Do you need a smack? Because I'd be happy to smack you if you do. This ER visit is gonna cost us. You better hope your grandfather will pay for it."

My father looks at me with the dead eyes. Sometimes his eyes go dead like the cat we found in the shed, and I know I better not say anything else or I'll get a beating.

I don't say one word the whole way back.

I remember the wooden woman at the bar and how she spoke to me and how it made me real peaceful inside.

But I worry. If someone else ran the bar they might take the woman away. Where would she end up if they did? Would she still be able to protect me?

Three

Jules, 6 years | Late August, 1967

THE HOUSE AT 18 ALETHEA ROAD

"I'VE BEEN TALKING with a developer and he says we can earn a fortune for the land. His company is planning more building in this neighborhood. We could sell the land around the house to pay it off."

I hear my father say this to my grandfather in his oily voice. He always uses this voice when he talks to my grandfather and the neighbors.

My father and I got back from the hospital about an hour ago and I got sent up to my room. I'm supposed to be resting, but I'm not tired. I'm sitting on my floor by the heat register, painting watercolors with the new Paint Rite set I got for my birthday. I'm listening to my father and my grandfather downstairs in the den. The den is filled with turquoise Naugahyde furniture. My father always takes people there to talk private. I can eavesdrop 'cause the sound comes up real clear through the holes in my radiator.

My grandfather's upset because of the stitches and stuff that happened at the bar and because my mother's not here and my father won't say where she is. She's probably at her friend Natasha's place. My father doesn't like Natasha. He says she's a bad *influencer* and calls her a bitch. My mother smokes smelly herb cigarettes when she hangs out at Natasha's. I like to go there because I like to play the drum set in the garage and my brothers don't know about it yet.

"You should count your blessings the *kind* will heal from this. Almost killed by a crazy man with a gun. Still you want to ask me for more money. This home is my wedding gift."

"If it's a gift why don't you transfer the title to us? It should be ours to do whatever we want with."

"This way it never becomes lost in maybe a poker game."

My father doesn't say anything, but I'm thinking he's real mad. He doesn't like it when he doesn't get his way. I imagine my grandfather sitting in the den. He probably thinks it looks silly because my father lets the people who come to visit him write their names on the walls with black magic markers, even though we're not allowed. Plus there's a moose head stuck over the TV and he put a pair of sunglasses on its eyes so it looks like Miles Davis. That's my father's favorite singer.

"We could make more money on the land than you paid for the entire house. It's a temporary situation though. This man could change his mind about where he wants to build and pay someone else if we wait too long," my father finally says.

"Yes. There's always a time limit with these golden opportunities. I give you the money to start businesses before this. The ad business, the fish and chips store. All have failed. After you purchased the bar, you told me you needed more money to expand. But, I see no expansion. The one thing that has expanded, as far as I can tell, is your wallet for brief times. I saw the *beyz* man who came into your bar to collect his money. I don't know what kind of trouble you found, but this kind of trouble doesn't go away when you throw money at it. Maybe you should call police."

"I'm not going to call the police. You don't understand, old man. The police can't do anything. I borrowed money and I have to pay it back."

"You borrowed? You lost bets? Which is? Borrow or lose? Never mind with the answer. You receive no more money."

My father says, "They might try to hurt Wendy or the kids. To teach me a lesson. You don't want anything bad to happen to them, do you?"

"Now you threaten with the *kinder*? I know you're mixed up in *meshugener* business. Money buys everything but good sense, my brother Oizer says. He warned me not to give more money to you, but I wanted you to succeed for the *kinder*'s sake, for Wendy's sake. I thought you would make a good husband. Now I see you're a criminal. You're going to drag my daughter and the *kinder* into it. Maybe it's good they kill you."

I suck my breath in. I've never heard my grandfather talk like that to anyone. My father gets mad when anyone talks back to him, and I worry he might try to hit my grandfather.

"Why don't you ask your family? Maybe your sister will help this time?"

"Listen. I can't ask my sister. She's got too many expenses. My family doesn't have the money, or I'd ask them."

"Maybe you ask too many times to them? Maybe they decide like I do. Enough is enough."

My father doesn't answer. I can hear him moving the big bottles on the bar, opening the small refrigerator in the den, then the tinkle of ice cubes in a glass.

"Chivas?" he asks my grandfather.

"No. No thank you."

The only thing I've ever seen my grandfather drink is the berry-colored wine at holidays, the *man-of-chivas* wine my mother hates.

"You have no money for paying your debts, but I see you still have money for alcohol and expensive furniture and televisions."

My grandfather sounds really angry now. His voice shakes and he's shouting.

"All the money. All the money I give to you. You waste on these things instead of making a good future for Wendy, for the *kinder*—your family. Wasteful things. All bought with my money. Never again."

"Calm down, old man. Sit down."

"I won't sit in this home; I won't talk *with* you again until you pay me back. Every cent of what you waste. Pay me back and pay your *shyster* friends back. I want nothing to do you with you. I am wrong to try to help you. I see now this *vas* not good, not best for Wendy or for you. This *vas* a mistake in the beginning. I will transfer the deed into Wendy's name. She can decide what to do with the home and the land. I'll not be involved in your business any longer. You are children when you started together, but you are adults now. No more money from me. Find your own money."

I hear my grandfather's steps already climbing the den stairs.

I'm afraid he's going to leave without coming upstairs to see me. I run out of my room and down the long hallway to the landing on the living room stairwell to try and catch him.

He's not coming to the front door. I run the rest of the way down the stairs to the living room. I can see him standing in the kitchen. He's staring around the room at everything.

"Hi Grandpa."

"Hello, Chavalah."

My grandfather calls me by my Hebrew name.

"Are you going now, Grandpa?"

"Yes, Chavalah, I'm going home now. Is your neck feeling better?"

"Yes."

My grandfather looks around the kitchen again and says, "You know, when I am a young boy we had a home that had two stories. Our entire home *vas* as big as this kitchen on the bottom and half this size on the top."

"Like in *Little Women*? Wow. That's a tiny house."

"It didn't seem tiny to me." He smiles.

We walk out to the living room and he walks over to the two big pictures of my great-grandparents that hang on the wall. They don't smile in the pictures, and whenever I notice it I want to behave better because it seems like they might be happier if I do.

"Grandpa, how come they're not smiling? Are they mad?"

"*Oy, oy*," my grandfather says and shakes his head. He does this all the time when he's playing with us. "They should be."

He starts to laugh. I'm glad he's laughing now.

"My parents are thinking they are in *Gehanna* with the *beyz* man here."

I'm not sure where Gihunna is or what baze men are, but I think he's talking about my father and it's not good.

My grandfather's leaning against the piano now and scanning the room.

"Did you know your mother used to play this piano when she *vas* a little girl like you? She practiced every day. She played recitals for us on Sundays after lunch."

"Really?" I've never heard my mother play the piano. David and I take lessons; otherwise, no one ever plays it.

"She *vas* a good girl, your mother."

He walks over to the bookcases on the living room wall. One whole side of the living room has books from the floor to the ceiling. It's like we have our own library. I point to the Bobbsey Twins books. "These're antiques. My mother read these when she was little," I tell my grandfather, although I'm sure he already knows.

"Yeh, yeh. Many of these books are hers. She *vas* such a smart little girl. Do you read them?"

"Absolutely. I've read all the children's books she read. Nancy Drew is my favorite. I've started reading the encyclopedias and the grown-up books now."

"You're a smart girl, Chavalah. Keep studying hard and you'll go to college one day."

"My mother goes to college sometimes. She keeps her schoolbooks on this shelf." I point to the crowded shelf above me where we have to remember not to touch.

My grandfather looks at all the books and says, "You're going to be a dedicated scholar, then you will become a great teacher and make me proud. Can we go see your room now?"

"Sure."

On the way upstairs he stops to stare into the dining room at the big wooden table and the china cabinet. I wonder if he's really not going to come back to our house. His eyes are all soft and sad.

We stop at the top of the landing where my parents' room is. He stands in the doorway and peeks inside. I'm hoping he doesn't go in because we get in trouble if we do.

"Are your brothers still playing outside?" he asks as we walk by their empty rooms.

"I think so."

"Do you know where you mother is?"

"We're not supposed to tell, but she's probably with her friend Natasha."

"Why can't you tell?"

"My father doesn't like her."

He leans back and stares down at the wood floor after I answer.

"Will you take me and David and Moses with you?"

He looks up. "Why would you want me to do this?"

I can't say why I want him to take us, I'm too afraid. "It would just be better."

I don't want to tell him about the fights where my father punches my mother and she throws things and screams and they say mean things to each other. I have a hunch it's gonna get worse. Especially if my father runs out of money, because that's what they argue about all the time.

Instead, I walk with my grandfather to the end of the hallway, to my room, and we step inside.

"Did you do all these paintings, Chavalah?"

All my watercolor gardens are spread across my floor, drying.

"Of course, and all of these." I spread my arms to include the drawings taped up on my walls.

"An artist."

"Yes," I answer. "I'm going to become a *great* artist someday. But first I have to get dedicated," I add seriously, remembering his earlier words.

My grandfather laughs and shakes his head back and forth between his hands and says, "*Oy, oy.*"

But then he stops laughing and leans in close. "You need to stay here and take good care of your brothers. Who else will do this?"

"But why? Why can't we come and live with you and Grandma?" I start to cry.

"We have no room for you in our apartment, Chavalah."

"Oh," I answer; then I'm crying big hiccups.

I throw my arms around his legs. I'm thinking maybe if he sees how much I want to go with him, and how sad I am, he'll take me.

"Oh Grandpa. I'll be good. I'll be so good."

He bends down and takes my face in his hands. "You are good. No one is as good as you children. But, still, I can't take you home to live with me and Grandma. Stay here with your brothers. Things will be better, you'll see."

He peels away my arms and smiles down at me.

"I love you, Grandpa." My voice still has a hiccup.

"Come outside with me," he says.

At the far end of the hallway, there's a door leading outside to a widow's walk at the back of the house. We step outside and onto the walkway. The wind is up again and slams the screen door closed after us. My hand makes a flap-flap sound across the railings as we walk. The salt air stings inside my nose and makes my eyes water more.

My grandfather and I stop on the edge of the walkway, right next to my bedroom window, and look down toward the ocean, out below the cliff. His eyes see something far away.

"I often come out here to *contemplace*," I say.

He reaches into his pocket and slides me a butterscotch candy. As I'm letting it melt on my tongue, he points toward the lighthouse. "When I came to America, I came from that direction."

Except for the island the lighthouse is on, there's just ocean as far as I can see. In the other direction is Boston. It sits like a huge mud pile. Down below, the rocky beach bends out to the land bridge connecting us to the other side of the island.

My neck starts to sting where it's got stitches.

"It's a good property. It should stay in the family and be a place for you *kinder* to come back to with your own families. I wanted to protect her, but I've prevented her from growing up. I'm going to sign over the deed to your mother to be rid of his greedy begging. She must learn to control her own future. I will make the home and the land hers, but she will receive no more help from me if she sells it. She will have to honor this. She cannot sell."

I don't think my Grandfather Samuel is talking to me, and I'm not sure I understand everything he says, but I want him to know I can keep a secret. "I won't tell."

Four

STOOGES AND CRIMINALS

"YOU FORGED MY name and sold half of our property to that crook so he can build more shitty bourgeois ranch houses all around us? You myopic asshole."

It's about eleven o'clock on a Sunday morning. My mother was sleeping before my father came to pick us up for his visit. He moved out last winter. They're getting a divorce. Sundays are supposed to be the day my brothers and I spend with him. He doesn't always show up.

"Whadya call me?" My father yells so loud it hurts my ears.

I can hear the smack of a fist on flesh and my mother's whiny scream.

"Where's my money?"

"It's not yours. It's my father's, and you're not getting any more of it."

In the midst of this, Moses knocks, then comes into my room and closes the door, which muffles the shouting a bit. I'm sitting on the rug my mother says is Persian, leaning forward to pencil sketch in a pad I laid out on the wooden floor. It's muggy hot and my shorts stick to the rug.

I taught myself to draw from a library book called *How to Use the Figure in Painting & Illustration* and I keep it *perpetuously* checked out. I'm still no good at it.

Although the door remains closed, my brother whispers to me. "Jules, I'm scared."

"It's all right . . . they'll stop soon. Go outside and play."

"I can't. We're supposed to stay in our rooms 'til he's ready to take us."

"Then you better go back. Where's David?"

"I dunno."

We stop talking. Louder screaming. I hear the crash of glass things breaking against a wall and my father yelling. "You're supposed to be here with your kids, not running around with that hippie bitch and those drug addicts."

"What about you, you're never with 'em. You're too busy sleeping with my supposed friends."

Their voices fade into growls.

"He's got a gun," Moses says. His eyes are big like a goldfish's.

"No Sir . . . H-h-how do you know?"

"I watched him. He put it here." Moses points to the back of his pants.

"Don't worry. He's just scaring her. He'll leave her alone soon. Go back to your room and shut the door."

Neither of us really believes what I'm saying. Moses scratches the crook of his arm where red itchy spots grow on him.

"All right," he says and leaves.

I wait for a second, then stand up and peek out in the hallway. I hear the shouting again—louder this time—and the sound of Moses's closet door closing. I know he's inside. His closet has become his hiding spot, but I don't think anyone else knows about it.

I step out of my room and run as quietly down the hall as I can. The noise and shouting is coming from their room, beyond the stairs, at the other end of the hall.

The master bedroom door is cracked open and I stop long enough to see my mother kneeling on the bed. She wears her butter-yellow silk Chinese brocade bathrobe. I can't see any other part of my father but his hands, grabbing her hair and pointing the gun at her forehead.

Run. Call the police.

I run down the stairs and through the kitchen to the den. David sits in the aqua Naugahyde lounge chair, staring, like he's hypnotized, at the black-and-white television.

"He's got a g . . . g . . . gun this time. We've got to do something!"

David continues watching *The Three Stooges*, then walks over to turn up the volume on the television as the screaming from upstairs roars louder and louder. He sits back down again.

"Call Freddie," he says.

"Who's Freddy? *Who is Freddy?*" I shout at him, but he ignores me.

He won't help. It's up to you. Like last time.

Frustrated, I go to the phone behind the bar. Crouching down, I close my eyes, trying hard to remember the number.

See the numbers like a picture in your head.

I open my eyes and dial, remaining hidden behind the bar. I know David can't hear me.

I never stutter when I pretend to be someone else, but my fingers shake so bad I have a hard time turning the dialer on the phone.

The woman at the police office answers.

"Yes. You need to come right now to 18 Alethea Road. My husband has a gun and he's pointing it at the children. You need to lock him up this time and not just take him for a walk."

She knows the address from the times before.

"Are you able to provide proof of abuse to press charges, Mrs. Finn?"

I don't know what she's talking about.

"N-no, I just want you to lock him up this time and keep him in jail for a few years."

"First of all, they'll never keep him in that long, and you're going to have to be willing to show proof he's been abusive—like letting us take photos of any bruises or cuts. That's the only way for us to keep him and obtain a restraining order for you. We've been over this . . ."

"F-fine. C-come and get him now."

I hang up before I stutter again, and I notice my hand on the phone. It's still shaking. I stand up from behind the bar and listen to the sound of my parents' argument, louder still, and glance over at David. The Three Stooges fight and bang each other around. This noise is as loud as the sounds of my parents' screaming. It's almost like the Stooges are making fun of my parents.

I'm too frightened to stay. I go out the back entry, onto the wide side porch. I still hear my mother's piercing screams and my father's yells as I climb down the stairs leading into the yard and around to the back of the house, which was built on the edge of a huge cliff overlooking the ocean.

I climb down to the shoreline and I hoist myself up on one of the rocks that form a jagged seawall. With careful footing and hair-raising jumps I make it out to my favorite place—a large, flat rock that juts out beyond the seawall and is surrounded by other huge, craggy rocks that form a jetty along the shore. My thinking spot. I can sit in this spot and be completely hidden from any angle except directly out to sea.

Down here I feel spits of breeze, and when I suck in the salt air it makes my insides soft. I lift all the hair off my neck to dry my collar and the back of my blouse.

I hate that my mother won't let me cut it short like my cousins. I have to wear it down on Sundays whenever my father comes to take us to our Aunt Doreen's. It ends up in horrible knots that kill my scalp when she tugs them out at night.

After a while I hear a police siren's shrill alarm winding up the long hill toward our neighborhood. I scramble over the jetty and climb the wooden ladder built from our backyard, at the top of the cliff, to the beach below. It's a quicker way up. The people who owned the place before us built the ladder, and the rungs are rotting and broken in a few spots, especially at the top. I only use it once in a while, when I want to spy on the house.

The shrieking siren becomes louder as I climb closer.

When I reach the top of the ladder, I poke my head over the top of the cliff, staying hidden behind the scrub at the edge. Two policemen, one I recognize as Officer Hennessy, who lives in our neighborhood, stand in the driveway. Officer Hennessy talks to my mother, and the other officer hauls my father into the police car. Officer Hennessy's holding a gun; it must be my father's gun. My mother's face is scratched and bleeding. The blood's running down her face onto her neck and the yellow bathrobe.

She's arguing with Officer Hennessy. "I'm telling you, I didn't make the fucking call. I'm sure one of the neighborhood morons did it."

My mother gestures to the neighbors across the road, who are just arriving home from church. They stop to stare at the commotion. The siren light blinks a huge fiery red reflection off the white paint on our house shingles. You could probably see it a mile away.

"The divorce won't be final until August, but he's not supposed to be bothering me. He's supposed to be here on Sundays to pick up the kids. Of course, he has a hard time remembering to do this unless he wants to harass me about something."

My mother's real angry with the local police because they've never arrested my father before today and he's beaten her up lots of times. But it's mutual: the cops don't like my mother because she's always calling them pigs and telling them they'd be criminals if they hadn't become cops so they'd be able to carry guns.

Officer Hennessy asks my father, "Is this gun registered, Howard?" He doesn't wait for an answer. "Listen, Missus Finn, you're going to have to come down to the station and let us take pictures of your face if you wanna press charges."

He leans in closer to her. "If ya don't put a stop to this for your kids' sake, I'll make sure we take you away next time and the kids'll have to go to live somewhere else. Do you care about that?"

"Of course I care, you imbecile."

First Officer Hennessy acts as if he might hit my mother, but then he says, "Good, we'll see you at the station in a little while."

"Let's take him in," he says to the other cop—then, to my father, "Howard, I can see how the woman tests your patience," and they all laugh. "I'm gonna have to book you this time, though, and you better not be coming back here except to see your kids. Make 'em wait on the front lawn, or down the road is a better idea, for Chrissakes."

I remember Officer Hennessy was a regular at my father's bar before my father lost it in the poker game, and I wonder if he's arresting him now because he can't get free drinks anymore.

I look up and I see Moses peeking out his window. He holds one hand up on the wavy windowpane and it seems like his whole body is crying.

Windowpain.

By this time, more of the neighbors have arrived home and are standing on their porches or on their lawns, watching as the police car leaves. Mrs. O'Connell, who lives across the road, still wears her church clothes: white gloves, a short, polyester pink coat that matches a polyester pink dress underneath, and a pea-green, pillbox hat. They're the kind of clothes my grandmother wears, although I think Mrs. O'Connell is my mother's age.

She walks up to my mother with Mr. O'Connell by her side.

"Fucking pigs."

Mrs. O'Connell pretends she didn't hear my mother's comment, but her face is all scrunched up.

"It's such a good thing you're doing for the children's sake. We've been afraid for them. Anything we can do to help?"

"He wasn't touching the kids, you dig? Mind your own business, you square." My mother walks inside and slams the front door.

Mrs. O'Connell asks her husband, "What did she call me?"

"It's that hippie talk they use in the city. I can't make sense of it."

"Well it doesn't make any sense."

Mr. O'Connell walks to his porch as Mrs. O'Connell stands talking, mostly to the air. "Those poor children. Mrs. Finn's been gone more now, since that beast of a man left, than when he lived there. Lord knows who'll take care of them."

I can't figure out why, but it feels worse to hear her talk about us that way.

Glancing back up at the window where Moses stood, I can see he's gone now.

My mother is screaming my name. I duck and step down a rung on the ladder, hiding. When I hear the sound of her and my brother's voices from the driveway I peek over the edge of the cliff again.

My mother, David, and Moses all pile into the station wagon. She guns the engine and screams at my brothers to hurry up so she can drive to the police station for photos of her bloody face.

I don't want to go to the police station and risk a run-in with the lady I spoke to on the phone. I hide my head behind the scrub again and creep back down the rickety ladder, which splinters off rotted pieces with every step.

Five

"AND DON'T FORGET to go through the stuff in the cedar chests downstairs," Wendy says. "There are old comforters that you can look through to use for your bed in the dorms."

I've been packing up, organizing, or trashing every item I own for days now. The dorm assignment papers that came in my freshman orientation packet last week stressed the fact that there's limited storage space and we might not have our own closets. So I've got to pare down everything I own to two suitcases, limited wall decorations, and bedding.

Wendy's taken my departure from the house as an opportunity to pawn off all the crap in the house she doesn't want but doesn't want to throw out. Piles of smelly, aged, ripped sheets and pillowcases sit on my bedroom floor. The frayed and bulb-burned lampshade from a long-broken lamp stem decorates my bureau.

"Here. A going-away gift," Wendy proudly offered, despite the fact I'd explained that my dorm room will come furnished with a desk and study lamp.

I wonder if David received the same "gifts" when he left for college a few years ago. I can't remember.

So much has been lost. So much has been denied, despite the evidence, the psyche marks, like cigarette burns on formica.

The moments that my brain does remember seem quite random.

Even now, after all these years, my memory of that moment with David and

The Three Stooges remains crystal. It's wrapped in a sort of warm insanity that, however peculiar, provides vague comfort.

It became clear to me, early on, that David had a unique method for dealing with the stress of our family. I think he figured he couldn't change the situation, so he retreated to a place where no one else could go. I, on the other hand, fought back. But it was a war no one but me knew I was fighting. I was a secret warrior. Incognito.

Over time, I developed the *voice of a mother*, the mother I imagined out of "Beaver Cleaver-land." In the beginning, I used it to call the police. Later, I used it to call in the absences and tardies my brothers and I accrued when my mother went to party with her friends and left us, sometimes for days, without supervision.

In retrospect, I don't feel bad about lying to the lady about Howard pointing the gun at us. He had, in the past, not only threatened but hurt each of us. He was a man filled with a rage he couldn't contain. It seethed and seeped out, sometimes in alcoholic bursts, sometimes with no alcohol and seemingly no provocation. He beat us with his belt or his large fists. His blows were uncontrolled and without concern for the frailty of our small bodies. He must have been unaware that his physical strength was much greater than ours, and I felt, when he beat us, that he wanted pure domination over us and, sometimes, the annihilation of our wills, our individual wills to defend, to argue, to defy, and even—at times—to live. In those moments, I felt his true intent might be to kill me.

We were smashed against walls, beaten against furniture, slapped down on floors, and left with no reactive movement. We learned to get there fast, to that place where we didn't react, feigning unconsciousness, disassociating from the pain because it caused response and response equaled more pain. The sooner I could leave my body, the sooner he'd leave my body alone.

Wendy beat us with the horsewhip she used on her rides at Withensea Stables.

I think the reason the police came that day when Howard had the gun—they didn't always come—was because I told them my father had threatened us, his children. Although the local police thought a good talk and a walk around the block was the correct way to deal with domestic violence, I don't think their morals stretched to allow child abuse. At least, not when firearms were being waved around.

In our community, hitting your kids isn't considered child abuse. This is "spare the rod, spoil the child" territory. Good old Puritan ethic. Massachusetts is, after all, the state that, in 1646, enacted the law allowing the death penalty for a rebellious child— the "stubborn child" law. People here look the other way when parents discipline their children. When we were beaten, we were left with visible welts, scratches, and bruises, but no one ever asked about them—and if they did, they were satisfied with an honest "my father hit me" or an obviously made-up version of how we'd gotten the marks.

They were minding their own business.

I knew Mrs. O'Connell was trying to be kind that day with Howard and the gun. For a New Englander, getting involved rather than maintaining a cold, silent regard was a grand gesture. But my mother didn't like the neighbors because they were "nosy." It must have been hard to ignore the stuff going on, though, and my mother never did get that.

"Who cares what the neighbors think?" was one of her favorite sayings.

I think there must have been many small fractures, but with no hospital visits and no x-rays, there's no way to be sure. When you're young, bones heal fast.

Complaining about a beating or the pain invited more of the same. Also, I knew my friends were being hit by their parents as well. I knew our situation didn't differ much from theirs. But I never believed that my friends were being hit as often or as hard.

Now I understand more about why Howard and Wendy were so mean.

For Wendy, we existed merely as a barrier between her and loneliness. I found out when I was about six that Wendy was adopted. I think, as an adopted child, she must have missed out on the crucial bonding in early childhood that deters sociopathy. I read an article about it in one of Wendy's *Psychology Today* magazines. Then, this year, I learned more secrets that explain why Wendy is so messed up.

She received an exclusive education at Girls' Latin School in Boston, where she distinguished herself as an excellent student. But she was never taught to take care of herself. Yetta waited on my mother like a servant. Wendy wasn't expected to do chores, let alone pick up the clothing she dropped on the floor as she removed it from her body. She was a pampered, spoiled child who never developed house-keeping skills.

Yetta loved to cook for Wendy, but refused to let her learn to cook herself. Later, in her teens, Wendy spent hardly any time at home with her parents and refused to eat most meals with them. Yetta began leaving Wendy her meals in the refrigerator to have when she wished. It wasn't until Howard and Wendy married that she began her education, instructed by Howard, in what were considered her wifely duties. It was a painful education that, had it been graded, would have received poor marks for execution and a failing score for effort.

Howard, ten years her senior, married Wendy when she was seventeen. He seemed entertained by her independent, nonconformist behavior before their marriage. Afterwards, he became scarily determined to subvert her personality and pull a Pygmalion-style miracle by transforming her into a suburban housewife.

They were both unhappy with the attempt.

Howard expressed his displeasure by having affairs, and, after several years of half-hearted attempts to please him, Wendy began to assert her independence. For this reason, my mother spent more time in the kitchen during the early period of my childhood than she ever did again. Howard demanded that she provide balanced, nutritious meals and bellowed if they were less than palatable. I remember a lot of bellowing around the dinner table.

That day with the gun marked the beginning of another chapter in my life.

My first seven years were filled with the fear of Howard's violence, but they were also filled with artistic and athletic activities. My brothers and I participated in most of the same activities our friends did. There was at least a semblance of normalcy in our suburban existence. We were kept busy with practices and lessons. My brothers played team football and baseball. We all endured piano lessons. I used to sit at the piano in my wet bathing suit in the summers, because I'd have run in off the beach just in time for the lesson. In the winter, I peeled off snow clothes before sitting down, having just come in from playing outside.

I hated my piano lessons because it meant I had to come back to the house and the chaos. My teacher, an older Italian woman who ate foul-smelling pepperoni sandwiches, beat time to the piano metronome with a baton, on my knuckles, as I tried to play. I still can't play the piano without thinking of the smell of pepperoni and that tapping baton.

I also attended ballet classes with the Boston Ballet on Saturdays. This remains the one class Wendy brought me to with regularity. She always got stoned with a friend in Boston while I practiced. I never wanted to be a ballerina, though I liked the formality and structure of the ballet studio classes. I possessed no real talent, and eventually the ballet master became honest about my chances for acceptance into the corps. He encouraged me to study tap dancing. But I knew tap wasn't my style. Tap was for people who smiled. Ballet was serious.

Summers were better. My father's sister, Doreen, owned a summer bungalow in Withensea and came to live there every summer. During the first seven years of my life I spent almost every summer day at my aunt's beach bungalow or on the beach with my other aunts, uncles, and cousins, and grandparents on Howard's side.

I felt freedom on the beach. It was my playground. My cousins and I spent all day in and out of the freezing waves, drawing and playing circle hopscotch with Popsicle sticks and building elaborate sand castles with our plastic pails and shovels. At lunchtime we were whistled in like dogs. We would run—pink-skinned, blue-lipped—to the spot up on the soft, white sand where there was a semi-circle of aluminum chairs and chaises. Once there, we were toweled off and fed warm peanut butter sandwiches, soft peaches, and icy water from a long, silver thermos. Afterwards, we were lectured to stay out of the water until we had digested. We always ignored those instructions and ran directly back into the ocean, where we played for hours, until the ice cream truck rang its bell at the edge of the dunes. Then it was a chorus of whines and begging until someone offered coins, which I would trade for blue raspberry Italian ices.

Howard, who, as I've described, disciplined us in a manner usually reserved for inmates or delinquents in a military school, displayed a paradoxical sweetness around his family.

After the divorce, when he remembered to pick us up on Sundays, we were taken to his sister Doreen's home and dropped off while he went elsewhere. Going to our Aunt Doreen's was a treat we looked forward to. We missed our long summers on the beach with this big Irish family and the nighttime barbeques and marshmallow roasts that followed.

Howard drank at one of the local tourist bars or spent Sundays out playing poker games.

During the winter, when Aunt Doreen went back to her winter home and we were alone with him, our visits were a different story. Without the audience of his family his mood was unreliable and often volatile. We spent our time either playing outside or cleaning Aunt Doreen's place for him, or sometimes I would read the Sunday newspaper from cover to cover—literally—in a corner somewhere while he watched sports on television and drank beer. He never let me bring a book to read. He said I read "too many books, like your mother." My brothers played ball outside or watched television with him. When his libacious sports television time ended he called us together and, usually inebriated, drove us back to Wendy, often without having offered us anything to eat for the entire day. We learned not to complain.

———

Howard drives us to a nearby restaurant and tells us to stay in the car. He hops out of the car, goes in, and comes back with a small bag. When he leans back in the driver's seat and opens the bag, he pulls out a lobster roll and proceeds to eat it without offering us a bite. David, who sits behind him in the car, makes the mistake of asking if we will be allowed to order something to eat.

"Didn't your mother feed you breakfast this morning?"

He always looks for ways to blame her for anything.

David replies, "We ate Wheaties for breakfast."

"Good, you shouldn't be hungry now; it's only been a few hours since you ate breakfast."

David perseveres. I'm sure hunger motivates him. But we all know not to cross Howard, as well as the consequences for not behaving well.

"But I'm hungry again. Aren't you going to give us lunch?"

Howard turns around and backhands David across the seat.

"There, that's lunch. Is it tasty?" he snarls.

We all freeze. I sit next to David in the backseat and Moses cowers in the front. None of us breathes at first. I steal a peek at David and see he's fighting back tears. I don't want to embarrass him by letting on I see him crying. I stare out the side window. Howard eats the rest of the lobster roll while we all sit in silence.

He says, "Lobster rolls are expensive. I can't afford to buy you all lobster rolls for lunch."

———

The cost of the lobster roll would have covered the cost of several less expensive sandwiches for all of us. I remember feeling shocked at his selfishness. I'd been a witness to it before, in many ways, but I'd never seen such a blatant display. That experience solidified my understanding of his nature.

Our stomachs were audibly rumbling, but he drove us back to Doreen's place so he could watch a football game while we played outside.

From that point on, we never complained about the lack of meals on those visits; instead, we ate tons of Raisin Bran and Wheaties on Sunday mornings, just in case. We never told Wendy, either, knowing she would cause trouble with Howard and fearing the retribution we might endure the next time we saw him if she did.

Before, we'd gotten glimpses of his softer side at bedtimes, holidays, and birthdays. At those times he became the magical father of our dreams. We celebrated birthdays with parades. These were elaborate productions with hats that Howard had intricately folded from newspapers, worn while we marched around hunting for presents and singing "Happy Birthday."

Christmas Day before the divorce was blissful. It was the one day that stayed argument-free. Whatever friction our parents held was put aside and temporarily forgotten. My father decorated the outside of our old Victorian with large, multicolored bulbs that made it look like a gumdrop-laden gingerbread house. My brothers and I hung stockings on our fireplace that were so big we could have jumped inside them ourselves. They'd be crammed with toys the next morning. Howard's friend owned a toy store, and at Christmas our living room became the previous year's "Toy Clearance" repository. We'd wake each other up in the middle of Christmas Eve night to go down and marvel at the toys stacked from one end of the living room to the other. Most were unwrapped, and we were unable to resist playing with them. These were the Useless Presents, as in *A Child's Christmas In*

Wales. We waited to open the Useful Presents. This is how our parents found us in the morning: already occupied with the toys. They didn't mind as long as we didn't open the wrapped presents—the Useful Presents— from *"aunts who always wore wool."*

Wendy made a Christmas pancake breakfast for everyone, and then we spent the day playing until dinnertime. Wendy complained we were being spoiled with toys, but she never made a scene about it on Christmas.

After the divorce, we rarely saw Howard's family.

Summer days were spent with friends or pursuing other interests. Birthday parades went away. Christmas became a lonely time. Wendy, who had been raised a Jew, didn't enjoy Christmas celebrations with the same spirit as Howard.

We missed our Christmas mornings and the *spoilage*, now replaced by a single, thoughtless, used gift from Wendy. No Christmas pancake breakfasts. Instead, after opening our present, we retreated to our rooms and met later for TV dinners. I learned to prepare them for myself and my brothers in those early years after the divorce.

After Howard left, bedtimes were not monitored. As long as we were in our rooms, Wendy could party with privacy. She never checked to see if our lights were off and we were asleep.

I developed a bad nocturnal habit of staying up late due to the noise level, which earned me tardy slips at school. This is where my ability to forge Wendy's signature came in handy.

Although Howard kept his Sunday appointments for child visits sporadically, there were a few times he showed up for other reasons. Once he came back with a gun—again—to threaten Wendy's new boyfriend. He also showed up when Wendy had a motorcycle accident, and once more during the Blizzard of '78.

After Howard left, Wendy changed. The house changed, too—after Wendy's redecoration it looked like someone had hired a lunatic as a designer, someone who had plenty of money to spend but had experienced a prolonged, visual anxiety attack during the process. The neighborhood changed; the land Howard sold off got developed into rows of aluminum-sided, raised-ranch houses all around us. We became less like children and more like neglected pets. We got intermittent feedings until I learned to cook, no affection, and almost no attention, except when we didn't behave in a way that pleased Wendy, which pretty much meant being in the same room as her and breathing. We developed independence beyond our years. Within our own pet universe we found hierarchy and function.

I still practiced my escape down the ladder, and the ruggedness of the beach kept our new neighbors from crashing my private retreat in the cove.

A huge meadow of wildflowers decorates the area surrounding our house in the spring and summer months. Another Victorian-era house, the O'Donnells', built the same year as ours, sits across the road. For years, nothing more was built around us on the cliffs with their sweeping, dizzying view of the rocky coast below.

The calm I found within the chaos was almost always instantly available to me there below the cliff.

I have been to church and synagogue. None of it feels personal. The pronouns are wrong. I think that place on the beach provided a kind of substitute church for me. I don't think I would have called what I did back then *praying*. I'd have called it *wishing hard*. I kept a hope I'd get over feeling so badly about things. I don't know why, but I anticipated that things would end up all right and I'd come out strong and feeling better.

When I imagined God's image I pictured the wooden woman, the ship masthead. When my father lost the bar, I was devastated to learn she'd been sold at an auction, yet I still believed she was watching out for me. Otherwise, I felt isolated. I felt a child's social understanding of existential loneliness. I felt different, but I couldn't name or describe my difference. All I knew was that my concerns, my needs, my likes, and my dislikes were different than those of my brothers and any of my friends.

At times, when I was recognized, I became embarrassed by the difference and tried to figure out a way to hide. I decided early on I'd learn to pretend to be like everyone else. But I couldn't seem to get a bead on how to respond spontaneously and still remain certain. When I could rehearse communication with other people, I felt fine, but in a situation where I had to improvise I became lost and grew quiet, which I'm sure made me appear even more unusual. I compared myself to my family members. Wendy seemed to have been born with an innate understanding of the dark side of human nature, while I grew into my teens needing a field guide for intention. My older brother, David, let everything roll off his shoulders. He hardly noticed and seemed to never get upset by the things that happened. Moses preferred to hide in his closet. I couldn't tune it out like David. I became angry and acid-tongued around my family. I needed to fight. I didn't believe anything could change otherwise, and I needed it to change.

I never believed my family made me different or that my difference grew as a result of my environment. I didn't even feel like a member of a family. Our house very loosely held a group of individuals who happened to share a space but no commonality. We were solely growing up together.

In the meantime, I decided I would try to be smart and strong. These were the qualities I strived to develop through the years of my childhood, though it got more difficult as I got older.

I began to see my life in parts. When something bad, or weird, or crazy happened, like my father having a gun and threatening my mother, I'd say to myself: *This is the part where my father points a gun at my mother's head.* Like in a movie or something.

I don't know why that made it seem better, but it did. It became more about watching the weirdness than contributing to it. Also, when you see your life as crappy in parts rather than crappy as a whole, it somehow seems easier to handle.

Six

Samuel Trautman, 69 years | August, 1979

BROOKLINE, MASSACHUSETTS

YOU ASK ME to write my story. This is not a story I will want you to read now, while you are starting out your life with hope. Later, after I am gone, I think. But I will write for you, Chavalah, my little Chava.

I have three stories. I will tell the first and the third story. I don't tell the second story. No one I know who lived the second story will tell the second story except to someone who lived it. Better to forget that story and live to tell another one.

You will find that most of the parts are lost. A few memories survive as fragments. Other parts are as whole and grounded as the earth of my *Bubbe* Chava's orchards. My boyhood home. I will put down every detail of these stories I can remember before all the parts are lost.

And so you will have my truth.

I will begin at my beginning, when I am still called Szaja.

September 5th, 1923. Ivnitza, Russian Empire.
We lived near the Teteriv River in a small village called Ivnitza, which is surrounded by ancient forests. Zhytomyr, the nearest city, sat north of us.

This is the day my *mater* and *foter* left the Ukraine, which had, in recent years, been swallowed up like a pig's dinner and become part of Russia. I am thirteen years old. *Mater* and *Foter* also left me, my two younger brothers Idel and your uncle Oizer, my two older twin sisters Ruchel and Sura, and my eldest sister, Reizel, your aunt Rose, eighteen and married to a young man named Berl. We are left on my *Bubbe* Chava's farm.

That day they began their long travels to Turkey and to the eventual sailing to America. They are going to make a new life for us. My *foter* promised to send for us as soon as he could.

Every night, for weeks, we spent the evenings helping to pack. This involved much more laughing, singing, and making fun of my *foter*'s terrible dancing than actual work. The day before, we had finished the last of the apple harvesting from our orchards. It had been a good year for fruit. First the cherries in the spring, and now the apples. We made more money in the markets these two past seasons than in the years before—the years of the famine.

Since they are leaving before the Rosh Hashana holiday, my *foter* said we should say the religious poems, the *piyyuttim*, together. *Mater*, Reizel and the twins made a feast of food—apples dipped in honey, *rodanchas*, potato *latkes*, and delicious challah bread, finished with a delicious *Lekach* cake with cinnamon and raisins. This I remember as the first time my belly felt full in nearly two years.

The three youngest children—including Idessa, still a baby of five months—would leave on the journey with my parents. I am to take charge of my two younger brothers; Ruchel and Sura would help with their care. Reizel and Berl would take charge of all of us. My *foter*, Abram, like most of the people in our village, spoke Yiddish, Polish, bits of Russian, German, and Ukranian. He helped to teach us all to speak these languages. You never knew who you might need to speak with. Knowing other languages could save your life.

My *foter*, a good-natured man and a hard worker, is also a dreamer. When he married my *mater*, his in-laws, my *Bubbe* and *Zayde*, gave him their orchards as a dowry. It is a good gift, but he never found happiness with his life as a farmer, and he dreamed of life as a wealthy man.

Meantime, the wars brought sorrow to our village. We lived in perpetual fear of arrest. Every day our enemies changed: the Bolsheviks, the anarchists, the White Russians, or the Poles.

The most recent local violence had been at the hands of the Cossacks. Budionny's 1st Army destroyed the bridges in Zhytomyr, wrecked the train station, and burned buildings, including the synagogue in our village.

No one knew what could happen to us.

These are the times of the pogroms. All around us in other parts of Russia, now called the USSR, we heard of whole villages of Jews being rounded up and marched out, homes burned or taken over by armies. This had been happening for years and years.

My *foter*'s boyhood friend, Mendel, traveled to America—to New York City—

and sent occasional letters filled with extravagant stories of American prosperity and opportunity. Mendel's family had already joined him in New York.

My *foter*, Abram, decided he should go to America and live the good life as well. He wrote to Mendel and announced he is coming. Mendel wrote back and told him he planned to move to Brooklyn, that he'd found a bigger apartment. He wrote that Abram should come and live with them, but he couldn't take all of us at once. My family, even in our village, where families are huge, is one of the largest.

And so, my *foter*, without waiting for an exact address—how big could the village of Brooklyn be?—would pack up himself, my *mater*, and the youngest children and begin the journey toward the paradise called America.

He'd decided a year earlier that my twin sisters—fourteen at the time—could go to America as servants to a rich American family. He saw advertisements in the Kiev market for such things. They advertised outrageous wages for young girls. This would provide passage for all of us at the same time. But, when Ruchel failed to recover fully from the typhus and Sura refused to go without her, he softened and decided to wait until he arrived in America and could secure a spot for them himself.

Knowing what I know now about those advertisements for young girls from small Ukranian villages, it would have been a bad gamble. But considering the alternative nightmare they endured, perhaps the odds would not have been as bad.

I remember being amazed he convinced my *mater* to leave her children and the farm she had grown up on and embark on this journey. *Mater* had always been the practical one.

———

Before they left, my *foter* walked me out to the apple orchard and spoke to me about his plan to go to America. I remember the sunrise that morning. The flaming orange and blood red reflections on the orchard leaves made them glow like lanterns.

"Why, *Foter?* Why do you have to go?" I scowled and dug my toe into a mound of leafy dirt.

"Once we are in America, we will have many opportunities. This family will be healthy and prosperous. We will find a good doctor to help your sister Ruchel. We will send for everyone to come and live with us."

"I should go with you and find a job in America. I can work and help save money for everyone to come. Reizel and Berl can take care of the children." I had become a Bar Mitzvah that year. I considered myself a man.

"Your *mater* and I need you to take care of your brothers, Szaja. Reizel and Berl will be busy with the farm and the girls. You need to make sure they stay out of trouble. You're a man now, yes. I need you to be a *schtark* man and keep the family safe. No matter what happens, Szaja, don't let anything separate the family further. Protect your brothers and your sisters. Now *Bubbe* and *Zayde* have gone, we are all the family we have on this earth. *Iberkumen*."

———

Iberkumen. Survive. Yes. This is most important. Abram's parents had died long ago, and he had been the sole surviving child, all the rest taken to their deaths by disease or war.

My *mater*, Tailia, had two sisters, much older, who had moved away with their respective husbands long ago and not been heard from in years. They had, no doubt, been buried by hard times of their own.

My *mater*, ever loyal, stayed with her parents, even marrying a man who agreed to work their orchards. She bore seventeen children after marrying Abram at fourteen. She lost nearly half the children she carried to disease and famine. We had recently lost my *Grandmater* Chava, and my brother, Gershon, to typhus. Gershon, two years older than me, had been my best friend and ally.

Losing him, for me, is a terrible grief, but to my *foter* it had been devastation. Gershon, as his eldest son, had been the one he'd pinned his hopes of a better life upon. When he died, my *foter* died a bit as well. I think this is why, when he began to talk of leaving for America, my *mater* agreed. This is the first light we had seen shining from my *foter*'s eyes in over a year.

Survival, I think, is some part of our genetic path. We are directed by our blood. Our ancestors survived countless trials and we are coming through a difficult period of poverty and hunger. If I tell the truth of what the world is like in that time, Chavalah, you may not believe. None of your history books will tell you this story.

Under the Soviet Communist regime, we suffered a famine that, contrary to what the history books say, is not solely caused by drought and crop failures. The famine had been concentrated in the provinces of Southern Ukraine, and this area is known for its abundant grain crops. More people lived there when I am a boy than all the people in China right now, but between the fall of 1921 and the spring of 1923 over a quarter of these people died of starvation and disease.

This is an abomination. Saving this population would not have been difficult. During the two years of the famine, the Bolshevik government stole from us many times the amount of grain it could have taken to end the crisis.

I hated the Bolsheviks.

You see, most of the confiscated grain got shipped abroad: the first year to Russia, the second to Russia and the West. The Ukraine is also ordered to send additional famine relief to the Volga and to feed over two million people who came from Russia as refugees, soldiers, and administrators. Our own area had been badly affected, but not to the extent the southern regions suffered.

Where we lived, Chavalah, in the north, there are many orchards. Fruits, which ripened and grew rotten in a relatively short time, are not required as a part of the government shipments to other countries. We are obliged, however, to give up a portion of the harvest, as well as a taxed percentage of profit from our sales. Remember, we had no refrigeration. Our transportation—a cart driven by our horse, Pavolyah. We sold the fruit from our orchards, mainly cherries and apples, in the local markets and sometimes as far away as Zhytomyr. During those hard years, we grew a small crop of potatoes, which we hid in a tiny section of the orchard. Survival became possible by using our own fruit and vegetables, eggs and meat from occasional chickens, and the meager supplies we bartered for with our neighbors. Many others are not as fortunate. Families are broken. Orphans wandered the countryside trying to find food and work.

Berl, Reizel's husband, came to us from the south, through the famine. One day, late in the winter, he appeared in the orchard like a starving ghost and asked my *foter* for work.

A boy of sixteen, he is lame, many of his toes lost to frostbite.

My *foter* eyeballed him and shook his head. "*Oy vey*, Tailia, what am I going to do with a lame cherry picker?"

"Put him on the tallest ladder under the ripest, fullest limbs. He will be a good worker," my *mater* pronounced. She could see already he'd be a loyal husband to Reizel. As we are giving him his life with the work, my parents didn't have to provide a dowry, an impossibility at the time.

Berl is hard worker, despite his disability, and also a kind husband to Reizel. Reizel never complained about the match, but I know she felt unhappy. She is smart and had dreamed of leaving the orchards to go to university somewhere where they allowed girls to study. As the eldest girl, however, she is caretaker to all the other children.

Reizel is the one who mothered me. By the time I came, my *mater* is busy working in the orchards, cutting, stringing, drying, and storing the apples and preserving and storing the other fruit and vegetables we grew. Although Yiddish and Russian are our spoken languages, Reizel helped my *foter* to teach us all to read and write Hebrew, Ukranian, Polish, Russian, and German. Berl taught us the English he'd learned. We would be ready for America.

Oizer is eleven. He is the second—still-living—son in our family and he is smart with money. He figured out a way to gain our market baskets for free by secretly exchanging our produce with the market women from Kiev. Fruit baskets are our main expense, and Oizer saved us such a great deal with this barter that my *foter* is able to buy tickets, papers, and supplies for their trip within the year.

We never told the Bolsheviks we didn't buy our baskets anymore. For what did they have to know? They'd make us pay more taxes.

———

"But how soon will you send for us, *Foter*?"

"Soon. Soon, Szaja. Be patient and your patience will be rewarded."

"Will I be able to go to school in America, *Foter*?"

"*Ye, ye*, all my children will be scholars in America. *Oy*, we will talk many long discussions regarding important matters. It will put your sister Idessa to sleep."

Idessa, the baby, is famous in our family for keeping us all awake with her fussiness.

"And I will learn to be a doctor, *Foter*? I will go to the University of America and study?"

"*Ye, ye*, you will be the doctor, Szaja. Reizel will study, and Oizer will be a *milyon* merchant. Make sure Idel stays out of trouble. The boy has marbles in his head for brains."

"I will make sure, *Foter*."

———

Idel, then eight years old, is a worry to me. A mischievous toddler, now he is a bit of a wild boy. He acted before he thought—if he thought at all. He is always getting into scrapes and the family is always bandaging him up.

Once, he decided to climb the tallest apple tree.

When my *mater* found Idel with his arm broken, on the ground and wailing with pain, she asked him, "Why did you climb the tree?"

Idel wept as he spoke. "To see the view."

"But what were you thinking? It's not safe," insisted my *mater*. "Didn't you think about how you might be hurt, or how you would climb down?"

"No, I wanted to see what I could see up there," Idel cried.

"So, what did you see?"

"Nothing but more trees."

"What did you learn?"

"I learned G-d doesn't want me to see the view, because when I turned around to see more in the other direction, I slipped and fell."

"G-d wants you to see, Idel. He also wants you to think carefully before you do things so you won't become hurt."

"Did an angel catch me, *Mater*?"

"An angel? Why should you ask this question?"

"Because after I hurt my arm on a branch while I fell, I felt someone catch me and put me on the ground."

That day, Idel's angel became a sort of talisman to ward off anything bad and to protect us. If there is a storm brewing while we are out on the road, my *foter* summoned Idel's angel to see the family safely home. Idel's angel is enlisted for every family illness, for protection from the soldiers, and to ensure our orchards good production. My *mater* even used Idel's angel to remember where she put her sewing basket.

The arm is set and healed quickly, but Idel still never listened. He is impulsive and carefree. I thought then it would take much more than a broken arm to lead Idel to reflect on his actions.

———

"Don't leave me with him here long, *Foter*. Already he won't listen to anyone."

"Don't worry, Szaja, it won't be long. It won't be long at all, you have my promise."

———

My *foter* had no way of knowing that my escape from Eastern Europe would take another twenty-five years.

That life, my boyhood life, is the sweetest time. The winters are long and harsh and the work tiring, but the reward of my family, together and laughing, is all I ever needed. I knew this, even then.

But my *foter* is excited and happy, and it is hard not to be happy with him. Standing there in the orchard with him, the late summer sunrise lighting everything golden as the sun began its slow climb into the day, I inhaled the scent of the ripe apple trees and the damp earth.

I stood there with a smile on my face, knowing with a dreadful certainty that I would never experience that kind of happiness again.

Seven

RECESS

I REACH FOR a swing on the school ground at recess when something hits me, hard, on the back of the head.

Whoever did this is going to be sorry.

The next thing I know, several people stand over me, watching me. As if I'm a bug. One of the playground monitors, Mrs. Hertiss, says someone has to walk me to the nurse's office.

I hate nurses. I hate needles and shots. They go together. Besides, recess ranks as one of my favorite times of the day, and today spring finally came. I can smell it in the warming air. It's the smell of old things heated and dried.

"I don't need to go."

I try to sit up but fall back again, dizzy.

"Oh, you're going to the nurse all right, but wait until you don't feel too dizzy to move. What happened anyway, Julianne?" Mrs. Hertiss asks.

"Something hit me on the head."

Mrs. Hertiss interrogates the kids around me.

"What hit her?"

A boy named Larry speaks: "Don't know. We didn't see anything."

"Were you standing near her?"

"Yeah, but we didn't see anything."

"How can that be? Maybe one of you accidentally hit her?"

There's a whole bunch of "Nos."

"All right—you," she points to Larry, "take her down to the nurse's office and make sure she doesn't fall."

Larry helps me up and walks me into the school and down the hallway to the nurse's office across from the cafeteria. The fifth graders are finishing lunch and I'm embarrassed. I tell Larry he can let me walk the rest of the way.

But he insists on helping. "You could fall again. No way I'm gonna let you fall down."

I'm surprised he's acting nice to me. I don't have any real friends at school. Friends are too much bother and kind of risky. I can't bring people back to our house because I never know what Wendy will do to embarrass me. She loves taking off her clothes and stuff and walking around the place that way.

The other reason I don't have any friends is I've been having trouble getting along with people. People make me mad. Kind of in general. Like Jo in *Little Women*, "I am angry nearly every day of my life." When anyone makes me mad, I slug them, which gets me in lots of trouble. I end up spending lots of my recesses standing against the punishment wall instead of running around. Once I even got in trouble standing *in detention* because I tried to talk to one of the girls in detention with me. She told me her name was Lily and she was "emotionally disturbed." I'm not sure what this means, but I'm curious if I might be too. I got fascinated talking to her. The teacher who watches the detention kids charged over to us and told me to stop bothering her.

I argued with her. I hadn't been bothering Lily; she was happy that someone was talking to her. The teacher kicked me out of detention anyway. I became afraid to talk to Lily after that, but I looked up *emotional disturbance* in one of Wendy's psychology textbooks (she was taking a psychology class at college). I decided I could have *emotional disturbance*, too.

When we walk into the office, the nurse, Mrs. Dougherty, asks what we want. Larry and I speak simultaneously.

"I got hit on the head with something, but I'm fine now."

"She got hit on the head and fell down and couldn't talk for a little while."

Mrs. Dougherty asks me if I think I lost consciousness.

"Huh?"

"Do you remember falling on the ground?"

She feels the back of my head, which now has a big, painful knot.

"No, I don't."

She leans over and peers into my eyes with a tiny flashlight.

"Do you know what hit you?"

"No, uh, I don't. . . Can I go back to recess?" I ask.

"Larry, *you* can go back to the playground," Mrs. Dougherty says.

Larry leaves and Mrs. Dougherty makes me lie down on the hospital cot in her office. I worry she might give me a shot or something.

"I'm fine, and I'm going to miss my class if you keep me here any longer. Can I go back now?"

"How old are you Jules?"

"In exactly one month I'll be nine"

"What's your address?"

"Ummmmh." I start to tell her, but then I worry about why she needs the information. Luckily she drops it.

The back of my head doesn't sting until Mrs. Dougherty dabs *mercurochrome* on it. There must be a big cut back there. I'm mortified and infuriated because I'm sure I have a big red stain, like a weirdo.

"No. I'm sorry, but—I think you may have a concussion, and the lump on your head might grow bigger and more painful if you don't let me put ice on it."

She fixes an ice pack and puts it under my head on the pillow. "Jules, what's your telephone number? I need to call your mother."

"Um, I don't remember."

She stares at me, trying to decide if I'm telling the truth.

Calling Wendy is not an option. She's probably gone to a friend's to party.

Probably high.

She's doing most of her partying at her friends' houses lately. She leaves for long weekends—pretends she's going to be gone for just one night, then calls the next day to check in and tell us she might stay another day.

When she parties on a night before a school day, she calls and pretends she'll be back the next morning to check on us and make sure we're at school. Then she shows up at dinnertime with fast food so we won't be mad at her.

We love fast food. Wendy loves it because it gives her an excuse to drive to the next town, where the new Burger King and McDonald's are—off the island.

Wendy is a terrible cook.

Anyway, when Mrs. Dougherty can't pull my phone number from me, she finds it in the school directory. I can hear the phone ringing. I pray she isn't there.

"Hello, this is Mrs. Dougherty, Julianne's school nurse. I'm calling because Julianne had an accident. She's been struck by something on the school grounds, and I think she might have a concussion. You may want to bring her to your pediatrician."

I hear Wendy's voice screeching through the phone. Loud music blaring in the background. "Can't you send her back to class?"

"No, she's not well enough to go back to class."

"We live a block away. Tell her to walk home."

"I see. I can't let her walk home, regardless of how close you live. You'll have to come and pick her up."

"I can't come." Wendy says.

"Do you have a car?"

"Yeeeees. I have a car." She sounds mad, and I could've told Mrs. Dougherty if she pisses Wendy off she can forget about her ever coming to take me.

"Well, I don't understand," Mrs. Dougherty says. She keeps rolling her eyes and winding one hand tightly around the telephone cord like she wants to use it to strangle Wendy. I'm worried she can tell that Wendy is high.

"It's all right," I say. "I really do live close by. Approximately five minutes. I don't mind walking."

"You sit tight, sweetie," Mrs. Dougherty says to me. "Mrs. Finn, you need to come and pick up Julianne."

"For God's sake, if you think she needs a ride, why don't you drive her?" Wendy screams.

"I can't drive her. I'm still on duty and I need to stay here on school grounds. You need to . . ."

Wendy must have hung up on her.

Mrs. Dougherty hangs up the phone and stares at it, not saying anything. Finally, she smiles politely at me. "Does your mother have a car?"

I nod.

"Does she have a problem driving?"

I think about that one for a bit before I answer. "Nooo," I say hesitantly.

She stares at me hard, then she speaks real softly and says, "Rest your eyes. I'm sure she'll be here soon."

She tells me to close my eyes but stay awake, and she will watch for my mother.

We wait like that for a very long time. During this time, Mrs. Dougherty speaks to Mr. Bellami, the school principal, about the conversation with my mother. His office is in the middle of a short hallway running between the main office and hers. I can hear everything, even though his office is closed.

Mr. Bellami already knows Wendy because she came to the parent-teacher meeting last fall. I can tell Mr. Bellami doesn't like her by the way he talks with Mrs. Dougherty now, but at the parent-teacher meeting he talked with her more than any of the other mothers. Probably because she was wearing one of her see-through blouses and a miniskirt. He stared at her breasts practically the whole night. It's mortifying, and I wish she'd stop showing up at our school, but for some bizarre reason school and our grades is the one thing she gets *parent freaky* about. She gets all As in her college classes, and if I don't pull As she's mad at me *and* my teacher. I got a B in Science and she argued with my teacher about it for like an hour. It was so embarrassing.

I keep falling asleep. Mrs. Dougherty keeps waking me up and telling me not to nap but to keep my eyes shut.

I start to think about the trip we took in February to Key West.

—⸺—

After all these years, this unexpected trip remains the only time I have traveled beyond Boston. Amazingly, on our spring vacation, we were flying to Miami, Florida and then driving south to the Keys. My grandfather paid for the whole thing, of course.

Once we got to Key West, I figured out why Wendy took us there under the guise of a family vacation: so she could be with her boyfriend, Jack.

Jack lives with us. He moved in about three months after Howard left. He grew up in Withensea—on our side of the island, down the road from us—and moved from his mother's house into ours. He hardly ever works, since Wendy supports him with my grandfather's money. He scores all his drugs, drink, and food for free, and Wendy takes care of him with a surprising amount of mothery care.

He's become a fixture, literally. He almost never moves from Wendy's bed during the day. He sleeps, watches TV, does drugs, drinks, and eats. All in that bed. Mostly he sleeps. He seems to sleep all the time. He barely speaks to us kids. He barely speaks at all unless he's really lit on alcohol. He's usually high.

There are a few things that inspire him to move from the bed. I'll list them in order of frequency: going to the bathroom, riding his motorcycle, and doing art projects. One day last fall he got out of the bed and actually started taking classes at an art school in Boston. He turned the basement into his studio, which includes a dark room. He works nocturnally. We barely see him.

Everything Jack produces is beautiful. He makes stained glass windows and lamps and sand paintings, and after taking the photography classes he started making great photos, which he sells to pay his bar tabs.

I like the creative part about Jack. I still draw and I've started oil painting this year. So we have something in common. But he hardly ever speaks to me, and I mostly avoid him.

The artistic part of Jack is the reason Wendy puts up with his lack of ambition, his sleeping around, and the fact that he's catatonic. She loves the idea of having an artist boyfriend.

Also, and most importantly—in Wendy's mind, at least—Jack is handsome.

I don't think he's heart-stoppingly handsome like Omar Sharif or Cat Stevens, but he looks like a surfer version of the Marlboro Man. This is important because even though Wendy has a lot of self-esteem about her intelligence, she was a fat kid, and she's really self-conscious about her weight, which is why she's always on a diet. I guess she figures people won't think she's that bad-looking if somebody she thinks is handsome, like Jack, likes her. So I think she overlooks the parts of Jack that don't fit with an ideal mate.

In my opinion, she looks just fine. People sometimes tell her she looks like Jennifer O'Neill when she straightens her hair with the big pink soup-can curlers.

She's weird about my weight too. People constantly tell me I'm too skinny, but whenever Wendy hears them say it she goes crazy. "She's perfect at this weight," she yelled at our pediatrician when he tried to lecture her about feeding me. I had to go see him for a tetanus shot when I stepped on a rusty nail and the whole way back from my visit she kept ranting that it was better to be thin than fat and I should consider myself lucky. She told me that even if I didn't turn out pretty, if I was skinny I'd be considered attractive.

I could care less about that stuff.

That January, when I was eight, Jack got hired to sail a boat from Massachusetts through the Panama Canal to California. Key West was a port stop for him. Wendy managed to weasel his sailing information from the boat's owner, even though Jack told her he wanted privacy, and she surprised him with a visit. Jack likes women, and Wendy grabs every opportunity to interrupt his "adventures."

It's a long drive down to the Keys, and when we checked into a hotel it was almost midnight. Wendy told us she was going to see Jack and we should go to sleep. Four hours later, she came back to the hotel a Complete Emotional Mess. She woke me up and proceeded to have a meltdown. She didn't bother to keep her voice down, but my brothers, in the other double bed, slept right through her yelling.

I guess when she arrived at the dock Jack was partying with the crew and his new girlfriend who had been sailing with them for a few days.

"I can't believe I trusted that asshole. He's fucking her while I'm waiting for him to call me. I will never trust that bastard again. Never trust men, you dig me? Their penises do all their thinking for them."

I didn't understand what she meant by "thinking with his penis," but I tried to give her good advice. I told her what I've heard my teenage neighbors say to one another when they get mad at their boyfriends: "You can find another boyfriend. You don't need him."

Wendy, apparently, thought this was a good solution. The next day, she paid for our breakfast and gave me the room key after we changed into our swimsuits to go down to the hotel pool.

"Watch your brothers and be good. I'll bring back dinner."

We had fun swimming and watching the TV in our hotel room, but Moses and I got sunburned, unlike David, who tans. When Wendy returned she carried in tons of bags with clothes she'd bought for herself, but she'd forgotten to bring dinner. She got mad at me for getting us sunburned and told me we'd better stay out of the sun the next day. Then she told us someone was coming to pick her up later for a date.

This is the part where we started calling my mother Wendy.

She told us to call her Wendy and pretend she was our sister—a practice I've continued since we got back from Florida. Calling her "Wendy" helps take the "mother" expectations away. She doesn't usually mind it, and it fits us better.

A very, very young man named Danny showed up a few hours later. I answered when he knocked. Wendy was still getting ready in the bathroom. When she came out she smelled like patchouli incense and was wearing a sheer, navy-blue blouse with a fringed vest made from a leather American flag. The miniskirt she wore barely covered her butt and her knee-high boots were a shiny, white plastic material. She wore her hair all curly-frizzy with a leather headband tied around her forehead.

I behaved like an obedient sibling. "Wendy, could we have money to order a pizza for dinner?"

David and I had already figured out how to charge food to the room, but they only accepted cash for pizza delivery. Wendy gave me a totally fake smile and handed me a fiver from her new purple-suede fringed pocketbook.

The rest of the week of vacation went pretty much the same way. The boy/man was different every night, though. She came back late every night except for one night, when she didn't come back until the next morning. Then she locked us out so she could sleep all day.

My brothers and I ate more pizza that week than we've ever had in our whole life.

Something interesting I discovered is that Florida has scads of elderly people. We met lots of grandparent types staying at the hotel who sneaked us forbidden food like Twinkies and Orange Fanta and slathered sunscreen on us. I got a splendid gift from one old lady, an art history book about Edvard Munch called *Things That Make You Want to Scream.* Her husband kept joking with me and asking if I was Veronica Lake's granddaughter. *Sullivan's Travels* is one of my favorite old movies. I was totally flattered.

We made one trip to see downtown Key West—mostly the bars Wendy had been hanging out in, and she got mad when we slipped and called her "Mom" in front of the bartender.

We also saw Hemingway's home. I had just finished reading *For Whom the Bell Tolls* and it made a huge impression on me to see his home and especially his writing room. He left lots of inheritance to his cats, which had extra toes and ran around everywhere. I met a cat there named Rothko, who is pretty much my favorite artist. I especially love his painting *Blue, Green, Brown*. The strange thing is, that very day, the day we visited the Hemingway Home, Mark Rothko died. One of the guides at the Hemingway Home told me. I wondered if Hemingway and Rothko were friends.

———

After about two hours of waiting, the final school bell rings and it's the end of the school day. Mrs. Dougherty calls Wendy again. The music on the other end of the phone sounds even louder.

"Hello, this is Mrs. Dougherty from the school. School is over now. We can't keep Julianne here any longer. You need to come now."

Wendy shouts, "I can't come. Let her walk home now. I'm sure she's fine."

"I still can't let her walk home. She's been struck and as I said earlier, I think she may have a concussion. You need to bring her to your doctor to examine her. She's got a large bump on the back of her head."

Wendy doesn't say anything, but the music blasts through the phone.

"Is there a problem, Mrs. Finn? Because I could have you talk with Mr. Bellami, our principal, if you would feel more comfortable."

Mrs. Dougherty is trying to scare Wendy with the principal, but I know Wendy isn't afraid.

Nobody scares her. Not even my father.

Wendy is wicked smart and belongs to a club for Einstein geniuses. Sometimes it takes me and my brothers a while to figure out her tricks, but after a while, we do. We're not stupid; we were all above average in intelligence according to the test she gave us, but we don't have genius IQs like her.

"It's not a good idea to coddle children when they injure themselves, you know," Wendy says.

"Excuse me?" Mrs. Dougherty says sharply.

"It's called negative reinforcement. Read Skinner. It's a form of operant conditioning. If you give kids attention when they become sick, they relate the injury to attention and manifest illness with more frequency. Surely you learned a bit of childhood psych development when you got your nursing degree? I mean you do work as a school nurse!" Wendy's voice rings out in the room.

I think Mrs. Dougherty's head might pop off she gets so angry-red in her face.

"Mrs. Finn, I do know quite a bit about children, their behavior, and their needs. Your job as a parent is to make sure her needs are met. Bringing her to the doctor to be checked out isn't spoiling her, it's protecting her. Your daughter needs your attention right now."

"I'm not sure," Wendy says. "I read Erikson, and I think he's been interpreted in too linear a fashion. The stages of development aren't necessarily sequential. There've been studies that show abandoned children manage to raise themselves in the wild. It follows that children, given food and shelter and surrounded with many more tools for survival, can raise themselves without the interference of adults who think they know what they're doing."

I have no idea what Wendy is talking about, but it sort of seems like she's winning. I figure the psychology stuff she's studying at Northeastern must be good.

Mrs. Dougherty says, "Children that have been cross-fostered by wild animals, like *wolves*, sometimes manage to survive in the wild. However, they fail to develop key human components like language or social skills, regardless of how long they're schooled following their abandonment. Surely your daughter deserves a better chance at survival than the Wild Boy of Aveyron, Mrs. Finn?"

Wendy quiets down. I don't know who the Wild Boy is, but I know I don't want to end up like him even if Wendy thinks it might be a better way to raise kids. But she agrees to come and shows up in the Country Squire a few minutes later. She beeps her horn so long and loud I hear it inside the nurse's office. I jump out of the cot and onto my feet quickly and I make myself dizzy. I have to sit down again.

"Let's go slow, Julianne," Mrs. Daugherty says.

She puts her arm around my shoulders, helps me up, and walks me outside to Wendy's car. On the way out to the car she says, "If you ever want to come down to my office and talk, I won't mind. You can talk about anything you like and we can keep it private, okay?"

She means well, but I've decided adults aren't to be trusted about anything they say. She and Mr. Bellami are likely in cahoots to get us taken away from Wendy and have her put in jail. Wendy told us what would happen if she went to jail.

Orphanages.

She told us she came from an orphanage before she was adopted and about how awful and mean the people were. I figure she's telling the truth about that one since she's mean and they must have made her that way. She never talks about it, either, and we're not supposed to ask my grandparents about it. It must have been horrible.

"Your mother should take you to the doctor and have him check you. If she decides not to, shut the curtains to keep it dark and lie down in your bed, but don't fall asleep. I'll tell her this when we talk," Mrs. Dougherty says.

She walks me over to the car and stands with me on the sidewalk, waiting for Wendy to get out. Instead, Wendy waves at her and reaches over to unlock my door from the driver's side. Mrs. Dougherty helps me slide in, and without saying a word Wendy drives off before I even have time to say good-bye and close my door. I hang on to the dashboard as Wendy swerves out and in again with the car to swing the door closed.

I turn and catch Mrs. Dougherty's face as we pull away from the school. She looks like Edvard Munch's *Scream*.

I know it's useless for me to ask, but I want an explanation. "Why didn't you come?"

"I have friends visiting, and I couldn't leave them."

"But I have a concussion. Do you know how mortifying it is to wait for you? I think the nurse might call the police on you."

I know I've gone too far. Wendy laughs. I can tell she's high because she's weaving the car all over the road. I'm glad we only have a few blocks to go.

"Are you going to take me to the doctor? Mrs. Dougherty says I should go to see a doctor."

"No. I don't think you need to see a doctor."

I'm not surprised by this. We have to be practically dying or dripping blood for Wendy to take us to our pediatrician. So I figure I should do what Mrs. Dougherty told me, to be safe.

"Mrs. Dougherty told me to lie down when I go back to the house, with the blinds closed, but not to fall asleep."

Wendy doesn't say anything.

"Just so you know, I don't want to end up like the Wild Boy."

Wendy laughs and reaches over to feel my head. I flinch because I think she might hit me. Sometimes she gives me a slap when I speak sarcastically. Sometimes she ignores it.

"I wanna feel your bump."

I direct her hand to the back of my head.

"Wow, big bump. Okay, lie down in your room if you want to. I've got friends over, though."

That's Wendy's hint to stay out of her way and outside, if at all possible.

My brothers and I make this possible for her since we don't like her friends. When she invites friends over, they don't do drugs—none that we're aware of, anyway. It's like a concession to a code of ethics related to her parental status. So far, anyway.

Eight

Jules, 8 years | April 15th, 1970

CODE CHANGE

WE PULL INTO our driveway. Music blares out onto Alethea Road from inside.

On almost every inch of our driveway and our now tire-marked front lawn: motorcycles.

I stagger out of the car, still dizzy, and start exploring the motorcycles. They say "Hells Angels." They have wild-painted designs in bright colors.

"What does 'Hells Angels' mean?" I ask Wendy.

Wendy says, "It's a club for motorcycle riders."

Then she walks inside and joins the party.

The smell of something moldy-sweet hits me as soon as I walk up the porch stairs. It's the same smell I remember from Wendy's visits to her old friend Natasha.

Inside, tons of people sit around the kidney-bean glass coffee table in our living room. They pass a cigarette with the weird, moldy smell back and forth to each other. I know its marijuana. I've smelled Jack smoking it when he thinks we're outside and I find tiny ends of them around all the time. As soon as I step into the living room, people scoop things up off the coffee table and stuff them in their pockets. They're hiding some kind of small tools from me, but I don't have a chance to see what they are. Everybody stops talking when I walk in the room. They stare at Wendy until Jill speaks. Jill is Wendy's newest, best friend.

"Jules, this is my boyfriend Billy, and these guys are friends of his and their chicks," Jill says, gesturing around.

"Hello," I say. "Are you all in the Hells Angels club?"

They all laugh hard. I can't understand why it seems like a funny question, but I figure Wendy lied about it's being a club or something. "Yeah, we're all part of the club," Jill says. I can tell she's trying to be nice, but it still seems like a joke on me.

Everybody seems sheepish. Probably something to do with the drugs they were doing and the fact a kid is there watching them. I scan the room. "Where's Jack?"

"He's taking a ride on a bike he's thinking about buying," Wendy says.

Jack's probably going to be joining the club, too, I'm thinking. Judging by the people in the living room, he'll fit right in.

Since Florida, Wendy's been wearing clothes that belong on the Sonny & Cher Show. When Jack got back from sailing, he was wearing the same style of clothes. Hardly anybody in Withensea, except maybe the teenagers, dresses like the two of them. Everybody in this room dresses like the hippies on TV. Only with more leather.

They fit right into Wendy's interior redecoration.

———

After the divorce from my father, Wendy went psychedelic with the decor. A bright magenta shag carpet now covers most of the floors. The kitchen has been covered in a vinyl pattern of large fire-hydrant orange, lemon-yellow, and lipstick-red daisies.

In the center of the living room is our same couch, reupholstered in a bright, rose-floral print. Next to it sits the formerly black, S-shaped chaise, now reupholstered in fluffy white sheepskin. On one side table by the couch is a lamp with a crushed velvet, scarlet-colored shade and tacky, dangling, scarlet-colored plastic jewels. On the other side sits a lamp with a round chrome base and a shiny, black-vinyl shade. Both lamps have blacklight bulbs.

All the walls are painted a pale shade of lavender. The antique framed pictures of my grandfather's parents still hang on the walls, but now they're joined with framed blacklight posters, most of them Peter Max creations.

The curtain rods are draped with moss-green, slubbed polyester fabric.

Scattered everywhere are random sculptures—donated by artist friends or created by Jack—and yard sale stuff that Wendy collects. The fact these things remain in place despite all the visitors who could have taken things without notice is more a statement about their "junkiness" and less about the honesty level of Wendy's friends.

In the den, the old black-and-white TV and phonograph are still there, but the TV and phonograph have become property of "the kids." Wendy uses a much more sophisticated stereo system, complete with a Pioneer "tape deck" set up next to a large color television she keeps in her bedroom. The bar, which used to hold my father's alcohol, has become a candle-making workshop. The top of the bar is littered with candle molds, spools of candlewick, boxes of dye, and bottles of scent. The planter, which before held his record albums, now displays the candles. Most were molded with the sand we've carted in pails from the beach. Wendy sells them at one of the town's arts and crafts stores with Jack's stained glass creations.

The exceptions to Wendy's redecorating are the bedrooms belonging to my brothers and me, and the dining room.

We rarely use the dining room since the divorce.

The money used to fund the entire redecorating job came from my father. Not that he volunteered it or anything: A week after the divorce was final, Wendy went to Sloane Sales, a big department store in Boston's South Shore, and used the Master Charge card he didn't know she kept in his name to buy over seven thousand dollars' worth of stuff.

Wendy charged furniture, carpet, appliances, bedding, drapery, clothing, a slew of art supplies for me, a bike for David, and a unicycle for Moses. She also bought new fishing rods and a small dinghy for Moses and me so we could go fishing in the bay, which was calmer than the ocean side of Withensea. She figured he owed it to her to make up for the money he'd gambled, the money he didn't share from the land he sold, and all the money he'd spent during the marriage.

My father got furious about the Sloane Sales spending spree, but Wendy got away with it somehow.

——

I hate the mess, the music, and the all noise from the people hanging around. Wendy and the hippie crowd don't even notice when I walk upstairs to the visual quiet and peace of my bedroom. The light there bothers my eyes, so I close the blinds, huddle under the covers, and, even though I try to follow Mrs. Dougherty's instructions, quickly fall asleep.

I wake up to the sound of my brother Moses shouting from downstairs. "She's dead, she's dead!"

Moses runs upstairs as he screams and bursts into my room. "Mummy is dead. She's dead." Somehow, oddly, I think he might add "Ding-dong."

"What are you talking about?" In two split seconds I've gone from sound asleep to high alert. "What happened? Stop shouting and tell me what happened."

Moses, breathing hard, sobs out his words.

"I saw her; she's on the ground at the corner. There's a motorcycle and another guy. She's not breathing and there's lots of blood."

Jack shouts from downstairs for Moses.

I answer, "We're up here."

Jack runs up the stairs and down the hallway to my room.

"What happened?" I ask.

"Your mother's been in a motorcycle accident. She went for a spin around the block with one of the guys, and I guess a car cut them off. Didn't see 'em. They skidded off the road and the guy who's driving got bad scrapes and maybe broke his leg, but your mother went flying."

"Is she all right?" I ask.

"She's in rough shape, but she's alive. She hit her head." He stops, then goes on. "She's on the way to the hospital now. Why don't you stay here with your brothers and I'll call you from the hospital and let you know how it's going?"

"Aye-aye," I say.

He turns, about to leave, then turns back to me. "Hey, what's going on here? Why are you in bed? Are you sick?"

"I got hit on the head at school today and got a concussion. The school nurse said to do this."

"Oh man, Moses, you'll have to take care of your sister for a bit until we get back."

"I'm fine," I protest.

"No arguments, man, you dig?" Jack says, and he leaves.

"See silly, she's alive," I tell Moses.

I sit up in bed and pull the covers back for him to join me. He crawls in. His body shakes.

"She didn't move, even when they put her in the ambulance car. She had puddles of blood around her head, and her mouth had dirt in it."

"If Jack says she's alive, she's alive. She probably got a concussion, like me."

"What's a concussion?"

"Come on, let's go downstairs and see if we can find something for dinner. I'll tell you all about concussions." I'm proud of my newfound head injury knowledge.

I start to push to my feet to go, but Moses grabs my hand and pulls me back down again. "I didn't tell anyone she's my mother—the whole time. At first she started moaning, then she didn't make any noise anymore. I thought she might be dead. I didn't tell anyone about her being my mother even when the ambulance car came. I didn't tell anyone."

I put my arm around him and pull him over to me, not knowing quite what to say. "Don't worry. There wasn't anything you could do anyway."

I'm still dizzy and sort of wobble up out of bed and down to the kitchen. David comes in. He's all sweaty from basketball practice. "What's going on?"

"Wendy's at the hospital. She got in a motorcycle accident and Jack's gonna call us later and let us know how she's doing."

"Who's gonna make dinner?" David says on his way into the shower.

———

I end up making us TV dinners.

This is the part where I take over making dinner.

Jack comes back from the hospital later that night and tells us Wendy might stay there for a while because she hurt her neck in the accident. She broke bones in her vertebrae. I study all the vertebrae information in our encyclopedias, but it doesn't make sense she would be alive if her neck is broken. I decide he didn't get the story straight. He tells us he'll call my father to come and take care of us. I argue we can take care of ourselves, but Jack won't listen, and he makes me call my Aunt Doreen. She's back in her winter home in Rhode Island, but she knows how to contact my father.

He stopped showing up for our Sunday visits a long time ago. The last we heard, he moved to Florida. Aunt Doreen tells me she'll call him, though. I try to assure her that we can take care of ourselves, but she has a rough idea of our situation, and she responds as I expect any responsible adult would: she tells me if he won't come take care of us, she will. I'm thrilled at the prospect of having Aunt Doreen come back to Withensea and stay with us for a while. We haven't seen her much since the divorce.

I figure my father won't want to come. He hates Wendy's parties, her friends, and the fact she smokes pot. He complains how "it's not good for the kids to see."

His absence, although I enjoy it, still seems like desertion. I think if he cared he would find a way to change the situation. Even when he was still showing up now and then for those Sunday visits, he never called to let us know either way, and Wendy refused to keep calling him to keep tabs on his plans. I know she loves the fact he's stopped visiting. He's rude, bossy, and occasionally even violent when he comes here.

He showed up once about a year ago, drunk in the middle of the day, waving his gun around. Jack was sleeping, as usual, when my father arrived, but he woke up quickly with all the screaming and ran downstairs. Moses and I were standing in the living room staring at Wendy and my father as they went at it.

Wendy yelled, "Shoot me, motherfucker, and you'll never see the outside of a jail cell."

"I'm not gonna shoot you, you lousy slut, I'm gonna shoot him." He pointed the gun at Jack.

"You're such an asshole. Whadya gonna shoot him for?" Wendy said.

Although Jack seemed shaken, standing there with my father pointing a gun at him, he acted equally shocked to hear Wendy in full verbal assault mode. She presents well most times and hadn't shown him her full colors until that point. He kept glaring at her and shouting, "Wendy!" every time she swore.

"Listen man, you don't want to shoot anyone. Your kids are here, and I know they don't want to see either of you this way. Why don't we all calm down?"

Wendy stormed upstairs and left Jack and us with my father. He didn't shoot anyone. I guess her going away calmed him down. He left soon after.

Tonight, I'm praying two prayers to the wooden woman, the old ship mast-head: First, that my Aunt Doreen will come take care of us. Second, that my father will stay in Florida.

Nine

Jules, 8 years | April 16th, 1970

HEMINGWAY'S MAFIA

I WAKE UP with the same huge lump on the back of my head and I'm still dizzy.

Jack has disappeared. I knew there was no way he would stay and take care of us.

Normally I go to Stillton Elementary, which is a short walk up the road. David takes a bus to Withensea Middle School, and Moses spends the mornings playing, while Wendy sleeps in, until the bus for his afternoon kindergarten session comes. But if David and I go to school, nobody will be there to babysit Moses. We decide we can *all* skip school.

This is the first time any of us have ever played hooky. It's warm outside, but we don't want anyone to find out we skipped. We stayed inside all day. First we play Life until we feel hungry. My brothers eat Wheaties, but I like Raisin Bran and we're out. I eat croutons from an old box in the cupboard while we all watch TV.

We're jumping on the sofa when the mailman comes. We scream and hide. That's fun. We play Hide and Seek 'for reals' inside our house, which we haven't done for ages. We play and laugh hard until Moses gets stuck trying to go down the hamper shoot. This is *really* funny until we have to pull him down by his legs to unstick him and he lands with a crash, tipping over the hamper. He's crying hard and there's a huge bump on his forehead. Now we both have bumps on our heads. Other than that, we're having one of the best days we've had in a long time.

Later that day we get a surprise. The wooden woman has ignored my prayers.

My father shows up. He doesn't just show up. He brings our new stepmother, Paulina. Until today, we'd no idea he'd remarried.

All my fairy tale ideas about ugly stepmothers shatter. Paulina is breathtakingly beautiful. She's tall, about six feet tall, with bangs and long, coppery-brown hair flipped up at the ends in big curls. Her lashes are unbelievably long, and she has big see-through blue eyes she's heaped loads of makeup on. She has a curvy body with long, long legs and big breasts. Her lips are outlined with a dark ruby-red pencil and painted in with a bright fuchsia-pink lipstick, and when she flashes her wide, white-toothed smile, she dazzles.

I've seen the Playboy magazines my father stashed under the bed when he lived with us, and Paulina looks like the women in those magazines, but with clothes on. Her perfume smells like lemon peels and nutmeg.

"Hello, you must be Julianne. Your father has told me so many nice things about you."

I wonder what nice things he might have said. We've rarely heard from him since his move to Florida, and he hasn't remembered to send birthday or Christmas cards for any of us for about two years, since the divorce. He puts his arm around Paulina proudly.

"I'd like you to meet my new wife, Paulina. We would have invited you to the wedding, but we decided quickly and had no time to bring you guys down to Florida."

His excuse doesn't fool me. It's clear we aren't part of his new life. I wonder if Paulina's figured out what a lousy father he is or if he's lied to her about how he treats us.

This is the part where we meet my father's second wife and we all play house.

The first thing he does is put us to work cleaning. Probably a good idea. Everything looks like a cyclone hit it and someone had a party with the debris. I don't think Wendy has dusted or cleaned anything thoroughly in the two years since he's been gone.

My brothers are told to clean their rooms. Since mine is already tidy, I'm on dusting duty. I am given a rag and a rusty can of Pledge and put to work in Wendy's room, where he and Paulina are, apparently, going to sleep.

My father was a neat freak when he lived with us. Many fights with Wendy were about her low standard of cleanliness. So I'm not surprised we're cleaning again. Still, I resent having to make things clean for him. Paulina pitches in and cleans up the kitchen while he makes several phone calls.

"Oh my," she keeps exclaiming from the kitchen. I'm not sure if she's reacting to Wendy's kitchen décor, the kitchen's state of disorder, or both.

My father makes a few crass comments about Wendy's credit card redecorating spree, but otherwise he seems happy. It seems like he's enjoying being back. After a while, when she sees we have nothing in the refrigerator, Paulina leaves for the store to grocery shop.

Wendy calls.

There are several phones spread around each floor of the house. My brothers and I each take our own extensions to talk to her. We all say hello. David is on the phone in the den and Moses is upstairs in Wendy's bedroom. I sit on the piano bench in the living room, where my father listens to my end of the conversation.

"How are you doing?" I ask.

"How long are you going to have to stay in the hospital?" David asks.

"Not sure. They *dunno* how long it'll take for my neck to heal. It's broken in two places," Wendy says. She sounds funny, like she's talking with her mouth full of food.

"But can't you come back home while it gets better?" Moses asks.

"No, the doctors *wammetuh* stay in the hospital case my breathing becomes worse. I *dunno* know how *longI'llbeere*."

Wendy begins to cry as we all listen on our various phones. No one knows what to say to her. Moses tries. "It's all right, Mummy. Dad's here and he brought his new wife, Paulina. They'll take care of us and you'll be better soon and come home."

We can hear her make a terrible gasping noise. "He brought *thadwhore?*"

Moses made a big mistake.

"*Puddyafatha* on the phone," Wendy says. I shakily hand the phone to him. "She wants to talk to you."

I can hear Wendy's scream through the receiver even when I cross the living room.

"You asshole! You bring that whore inside my house? *Getherouttathere!*"

At first he talks quietly back to her even though he says nasty things. "You're lucky your neck is already broken. If you think you can tell me what do, you're a crazy bitch! She's my wife, and she goes where I go."

"Get your ass out!" Wendy screams, completely clearly.

Now he loses it. "I gave you this house. Don't you talk to me that way! You better shut your fucking mouth or . . ."

"Don't you dare threaten me or I'll mess you up so bad you won't know your ass from your elbow!"

"You can't do shit from a hospital bed. You're going to have to shut up and let me take care of my kids. Do you understand? This wouldn't have happened if you stayed home where you belong instead of riding around like a teenage imbecile on a motorcycle!"

He hands me back the phone. "Say good-bye to your mother."

I accept the phone from him, still shaking. "Goo-good-bye, Mom," I say quietly. "W . . . w . . .w . . . will you call us tomorrow?"

"I will," she says.

My brothers say good-bye and we all hang up our respective phones.

I worry about what will happen. Wendy and my father are at it again, and it seems clear neither one is going to back down.

I'm not happy about having him here again. He's been here barely a few hours and he's created a war zone. Paulina seems decent, though, and it's good to have a semblance of parental intervention again. We've gone two years without any and managed to remain safe, but I know it might become a dangerous situation for my brothers and me. I'm afraid Wendy will make him go away again, as much as I'm afraid of his terrifying temper, living here with us.

When Paulina gets back, my father helps her unload tons of bags from the grocery store and she starts making us dinner. This is a treat. We are told dinner will be at six thirty sharp and to wash our hands, change our clothes, and brush our hair, which no one has told us to do for years.

At six thirty we all sit at the dinner table, wide-eyed with gratefulness, and wait for the signal from my father to begin. After he lifts his fork we're allowed to do the same, and not a moment sooner.

Dinners with my father were usually tense. His idea of parental responsibility included a strict manner code for meal etiquette. We had been trained to eat as though we were attending a banquet held by Emily Post.

After the age of five, any etiquette infraction got "corrected" by the swift poke of a fork tine, which, I'm certain, is definitely not Emily Post behavior.

I have tiny fork tine scars on my upper arms. Apparently, I'm a slow learner.

We eat silently, remembering the "children should be seen but never heard unless addressed" dinner rule from earlier days.

Paulina has prepared baked chicken with a can of mushroom soup, green beans, and homemade macaroni and cheese. A feast. It's been a long time since we've eaten a dinner of something other than frozen or fast food. Or our staple, cereal.

"She's broken bones in her neck? Won't she need a surgery?" Paulina asks.

"She didn't say." He meets her eyes and motions toward us before he continues. "We won't know much more for a few days. In the meantime, let's do the best we can to put this place back in shape and take care of you kids."

My brothers and I glance at each other with faces reflecting a vocabulary of emotions. I know they are as confused about all of this as I am.

David asks, "If Mom isn't better soon, will you be living here for a while?"

"Would you like that?"

David stares at his plate before he answers. "Well, I want my mom to get better."

Paulina speaks. "Of course you do. This is a hard time. We'll all do the best we can. Did you know I have two children? I have a boy and a girl. They live with their father now, but soon they're going to come and live with your father and me."

This sounds unusual to me. I wonder why she doesn't have her kids with her. Isn't that how it usually goes with a divorce? The kids live with the mother.

Paulina smiles at me. I ask, "Why don't they live with you now?"

Paulina starts to answer, but my father interrupts, "Ix-nay on the explana-tion-ay." Sometimes he speaks in Pig Latin, like we can't understand what he's saying. "Not your business," he says to us.

We spend the rest of dinner in silence.

After dinner, Paulina asks me to help her with the dishes. I know we'll have the kitchen to ourselves, and I'm curious to spend time alone with her. While we wash and dry, she tells me about her kids in Scituate and her life with my father in Florida. They live in a town called Destin.

"Where is Destin? I've never heard of it." I've never done dishes like this, with someone else. I'm careful when I lift the warm, slippery dishes from her fingers. I dry them with the new pink dish towel she bought at the store and stack them in the new dish rack.

"It's south of Niceville," she says.

"Niceville?" I ask. "What part of the state is it in?" My nose is itchy. I can't tell if it's her "lemony scented rubbing alcohol perfume" or the dish soap. Wendy never buys this soap. I put the dishes into the automatic dishwasher with the Cascade.

"South. It's in the southern part by the Gulf of Mexico. I'm not sure how I ended up down there. I grew up in Maine, but I love it down there. Florida's kinda pretty."

"I know," I tell her. "My mother brought us to Key West this year for spring vacation."

"Oh, I love Key West."

"Yeah, I liked it too. My favorite is Ernest Hemingway's house. I love that he left his money to his cats," I say.

I think Paulina might have been to Hemingway's.

"Ernest who?" Paulina asks me.

"Hemingway. The writer?"

She seems confused. I continue: "*For Whom the Bell Tolls?*"

Her eyes get bigger and rounder.

———

What I didn't understand at eight is that most people don't enjoy reading as much as I do.

Wendy is an avid reader with a wide variety of interests. She's had lots of time during these long New England winters to do nothing but party and read. She has also, as long as I can remember, taken sporadic college classes, mostly related to psychology. So the shelves are stacked two and three deep with everything from Chaucer and Freud to Erica Jong. I took full advantage of the books. Books are my antidepressants.

By the age of eight, I'd consumed a literary buffet including an assortment of Steinbeck, Thomas, Carroll, and several books of poetry. Ever since Key West, Hemingway has been my favorite.

———

"I've never heard of that book. I'm not much of a reader. I like movies though. Do you like to go to the movies?"

Ahhhh, movie friend. I love going to the movies. "Yes. Did you see *Dr. Zhivago*? It's one of my favorite movies," I say.

"Ummm," Paulina looks confused again, "no, I didn't. I loved *Airplane*. Did you see *Airplane*?"

"No. What's it about?" I ask.

"Ummm, well, you've got to see it. It's so funny. It makes fun of other movies. It's so funny."

I'm beginning to wonder about our being movie buddies.

She asks, "Do you like to go bowling? I noticed there's a bowling alley here in Withensea."

I nod. "Yeah, I like to go bowling."

The bowling alley, Withensea Shore Lanes, is one of the only year-round businesses where kids are allowed to hang out. Saturdays, after the leagues finish, anyone can play. Besides the bowling there are candy and pop machines—items that are not allowed in our diets. We use the money we get from our grandfather for treats like these.

"It's 'candlepin' bowling. I read recently that candlepin bowling was invented in Massachusetts. Are you familiar with candlepin?"

Paulina shakes her head no.

"It's similar to ten-pin bowling, but each player uses three balls per frame, the balls are much smaller and don't have holes, the downed pins aren't cleared away between balls during a player's turn, and the pins are thinner and harder to knock down. At least, that's what I've heard. I've never played ten-pin. Maybe we could go bowling this weekend?" I ask.

"Well, let's see what your father says. On Sunday we're gonna try to go visit my kids at their dad's. They live in Scituate. Maybe we could go on Saturday if your father says it's okay."

I can tell she's making a big effort to get me to like her, and I'm not going to stop her. It's nice to have her falling all over me that way, but I wonder why. Is Wendy going to be in the hospital for a long time? Are we going to be able to stay with her when she gets out? I wonder about the hospital surgery my father doesn't want us to know about. Everything's shaky.

———

A few weeks later, after school, things get even shakier. Outside our house, my father's car is gone. Inside, Paulina is sitting in a cigarette fog on the piano bench, mascara running down under her eyes. Beside her on the bench sits a pack of Pall Malls and a half bottle of Chivas Regal.

She's flicking ashes from her cigarette into an ashtray on the piano.

It's Wendy's ass ashtray. When you press a plastic button on the side of the tray, which is shaped like a giant butt, it opens and the ashes go inside the ass crack. Paulina hasn't figured out how to use it because the ashes sit on top of the butt in a huge pile, about to topple over onto the piano.

Her face is all wet with tears, but her eyes are blank like a doll's.

"Hi Julianne."

"Hi. What's wrong?"

"Come over here. I've got something to tell you. I've got bad news."

I steel myself and walk over to where she sits, clutching my school book bag against my side. "Where's my father? What's wrong?" I ask.

Paulina peers intensely at me, like she's searching for an answer in my face. "Your father left. He went for a drive."

I can tell she's left something out that has nothing to do with what she's about to tell me. So there are at least *two* bad things going on.

"It's your mother," she begins, but she stops and stares at her lap.

She's not supposed to be telling me what she's about to tell me. My heart pounds and I have a hard time finding the breath to speak. Tears start stinging my eyes. I squeeze them shut for a second to keep them from coming out.

"Is she dead?" I ask, staring at her face.

Paulina looks at me with the same blank stare. "No, she's not dead, but she's not doing real well. The doctors don't think she's going to live. So, she might die."

My head zings with a million thoughts.

I don't trust grown-ups to tell me the truth. Has Paulina told me something that's going to happen soon, has already happened, or might happen sometime in the distant future? Grown-ups aren't supposed to say scary things to kids, and this sounds scary. Here's Paulina telling me my mother might die, so it must be true.

I wonder if she wants Wendy to die. Does she want to take care of us? What about her own kids? Is she going to be allowed to have her own kids come live with her if she has to take care of us, or are we going to go live with my grandparents? I still hold out hope that we'll get to live with my grandparents, although Wendy laughs whenever I suggest it.

Worse, will we be sent to one of the orphanages Wendy threatened us with?

"So what's going to happen?"

Paulina jumps right in as though she's been waiting for me to ask. She seems excited, which is weird.

"If she dies, your father and I will stay here with you kids."

"You won't want to go back to Florida?"

"Florida? No, we haven't lived in Florida for the last—" she stops to count on her fingers, "—six months. We've been staying at your Aunt Doreen's."

I'm stunned.

They kept a secret.

My father has been living in the same town as us for six months without bothering to visit? We didn't see my Aunt Doreen this past summer because supposedly my father was out of town, and we never visit his family without him.

They all knew he lived there and kept it secret.

"H-how come he didn't come and see us?"

Paulina's face turns magenta. I can tell she feels caught and doesn't want to tell me the truth.

"Well, your father didn't tell you he was here because he was afraid your mother would ask for the child support payments, and he doesn't have a job yet." She stops for a second. "There's no money for that. I'm sorry, honey; I didn't mean to make you sad. It's . . . every spare dime has gone to the lawyer who's working on bringing my kids back to me. You're gonna like my kids a lot. My boy, William, is a year older than you and handsome. My girl, Lucy, is Moses's age. Just think, you'll have a sister!"

Paulina doesn't seem sorry to make me sad. As a matter of fact, she perks up as she tells me all this, half a smirk on her face. Probably drunk.

She wants to hurt you.

Two things became clear to me in this moment.

One: My father cares more about losing money than he does about seeing us. Two: Paulina is too selfish and stupid to care how we feel—and she believes it's okay for a father to act like this with his kids.

All I can think is "it stinks."

She looks pretty, but she's ugly inside.

I decide not to give away anything about any of it. Instead I say, "Thanks for telling me. Let me know what happens with my mother, all right?"

I turn and walk toward the front door. When I turn around, Paulina stares at me, confused.

"I'm going over to my friend's. I have a homework project. I might be back late."

"Not too late I hope. I'm making dinner. Come back by six thirty for dinner, okay?"

"I will."

You thought she was the mother type, but she's a freak.

Paulina struggles to scoop the cigarette ashes off the piano where the ashtray overflowed. I walk back over to her. "Do you think we could call Wendy later?"

I say it politely while I push the button on the side of the ashtray. The butt opens and the ashes spill in.

Paulina sits, amazed by the ashtray. "I don't know, honey, I'm not sure she can take phone calls."

My heart pounds through my blouse again and I can't find my breath to say anything else. I stare at Paulina's face. She seems pissed off. I guessed she's mad at me because I didn't show her the butt button before. I don't care.

I walk out with my book bag, but I don't know where to go. I have no friends. I do need to write an English paper, but since it's Friday, I have all weekend to finish it.

What I want is to call Wendy to tell her I love her, but I realize that if Paulina is telling the truth it might never happen. I've been angry with Wendy, but at least she didn't leave us and pretend to be living in Florida.

I can't breathe.

Stashing my book bag behind the juniper bushes by the front porch, I walk along the cliff then follow the path down to the beach to my favorite sitting rock on the jetty. Before long, I'm breathing again.

I come up with a plan. I resolve to make sure that even if Wendy dies, my father and Paulina are never going to want to stay in Withensea and take care of us.

You're better off in an orphanage.

Paulina seems to have a difficult time keeping secrets. I'm certain my father never wanted us to know he'd been staying in Withensea all this time. I also think Paulina shouldn't have told me about Wendy. I remember how weird it was that she'd been crying when I came inside but got excited when she talked about the prospect of moving in, even after telling me how Wendy might die.

Her sadness didn't have anything to do with Wendy's dying. She was upset about something to do with my father's leaving on a "drive." What did he do to make Paulina cry? Whatever it is, it's time for him to pay for all the bad things he's done to Wendy and to us, and I am going to be the person that brings him down. Like Vito Corleone.

You, Jules Finn, will bring Howard Finn to justice, gangster-style.

———

We'd overheard many stories from Wendy regarding my father and his illegal activities. Mostly she listed petty crimes involving bilking people out of investment money for fake business enterprises. Wendy called him the "biggest con artist on the South Shore." I wasn't positive what this meant, but no one, not even my Aunt Doreen or the rest of his family, ever argued with her about this point.

I'd read one of Wendy's books, Mario Puzo's The Godfather, recently, and I imagined my father lived a life out of the pages of the book, although I was pretty sure there wasn't an Irish mafia. His personality fit the violent Corleone family profile, and once he'd practically murdered Wendy—we thought she was dead after he choked her unconscious in front of us during a fight they had in the car. My Aunt Doreen pounded on Wendy's chest to make her breathe while Moses and I were trapped in the backseat. We had to watch the whole thing.

When he was choking her, her face turned all crimson-blue, and when she started breathing again it sounded like she was choking all over again.

Looking back, I had no idea that justice had already introduced itself to us. It turned out that my father was on probation for one of the petty crimes he'd committed in Florida. Probation created a fortunate and ultimately fate-changing chain of events, shaping the next few days and the rest of our interactions with him for years to come.

———

I need a dead fish.

First I go back to our shed to gather my fishing gear. Next I hike down to the dock at the yacht club, where we keep our dinghy tied. Jack, who sails, has been gifted by Wendy (which means my grandfather gave her money for something else) a Hobie sailboat he keeps anchored at the yacht club. We use the dinghy to fish and Jack uses it to row out to where the Hobie stays moored in the bay.

It's a sixty-degree day in April. Warm for April in Massachusetts. But it gets cold fast when the sun goes down and near freezing at night. It's about four o'clock and already chilly by the time I make it to the dock.

My school clothes are dirty because I stopped to dig earthworms. Moses and I use earthworms as bait because we can't afford to buy sea worms.

I know I only have a little time.

There are rules about the dinghy—not the ones Wendy and I made, but rules the coast guard and the yacht club enforce.

Nobody has to wear a life preserver, but we're supposed to have them on board for each of us. We follow the rule, and it's good because Moses is a poor swimmer.

We aren't allowed to use the dinghy from dusk to dawn. This rule is broken often. The best catches happen during the dusk and dawn, and we're too focused on fishing to follow this rule. Besides, this one is Wendy's rule and she never wakes up until ten in the morning. Later, at dusk, we know if she isn't around she'll never know, so then it doesn't matter either.

One of the other rules I make Moses follow is that we, the ones who use the fishing dinghy (besides Jack), can't go out without each other. I never break this rule because I try to set an example for Moses and I enjoy Moses's company on our fishing adventures. We're great fishing buddies. Besides, he's only six and too little to go fishing on his own.

Anyway, I decide to break the rule and go by myself, but I plan to make it back by the six thirty dinner deadline Paulina set. I can't risk any trouble with Paulina or my father.

You need to be the perfect daughter to make this work.

First I toss my pole into the dinghy, unscrew the oars, and row myself out across to our favorite spot, a rocky cove by the edge of a small island that sits east of ours. Within a few minutes I bait my hook with the worms from my pocket, put my line in, and wait for a bite.

I'm hoping for a rockfish, maybe a schoolie, but after fifteen minutes I've hooked a flounder that flops on my line in the dinghy. It'll do. Catching anything is easier than I thought it would be. I start rowing back to shore.

I was nervous when I rowed across the bay because most of the folks at the yacht club know Jack, and they also know I'm not allowed out on my own. I can't risk anyone seeing me and ratting me out. For this reason, I choose a longer route back that will leave me out in the open for a shorter time. I follow close to a row of saltboxes built out over a land bridge close to the end of the island. It's a rougher job rowing back in because the tide runs in many different directions in this stretch. Originally the water flowed freely from ocean to bay at this spot, which was no more than a sandbar before the concrete walls and pavement were built to connect it to the rest of Withensea. But the bridge, which forces the existing currents to wind around its edges, has created complex wave and tide patterns.

By the time I make it back to the dock, I'm exhausted. My clothes are wet with mud, saltwater, and fish juice.

I've learned to guess time from the angle of the sun and the shadows it throws, and I see I have about half an hour to make it back in time for dinner. Somehow I manage to tie the dinghy, secure the oars, run to our backyard, bury the fish in the garden, return my fishing gear to the shed, grab my book bag in the juniper bushes, and sneak back in with time to spare.

I use my secret entry route, which involves scaling a trellis nailed to the shingles directly under the bottom of the widow walk ledge on the second floor. From there it's a quick balancing act along the ledge to my window, which I keep unlatched.

It's funny the things you do when you aren't afraid.

I shower to wash the fish smell off me and change into clean, dry clothing. At precisely six thirty I tie my sneakers and walk downstairs to join everyone for dinner.

Ten

Jules, 8 years | April, 1970

SALAD TRAUMA

IT BEGINS WITH iceberg lettuce.

Paulina prepares a huge salad as an *appetizer*.

We are as unfamiliar with the concept of appetizers as we are with fresh salad. We've only seen both at restaurants, where we rarely go.

Wendy considers appetizers needlessly fattening, appetite-spoiling foods. We're never allowed to order them and we never order or eat salads, except whatever garnishes might be present on our plates. Also, Wendy doesn't eat fresh fruits or vegetables, so she never buys them. Most of the fresh ones we've eaten have been at meals with our Aunt Doreen.

When we were younger, before the divorce, when she still cooked for my father and us, Wendy served canned peas, carrots, and beans. The worst was the canned asparagus she forced us all to try once, exclaiming, "Asparagus is a delicacy."

Delicacy, I decided, is code for disgusting. I got sick after swallowing it.

I haven't eaten a vegetable—besides the corn they ladle into school lunches— in years.

Judging by their obvious tentativeness as they stare at their own bowls, I doubt my brothers have either. Yet here we are, sitting in front of bowls filled with several different vegetables we know we're required to eat every bite of. My father expects us to do this as a courtesy to Paulina.

Nestled in the iceberg lettuce lay sliced tomatoes, square-cut cucumbers, chopped green peppers, pink-laced onions, cut carrots, and an as-yet-unidentified small white vegetable whose variety and type I have never seen.

I wait for my father to pick up his fork, our sign to begin eating, when David yells out, "Ahhhhhh!" and thrusts his fingers into his bowl, extricating a wiggling white grub.

I stare at the grub in David's fingers.

Paulina screams and jumps out of her seat.

Moses says, "Wow." Moses likes bugs. I think he's excited to have one join us at the table.

My brothers and I are simultaneously reminded of David's potentially punishable etiquette breach. We all gape at my father while Paulina continues to scream.

My father, although rattled by the wiggling grub and Paulina's screaming, manages to maintain his authority for the moment by asking David to remove the grub from the table. But as David pushes away from the table, my father makes the mistake of glancing down into his own bowl, an inevitable thought having crossed his mind before ours. He's unprepared for what he sees. Evidently, crawling in his bowl are several of the same grubs.

He yells, and as he attempts to push his bowl away he dumps it across the table, where the grubs from his bowl lie wiggling between the dinnerware.

It's really funny, but no one laughs.

Paulina begins a new round of screams, and Moses and I begin the excavation of our own bowls for grub family members. We find them easily. They are the (now-identifiable) small white vegetables I was wondering about.

"What's the matter with you? Are you some kind of a moron?" my father snarls.

Paulina stops screaming and makes a small moaning sound, holding her face in her hands as she leans over and clutches the table.

David sits still in his chair, the wiggling grub in his fingers.

"Didn't you wash these before you served them? How could you miss bugs crawling around in a salad? Clean up this mess, you idiot."

Any pretense of polite behavior toward his new wife disappears. We scan Paulina for a reaction. She casts a dejected look downward. "Yeah, I guess I forgot to wash the lettuce."

He snorts.

When he rages, he makes me think of an angry moose. His nostrils flare and his head goes down as though he's ready to charge. We all wait, adrenaline pumping, to see what direction he's headed. He stomps out, grabbing his keys and jacket on the way.

"I'm going out to dinner for a good meal. Maybe you'll think about how to be a better cook while I'm gone."

Instead of arguing, like Wendy would have, Paulina nods. "I'll do better next time."

"Good!" he shouts and slams the door.

After a few moments of silence, David yells, "Call Freddy!"

Moses and I laugh. Paulina sits there, confused.

We're all relieved and thankful for his exit. This is an improvement from his behavior with Wendy. My brothers and I stare at one another, a bit shocked. We aren't shocked at the shouting; we're shocked Paulina didn't get beaten. Our father's verbal violence usually escalates. His previous exits usually followed a physical attack.

Paulina notices our shocked expressions. "He's mad because I don't know how to cook real good," she says. "He's been real patient with me. I'm still bad at it, though."

———

Where all of my father's traditional expectations for his wife to prepare well-made meals came from has always been a bit of a mystery. His sister, Doreen, is a great cook, but I've heard many times that his own mother wasn't. She was a working mother and had no time to prepare meals. Doreen was the one who cooked for the family and took care of my father. Perhaps it fulfilled a fantasy for him—maybe he was trying to create the mother he never had out of his wives.

———

"Last night's meal tasted good," Moses says sweetly. David and I agree.

Paulina hangs her head.

Moses remains unfazed by the grubs.

David jumps up to clear the plates. "I'll throw this all in the trash in the garage."

Paulina heads into the kitchen. Before David leaves the table I whisper to my brothers, "Did Paulina say anything to you guys about Mom?"

"You mean that she might die?" David says casually.

Moses's head snaps up. "What? Mom might die?"

"No sir. I don't think it's true," I say, more for Moses than anything.

"No, I don't think so either," David adds, realizing the way his words are hitting Moses.

Moses's eyes fill with tears and he pans from one to the other of us and shakes his head, not knowing what to believe.

I push back my chair and stand up from the table. I meet David's eyes and roll mine at him. He rolls his back at me then gathers all our grubby salads and leaves for the trash.

"Don't worry, Moses. She'll live. We're gonna call after dinner and talk to her."

He lays his arms on the table and puts his head down. He needs dinner.

I follow Paulina into the kitchen to see what else she's prepared. Something that smells like spicy bacon saturates the air and I'm hungry. I'm also certain I'll eat about anything as long as it isn't moving on my plate. I talk Paulina into serving us the rest of the dinner.

The four of us go back to the table, where Paulina tells us her family is part Polish and she's cooked us a traditional Polish dinner. She calls it "boiled dinner with red cabbage": thick-cut potatoes and a speckled, chopped meat called *kielbasa*. "Polish sausage," she explains. It tastes spicy and exotic. We all love it.

—

Sometime later, my brothers and I try to phone Wendy in the hospital. Paulina sits on the couch beside me. A nurse tells me she's checked out, the details of which remain a mystery until I phone Jack, who's been staying with his mother again, for information. Jack tells me Wendy has been moved to Mass General Hospital, where there are specialists for her type of spinal injury. My brothers listen on the other extensions when I ask him about Wendy's chances for recovery.

"Whadya mean?" Jack asks.

"I heard she might, she might . . . die," I say, unsure about my brothers' reactions to this.

Jack remains silent for a moment. "Who told you that?" he mumbles. His usual vocal response.

I can tell he's genuinely surprised, but he hasn't answered my question. I persist, "Is sh-sh-she going to die, Jack?" Besides the stuttering, my voice rises into a trembling, high-pitched tone.

Jack must sense my panic, and he somehow manages to come up with calming news.

"No," he says, "don't even think that way. I don't know what you heard, but your mother is fine—much better today. She still needs the doctors to take care of her, but she's going to be better and come back home soon."

I'm certain Jack's telling the truth. It's Paulina who lied.

In this one moment, I've got a mix of emotions: Surprise at Jack's niceness and how he's talking in complete sentences, and happiness to hear that Wendy will recover. The third emotion is fury at Paulina, who clearly invented her story about Wendy.

My emotions jumble into one single, overwhelming sense of relief. I thank

Jack, sign off the phone, and repeat Jack's words to Paulina, whose expression I watch carefully as I tell her about Wendy's positive prognosis. She seems embarrassed, but offers no explanation for her earlier tragic warnings.

I don't know your particular brand of crazy, but I know crazy when I see it.

Although I'm certain my father and Paulina will be banished when Wendy comes back, I'm more determined than ever to make sure they're gone as soon as possible.

I'll put my plan into action tonight.

———

I wait until later, long after my father pulls into the driveway, walks in, and follows Paulina, who has been waiting for him, to Wendy's bedroom.

I remember an old daily racing form from his horse racing days that's tucked into one of Wendy's family photo albums. When I find it, I don't bother to consider the almost cryptic importance of her having kept this particular racing form, considering her incredible anger at the financial losses he incurred at the track over the years. I think it might be an old memento of *his* that had been left and overlooked.

I put the racing form into the band of my pants. Next, I creep through my window and out onto the ledge, down the trellis, and around to the backyard, where I buried the fish.

After locating the flounder—a difficult task in the darkness of the backyard—I wrap it up inside the racing form and carry it back to where the trellis is nailed to the wood shingles. I have no choice but to stuff the bundle in the back of my pants and hope that the slimy, muddy fish stays contained within the racing form.

After making it back to my room, I prepare for my next mission. I leave the wrapped flounder on my floor and creep downstairs to the kitchen, where I get a knife from the drawer. As I pass the front door, I unlock and open it. I carefully cut a hole in the screen, directly in front of the front door's lock and deadbolt. I leave it ajar, so it looks like a break-in, and put the knife back in the kitchen drawer.

Next comes the final and most dangerous element of the plan.

I creep back upstairs, carefully cradling the smelly flounder, and edge my way down the dark hall toward Wendy's room, where my father and Paulina sleep.

The door is closed, which is a surprise.

Wendy keeps it open, even—to our strong embarrassment—when she's enjoying "private moments." I've never discussed the things I hear coming from there or the things I've seen with my brothers, but I'm sure they've gotten an earful and an eyeful as well. Wendy has a problem with boundaries.

In front of the closed door, I start to panic and try to think of a different method to achieve my goal. I stall there, trying to drum up alternatives, but come to the conclusion that there is only one way to complete my mission. I hope I don't wake either of them. I hear a faint snoring coming from inside. My mouth tastes like iron.

Wait for him to snore again.

During the next rumble I turn the handle. Magically, the door makes no sound as I open it. I creep inside in the darkness, across the floor, until I find the foot of the bed, where I deposit the wrapped fish. I wait until his next snore to make my escape. I see no reason to close the door behind me. I sprint back down the hallway, scramble into my pajamas, and stuff my clothing into my hamper with the clothes I wore to go fishing. They stink. I drag the hamper down into the basement, which is creepy at night—this is practically the hardest part of the whole scheme—and throw everything into the washer. I know it won't be heard upstairs. I start the cycle.

When I sneak back upstairs I jump into bed, amazed I've managed to do what I did. My plan went smoothly. I'm nervous and it takes me quite a while to fall asleep—but tomorrow is Saturday. I think I'll be able to sleep in a bit.

———

When I wake up the next morning, groggy, I think I've dreamed the entire night's events. Then I hear the combined voices of Paulina and my father travel down the length of the long hallway from Wendy's room. I can't make out what they're saying, but his voice booms out over Paulina's whine. I hold my breath. I have no idea what will happen. After a while I hear the sound of a door slamming somewhere downstairs and his voice shouting at someone. I can tell he's on the phone. A few seconds later, there's a soft knock on my door. I nervously open it, and I find Moses standing there. I pull him inside.

"Somebody broke in and left a fish on Daddy's bed," he says.

"How do you know?" I quiz him, wanting to be certain.

"I heard them talking, and Daddy said he got a message from one of his rookies."

I become confused. I'm afraid my "mafia message" has been misinterpreted and will lose its intended effect. But then I realize Moses misheard the word. My father said "bookie." I know this because he repeats the word several times to various people on the telephone as the morning goes on. I know what a bookie is, having read The Godfather, and I become satisfied he's made the right connection from my message. I can't remember any specific mention of my father's bookies, and I don't know enough about bookies to know why they might be blamed for the fish delivery. But I do have a clear understanding that he lost more money than he won at the track, and that caused trouble for him. In using the old racing form, I somehow hit the jackpot of my intention.

An hour later, my father and Paulina drive away without a good explanation regarding their quick exodus. He tells us Wendy feels better and might get back from the hospital in a few days. He feels sure we can take care of ourselves.

He also tells us he's arranged for Jack to visit us and check in once a day to make sure everything is all right. This seems unlikely, but Jack shows up, and he ends up staying with us until Wendy's discharged from the hospital two weeks later. Maybe he just wants to be sure he's still got a free place to sleep, or maybe he thinks Wendy might die after all and he feels bad about the possibility we'll be put in orphanages.

Jack teaches me how to make spaghetti and tomato sauce from scratch. It's his one culinary masterpiece—he learned it from his Italian mother—and I become equally masterful. He also takes us to the drive-in movies and go-cart racing, and he buys a huge carton of vanilla ice cream that my brothers eat in about ten minutes.

People can be very surprising sometimes.

When Wendy comes back from the hospital she wears a neck brace and is still fairly immobile. She stays either on the couch or her bed. She holds court from both places to a constant stream of visitors—her new friends, the Boston chapter of the Hells Angels.

One day, I overhear her telling the true story behind my father's quick exit.

———

Not surprisingly, Howard originally left Withensea after having accrued immense gambling debts, which was his biggest reason for not announcing his presence for the previous six months. When he got the "sleep with fishes" message I left wrapped in the racing form from the day of his biggest single loss—which Wendy had spitefully kept without his knowledge—he assumed his bookie had found him and that *he* had sent the death threat.

Before that day at the races, my grandfather had given him twenty thousand dollars as an investment to build-on a restaurant next to the Little Corporal. My father lost the money at the track, and Wendy said he'd doubled the loss in loans he took out with a particular bookie named O'Reilly in an effort to try and win it back.

Wendy, the only other person besides his bookie who knew about the loans, still lay in the hospital the day he found the fish in his bed. So he ruled her out as a suspect. Which left only O'Reilly.

In an arrogant attempt to bully the bookie into backing off from what he thought was a death threat, he called O'Reilly and announced he wasn't going to be "intimidated by some two-bit thug." O'Reilly, confused about Howard's fishy accusations, at first denied his involvement, but he must have felt it an opportune time to collect on the loans he'd made to him.

Howard had been laying low in Withensea while he was under probation for petty larceny in Florida. He'd been flying down there every few months to meet his probation officer and pretend he still lived there and was looking for a job. O'Reilly had heard about Howard's situation through mutual friends, and now he threatened Howard with exposure to local law enforcement for violating the terms of his probation in Florida. I guess he also threatened to break his kneecaps, or at least that's what Wendy says.

———

Howard fled Withensea because a dead flounder convinced him O'Reilly had his number.

He went back to Florida and served a short prison sentence for skipping probation, and when his new probation terms were met, he moved all the way to California. So we didn't see Howard again for a while, which was fine with me. The next time we saw him, Paulina wasn't with him. They were divorced.

Wendy told us Paulina's kids had been living with her ex-husband because she lost custody of them during her first divorce. Her husband left because she'd been having an affair. Paulina developed a drinking problem, the kids stopped going to school, and the neighbors called Social Services. The kids were put into foster homes temporarily, and afterwards Paulina's ex-husband won custody.

Howard met Paulina two years after this sequence of events. I think he felt embarrassed by her status as a deadbeat parent and how it reflected on him, which is why he was paying for the lawyer to help Paulina regain custody. I thought it was pretty hypocritical—he never seemed embarrassed or apologized for his neglect of us, after all.

After Howard and Paulina moved to California, he found a job at a car dealership. The two of them socialized fairly often with his new boss and his family. They even spent time at his boss's beach home on weekends. I guess this guy had a teenage son, and Paulina and the teenager spent a lot of time alone. Paulina's inability to follow adult conversation may have influenced this activity.

One day, Wendy told me, Howard's boss walked in on Paulina and his son in the bathroom. Paulina was sitting on the edge of the sink, and his son was bent over, his head under her skirt and between her legs. When Howard's boss demanded to know what they were doing, Paulina claimed she was showing him a birthmark on her thigh. I guess he didn't buy it, because Paulina got arrested for child molestation and Howard got fired.

Wendy loved to tell that story.

Eleven

Samuel, 69 years | August, 1979

BROOKLINE, MASSACHUSETTS

UNTIL NOW I thought I am writing this for you, Chavalah. Now I know I am also writing this, my story, for myself. This is the way I write all the things I would not ever say. All the things I could never speak. Maybe these things will remain on the page and leave my brain.

September 19th, 1924. Ivnitza, Russian Empire.
"Look at me, Szaja!" my younger brother Idel shouts at me.

His dark head is bobbing and shimmering a brilliant bronze glow in the sunlight.

My sister Reizel, her husband, Berl, my brother Oizer and I have been pulling potatoes since dawn in the fields of what used to be my bubbe's vegetable gardens. We pull potatoes while my twin sisters, Ruchel and Sura, make soap back at home. This new trade, soap-making, we began this year to make ends meet.

It has been a year since my parents left with the young ones for America. It feels like forty. Much has changed.

Potatoes grow easily, and they have become the one crop we can legally grow since the Red Army seized control of the village farms. The apple and cherry orchards remain. They stand like silent soldiers. Their limbs produce more fruit than our family can harvest, and we can no longer pay workers. Now the orchards are framed by rows of long earthen hills. Within those small hills we grow our farm's main crop—potatoes. I hate potatoes. They smell of drudgery. When we dig them, they create small *kartofl* blisters on my fingers. Their smell ekes out of my pores.

But they feed us. We are left with almost nothing after the tithing we are forced to offer to the Russian armies.

Berl works beside me. He has become more than a brother-in-law this year—he has become my good friend. Berl, a man who usually remains composed, is kind and gentle.

I think of an evening early this spring when we rested wearily in the field after digging potato trenches all day. The sky had begun to darken into the color of steel, and we waited for the first spittle of the rain that had teased us with its entrance all day. I asked Berl about his missing toes and, with great sadness, leaning his chin against the handle of his shovel, he told me of what he and his brother had endured in Poltava, in Southern Ukraine.

"My father was led away to join the army, and me and my younger brother suffered the agony of our mother's eventual death during the droughts and the famine. We became two of the *bezprytulnimore*—the orphans who sometimes rode on top of the trains from town to town—searching for work and food. One freezing morning, I awoke with terrible throbbing pains in my feet; my toes are numb." Berl dropped his forehead to the handle with an exhausted thud. He wept as he continued his story. "I tried to wake my brother and realized his heart had stopped. Hundreds of children died a frozen death that night on top of the trains."

My fingers, hands, arms, and back ache. This pain distracts me from my memory. Reizel and Oizer use the potato forks while Berl and I dig, twist, and pull with our hands.

"Look, look at me Szaja; I am the red-haired basket maker in the market," Idel says. He stuffs two large potatoes into his shirt, and with the one arm not hanging in a sling he holds his potato breasts as he dances in the muddy field.

I stretch up and arch my back, straightening the square of my shoulders and flexing my fingers into my palms. I feel too cross and tired to laugh, but his show is too funny to stifle a smile.

Idel giggles with joy and runs to Oizer, Berl, and Reizel to show them his new body.

Idel.

He is playing in a wheelbarrow with neighbor children a few weeks ago and broke his arm. Not the same arm he broke when he fell out of the apple tree, his healthy, good arm. I worry what to do with Idel. He's trouble. Why didn't *Foter* take him to America? He is useless as a field hand. Still, he does provide wonderful amusement, and I feel gratitude for any distraction offered.

This is our life. We grow vegetables and fruits for the Volga—the Russian

Army and the administrators who occupy our village—and they let us keep a part of our property.

———

AFTER *FOTER* LEFT, we are visited by the new general's officers with an official deed stating that our property had been divided for the "benefit of the community." And it is so. No explanation. No financial compensation. Our return comes in the form of our lives. We hear of the families sent to prison camps—or worse, killed—because of their disobedience.

We are Jews. We are easy marks.

The administrators have begun what will be a focused program for the Volga regime: the "redistribution" of almost all the land in the Ukranian countryside. It is not only the Jews who are being forced to give up our lands. Our farm is one of the few remaining working farms dotting the countryside.

We enjoy a more fortunate life than anyone we know here in our tucked-away village hidden by forests. We have been spared many of the tragedies that have torn apart our neighbors' families. We are simple farmers and until the last few years the politics and wars around us hadn't influenced us in ways that caused much change to our daily lives. Now, with our village's new Russian military presence, everything has changed.

Yes, Gershon died, and Ruchel still suffers from frailty caused by the same typhus epidemic, but the rest of us have been spared this and other illnesses plaguing the Ukraine. Besides Gershon, my only other true sadness has been the loss of our beloved *bubbe*, who died an old woman and who lived a good life with our family and our love.

But now we live on a tightrope.

Wars and the pogroms have taken many Jewish lives in these years. It is ironic that Jews feel safer under our current Soviet rule than we did with the Ukranian nationalists, who rarely protected us. The Polish army massacres Jews as they retreat from the Soviet forces in Kiev. As though the Jews are responsible for their defeat.

Idel has his ideas, however. He remains certain that we will be left alone if we befriend the Russian soldiers. He often goes to visit with them. They live close by and occupy the largest estate in the countryside, the former home of the great Russian entomologist the Baron de Chaudoir, who died long ago.

Idel, an ingratiating spirit, entertains the soldiers, who are weary with war. They enjoy the presence of the dark-haired, blue-eyed young boy with the engaging smile and silly antics. He must remind them of their own young brothers. Or maybe he reminds them of themselves before the war, before this terror.

Oizer digs in the row next to me. He looks like an old man with his spectacles, although he is a year younger than me. He is the resourceful one and has the financial brains in the family. Oizer has arranged a way to channel almost half of what we produce on the farm to a marketer from Zhytomyr, who sells the produce for half the price to yet another distributor. We never declare this income when we pay our taxes. We save at least twice what we lose on these half-price sales. Oizer's plan has brilliance, but the interchange holds risk. If the Russians find out, we might all be sent to prison, or worse. Oizer set the plan in motion without consulting anyone. He came home with the rubles in his pocket and told us we could start to plan our departure to America with the money we would be saving.

We will not have to wait for *Foter* to send for us. We will send ourselves after we save enough.

The money makes us jubilant and careless.

———

Idel prances in the potato field. Reizel tries to usher him back to her row, to rein him in and focus the rest of us back to the task of pulling up the crop.

Harvesting potatoes is dirty, backbreaking work. We use wooden, spiked forks and our fingers to turn the potatoes up. We start at dawn, fortified with the latkes Reizel makes from the same potatoes we pull each day.

Latkes. I've grown sick of latkes. Even the slices of dried apple Reizel adds are not enough to sweeten the taste of the starchy wafers.

We will have them for dinner as well. This has been our meal for weeks. We wait until the next market day to bring us the more varietal foods our taste buds and our bodies crave. I dream maybe we will have a chicken. The ones we've bred have been requisitioned by the army. Requisitioned. I envision the chickens wearing uniforms and caps, marching in formation, before meeting their eventual doom on the chopping block.

We could use another horse. Our one remaining horse has become sick and weak and is barely able to till the soil. These are the things I am dreaming of before I see them coming.

The soldiers of the Red Army.

They come on horseback, and the horses are big and healthy. I know the soldiers are not from our village. Their horses are war-starved and skinny. These are soldiers from another village, another city—maybe Kiev.

This cannot be good news they bring. This might be another edict, an eviction, or an arrest—or worse—if Oizer's secret dealings have been uncovered.

We motion to one another as they approach over the hill marking the new border of our property and gather as they come closer.

Berl steps in front of Idel, taking a protective stance on his missing-toed feet. Soldiers pass our family home. There are at least twenty of them. I see several horses turn toward our home, where Ruchel and Sura work. I start toward them, my own protective instincts already powered on.

Berl stops me. "Stay. It's safer if we all remain together."

"But *mayn shvesters*," I begin.

"Stay now," is all Berl can cough out.

I glance at him. He wears an expression I've never seen before. A thin grimace of fear.

I watch my family, afraid to watch the approach of the soldiers. Reizel stands with an arm around Idel, who still holds his potato breasts.

"They will shoot you if you interfere," Berl says.

I am frozen, my entire body as cold as the hands I've been using to dig into the earth for the icy mounds in the basket at my feet. I stand, rooted.

Oizer stands next to me. His arm brushes my own. I feel his entire body trembling.

I glare at him and he flicks his eyes to mine and back at the approaching soldiers. I am thinking that if they came on his account he is responsible not only for his own terrible fate but for that of our family as well. My anger at him in this moment helps me feel less fearful.

"This is your fault, Oizer."

"There is no fault, only sacrifice," Berl spits.

"Time for Idel's angel," Reizel whispers.

She says it with a tight, dry tone and it gives the moment a strange levity. I can feel us take a breath.

Breathing. We breathe in this moment.

Idel must have taken Reizel's words as a cue for play although I know he must also be afraid. The soldiers, with their guns and swords and horses, are all strong, powerful, and frightening. All of it, *meant* to be terrifying. But before he can be stopped, Idel starts dancing with his potato breasts again, in the direction of the advancing soldiers, within a few yards of us now. He skips around Berl and runs forward to entertain them with his nonsense.

"Idel," Reizel and Berl shout.

Then the terrible confusion begins.

Startled by the small boy and the shouting, two of the horses rear back, throwing the soldiers off balance. One soldier falls to the ground, creating chaos in their formation.

Another soldier, the captain, jumps off his horse and moves to intercept Idel's approach on foot. He catches Idel by the collar of his coat and holds him roughly there.

Behind him, the soldier who has fallen lies still on the ground.

My family moves forward to collect Idel from the captain, who snarls at him. Idel, quite frightened, cowers in his grip.

Berl reaches them first. He speaks his excellent Russian, explaining that Idel is playing, that he hasn't meant to upset the horses or the soldiers. As he speaks, the two of them, Berl and the captain, keep craning to look at the soldier on the ground.

Berl and the captain, who is still dragging Idel by the collar, move toward the soldier. Reizel, Oizer, and I follow them to where the man, bleeding profusely from the head, lies motionless, his eyes glazed and unfocused.

I have never seen so much blood. The right side of his head is open like a black tomato, and what must be his brains spill out and cover the side of his face. Blood pools out around his head and stains the muddy earth of the potato ditch a deep purple-red.

He is dead.

He is dead.

What happens then happens quickly, before anyone has a chance to drag their eyes away from the staring corpse.

One shot drawn from the captain's gun.

One shot.

Point-blank, I think it's called, when the gun is as close as it is to Idel's poor little head.

Idel shot in the head.

Then not even a head. The force of the bullet at this range, the space of about a foot, blows half of Idel's head off.

Idel's body falling.

Berl, who is standing behind him, falls. Berl, we realize, has taken the same bullet. It lodges somewhere in his heart, stopping it in that second. Berl and Idel fall together in a bloody, smoky mess to the mud.

Berl wears the same glazed, wide-open, horrified stare as the soldier with the spilled brains, his chest open and bloody with the wound.

Idel's blood everywhere.

I cannot not bring myself to look at what is left of his face.

Reizel is screaming.

Screaming.

The captain is saying something.

I can see his lips moving. I stare into his face. The captain has a face like a broken brick. Although I understand Russian, I cannot understand these words.

The sound seems far away.

Something. Something about the farm being taken for the army; our family, the entire village, being resettled in a Jewish district in the south.

The words—like ice picks hacking my frozen thoughts apart.

You must gather your things at once and join your neighbors who are also going.

Reizel still screams.

I try to collect my wits. I cannot find where my wits are, but somehow, somehow my legs move.

I am pulling Reizel away from something horrible.

From the horrible spot in the mud.

Oizer, still standing there. Still staring.

I hear the voice of my father clearly, as though he speaks the words again, standing next to me there in the orchard.

"Iberkumen," he says.

Survive.

I shout, but the voice which comes out is not my own. I order Oizer to help me pull Reizel away, to help me take her back home, where we need to gather as many of our things as we can carry. We grab her. I order Reizel to stop screaming. She tears her way out of our grip to run back to the spot where Idel and Berl lay. We try to take her again, but the soldiers pull us apart and fling her into the arms of two soldiers who threaten her to stop screaming with their guns and swords and turn her away to march toward home. Reizel, finally frightened into silence, lets herself be dragged by the soldiers.

As we approach, soldiers come out of our home. Four, five? I can't remember now how many I saw coming out.

More screaming from inside.

Ruchel and Sura.

Inside—at least ten soldiers. A few on the main floor where our small kitchen and main room are. I can hear their boots in the bedroom upstairs, above us. They shout and laugh over my sisters' screams.

Ruchel and Sura upstairs with the soldiers.

The first punch of rage begins to drive the shock from my body. Every cell of my body strains to grab one of the swords hanging on a soldier standing nearby.

I want to kill every soldier. I picture them like small shrubs. I will chop them down to twigs.

The captain, who followed us on his horse, enters. His brick face barks an order, bringing the soldiers who have been upstairs flying down like locusts. They are half-clothed, rapidly dressing themselves, and sheepish. The captain barks at the men to go outside and motions at me.

"Go to your sisters and tell them to gather their things. You have five minutes."

Five minutes. This is the time they give us.

My rage carries me into the completion of this impossible task.

———

We heard stories later, after our month-long journey to the settlement camps in Southern Ukraine, of families ordered to leave with no possessions, or to give their belongings to these soldiers in exchange for their lives.

I would have given my life to erase the pain that my sisters and the rest of my family endured on this day and in the days that followed.

I don't remember how we managed to collect our things, preparing for what we thought might be an overnight hike to a nearby village or city. We had seen many immigrant camps on our way into the Kiev market. We remarked to each other how poor, how bedraggled, the people who lived in those camps appeared. We had no idea how much worse things could become. We would learn.

Ruchel and Sura. They never recovered from their attack.

Ruchel had already been frail and thin from the typhus. Sura, her twin, had been stronger, but now they are tiny mirrors. They lost light on that day. They became the ghosts of my sisters.

None of us talked about it. None of us dared ask any questions. It seemed too terrible, maybe as terrible as what happened to Idel and Berl. Maybe more terrible. They'd been killed by the attack as surely as if they'd been shot. This is how things are in those days. For women—girls, really, they are fifteen—to be raped felt the same as death.

Their ghosts died as well. The ghosts of my sisters left world a few weeks later. They starved to death. Both of them. Both deciding they would refuse to eat the meager rations the soldiers provided us on our journey to the resettlement area. We begged the girls to eat the grains offered. Reizel, Oizer, and I begged. Nothing worked. They'd made their decision. Each day the walking contributed to the eventual loss of all energy. Their weak bodies gave out.

We woke one morning and found them clasped, arms around one another, under their coats, which we used as blankets on the cold ground. They had gone together in the same way they had been born.

Reizel led us in the prayers. We had no *Shomer*, no *Chevrah Kaddisha*, and no *Tahara*.

They gave us five minutes to say the prayers. Five minutes more than I needed. More than I wanted. Five minutes longer than I could stand to acknowledge the pain of this loss without losing what remained of my mind.

The soldiers on their horses, waiting, ordered us to leave their bodies shrouded in their coats, and without a burial, by the side of the road. They told us they would assign soldiers to bury my sisters.

I did not believe them. I no longer believed anything.

Life began its bad dream. There is no color. Shapes are a deep, flat gray, shadow. Sounds are muted or clanging in distorted decibels. At first, everything hurt my skin. Then I no longer felt my body.

I could not tell you what we ate, how long we marched each day, what people we met, what the weather is like—nothing. None of these things can be remembered. It is as though I am sleepwalking.

To continue to live in a world where people behaved like these soldiers seemed impossible to me. I had great shame, guilt, and anger at myself for not being able to prevent the terrible murders of Idel and Berl. The deaths of my sisters had been as much my fault as the soldiers'. I had failed to do the one thing *Foter* had charged me with: protect my brothers and sisters.

After her breakdown upon Idel and Berl's murders, Reizel grew much stronger than Oizer and me. She took us by the hands as we left our sisters there. She led us away from that place. She managed to follow *Foter's* edict to survive and taught us how to do the same.

Reizel became the reason I didn't join my ghost sisters in their starved exit from this life. In her strongest spirit, she led us through that terrible time and eventually to a place where we found peace.

Twelve

SEAGLASS

MY BEST FRIEND Leigh and I stroll to the school bus, after school. I half-listen to her going on about her newest crush while I focus on the magnificence of the tree leaf colors.

Withensea is filled with trees, and trees, in a small New England town, are serious business. The people of Withensea passed one of the New World's earliest environmental laws when they voted against cutting down any more small trees on the island. (The island timber was being used to build homes in Boston.) The result of all the tree hoopla is that Withensea is a green paradise. Maple, balsam, oak, and white pine grow everywhere. They stand around homes and businesses, lining every roadside that doesn't border the sea with its ferocious winter winds.

The fall beauty is particularly spectacular. All this week the colors have been coming, and the golden yellows, burnt oranges, and scarlet reds sparkle out against the old faded lime green leaves like they've been colored on. When the sun begins to set, its reflections light the leaves as if they have tiny light bulbs inside them. I drink in the intensity of the colors and remind myself to memorize its reality and its essence. I'm saving it all for when I'm older—for when I leave Withensea.

Beauty. If only I possessed a sliver of the gorgeousness. Wendy says although I'm not pretty, I'm not unattractive.

I have long, straight brown hair and dark, cucumber-green eyes with pale skin and freckles. When I'm scared the color of my skin gives me away more than my eyes, because my freckles stand out like tiny brown pebbles on white sand. I don't match the weight or height for my age in those standards charts—I'm in fifth grade and barely break four feet, plus I'm too thin. I get teased all the time as the smallest girl in my class.

My best friend, my one friend, is Leigh Westerfield.

———

One day after school, I had a fistfight with one of the girls in my class. It was one of those weather days where the rain comes in twenty-second pelts and then quits. I'd been having almost daily fistfights since school began, and I had learned to draw blood as quickly as possible. Best way to end it.

The girl grabbed my hair and swung her fist toward my head, but I caught a lucky break when she lost her footing. Her fingernail caught the edge of my ear as I pulled away, giving me a perfect shot at her face. She got a bloody nose, and I got a ripped earlobe. She called off the fight.

Leigh hung out as the small crowd of kids moved away after the fight ended. She'd moved into my neighborhood the week before school started that fall, but I hadn't talked to her until then. All I knew was that she was one of the few girls in my class that was already wearing a bra. This is something I hope never becomes a necessity for me, despite the way my brothers tease me about my lack of breasts.

I knelt on the ground, searching for the tiger's eye earring the girl ripped out of my ear. Leigh offered to help and began scrambling around with me in a muddy puddle.

She wore the coolest purple jeans I'd ever seen.

"You're destroying those." I jutted my chin at her jeans and spoke in an angry tone.

I expected her to take off.

"You just beat up the toughest girl in our class. I thought you were way too small to take her."

I ignored her.

"You won't have to fight anyone else again now you've shown you can beat her up."

"You think?" I asked.

"Absolutely. I wouldn't mess with you."

I thought she might be making fun of me, but a goofy smile spread over my face. I couldn't keep it in.

Leigh smiled back, offering the kerchief she'd been using to tie back her wavy, strawberry-blonde hair.

"Your ear is bleeding. Wipe it off unless you're trying to look *really* tough."

———

I never found the earring, but that was it. We were best friends. And she nailed it: no one ever bothered me again. Leigh's smart about people. I'm happy around her in a way I've never been before. I'm still like an alien, but with Leigh beside me it's okay, even wonderful, to be different.

After the bus drops us off, we stop at her neighborhood playground for hours, swinging on the swings and talking. We wait until the sun begins to drop behind the big oak trees that tower over the playground before starting the walk back.

"Watch out. He's got a water gun and a big crush," Leigh warns me about the boy riding his bike toward us.

"On you?" I ask.

"No, not on me. On you!"

"He does not. He hates me. He punches me every time he walks by me in the hall."

"Exactly! When he develops a vocabulary, he'll ask you out."

I laugh. "You're loony. He loathes me." I pronounce "loathe" in a way that rhymes with "cough."

I have gotten into the habit of sprinkling words I've read—but have never heard spoken—into my speech. The result is something Leigh labels the Jules Finn "Say-It-Like-It-Looks Dictionary."

Leigh peers at me oddly. "Huh?"

"I think he hates me cuz I fought him in the third grade and threw him over the cliff in front of my brother and all his friends."

Leigh laughs.

The boy, Jeff, rides by us, circles, and squirts me until I'm soaked and screaming. Leigh steps over to his bike and wrestles the water gun out of his hand while he tries to keep his balance on the bike. She grabs it, and he peddles away, cursing, after she turns it on him.

"Thou lump of foul deformity!" I shout after him.

"What did I tell you? He wants your attention," She squirts the water gun into her mouth.

"Well, that was fun, now I'm totally in love," I say. "How come only the weirdos like me?"

"Anyway, what I was gonna tell you . . . Andre asked me to the all-school dance at the high school tonight!"

"No way. Are you gonna go?" I ask.

Neither of us has been to a school dance before.

"Duh! What do you think? And you're coming! We can go together and meet him there."

"No, it'd be way too freaky. You go."

A plane coming out from Boston Logan flies overhead, nearly drowning out our conversation.

"No, come on, it'll be fun," Leigh shouts over the noise. "I stole cigarettes from my sister, and we can bum more at the dance."

I think about it as the plane moves farther away, leaving a streak of puffy white across the sky. We stand in front of her house.

"Okay?" Leigh asks.

"Okay," I answer.

"So you can sleep over tonight and we can walk to the dance from my place," Leigh says, moving across her lawn to her porch steps.

"Great," I call out.

She lives in one of the ranch houses built by the developer who bought the land Howard sold. With the exception of the land supporting the O'Connells' home, my grandfather purchased all the available land around our house. The land was cheap at the time, and he saw the potential in the real estate of the neighborhood long before the developers who came later making offers to Howard. The developers built the ranch homes well, but with no imagination: they're clad in different colors of aluminum siding, but they're built exactly the same.

The spicy, sweet smell of Leigh's mom's tomato sauce sneaks out the door as Leigh holds it open. The juices in my stomach give a gurgle and my mouth waters instantly.

Eggplant parmesan—my absolute favorite!

"So, are you gonna go home or do you want to eat over first?"

Leigh knows that, 90 percent of the time, our refrigerator holds two staples: nail polish and film canisters. The film canisters alternately hold Jack's film and various drugs that Wendy insists are vitamins.

Wendy started a lifelong diet at fifteen, and she figures the best way to avoid overeating is to avoid grocery shopping. The fact that she has three growing children clearly doesn't stand in her way.

My brothers and I, not coincidentally, befriend people with generous families who feed us regularly.

"I gotta go back and see what I can feed my brothers," I say. "And I gotta grab nicer clothes. This isn't a good thing to wear, is it?" I say, motioning to the farmer jeans I'm wearing.

A few months ago, Wendy started modeling clothes at trade shows for a friend who owns a clothing design business. She gets to keep most of the clothes she models and she's collected an enormous wardrobe of trendy clothes, like the stuff rock stars wear on shows like *The Midnight Special*. Leigh loves coming over when Wendy leaves because we can open her closets and dive into the rayon, paisley-printed blouses with billowy butterfly sleeves, glittery, multicolored, rhinestone-studded denim shirts, and crushed velvet jackets. The bellbottoms drag the floor on me, but Leigh can almost get away with wearing them when she's got Wendy's high-heeled black vinyl boots on. Leigh even borrows some of the clothes from time to time. Left to my own devices, however, I choose plain, ordinary clothes and wear the same things with great frequency. This is the second time this week I've worn the farmer jeans.

"You should wear that purple suede vest your mom has with the beaded fringe. Do you think I could borrow the one with the American flag on it? I'll fix you up, it'll be fun."

"I'll see you in a bit," I say to Leigh. I wave and make my way up the avenue and around the corner to the edge of my neighborhood.

Leigh has a great eye for fashion. I trust her opinion. I know talking Wendy into letting me borrow her clothes is out of the question, however. She gets multiple samples of the clothing she models at trade shows, in several different colors, but I'm still not allowed to touch them unless she doesn't like them or grows tired of them.

I don't come close to filling out most of the things she wears unless my grandfather tailors them, anyway—but the vests are one-sizers Leigh and I can both wear. The tricky part will be swiping them without her noticing, although given the normal chaos and level of distraction in our house, it might not be that difficult.

Cigarettes are not the motivator for me to go to the dance, though I let Leigh think they were. The truth: I am dying to go to the dance. I have a fantasy I will meet the guy of my dreams and live happily ever after there. And I'm certain the guy of my dreams does not live in Withensea, so he will have to be visiting someone and have been brought to the dance, like me. We will have that in common.

Leigh is the only girl close to my age who lives near our neighborhood. Before she moved into her neighborhood, when I wasn't playing sports with David and his friends, I hung out with some of teenage girls on my street once in a while, smoking cigarettes and listening to their stories.

When Wendy learned about my smoking (David told on me in a moment of revenge), I became known as "stupid"—the worst thing you could possibly be. Stupidity, in our house, is the ultimate sin. Stupidity trumps thievery, substance abuse—anything you can imagine as a normal ethical, moral, or legal breech, actually. Stupidity, in Wendy's mind, is the lowest rung of human behavior.

There is no rule-setting or punishment regarding my smoking, however. There is, instead, an almost constant admonishment about how ignorant I must be to continue damaging my lungs, stunting my growth, and ignoring the fact that my behavior will permanently mark me as a person incapable of making any respectable, responsible, or intelligent choices.

I still smoke, however, and sometimes I light up in full view of Wendy to spite her. I've always been stubborn. Leigh and I both smoke, but her mom will kill her if she finds out she's been smoking, so we never smoke anywhere in public.

We live on the end of the island where the high school is, and Leigh's house is closer to the school than mine. I don't have to ask permission to sleep over and Leigh knows it. Wendy is rarely at our house, and even when her body inhabits the place, her mind rarely checks into our reality. Ever since she got back from the hospital, she and her friends have been having a party that never stops and involves every conceivable painkiller and psychotropic drug. Pretty much anything that might create an altered state.

A few months ago, I found Wendy and Jack tripping on acid and hunting for her face in the living room rug, under the piano. Wendy stared up at me and said, "Oh God Jules, I'm glad you're home. Could you help us? Help me find my face? I lost it somewhere here in the rug and I've been searching a long, long time."

The situation was hysterical: Wendy, the card-carrying Mensa member who lorded her intelligence over everyone, was carrying on like a fool. But it was also scary. I had complete control over this particular situation, and I didn't want it. Wendy was tripping her brains out and depending on me to produce a happy ending. I wanted to rescue her and I also wanted to let her suffer. My protective instincts won, as usual.

"Well, you've been searching in the wrong place. It's right here under the piano, and if you weren't doing drugs you wouldn't have lost it in the first place." I pretended to scoop it up and handed it to her gently.

She tore the imaginary face from my hands breathlessly, patted it to her cheeks and thanked me.

Sensing an opportunity for a real connection, I asked, "When are you going to start being a good parent? It's time for you to grow up. Don't you care about us?"

Wendy became oblivious to me. She started touching her face and moaning. She never answered me. She got lost in her trip again. I stomped up the stairs and slammed my door.

I heard Jack say, "Jesus, what a drag."

I slam lots of doors these days.

I'm pissed with Wendy for not being a parent, an adult, or even a semblance of support for us. At ten, I have become what she needs—her mother.

My brothers and I make the choice to rebel and not be a part of the drug-induced party, although we are constantly, inappropriately, invited. I figure this is the greatest annoyance to Wendy—for us to be "square," as she calls it.

A few weeks after the "lost face" episode, Wendy's retaliation for my refusal to embrace her lifestyle was to slide a hit of acid into a bowl of Raisin Bran I left on the counter.

After I finished my bowl she made up an excuse to punish me, telling me I hadn't put away the dishes fast enough, sent me up to my room, and let me go through the acid trip without knowing what was happening to me.

Up in my room, I grabbed a book and lost myself in the story. A bit later I found myself unable to concentrate on the words, which were sliding over the pages of the book and dropping to the floor like small seeds. Next, they came alive and turned into tiny bugs. Having no idea what Wendy did, I thought I was going crazy. I became terrified. My hearing magnified—at one point I thought the airplane flying overhead would crash into our house. It sounded like it was making an unusually slow descent, and the sound grew deafening. I felt my floor begin to shake. I ran out past Wendy and Jack, who were getting stoned in the living room, and into the road in front of our place. I felt convinced the house would erupt into a firestorm any second. But I couldn't see a plane anywhere.

Once the deafening noise of the passing plane faded away and I was done shaking, I wandered into our backyard, which felt like a safer environment. I sat on the grass beside the back porch, but soon I realized the grass appeared to be breathing. I freaked out, and the thought crossed my mind that I'd fallen through the rabbit hole, like Alice. The thought of calling for Wendy occurred to me, but then I remembered she and Jack were stoned. I didn't think she'd be any help. My brothers had gone out that morning.

I sat alone in the breathing grass and craned my neck up at the huge weeping willow tree in our backyard, which has long been one of my refuges. I jumped up and began to climb the wide limbs, but my legs were uncoordinated and slow. I talked my way through the action of climbing. "Step here. Slide your arm up the bark. Hold on to this branch and pull. Oh, so heavy. Lift this leg. Higher. Higher. There. Step here now. Reach this arm up. Grab this branch."

This occupied me until I found myself at the top limb of the tree. Time became quite fluid. I began to relax and enjoy the view from my perch, which sat above the roofline and offered a breathtaking view of the ocean. Leaning back against the bark, I let go of the branches I'd been holding and let myself sink into the tree limb. I felt myself become part of it, the tree bark a part of my skin, part of me. The leaves, grass, fence, ocean. The lighthouse in the distance. I could feel the air moving through my body. I became the center of a large figure eight. All of life seemed to flow through me in the center of that design, spiraling like a huge DNA strand.

Later I learned it's the symbol for infinity.

At some point, I became convinced I was weightless and capable of floating. I stretched out my arms, Superman-style, and began to lean over the edge of the branches. At that moment, Moses came into the backyard. I could see him down in the yard, but from my vantage point, high in the tree, he seemed like a small speck. I couldn't make out his features clearly, and his hair looked like it had been dyed a deep brown. It glinted with bronze shimmers in the sunlight.

He was standing in the shade of the willow.

Jules, what are you doing? You better come down or you're going to fall.

He sounded funny. Like a lady.

I wondered how he knew I'd climbed up there. I knew the foliage hid me well. It seemed impossible that he could know about my hiding spot, and yet I had watched him walk straight to the tree and gaze up to exactly the spot where I lay.

I balanced in the center of the limb.

"I'm going to float down to you," I shouted down to him. "Watch me."

No!

I let my body fall forward as he screamed.

I still remember the scream. It sounded strange. Like an echo.

It frightened me and caused me to jerk into an adrenalized awareness. I felt myself hitting the branches and instinctively grabbed at them as I bounced from one to the other on my way down.

I slammed chest-down into one of the lower limbs of the tree. Stunned, I lay there for a moment. Moses, who had been screaming, stopped. The wind had been knocked out of me. I choked for a few seconds before I could catch a painful breath. When I could breathe normally, I peeked my head over the edge of the tree limb to see how far I was from the ground.

Wendy and Jack stood below and I, about halfway up the tree, could see their anxious faces.

"You need to come down now," Wendy said.

"I'm fine. I'll be down in a while."

"Why were you screaming if you're fine?"

"I wasn't screaming," I answered. "Moses screamed."

"What're you talking about? Moses isn't here," Wendy said.

I glanced down to where he'd been standing, but he'd vanished.

"Come down and we'll have dinner," Wendy said.

Dinner?

That seemed weird. It had been breakfast a bit ago. Where had the time gone? I climbed carefully down. I felt bruised everywhere, and my body was scratched from head to toe, but—miraculously—not a single bone was broken.

I came in to make dinner. I decided it would be TV dinners that night. It meant less time in the kitchen. I had an aching body and an aching head. The brightly colored daisy flooring of Wendy's kitchen renovation made my head hurt even more. The countertops were still covered with the old flesh-pink linoleum, and the pattern seemed to be shifting. The walls, recently painted bright orange, seemed more intense than ever.

As my brothers and I sat at the bar eating, I asked Moses, "Where did you disappear to after you were screaming at me in the tree?"

"Huh?" Moses stared at me like I was nuts and scratched the inside of his arm.

He told me he'd been with David until he came in for dinner. I could tell he wasn't lying. I attributed the "Moses mirage" to sudden insanity. Or maybe it was another kid who looked like Moses. I remembered I wasn't able to see him clearly.

But what was that other kid doing in our yard, and how did he know I was up there?

The experience made me believe I might be capable of random crazy thinking. Being crazy, in our family, would not be unusual or particularly noteworthy, but I didn't talk to anyone, even Leigh, about it. I've been determined to appear normal, even if I'm not. And for the past few months, I've been afraid it might happen again. Then, the other day, I overheard Wendy tell a friend how she gave me a hit of acid in my cereal.

I hate Wendy more than ever. But I also haven't forgotten the feeling of being somehow connected to the world in a way I'd never experienced before that day.

———

As I continue the walk toward my street, the setting sun bounces off the multi-colored leaf reflections in the glass windows of the surrounding homes. The scene paints "idyllic New England" until you turn the corner and see the sight our place has become.

The Victorian still sits alone on the cliff. It faces the one where the O'Connells still live, but now another row of the aluminum-sided ranch homes stands—gleaming in all its pastel glory—along the O'Connells' side of the block.

Our house was recently painted a vivid shade of periwinkle blue. Wendy picked the color from a Peter Max poster, and although the painter tried to talk her out of it, telling her that home exteriors shouldn't be painted that particular shade, she was adamant. One of the most bizarre consequences of her choice is that the color glows in the dark, which makes pointing it out to people who drop us off at night easy—and embarrassing.

As if the color isn't enough to distinguish the house, Wendy hired a company to blow insulation into the walls to help weather the winters and save money on the heating bills. This particular insulation method involved creating round, base-ball-sized holes in the wood siding to allow insulation to be blown in. When they finished the job, they covered the holes with small, louvered, silver discs. She never bothered to have the discs painted to match the wood shingles, and the end result is an electric blue surface dotted with silver discs. Our house now perches on the cliff like a psychedelic Victorian spaceship.

The first sense irritating me as I turn the corner onto our street, however, is not my sight but my hearing: the music coming from our place is blaring at concert level, and it grows louder with each step.

I hate the song that plays—"Every Christian Lion Hearted Man Will Show You," by the Bee Gees. Jack's favorite song. It's dirgelike, unlike any other music the Bee Gees have produced. Jack used to play it over and over while David chanted, "Play it again. Play it again," in a failed attempt at reverse psychology. I say *failed* attempt because Jack kept obliging David, I think because he wanted to bond with him and believed that he really loved the song as well.

VW vans, Beetles, and other cars and motorcycles painted with bright colors crowd our front lawn and line Alethea Road. The crowning glory of "freak," however, is the 1947 Daimler Hearse bearing the logo *The Hop Shoppe* in an ornate, psychedelic design, which has taken up residence in the driveway. To say it draws attention would be an understatement.

One of Wendy's friends owned the first head shop in Boston, and they used to use the hearse to advertise it. They originally parked it out on the city street in front of the store. But when the store began attracting attention from the Boston police, they repeatedly ticketed the hearse and finally towed it. After Wendy's friends rescued the hearse out of its towing debt, it ended up permanently parked in our driveway.

Our neighbor who purchased the ranch house located diagonally across the road from ours is agoraphobic. I totally understand why she has a fear of going outside.

As I walk closer, I can see the party is pulsing in full chaos mode. People spill out onto the lawn and wander down the cliff toward the beach. Wendy's parties are notorious and sometimes last for days.

When I reach the porch, more people pour out the door. They're laughing loudly. One of them grabs my arm as I brush by. It's Dorothy, Wendy's newest best friend.

Dorothy used to be a Rolling Stones groupie and likes to tell stories about the time she had sex with Keith Richards. She smiles at me and stays, still holding my arm, while her friends keep going. She waves off her boyfriend, a quiet guy named Decker, who lingers on the porch with her.

Decker, a major drug dealer for the Boston community, and Dorothy, a nurse who steals meds from the hospitals she works for, have, like the hearse, become fixtures at our place. Hospitals fire Dorothy when they find out she steals, but she's never arrested. Sometimes they rehire her. Dorothy has charisma. She's friendly, and when she isn't stoned she's interesting to talk to. Dorothy talks to me in a way that makes it seem like I matter, like my opinions are important.

I can see she's buzzed. She yells over the blaring music, "Hey, little woman. How are you doing? You getting back from school? Do you wanna go for a quick swim? The seaweed is good for your hair, you know."

"No thanks. It's a bit cold for me right now," I say, laughing.

It's the middle of September in New England. People who swim in the freezing cold ocean past Labor Day are surfers or nutty.

"Besides, I've got chores to do," I add.

"I dig it. See ya later," Dorothy says.

I watch her run down the road to catch up with her friends. Dorothy tears her clothes off as they go, as though she doesn't know it's chilly.

Wendy and her friends love to take off their clothes. There's a lot of nakedness that spills out onto the porch, the lawn, and the street, and I'm sure it shocks and amuses our neighbors. It embarrasses me.

"Oh, brother," I say under my breath. Three more people step out onto the porch. They're high school students with baggies of dope in their hands, which they hastily hide when they see me. One of them speaks to me.

"Hey Jules, you're looking foxy. You won't forget about me when you grow up, now, will you?"

"Not in million years. How could I forget you?"

I talk in a sweet voice he doesn't recognize as sarcastic. He smiles as he walks away.

———

It makes me mad that Jack sells marijuana out of our house, especially to high school kids. It's risky and stupid. He could potentially blow our family apart if Wendy's arrested.

Occasionally, one of the high school kids will ask me if I can score them dope, and it pisses me off. I'm anti-drug, as are my brothers, and I resent being asked. Jack has started telling them to hide the marijuana and pretend he's not selling to them anymore.

It isn't just the high school kids who know our house is a great place to score pot. It also hasn't escaped the attention of the local police, who cruise by with regularity but never bust anyone. It's like there's a conspiracy to ignore Wendy's behavior. I don't mind, because allows my brothers and me to remain together—but I am obsessed with the possibility of being arrested along with Wendy and her friends.

I can't count on my grandfather anymore. My Grandmother Yetta died last summer, and my grandfather seems to drift in a depressed haze. Our visits with him are random and brief. Once Wendy drove us into Boston to collect a check from him and then drove us right back to Withensea. We didn't even stay for dinner, and what's worse is my grandfather didn't seem to mind. So I don't think there *is* another place to go anymore if Wendy gets arrested and sent to jail.

———

I survey the scene inside. People pack the room wall to wall, and the air stinks of pot and cigarette smoke. People occupy every piece of furniture, sit on counters, sit on the floor. A man hangs off the bookcase like a chimpanzee. Everyone shouts at each other over the music.

The coffee table overflows with pipe paraphernalia, a large bowl of dope, roach clips, rolling papers, empty prescription bottles, and film canisters. The piano has been shoved in the corner next to the fireplace. Sadly, it's become scarred with more glass rings, scratch marks, and cigarette burns with each successive party. People sit on top of it as though it's a throne, and other people sprawl around it like subjects.

I wind my way through the crowd toward the stairs.

Wendy's still taking occasional classes at Northeastern University, and lots of her young college friends come to these parties.

"How is school?" they ask. "Are you still drawing?"

They question me as if we're all at a parent-teacher meeting. It's all formal and stiff and stupid to talk to them this way when I know they're all high and won't remember the conversation anyway.

Then someone asks me the dumbest question: "Do you have a boyfriend?"

I hate this question. "I'm ten years old and I don't plan to have a boyfriend for some time," I answer.

I smile politely and continue on. When I climb to the top of the stairs, I pass a few people who have just emerged from Wendy's room. I peek inside to see if Wendy is there. She isn't. I step inside and chat with the people who are still hanging out until they leave the room.

I close the door and open a window to air out the heavy pot stink. Then I open one of Wendy's closets. I pull through several racks of clothing before finding the two vests I want. I stuff them under my blouse and am starting to leave when I see the handle turning and hear Wendy's voice. I step back into the closet, pull it closed, and push the racks of clothing in front of me. I hear Wendy shouting over the music to someone.

" . . . fucked me, then he told me he was taking off to sail Saul's boat through the Panama Canal up to California and left the next day."

"No shit? Far out! Why didn't you go with him?"

It's Dorothy with her. She closes the door behind them, muffling the sound of the music so they don't have to yell.

Wendy opens the closet and lifts the laundry chute in the floor beside me with a rope hanging from the ceiling of the closet. She drops Dorothy's wet T-shirt and jeans through the chute, inches away from my feet, and grabs another shirt and pair of jeans from the edge of the rack I'm standing behind.

Wendy's motorcycle accident a year and a half ago left her with neck herniations that make it difficult for her to turn her head completely without pain. She doesn't see me standing behind the clothes in the closet.

"I don't have the dough to go with him. He kept the money from last year's weed crop and Samuel already gave me money for this month's bills. I fucking hate asking him for money. I have to make up shitty excuses and I've already had enough car trouble for this year, you dig? He takes a fucking pound of flesh, believe me."

A year ago, Wendy signed us up for welfare checks and food stamps from the government even though my Grandfather Samuel totally supports us. She never reports his money. This embarrasses me and my brothers and leaves our closest friends confused as to how we can afford expensive clothes and summer camp but still qualify for free lunches at school.

I can see through a parting in the clothes as Wendy walks to her bureau and opens one of the top drawers.

I'm familiar with this drawer. Wendy's pharmacy, a shallow drawer stuffed with pill bottles. I know from my nosy explorations that the bottles hold multicolored pills with prescription labels wrapped around the exteriors that sometimes have Wendy's or Jack's or other people's names on them.

The contents of the pills and their effects remain a complete mystery to me. I have no intention to check any of it out myself, but it's an impressive collection.

I watch as Wendy opens one of the bottles, shakes a few pills out and throws them back in her throat.

Dorothy asks, "Downers? Benzo?" and when Wendy nods, she holds her hand out and waits while Wendy walks over and shakes one into her hand. Wendy puts the bottle back, shuts the drawer, walks over to the bed and lies down on it. Dorothy lies across the foot of the bed. Completely naked. I wonder if she came in from the beach through the wall of people at the party without putting clothes back on.

Dorothy rolls herself up, pulls on the T-shirt, and tries on the jeans Wendy pulled from the closet, and I watch as Wendy lights a sandalwood cone in the brass cup on the bureau.

"I wish I had a sugar daddy to take care of me, lady. You don't know how lucky you are!"

"My father? Samuel's a bastard and a bully. He's lied to me my entire life. He acts like he's penniless but he's got a fortune—and he wants to dole it out in pennies so he can keep me attached at the hip and begging. Ever since I found out they all lied to me about my parents he's been afraid I'll try to find out who my real parents are and tell them to fuck off."

Wendy never talks about my grandfather this way in front of us kids. I inhale the sandalwood scent that drifts into the closet and remind myself to stay still so I won't be found.

"You never told me you were adopted. Would you do that . . . tell them to fuck off?" Dorothy asks.

"Absolutely. They're crazy. I grew up believing my grandparents were my parents until I was ten and they were too old to take care of me. That's when I went to live with Samuel and Yetta . . . who acted like they hated each other. He barely tolerated me, and Yetta smothered me until she drove me crazy."

My nose tickles from the incense and the wool inside the closet. I think I might sneeze, so I hold my nostrils shut.

"Nobody told me the truth about anything, and when I asked they screamed at me that I was nosy and ungrateful. When they did tell me anything . . . it was always a lie. Lies on lies. Fuck them all."

"Well still, it's nice to have someone to go to when you're in a jam. Jack's an asshole, Wendy. I don't know why you stay with him. I would have left after he banged that stoner chick."

"He's so fucking adorable . . . and not just because of his dick," Wendy says.

They laugh.

Dorothy says, "These are too fucking small, I'm gonna grab another pair."

She peels the jeans off and walks over to the closet. She stops directly in front of me.

"Your clothes are far out! You could sell the clothes you never wear and raise money that way. Jesus, you've got twenty million things in here."

Dorothy reaches up and grabs a bunch of jeans off the rack right in front of where I'm hiding. She sees me standing there, staring with eyes as frightened and surprised as hers. She whips the hangers back up on the bar and pulls the closet closed before Wendy can see me, although I can still see a sliver of them.

"If you think that's a lot, you should see the shitload of stuff I have downstairs I never even wear. It's all in storage in the basement," Wendy says.

"Far out! Let's go see. I'll bet you've got stuff you could sell for lots of cash!"

"Now? I'm tired, Dorothy, I wanna . . ."

Dorothy walks over to the bed, grabs Wendy's arm, and pulls her until she rolls off the edge of the bed onto her feet.

"I know you wanna take a fucking nap, Wendy— you fall asleep at every party. Don't be a drag. Get your ass downstairs and pick out some shit to sell."

Dorothy pushes her toward the door.

Wendy argues, "How am I gonna sell the clothes?"

"You're shitting me, right? You've got a crowd of buyers right here, right now! Go sell, Mama! Hell, I'll buy a pair of jeans if I can find a pair that fits me."

Dorothy stays in the middle of the room.

"Aren't you coming with me?" Wendy asks.

"You go ahead; I wanna start here and try on a few things. I'll meet you down there to help you haul it up."

"All right, all right. You don't have to pay me for the jeans, only no Raindance or Old Glory labels. Those're new threads from the last show."

Wendy leaves.

Dorothy waits a beat, then opens the closet and pushes the clothes aside. "You can come out now, Jules. What are you doing in the closet, little woman?"

I pull my blouse up to reveal the vests I've taken.

"There's a school dance tonight and my friend and I want to wear these."

"I don't think she'll miss anything in this mess, but you better bring them back in case she does and thinks I took them. Throw them on the closet floor when you're done. She'll think I dropped them. Have fun at your dance."

I don't know what to say, so I say, "Get thee to a nunnery."

Dorothy laughs and I do too.

I make my way toward my room at the end of the hall. As I pass the bath I see two people sitting in the empty bathtub while someone sits on the toilet.

I open my room and breathe a sigh of relief. No one in here. No pot stink. Just the smell of the sunbleached shells I left on my window ledge.

I post a huge sign on my door: JULES'S ROOM - KEEP OUT OR SUFFER EXTREME PAIN.

Most of the time the sign preserves my privacy in our very public house, but occasionally I find people using my bed. Not for sleeping. It grosses me out.

I stuff the vests into my overnight bag, along with a pair of underwear, socks, pajamas, a shirt, and—as an afterthought—my swimsuit, in case it warms up again tomorrow.

Before I leave, I check my art supplies and set up the trap I created to alert me if someone ignores my sign and tries to sneak in: a rubber band tied to a ribbon that stretches from the back of the knob to an old hook nailed into the wall. I cover the knob with half a rubber ball pushed through with straight pins that stick out like porcupine quills to thwart the efforts of anyone who tries to release the band from the inside. I love inventing things.

At David's room I knock. We practice this courtesy with each other. Wendy completely ignores it.

"Yeah?" he yells.

David, thirteen, looks more like Wendy than Moses and me. We all have her almond, almost Asian, eye shape. But he also has her olive skin, brown eyes, and kinky, dark brown hair.

He lies on an unmade bed reading a comic book and eating a Butterfinger candy bar. The room smells like moldy socks. Dishes, books, magazines, even his muddy football uniform, cover the floor. I yell over the blare of the music. "What are you doing? You're not supposed to be reading those."

Comic books are forbidden. Wendy considers us immune to abuse, neglect, drugs, and alcohol, but adamantly swears that comic books will rot our brains. We're all punished if they're found and one of us doesn't confess to the crime. David never does.

"Have you done your homework? Where'd you get candy? Make your bed, pick up your clothes. Put your uniform right into the washer, please, and put those bowls in the sink or you'll attract ants again."

He jumps up toward me. "Out of my room, you bossy hen. It's Friday and I don't have to do homework until Sunday night. Moses got the candy at the store. You can't have any and you're not my mother."

He slams the door in my face. A second later he whips it back open, smiles, and says, "Did you do the laundry? Did you wash my blue shirt? I wanna wear it tonight. Oh, and Dad called. He said he's coming back into town for a while to stay at Aunt Doreen's and he's coming to pick us up on Sunday."

"Your crummy blue shirt's done. It's in the laundry basket downstairs. You're welcome. Oh, and I'm not making dinner tonight. You should make sandwiches or a TV dinner, okay?"

"Thank you, Julie-Bo-Bulie, you're a skinny ninny. Too bad you have no boobies." He points to my chest, laughs hysterically, and slams the door again.

I open his door again without knocking.

"And feed Moses dinner. And feed Felix. I'm sleeping over at Leigh's. I can't."

I smile, satisfied. I know dinner for Moses and David will be meager. TV dinners or spaghetti. But we have all existed—during the two years post-divorce and before the motorcycle accident—on not much more than cereal, school lunches, and the kindness of our friends, and we've done okay.

I'm not sure David will feed the cat, though. I make a mental note to do that before I leave. We smuggled Felix inside a while back. Wendy didn't notice we were living with a cat for a long time—a good thing, because she doesn't like animals. But for some reason, she's letting us keep her.

David is three years older than I am, yet Wendy leaves me in charge of him and Moses. This creates still more anger between us. He's pissed that I'm in charge. I'm pissed he isn't more grateful. David can be crude and annoying. He never listens to me. He speaks like a robot, asks ten questions at once without waiting for answers, and ends conversations abruptly. At times, he makes loud, nonsensical pronunciations to no one in particular. He avoids doing anything he can cajole me or pay Moses to do. Sometimes I hate him.

Howard's call surprises me. We've hardly seen him since his hasty departure during Wendy's hospitalization. He lives in California now. Wendy says he's started a new scam with business card placemats that he sells to restaurants.

After Wendy came back from the hospital, she pretty much put me in charge of running the house while she recuperated—doing all the laundry, cooking, cleaning, caring for and keeping tabs on my brothers, and feeding Felix.

It's been over a year since her accident, but when Wendy became mobile again, she never resumed the chores she handed me. She tells me I'm "obviously old enough to handle it," because I'm doing "such a good job." She's the queen of manipulation.

I never receive or expect anything resembling an allowance in return for my service, but I've progressed in my cooking ability from TV dinners to boiled pastas and broiled meats. I never explore beyond these simple dinners. Salt is my main spice for taste, and when I feel especially daring, I add pepper to the recipe. Still, my cooking is more proficient than Wendy's. My brothers are, I think, happy to have regular dinners prepared for them.

I've also become a pretty good baker. I bake casseroles and lasagnas, as well as occasional treats. Even though we buy them at the store all the time, sweets and soda are not really allowed. Our "dental health" is the excuse Wendy gives, although we know the real reason: her inability to control her binging if they're present. However, if I *bake* something sweet, like lemon cake, chocolate-chip cookies, or raspberry tarts, the rules are off. It's as though "home baking" makes sugary things somehow healthier. Maybe she can't resist home-baked food. But it's probably Jack, with his sweet tooth, who she tries to please by allowing it.

The laundry is done with much more regularity, and the house, though a mess most of the time due to the almost constant party of people, is generally cleaner and more organized than it was before the accident.

I don't understand why Wendy, who rejects the social rules for women's behavior, gives me all the stereotypically female chores while my brothers are left with a minimal amount of stereotypically male chores. They split taking out the trash and mowing the lawn in the summer months. Everything else falls to me. I argue they ought to help out with laundry and dishes. Wendy says they're "women's jobs." Until my friendship with Leigh, I had plenty of time to fulfill my role as mother to the family. Now, I'm ticked off I don't get to be a kid and my brothers aren't helping out more.

I knock on Moses's door. He doesn't answer, and when I peek in, he isn't there. I step inside and snoop around.

Although I cherish my privacy and guard it with small weapons, I'm nosy and often sneak into the stuff that belongs to the rest of my family.

Moses is seven and, like me, small for his age. This makes him seem a bit younger than he is, but his eyes are the eyes of an ageless person. Wise and sad. His eyes are navy blue, not muddy brown like Howard's, Wendy's, and David's. No one else in our family has blue eyes except our Grandfather Samuel. But I know he isn't our real grandfather because of Wendy's adoption.

Somehow, despite all the meanness in our family, Moses remains remarkably sweet in nature. He idolizes David, almost six years his elder, and spends too much time and energy trying to win his approval. He does most everything David asks, including regular runs to the local grocery for David's junk food desires.

But Moses did figure out how to profit from David's laziness: he developed a financial deal involving a percentage split and transportation allowance for any errands he runs for anyone, including myself, Wendy, and Jack. I admire his business sense. Moses is a whiz at saving money. He buys himself expensive items for a young kid, like bikes, with the money he saves. He also loans the money he saves back to us (with interest, of course). I think Moses is going to grow up to be a multimillionaire or something.

I wonder where he could be. Moses has one friend—a school friend who lives on another part of the island. He doesn't see him outside of school unless his friend's mom arranges to drive him back afterwards. Wendy doesn't drive us around anymore, and she doesn't arrange carpooling. This would mean a call to another parent, which she avoids. No doubt she finds it too parental. She calls stuff like that "suburban rituals." As a result, we walk, ride the bus, or ride our bikes everywhere.

Moses hasn't mastered the bus schedule yet. His choices are to play by himself or to hang around our neighborhood. But our neighborhood harbors an unusual demographic for an Irish-Catholic town, where Catholicism and the rhythm method usually produce an abundance of girls. Our neighborhood has an army of boys—and tons of them are David's age, but none are Moses's age. He sometimes tags along with David, though the arrangement is less than desirable for David.

———

I close my eyes for a moment in Moses's room, savoring its peacefulness. It smells like Nilla wafers and old pennies. His room, the smallest, was originally the nursery. Moses never got the upgrade David and I enjoy. But it stays warmer than the rest of our rooms. Wendy used the maroon remnants of the downstairs rug to carpet it. It's also the quietest.

Moses's space amazes me. His shoes are lined up under his perfectly made bed, with a faded old race car bedspread Wendy purchased years before during the "Sloane Sales Master Charge Buying Spree." Stacked and labeled shoeboxes and milk cartons line the walls, displaying his various collections of matchbox cars, trains, action figure heroes, and Tinker Toys.

I walk toward the large bureau pushed up against one wall. I brush my fingers over the dinosaur models, glass figures, and small pebbles and feathers decorating the top of his bureau. I know he hides large, lidded coffee cans on the floor of his closet that he's stuffed full with pennies, nickels, and dimes.

His unicycle leans against the wall. He told me he asked for the unicycle because he thinks he might never grow taller, and if he doesn't he'll be able to make a living in the circus, riding his unicycle. He's preparing for that career path. For the same reason, he taught himself to juggle.

While turning off the power on one of the walkie-talkies he shares with David, I notice a small shoebox next to one of the milk crates on the floor. After a moment's hesitation, I open the lid. Inside, a small, furry fake mouse lays in layers of grass. I let out a sigh of relief and pick it up with my other hand. As I examine it, a banded garter snake winds up out of the grass and across the mouse in my hand, flicking its tongue at me. I let out a loud yelp and slam the lid of the box on the snake's head, pushing it down and back into the box. The fake mouse lies on the floor by the box. Breathing hard, I inch open the lid a bit and squeeze the mouse back inside. Standing up, I shoot one last glance at the box, open the door, and step into the hallway.

There is almost always something living in Moses's room besides Moses.

———

Of all Moses's collections, there's one I especially love: his collection of sea glass, stored in one of his shoeboxes. Older sea glass has a white frosted glaze over it, a sand tattoo that, over time, rounds the rough edges.

Sea glass, more than anything else, reminds me of Moses.

I still have the box. It reminds me of our childhood here by the ocean and how the ocean, with time, transforms broken glass, something capable of causing injury, into something touchable. The ocean makes glass precious. Something you can keep.

Thirteen

I, SZAJA, AM now called Samuel. Samuel Trautman.

At thirty-eight years of age I finally arrived in America to reunite with my family. Two years later I sat in a Brookline, Massachusetts apartment I shared with my sister Rose and her second husband, Mocher.

This story tells of the night I arranged a marriage with my first wife, Yetta. It is a night I referred to later as our first date. This is a small joke between us. In another time, in another household, it could have been a date. If it could be called this then it is the first date of my life.

My sister Reizel, now called Rose, lit the festival candles for Seder and placed a bottle of Manichevitz on the table with what I knew is her best linen. I can still remember the fabric: light blue cotton printed with a woman and man dancing in the middle of ladies' fans.

Rose also put out the Seder plates and silverware and the crystal glasses my parents brought all the way from Zhytomyr. Given to Rose for her wedding to Mocher, they are one of the few remnants of our lives from that time. Although I valued the beauty and craftsmanship of the delicate design, they brought nothing but pain to me. If the glass had been broken into shards and stuck into my eyes, the pain would not have matched the pain I felt in my heart looking at them.

"Please, *zay azoy gut*, Rose, take the glasses off the table," I say when I find her folding napkins in the dining room.

"Why, why Samuel? They're made for such an occasion as this."

"Rose, the table is fine-looking, and I know you're trying to be kind, but the woman is going to think I'm a *faygeleh* with all this."

Rose laughs, and as usual, she gets her way.

Rose has been calling me Samuel since I came to live with her and Mocher in Brookline. I am glad to leave that name, that boy—Szaja. My assimilation to American culture is made easier with the new name. Samuel could be anyone. He could be a Jew, a Catholic, or an Englishman. Samuel could be a man with nothing bad in his past. But I know that Samuel is not who I truly am. I am Szaja, a Jew who has survived the wars by forgetting I am a Jew. Now I will spend my life remembering.

Foter and *Mater* had written to us a few weeks before we are attacked on the farm, and Reizel corresponded from the camps in the Ukraine to let the family know about the tragedies and where we had been sent.

After the attack, Reizel, Oizer, and I spent time working in the Ukranian camps. Reizel learned to be a seamstress, Oizer and I became apprentices to a tailor. We learned to sew as well. After six years of finding ways to work and stay together as the work camps became more and more regimented by the Red Army, we are ultimately separated in 1930.

It had been impossible for us to save money in the camps. They didn't pay you for the work, only gave you food and shelter, and my *Foter* still had no money to send for us. They are struggling with the American Great Depression. There are many mouths to feed and not much job opportunity for *Foter*, a cherry picker.

Oizer and Reizel are selected for a work camp near Cyprus, Turkey, where they would live a better life under the British rule. There are actual wages for their work there, and a huge community of Jewish settlers. They are jubilant. Life in the Ukranian camps is a desperate one. Any way out made a better life possible. When we got the news, we knew that they are one step closer to being reunited with our family in America.

On the same day, I am recruited by the Red Army. They told me it would be a year before I could join Reizel and Oizer in Cyprus. Within a few days of my recruitment, I am sent back to work near Zhytomyr, on the border between the Ukraine and Poland, where they are building railroads and army headquarters. It seemed impossible to me that I would be returning to the place from which we had traveled so far away. I worked four days' travel away from our farm and yet I never visited. I would not have been able to bear it.

It is difficult and dangerous work, and until the day I am arrested and sent to the prison at Majdanek I found it impossible to remember and honor my heritage.

The Russian soldiers forgot that I am a Jew as well.

Rose tells me that they tried to contact me several times. All their efforts are futile, and I never tried to contact them. It is s better that way. I had cut off communication with my family in America as well. I still held deep shame for not preventing the deaths of Idel, Berl, and my sisters. I also had shame for my predicament as a member of the Red Army, their murderers, and I thought it best to pretend I had no family and travel alone in the world.

My life is a shadow.

It took Rose and Oizer eight years to save the money for the ship to America from Turkey in 1938. Rose is thirty-two at the time. It had been almost fourteen years since we are attacked at the farm. Oizer had turned twenty-six.

They emigrated before President Roosevelt made his proclamation on immigration quotas, which limited immigration based on race and a person's place of origin. A mere two months after their immigration, the annual quota for Turkish immigration is reduced to two hundred and twenty-six people.

While on the ship that carried them to America, Rose fell in love with Mocher, a tailor eight years younger than her. In Mocher, Rose had found her *bashert*. He joked and teased her into a contagious happiness she had never known before. When they stepped off the ship to meet the rest of the family, Rose introduced Mocher as her new husband—they'd been married by the ship's captain. Our parents insisted they have another wedding with their rabbi.

Meantime, my years as a soldier dragged on. 1944 marked twenty years since the murder of my family. I couldn't tell you what triggered my decision, but I decided I would escape. In the middle of the night I left the tent camp on the border of Poland where we had built an army outpost. I simply walked away and into the forest. Three days later, lost and sleeping under an oak tree, I am found by the Germans, and as I have no papers and I am dressed in uniform, they assumed I am a Russian defector.

They put me on my knees in front of the oak tree and pointed a gun at the middle of my forehead. I don't remember feeling anything. No surprise. No fear.

————

"Is that the *Sturmgewher*?" I ask in German. We have recently heard stories about this assault rifle and its frightening ability to shoot multiple rounds.

The soldiers break into laughter.

"I'm about to kill you and you want to know what kind of gun I will use?" the soldier asks.

I nod.

"Where is your gun?" he asks.

"I have no gun. Kill me."

"You're a filthy Russian deserter."

I give no response.

"You amuse me. I won't kill you today," the soldier says.

Instead, they arrest me. If the Russians had found me first they would have taken a leg, as they do with all defectors. As they did to Pieter. The Germans spare my leg but send me to Majdanek.

It is the final months of the war. We are among the last trains full of people to arrive at the Lublin station outside the camp. The train is filled with Byelorussians—that is their name for the White Russians—and members of the Polish Home Army.

First they line us up and separate us according to our religion and race. I am still wearing my Russian uniform when I am captured, and I am sent to the Russian POW quarters. When we are questioned about our skills, I decide not to tell them about my talent as a tailor. The Jews are tailors. I tell them instead that I farmed an orchard before I became a soldier. When the German guards choose men to work in the prison fields, cultivating the fruits and vegetables, I am selected.

In April of 1944, a few months before the liberation, they line us up and march most of the prisoners away. They tell us they are taking them to another camp. I am told to stay. I think this will be my last day on earth. Someone has discovered I am a Jew and they will shoot me in that moment. Instead, I am given another job for the last three months of my imprisonment.

It feels the same as being dead, this job. It is the job where Pieter and I make our deal.

After the war, the Romanian Rescue Mission offers to send me to Palestine, but while I recover I write to my parents at the last address I kept for them in Brooklyn, New York. Miraculously, it reaches them. They respond with a telegram with instructions to contact a man in Paris who will help me to immigrate to America to join them. They send the man money to be used as payment for my passage to America. They also send me money, the last of their savings, to arrange my travel to France.

I spoke no French, and the man my parents have arranged for me to connect with turns out to be a shyster—he steals my parents' payment and puts me to work in a Paris sweatshop sewing ladies' fur coats.

Taking advantage of Jewish refugees has become its own industry. They know we are desperate.

This sewing skill I learned in the Ukranian work camps has become my new trade. As I learned in the camps, to have a trade means life. I work in the sweat-shops for two years, and then find a job working in a huge Parisian couture house on the rue Matignon, off the Champs-Élysées, sewing ladies' gloves for their collections. I save my money and wait to see my family in America.

—·—

One day—I've only been working a month or so in the couture house—a finely dressed older man approaches my workbench and stands peering over my shoulder, watching me work. He smells like coriander. I am nervous, thinking I will be fired. Everywhere in Paris people point fingers towards those who did not protect the Jews, yet still there is hatred for our people here.

"You have very fine stitching. Where did you learn to sew this way?" he asks me.

I look up into a most startling pair of ice-blue eyes.

"In the work camps in Cyprus, and then . . ." I pull up my sleeve to show him the numbered marks on my arm. I have no idea why I do this. I had never shown the shameful tattoo to another soul.

"I would be grateful if you would teach this skill to others," he says. "I am honored to have you here"

"I am honored to work for you," I respond. "I would be happy to share whatever skill I possess."

This man turns out to be the great fashion couturier and parfumier Lucien Lelong, who stood up to the Germans when they tried to force the Paris ateliers to move to Berlin. His former wife, a Romanov princess, lost her father and brothers to the Bolshevik murderers.

Only a few years later, M. Lelong closes the doors to his family business and retires. Luckily, having worked and taught for one of the most renowned designers in Paris, I have no trouble securing work with another atelier.

Always there is another goal: to be reunited with my family. But besides the money required for my travel, I have encountered another obstacle. Immigration to America has been tightened. Quotas put in place. Eventually, however, I am granted the right to immigrate because of the enactment of the 1948 Displaced Persons Act. This allows a select number of Jewish immigrants—Nazi death camp survivors, those who have family members who are American citizens, or those who can offer trade services needed in the US.

I fit all the categories.

—·—

I am one of 400,000 people who are allowed to immigrate in those last few years. President Truman made sure we are allowed entrance. The day my letter from immigration arrived, I saw an ad for Air France plane travel to New York. I had never been on a plane and I am terrified by the idea, but it seemed my best option, as it proved more difficult for me to think about boarding a ship again. It is unbelievable to think I could see my family within twenty hours of getting on the plane, although the ticket cost me a fortune. I flew to America from Paris in 1948, nearly four years after gaining my freedom from the camp, at thirty-eight years of age.

The sole detail I remember about my flight is that a button on my coat popped off as I bent to sit in my airplane seat, and one of the hostesses is kind enough to find me a needle and thread so I could sew it back on during the flight. In those days, the airplane hostesses are trained nurses because the idea of taking a flight is dangerous. People worried about altitude sickness and other, more serious disasters. When she returned with a needle, this hostess, this nurse, noticed my skin pallor and asked me questions about my health. She suggested I see a doctor in America. As it turned out, my years in the army and camps had left me sick with anemia and malaria. I had been suffering with these diseases for years without being diagnosed and treated.

When I first arrived, I settled in Brooklyn with my *foter* and *mater*. They had been living in the same Crown Heights apartment since 1924—a miracle that allowed me to find them after all those years.

When they arrived in 1923, there are more than 75,000 Jews living in the Crown Heights neighborhood alone, yet my *foter* found his friend Mendel in the "village" of Brooklyn—another miracle. Mendel helped him find occasional work as a machinist in the factories, and my *mater* washed and sewed clothing in the Brooklyn brownstone they shared with Mendel and his family.

It is inevitable that Oizer should have taken the role of the eldest son in our family after arriving here in America. *Foter* and *Mater* are old when Oizer and Rose arrived, and I, the oldest living son, I am still a soldier and living in Russia at the time. Oizer did the job well, and I possessed no spirit, no will, to displace him from his role when I arrived. He had become a great protector and provider for the family, and I am content for him to continue to fill that role.

Although my *foter* and *mater* seemed overjoyed at my arrival, I felt broken inside. I still mourned our losses and blamed myself for not preventing the tragedies back in the Ukraine.

Soon after I moved in with my family, *Foter* sat talking with me late into the night. We swirled cheap brandy in our glasses and reminisced about our old life on *Bubbe* Chava's farm. I felt safe. I felt a brief sense of lightness as we sat watching the fire dance with the last embers.

"Those are the best moments in my life. All of us together in the orchards," I said.

My *foter* had taken up pipe-smoking—a habit I thought made him look like a gangster. He tamped bits of spicy tobacco into his pipe as he spoke.

"The best is coming, Szaja."

I said nothing as he lit the pipe and drew in slow, rhythmic puffs of smoke.

"Szaja, no one could have prevented what happened. Never mind a young boy."

I am startled by his comment. Before I could answer, he continued.

"Let's not talk about the past again. It's best to let the past go, otherwise it will imprison you. You're a free man, Szaja. See a future, create a plan, work hard, and you will realize your dream."

———

But I had no dreams. Only nightmares.

It is Rose and Mocher who convinced me to move to Brookline to start a tailoring business with them. Rose told me they needed a skilled worker. I had been working in a large sweatshop in Brooklyn with them and I am nearly recovered from my illnesses, thanks to Rose's ministrations. I knew she felt concerned about leaving me, and this knowledge pressed me into going with them.

I am torn, though. I wanted to stay with the family, this family my eyes are drinking in with thirsty gulps. For years I had dreamt of nothing more than being reunited with them, of seeing my dear *mater* and *foter* again. I thought, in the last days of my work in Paris, that if I could just see them again in America, I would be able to die in peace. This is the thought I lived for.

But then, living there in Crown Heights with them, taking their love and re-building my soul, I felt more like a stranger—a ghost, than the son—the brother, I had once been.

I am changed, I knew. And I could feel that it is not a change that would be reversed through love or time. There is some missing faculty; a part of me seems gone forever. I felt as much an imposter in my family as I did in the days I am hiding the fact I am a Jew.

Rose understood this. She is the one person who helps me find myself. She reached into the parts of me that are still intact and drew them closer to the surface. At times this felt healing—I am moving toward a less painful, lighter way of being. I smile and laugh with her teasing and through our laughter my soul breathed air. But at other times, the push toward the surface is a struggle that sent me back into myself, somewhere safer and hidden from even my own conscious thoughts. One day Rose asked me about the camp. I could not answer. That day I realized I could never answer or I would lose the bits that had survived. And this would break my deal with Pieter.

In the end, after a year living with *Foter* and *Mater*, I decided to move with Rose and Mocher to Brookline, Massachusetts, leaving my parents and the rest of the family behind in New York in Oizer's capable care. I slept on the couch in a tiny apartment we shared.

———

"The couch smells like you now," Rose tells me.

I laugh. "Not a bad smell. Not the smell of your oily latkes on those winter mornings on the farm."

Rose snaps the dishtowel she uses at the sink at my head.

"Shush. Those oily latkes tasted good enough for you to eat more than your share of helpings, as I remember."

———

About two years after our move to Brookline, Rose and Mocher decided the time had come for me to move into my own place. As I could not cook for myself and possessed only meager home management skills, Rose decided marriage is the most convenient and efficient solution. Rose met with a *shadchen* who found a woman for me to marry and procured a marriage contract for us. The *shadchen* arranged for me to move into the apartment this woman, my wife-to-be, had formerly shared with her now-deceased parents. The whole plan is hatched, agreed upon, and finalized in a matter of two weeks.

Yetta, this woman who lived two floors above us, had recently lost the parents she'd spent most of her life caring for. I had barely noticed her presence in the building before the night we met, except to note that she seemed exceptionally short. She is a formless shape passing on her way up and down the stairs. I'm not sure we had exchanged a single word in the two years I'd shared the apartment with Rose and Mocher.

I am a single man, nearing forty, who had never courted a girlfriend. This fact my sister and her husband are unaware of. They assumed that along the way— from camp to war, from town to city—I had found at least some women. They assumed I had done what most men do without a wife. But they are wrong. There had never been a time, never been a moment, where I found myself wanting sex with a woman. I had been curious, yes, and often aroused, especially when I am a young man. But the early time in my life had also been spent in a place with no normal outlet for expressions of those sorts.

Sometimes I overheard conversations between men about the women they bedded. But in my travels I always avoided discussions of women, of anything leading to the merest threat of my great secret. The secret that would reveal the fact that I am a Jew. I worried about this constantly in those years. The secret about my body terrified me in the men's urinal.

It is a miracle that, upon my arrival in the camp, the German guards did not examine me more carefully. They took me for a Russian soldier—a Catholic Russian soldier. I would have been murdered as a Jew if anyone had found the truth out. I never fully undressed after the first day's purification process.

For me, there are no pissing contests, no drunken size comparisons. Most importantly, there is never any sex. No women. Discovery could equal death. When I had those feelings, I took care of things and told myself I would save myself for marriage and live a pure life. I never dreamed it would take me this long to find a wife.

———

This night, I am seated at a table waiting for a woman I don't know—a woman who has already sat with the *shadchen* to determine what assets she will bring into the marriage. Our contract has been drawn and signed already. This night is a mere formality for this woman, a romantic gesture pushed forward by Rose and the *shadchen* so she will have an event to point to as her formal engagement date.

For me, it seems a good business arrangement.

———

I am a man with a business now. Rose, Mocher, and I owned our own tailoring shop. We ran a brisk business in a storefront off of Commonwealth Avenue in Boston. The building is cramped and drafty, however, and we shared a back room with a cobbler, so we had recently begun hunting for a new building with more space and light. Mocher and I worked directly with the customers at the cash register. Rose sewed in the back. We made money hand over fist.

Life had become a better prospect for me. I kept a new secret: I saved the profits from my paychecks and had become an *anlegen*, an investor. It felt like gambling to me. Gambling is a sin, I know, but this is different in its actual design. It is accepted and encouraged, even. Oizer, now married, had become a successful banker. When we wrote to one another, which we frequently did, he gave me tips for buying shares. I started out buying nickel shares in well-known, established businesses. Small investments in safe, conservative businesses that offer small gains and minor risks. But then I began to ask Oizer questions about bigger ventures. I felt confident, and with a low overhead on our business, free rent on Rose's couch, and no other financial responsibilities, I grew riskier.

With Oizer's guidance, I branched out into investments in the new utility companies and heavy machinery manufacturers. Electricity companies and the farming industry are growing at rapid rates. I found two small companies I liked, Eastern Bell Telephone and John Deere. I began with nickel shares, but gradually increased my monthly contributions as I watched my shares grow. Oizer said the market would take a long time to recover from the fall in 1929, but he could foresee a time when it would make many millionaires again. I want to be one of those *milyon* merchants. Oizer had already gotten close to achieving this goal, no surprise to any of us. He had always been the financial brains in the family, and now he made sure we all possessed everything we needed.

———

"It's time for you to start a new life, Samuel," Rose says, as we head toward the living room to wait. "We love you and love having you near us, but I want to see you happy. You need a wife, and maybe children?"

"*Oy*, Rose, please. A wife? Children? How could I do this? I have nothing to offer a wife. I am a ghost of a man."

"*Hak mir nisht keyn tshaynik*. You are a fine man, Sam. You are a strong, *gezunt* man with a good mind and a stable job. You've suffered enough. Now is your time for joy. Your eyes have been dim with tears and now it is time to open them and see. You are free. You are a free man now, Samuel Trautman."

I begin to laugh. Rose stares at me in shock. I can't resist.

"Rose, if I'm a free man, why am I being forced into marriage? I won't be a free man with a nagging wife."

Now Rose laughs.

"I don't think she's a nagging woman. I don't think she's a woman with much of a voice at all. I've never heard more than a peep out of her mouth, and she stayed with her parents even after the rest of her sisters left for marriages."

"Maybe no one wanted to marry her?"

"*Sayhak mir nisht keyn tshaynik*! She's a good woman, I'm sure. You don't want a looker, a *shaina maedel*, that kind of woman will give you a nervous condition. No, this is a woman who will make a good wife and a good mother. But, best news of all, when you move into the flat in 4C, this will be the woman who will get you off our couch and give us privacy, *mirtseshem*."

We are laughing as we hear a timid knocking.

"I'll answer it, you sit and behave yourself," Rose instructs me.

"*Oy*, yes, I'll sit and behave and ask the *miaskite* upstairs to marry me, yes."

———

As I remember it, the evening is brief. Yetta shyly answered me when I spoke to her. Good, I thought, she'll be a quiet wife. A wife with nothing to say is a perfect companion. I thought all I needed from this woman is cooking, cleaning, ironing, and someone to run the errands. Children are not necessary. Children are expensive and noisy.

Yetta seemed older than the *shadchen* told us. We are told she is only a few years older than me, but she looked at least ten years older. Her face is marked with deep wrinkles like the folds of a fine, ancient linen. A black hairnet held a thick bundle of dark, graying hair at the back of her head. I thought she might be close to fifty. She might be too old to bear children. Less to worry about. I would be closer to my *milyon* goals with no children to feed and clothe and send to school.

———

We finish the dinner Rose prepared and Mocher ushers us into the living room. Mocher goes into the kitchen to wash the dishes with Rose. This is when Yetta speaks—her first pronouncement since the answer she gave to my scripted engagement question earlier in the evening. She casts her eyes into her lap and blushes.

"What time do you go to sleep?"

I can't help laughing. "What time do I go to sleep?"

She nodded.

"I sleep at 8:30, why do you ask me this?"

She blushes and explains, "I want to know how long I might have in the evening for chores before you go to sleep. I don't want to be noisy."

She looks directly into my eyes. I notice for the first time they are a deep cocoa brown with tiny, barley speckles. Like the leather buttons on a man's tweed coat.

I nod. "I see. You should feel free to make your own schedule for the household. You will find I'm not a demanding husband."

Yetta gives a tiny smile and glances away.

The evening wraps itself up like its own small engagement present—simple and practical. No frills and bows, simply useful information and straightforward discussion.

———

I learned later it is the time after I went to sleep that Yetta is more interested in. Her parents are the only other people in the building who owned a television in those days and Yetta loved to watch television. She already knew my tastes are going to be quite different from hers.

Yetta is a most uncomplicated woman. The most important detail of our cohabitation for her would be how much time she would have to watch the TV programs she loved. One of her favorite is a show featuring short educational films called *The World in Your Home*. She loved to sit and watch this show, and others, during the week in the evenings. This didn't bother me. Mocher and I loved to watch wrestling on the TV and spent many happy Sundays doing nothing else.

Our wedding date had already been set before we met. The *shadchen* and the rabbi arranged for it to fall before the Rosh Hashana holidays in August. We made a small wedding. The entire family had been invited but told not to bother with the expense of coming from New York for the simple ceremony. We are too old for a big celebration, and Yetta's parents, who might have appreciated the fact that their spinster daughter had finally married, are dead. However, her six sisters are all there. They lived in the Boston area. Seven sisters in a family. *Oy.* Their poor *foter.* He must have been driven mad by all those women.

The day after our engagement dinner—to my surprise—I received a letter from Yetta. I found it stuffed under the doorframe, sticking out from the hallway rug, as I left for work early the next morning.

From this day until her death twenty-seven years later, this is the sole written missive I ever received from Yetta.

Dear Samuel,

I am writing to say to you how happy I am with this decision to marry with you. I am making ready to marry you with an open heart. This marraige my parents would be blessing with joy. They are gone now but I want you should know how much they wanted this for their daughter one day. And now you make good this dream of theirs. Yours is a good strong heart. This I know and the shadkhen she tell me also. So, I go forward and give you my dowry, which I not tell the shadkhen is more than she sees or hears from me. You will be a rich man with this marraige to me I can tell you now. I will give you the savings of my parents. This is what I have to offer you. I know I am a funny woman with a diffecult face. This I know. But for you, you can make a smile for me and this is a good thing.

Yours truly,
Yetta

I folded the letter back into the envelope and kept it in my pocket throughout the day. I kept pulling it out to read it again. It is a strange letter—an honest letter with a gift, the offer of wealth. This is what Yetta felt she could offer in exchange for the security of a marriage. Could I offer her security, I worried? Could I be a secure man?

I am a man with many names. Now, I am Samuel, the tailor. Samuel, the investor. An investor with more money to invest now.

Yes, I decided that day I would become a secure man to marry. I would make myself the man she wanted me to be and fill the role. I watched Mocher with Rose and I knew how to behave the husband. I could do this and it would be easy. I would be true and loyal. Fidelity is a given. I had no need for this woman. Why would I need others? I would be dutiful and prompt. I went to work and I came home from work every night at the same time. No stops for a drink or a chat. I made few friends outside my family. No one else to visit.

Oizer invested the dowry Yetta brought me. Twenty thousand dollars, a huge sum at the time. It is indeed a large dowry inheritance from her father, who had a good real estate business before he passed. It made us a fortune. Still, I never stopped working. You didn't stop working. Who knew what would happen? There could be another market crash. There could be a war to try and save oneself from. There could be a person to bribe in exchange for your life or your family's life. There are always things you needed more money for. This is the one thing certain.

Yetta knew we are wealthy, but she never asked me questions or asked to see our financial books. She is a thrifty woman and never wasted a dime on anything we didn't need. She never asked for more money than the household allowance I gave to her each month.

For the first year our marriage remained uneventful. The exceptions are the fumblings of our wedding night and the sad attempts at improvement that followed.

———

We are virgins and had absolutely no idea what we are doing. I suppose Yetta expected me to be practiced in the deed, but I had a paralyzing fear of seeing her naked body in a bed.

I saw many naked women in the camp at Majdanek. Dead women. My mind became so tightly shut against this horror it simply registered their anatomy as skin and bones.

I also felt quite self-conscious about my own body. Since my days in Paris, I'd spent most of my time sitting at a sewing table. My posture is terrible. My muscles are underdeveloped. My body is thin and, like those of most of the Ukranian Jews I knew, hairless. Not like the men I saw on my wrestling shows. I am embarrassed and ashamed of my body.

Yetta is, as most virgin brides are, shy and modest. She spent a long time in the bath on our wedding night and emerged wearing a peach negligee with so many layers I am worn out by the time I found the appropriate seams to open. She lay back on the bed, rigid. She never opened her eyes and spoke only two words the entire time we are consummating the marriage.

———

"Wrong hole," Yetta mutters.

I am having a difficult time and don't understand her. I whisper, "What?"

"Wrong hole," Yetta says a bit louder, in a strangled voice.

All at once I lose my embarrassment. I am mystified and want to discover what she is talking about. The idea that there is more than one hole seems aston-ishing. I need to see this.

Until this point I have been using my penis as a sort of shovel against the fabric between her legs. Now I lose my shyness and use my hands to part the onion folds of her negligee and at last see what she is referring to.

Another hole. A hole of a different sort altogether—unfamiliar and covered with a pubic hair similar to mine, but surrounded by lobes of skin and a small bump that sits above a different hole than the one I tried to breech.

Eureka! I almost shout my excitement in the discovery.

I realized my actions expose my lack of knowledge, and I am shy again. I man-age to keep my erection long enough to deflower Yetta, but then roll over in a heap beside her and stare at the ceiling while I wait for my body to relax.

I wait for her to talk, but realize she's waiting for me.

"Are you all right?" I ask.

She never responds, and I fall asleep. I have no idea how she feels. Did she enjoy what I did, or—if what I managed to glean from other men is true—is it a painful experience for a woman on her first time?

When I wake the next morning, Yetta is already in the kitchen making break-fast. I see on the sheets that she's bled a bit. I think she must have experienced pain.

———

We made attempts a few more times over the next several months, but we never managed to find the right rhythms necessary to enjoy the act. And, of course, we never talked about it.

We shared no chemistry—so, after those first attempts, we stopped trying. We stopped trying and never exchanged bodily contact again, with the exception of an occasional misplaced foot in bed. I managed to satisfy myself, when I found privacy and time, in our bath. I've no idea if Yetta ever found any satisfaction on her own. I doubt it. To be honest, at the time, I had no idea women enjoyed any sexual contact beyond kissing.

I think if we had managed to find a way to satisfy our physical needs with each other, things may have gone differently for us. Maybe we would have created a more pleasant marriage experience or at least managed to become friends. But this is the beginning of what became a strained and combative relationship. We never talked to one another at all except to manage day-to-day details or share important information.

Later, after the child, Wendy, came to live with us, we used her to pass infor-mation back and forth. She is ten at the time, and we found we could communi-cate through her and didn't have to bother with direct conversation. It is only after the child left—young, married, and pregnant with her own child—that we began to find it necessary to talk to one another again. And it is only then that we found peace and comfort with one another. It is only then, many years into the marriage, that I begin to tell Yetta about the boy I had been and to share with her the man I had become. A man with his own mind and body who had been forced to leave a heart beating in a ditch.

All the while, she had waited, patiently, like the earth waits for the winter to end and the soil waits for warmth to bring spring growth.

Fourteen

Jules, 10 years | *September 19ᵗʰ, 1971*

SUNDAY MORNING

I WAKE UP and lie resting in Leigh's bed. The twin-size bed is too small for us. Still, it's always a good night's sleep at her house without music blaring and people stumbling into my room in the middle of the night.

The dance was fun. Leigh and I danced almost all night and Leigh's new boyfriend kissed her for the first time. With so much to talk about, we hung out all of Saturday. It was one of those rare warm September days so we went swimming at the jetty and came back to her place to play Monopoly in the late afternoon when it started to feel chilly. Leigh asked her mother if I could stay over again and she agreed. We had the eggplant parmesan leftovers for dinner. My favorite.

Being at Leigh's is like having a vacation from my life—no chores, no loud parties with foul-smelling illegal things floating about, and only doing stuff kids are supposed to do. Lying in Leigh's bed, it's like I can feel my body—all my limbs connected, heart beating—for the first time in ages. I notice my fingernails need trimming and the hairs on my arm are bleached a light blonde. It's the first time I've paid attention in a while.

Ms. Westerfield, Leigh's mom, never likes anyone to call her *Mrs.* It's a women's libber thing. Wendy has started making everybody call her Ms. Finn too.

Ms. Westerfield also makes the best pancakes in the world. She obviously has an understanding that things are not great at my house, and she tells me, when I help her wash the dinner dishes in their cozy avocado green kitchen, that if I ever need anyone to talk to, she will listen and try to help. I appreciate her kind words, but I can never share the things that happen in my house with an adult. I worry we'll be taken away if someone responsible knows. I thank her and smile and tell her "everything's all right," even though we both know it isn't.

———

I called, after dinner last night, to let my brothers know I'd been invited to sleep over again. They need to know to make their own dinners and feed the cat. Someone I don't know picked up the phone, and when he set the phone down to search for my brothers I heard the party still going on.

Moses came to the phone and told me that David had gone out with his friends, but he'd be okay. Moses said he'd managed to talk one of Wendy's friends into taking him to Burger King for lunch. He'd gotten a ride there on a motorcycle.

"Geesh, Moses. Did Mom know? Did you wear a helmet?" I gripped the phone cord.

"Yeah, she let me go. I wore a helmet," he said hesitatingly.

"She's high. What a stupid idea. Please don't do it again."

"Don't be mad, Jules. I won't do it again."

"Good. Remember what happened to Mom?"

"I won't do it again," Moses said, almost whispering.

"What have you been doing besides riding around on motorcycles today?" I asked.

"Hanging out, playing. I set up my car racetrack in my room and now I'm organizing my Hot Wheels. Hey, Dad's coming to pick us up tomorrow. He called and talked to David yesterday and said he's coming back to live at Aunt Doreen's. We should wait for him in the morning."

"He probably won't show up, Moses."

"Why?" he asked.

"Why what? Why do I think that, or why won't he show up?"

"Never mind," Moses said dejectedly.

Moses, the only one of us who still looks forward to seeing Howard, is too young to remember the horrible way our father treated everyone when he was around. Moses still thinks good things about him and doesn't like for David and me to say anything bad.

"Hey, if he doesn't show up, let's go fishing tomorrow. Deal?"

"Yeah," Moses shouted back. "Yeah. That would be fun."

I hung up dreading the next morning and the possibility of seeing Howard and spending a boring Sunday reading the newspaper while he watched the football game. I hoped he wouldn't show up and I would get to spend time out fishing with Moses.

I lie on my side, my back to Leigh, her knee pushed against the back of my calf and her elbow pushed into my ribcage. I'm afraid to move because I know it will wake her. I lie still and listen to the sound of her breathing. Leigh sometimes skips a breath or two and gives a bit of a snort on her sudden inhalations. It sounds funny.

I think about the day ahead. I should head back after pancakes to see Howard. Sadness starts to creep in and ruin my brief happiness.

I realize that if I don't go back he might not hang around and wait for me. It might be risky because Howard's temper doesn't have a predictable pattern. If he's angry, and I'm not there waiting, I'll be punished. Then again, he might not care if I don't show up.

Leigh stretches and rolls over, bumping against me as she turns.

"Morning," she mumbles.

"Aloha."

"You're so weird." Leigh calls me weird a lot, which I don't mind, at least not when *she* says it.

"Greetings earthling," I add.

"Come on. Let's go downstairs and watch TV until my mom wakes up for breakfast."

I follow her down the stairs and into the family room, which smells like Pine-Sol, where we watch *Bugs Bunny*, *Scooby Doo*, and *Harlem Globetrotters*.

I'm thinking how much I love hanging out at Leigh's as I hear her mom walk downstairs and start cooking in the kitchen.

"You're lucky," I say to Leigh.

"Why?" Leigh asks, not taking her eyes off the TV.

"Because . . ." I pause, still staring at the TV—I want to be nonchalant, but don't have the words to describe the things she takes for granted.

"Because your mom makes breakfast."

Leigh's older sister, Annie, stomps downstairs and across the room in front of the TV without saying anything to anyone. She slams the front door on her way out. Annie is six years older than us and a sophomore in high school.

"She hates everybody. All she wants to do is skip school and smoke weed with her friends," Leigh says.

Wendy acts a lot like Leigh's sister. I realize I have a teenage sister too.

"You're lucky," Leigh says.

She's staring at me.

"Why?"

"Because you can do anything you want and nobody bugs you. You never have a curfew. Your mom has groovy clothes to wear and you eat pizza and Burger King all the time. My mom never buys Burger King. She says it has poison in the meat and sugar in the French fries."

"It's not as fun as it seems," I say.

———

I wanted to tell Leigh that along with the fast food came stomach upsets. Most nights Wendy forgot to pick something up, and there was only cereal in the cupboard. And those nights were actually better than the rare nights *she* tried to cook something.

Once she tried to bake an Angel Food cake. David couldn't even manage to make a saw cut through the thing.

But the worst times were when absolutely nothing remained in the refrigerator or the cupboards. And this was happening more and more frequently. On those nights David and I sometimes found a way to get invited to our friends' houses for dinner. We both tried to bring back leftovers for Moses.

I definitely couldn't tell Leigh about the sex parties Wendy had been having lately after she thought we were asleep.

Several nights that summer my brothers and I had been awakened by naked, sweaty people piling on one another and doing all sorts of gross things in Wendy's bedroom or right in the living room. After seeing that, I was sure I would never have sex as long as I lived.

All this information I needed to keep to myself. Once I started talking, I wasn't sure I would be able to stop. But mostly, I didn't want Leigh to have to keep those secrets too.

———

We sit in her kitchen and I gobble down my three plate-sized pancakes when I realize it's close to ten o'clock. I jump up to call my house, but no one answers. I don't know if it means that David and Moses are already with Howard, or that he isn't coming and they've already gone off to play somewhere.

I hope Moses didn't take off with David. I'm still hoping we can go fishing together. But, I figure I can track him down somewhere in the neighborhood if he did.

I wish I could stay here in the avocado green kitchen with buttery pancake smells. My body is present here. My skin absorbs oxygen. The pebbles in my stomach evaporate. It's only now that they have disappeared that I realize they have been inside me all along. I realize this is what it feels like to be safe. But I know I'm only borrowing the feeling.

I say thank you to Ms. Westerfield and Leigh walks me to the door. She remembers the leather vests we stole from Wendy for the dance the other night and runs upstairs to find them while I wait.

"I'll see you at school on Monday," she says when she comes back, handing me the vests.

"Splendid," I say. "Oh, I might call you tonight about the science homework if I'm stuck." Leigh loves science and understands the assignments. For me, science is like a different language.

———

It's about ten thirty when I round the corner to our road, and it seems unusually quiet. All the neighbors are at church, which usually provides a good opportunity for Wendy to play her music really, really loud. I see all the cars and motorcycles are gone from our yard, as well.

When I walk in, there isn't anyone around.

In the kitchen, stacks of empty pizza cartons and Burger King trash sit piled up on the garbage can. Tons of glasses and dishes cover the counters and fill the sink. I decide I'm not going to clean up Wendy's party dishes anymore. I am "on strike." When I check Moses and David's rooms, they aren't there. Next, I check Wendy's room to make sure no one's in there sleeping or something. No one. I drag the leather vests Leigh and I borrowed out of my overnight bag and throw them in the back of Wendy's closet. I'm disappointed Moses left and we can't go fishing, but I don't want to go find him in the neighborhood.

It feels wonderful—rare to have every corner to myself. I decide to spend time doing what I love most. Drawing.

In the den, I find my favorite record, *Tea for the Tillerman*. With no one there I can listen to the music I love all day. I go to work, drawing. I'm concentrating on a series of drawings of our cat Felix. Felix, a black-and-white long-haired tuxedo cat, seems to enjoy posing for me although her occasional position changes make things challenging.

It turns into an unusually hot morning for September. Later, it rains and the dim thought of fishing occurs to me. Fishing is better in the rain.

As the day wears on I lose myself in the process of drawing and fall into a trance-like state that I understand as precious and necessary. Time, in the physics sense, turns to energy, changes, evolves, and then disappears. I let myself become lost and found in it.

At about five o'clock, still sitting there with a floor full of Felix on white paper, I hear sounds from the kitchen. Cabinets slam as someone searches for food; a plate and utensil are pulled out of a cupboard and drawer.

Stretching, I hear the distant sound of the TV from the den. Must be David. He usually heads straight to the den for TV. It's basically his den, except when Wendy's making candles. I wait to hear Moses's footsteps on the landing upstairs or the sound of his door opening and closing, but I don't. I figure he must be watching TV with David. Moses never gets a vote about what to watch with David around, but he doesn't seem to mind. I think David gets lost in his own version of time-suspension world when he's watching his shows.

I gather the drawings scattered on the floor, balling and ripping the ones I don't care for. It's like I'm assessing someone else's work, like I'm removed from the process that created them. The selection goes quickly. I put the ones I like in a large binder I keep stored in my closet, shoot a last glance around, and satisfied with the tidiness of my room, make my way downstairs to pour myself a bowl of Raisin Bran.

I'm starving. I haven't eaten since the pancakes at Leigh's. I never know if Wendy will bring back take-out or if we're on our own for dinner, so, as I'm removing the cereal from the cabinet, I make a note of what is currently in there that might suffice for dinner.

Wendy and Jack rarely eat dinner. As far as I can tell, they exist on alcohol and drugs with occasional hidden-cookie cache indulgences for Jack. Wendy's most current fad diet food obsessions range from grapefruit to the grass in our yard.

I walk to the other side of the kitchen and peek around the corner into the den. David sits in the aqua easy chair staring at the screen, but Moses isn't there.

"Hey, do you know where Moses is? I'm gonna make dinner soon if you're hungry."

David pretends he can't hear me, so I yell: "Hey, hard-of-hearing, do you know where Moses is? I thought he went with you today?"

David breaks his silence to say, "Ask Freddy." He still answers this way sometimes. It's bizarre and I hate it when he does it. I'm outnumbered by the loony people in my family.

I'm frustrated now and a bit worried that maybe Howard did come here but David avoided the visit as well. I ask again, "*David*, did Dad come today and take Moses? I stayed at Leigh's until late this morning and when I got back there wasn't anyone here."

"No, Dad never came." He scowls. "I called Aunt Doreen and she found out he's not flying back. He cancelled his flight. She doesn't know when he's ever coming back."

"Figures. So where is Moses?"

I guess David is starting to worry now too, because he actually speaks nicely to me. "When I left, he wanted to keep sitting on the front steps to wait. I told him Dad wasn't going to show up and he could come play ball with my friends, but he said he'd rather hang out here and wait for you to go fishing. What time did you come back?"

"Around ten thirty. What time did you leave?"

"About nine. Maybe he's out somewhere on the beach?"

"Maybe." It's been a long time for Moses to have been alone this whole time. He usually tags along with David during the day. I decide to hike down to the beach and search for him.

I tell David, but he only nods, already lost in *Lost in Space* again.

———

Down on the beach, the sun dips below the cliffs. The sun shines out in the ocean to the east, but the cliff casts shadows on the beach and it's chilly. I shiver in my T-shirt and wish I'd brought a jacket with me.

If he's down here he'll be cold and come back soon.

Still, I walk the beach all the way past the rocky cove toward my hiding spot. Moses may have found it. But he isn't there. Past the cove the tide swells against the cliffs. I turn and head back.

———

I find David still sitting in the den, watching TV.

"No Moses yet?"

David shakes his head.

"He's not down there," I say.

David stares back and I can see the realization cross his face that something must be wrong. It's starting to darken outside, tomorrow is a school day, and it's rare for Moses to be doing anything on a Sunday night except playing in his room or finishing homework. "I'm gonna check around the neighborhood," he says. "Maybe you should call his friend? Do you know his number?"

"Good idea," I say, and as I'm standing there trying to remember his friend's last name so I can look him up in the phone book, it hits me, hard. It hits me so hard my body goes numb.

David tries to move past me on his way out.

"What is it, Jules?" he asks, impatient.

"The b-b-boat," I stammer.

"You think Moses used the boat by himself and went fishing without you? Well, if he did, he might still be out there! Let's go down to the yacht club and check. But I don't think he'd do it. He knows he's not supposed to. Come on."

He grabs my arm and pulls me towards the door.

—

I'm grateful to David for many things in this moment. The terrible dread I feel makes it difficult to move my limbs. Normally I am all action in a bad moment, but standing there on the steps it's as though my body knows something my mind is finding it difficult to believe. I'm grateful for David's kindness in ignoring my stammer. I'm grateful because he's helping me move toward a moment when we will both be present.

He pulls me toward the front door, but I struggle to go outside through the den.

The shed.

In the shed, I think, I will find two fishing poles, and then I'll know he hasn't gone to the boat. I try to loose myself from David's grip, but he holds me too strongly. When did he get so strong? I don't have the strength to pull myself away. I have to talk again.

"Th-the sh-sh-sh . . ." I point toward the backyard and David understands. He runs ahead of me now toward the back of the yard, under the weeping willow, where the shed stands. He pulls it open and we search inside. Moses's fishing pole is missing, along with the tackle box.

"No t-t-tackle."

My body gathers energy. David and I run down Withensea Avenue toward the yacht club.

I run faster than I've ever run before. David stands over a head taller than me and is three years older, and I'm running as fast as he is.

I think how angry I'll be with Moses for using the boat without me. I imagine what I'll say to him, how he should be punished, even how it might benefit me to keep the secret and hold it over him. I know David would do this. David might demand twenty trips to the store for candy, for free. No splits.

Those thoughts alternate with others. Hope that he's back at the house, maybe hiding someplace, playing a trick on us? Hope that he decided not to take the boat after all. Hope that he followed the rules, that he was good and waited for me to show up at the yacht club when I didn't find him. Maybe fished on the dock all day.

Why didn't I think of this before? Why didn't I check the shed when I got back instead of thinking he'd be with Howard or David?

I was entranced with the quiet. I wanted—needed—a day to draw and enjoy some solitude for once.

Howard disappointed him by not showing up and he didn't want to wait for me, because I might disappoint him as well.

If the boat is there, make Jack put oarlocks on the boat. Then Moses can't take it out without someone. When he shows up, don't leave him alone again. If Moses is okay, be nicer to both of your brothers. If he's okay, be a better person.

David and I run around to the back of the club where we moor our dinghy, right next to a fishing boat named Elysian Fields. This makes me think of the wooden woman.

You said everything was going to be all right. You promised. Please let Moses be all right. Please. If you're really an angel, show me now and I won't ever ask you again.

We stop in front of the empty space our dinghy usually occupies and we simultaneously look out to the spot where Jack moors his sailboat, hoping the dinghy sits anchored there instead, which would mean Jack is using his boat today. But the sailboat is there.

The sailboat is there and the dinghy is gone.

Every ounce of energy and hope I keep in *not* finding this fact pours out of my body. My body freezes again. David seems frozen there too. We stand like statues on the dock, squinting out across the bay as the fog begins to roll in, scanning for Moses in the dusk light.

I want to make a plan. I want to take care of the situation and I want to fix the fact that this is happening. I want, badly, to see Moses rowing his way back on the horizon, and I know David does too because we run toward the end of the dock together, scrambling as close as we can to a place where we might see him.

I run, but I can't feel my own legs moving.

We're screaming Moses's name, but my voice doesn't sound like my own.

We call and call and stop to listen. Our voices echo back to us across the water. Mocking.

We stand there calling as the sky loses all the light. The dusk turns from an inky blue to an iron black, the buoy lights ghostly against the rolling fog.

There is never an answer.

Part 2 | The Hour of Lead

Fifteen

Samuel, 61 years | September 22nd, 1971

WEST ROXBURY, MASSACHUSETTS

I STAND AT the *keyver* with the rest of the mourners.

The child. Moses.

I am aware of the *shomeret* standing at the gravesite. I find comfort in her presence. She was recommended by the rabbi, and there is something strangely familiar about this young woman, although we've never met before. She sat with the child at the mortuary since the death three days ago.

It is too long. We waited for the father to catch a plane from California where he lives now.

Despicable father. Disgraceful father.

It is well past the accepted twenty-four hours customary for a corpse to wait before entering the earth. But it also gave us time to find the proper *Shomer* and *Chevrah Kaddisha* to perform the washing ritual, the *Tahara.*

We stand for the service as the *cantor* chants.

I look to find the father. He stands to my left, head bowed, wearing the *kipah* handed him as he approached the *keyver,* but his black suit is intact. He has not performed *k'riah.*

I stare at him. When he glances up, I will point to his suit and remind him, but I realize he may not understand. This thought makes me angry—angry for his ignorance, his lack of respect, and angry for the arrogance of the modern Jews whose freedom came at such a terrible cost to the generations before them. But this man is not Jewish, I remind myself. No, he is not a Jew at all. This man is *shlekht*.

As though my anger has turned to poison, all the numbness in my body melts away and I am filled with a searing, crushing pain that courses from my head through my body and down to the soles of my feet.

I find myself standing in front of the father, and without thinking I am tearing off his left lapel—the fabric directly over his heart. He seems surprised and a bit afraid.

I think to myself, *This is good.* I want him to feel fear.

I am thinking if I could tear his heart out with the fabric, I might avenge this child's death somehow and make this pain abate.

There is pressure of a hand at my elbow. It is the rabbi. He leads me away from the father. I let myself be led. I am too weak to tear the heart from this man. I am an old man at sixty-one years. I have barely the strength to tear anything, including the thread from my needles.

At the thought of my hands tearing thread, the arthritic pain in my hands intensifies. I shove them deep into the pockets of my mourning coat to hide the intense shaking that has begun with the pain in my joints.

This same arthritis paralyzes my body at the end of the day and meets me when I wake in the morning. It is worst on these cold New England days.

For the past week we've been in the hottest days of summer. But today, the fall came like lightning. The sky is like a city sidewalk. Gritty and grainy-gray.

I wear the mourning coat made for me a few years earlier by Rose.

Rose.

She passed two months ago, a year after Mocher's death and ten months after Yetta's death.

Rose and Mocher lived in Florida for years, but with her passing I have a deep sense of desolation. Rose was the one who helped me carry my sadness. Somehow she managed to survive our sorrow and taught me to do the same. Standing there at Moses's *keyver*, I realize when I lost Rose, the light in my world switched off. When Rose is alive, she helped me see that my life had been a difficult struggle, but that I could also boast having fulfilled my father's main directive: to survive.

With her passing, however, life became nothing but an expanse of nothingness once more. The same way it is when I arrive in America all those years ago after the war. I have become unable to control my thoughts or my actions toward others with any consistency. I can't fully breathe. My sorrow forms a thick blanket over my body, protecting me but also isolating me from my own experience. I felt broken all those years ago, and the pain is doubled now.

Oh, Rose, here I am in my grief, my *tsar*, mourning the loss of this child. Please let the World to Come be a good one. This life has been hard for me to shoulder on my own. Or join me there, in our World to Come. I am certain that with you by my side I can walk forward without fear or anguish.

I am reminded of a time, long ago, when I made a similar prayer. I stood at another gravesite. I functioned as *cantor*, singing the prayers for the ceremony. I prayed with many Turkish Jews who came to pray by the grave, spoke the Prayer For The Dead, and sat *shiva* in a Turkish synagogue for the days following the ceremony. I arranged for the service when I got released from the hospital.

The *keyver* held the bodies of several hundred bodies drowned nearly two months before, stacked, one atop the other, in a shallow grave. As it had been at the camp.

The survivors of the blast and the Jewish community living openly there in Turkey begged the British officials not to burn the bodies, which had been their custom in these situations, but instead to honor and respect the religious practices of these people, these Jews, for whom cremation is a sin against G-d. Despite their terrible cruelty against these people, the Brits listened and for once behaved in a civilized way, allowing us to bury them.

But I do not want to think about another terrible day. This is the terrible day I must live now. The death of this sweet child, the death I mourn today. My hands tremble in my pockets. The bottoms of my pockets are shredding with wear. Perhaps I will repair the pockets. But why? Why should I repair a coat I never want to wear again?

This life is filled with too much sorrow.

I pray I will not wear this coat again, *kehnahore*. I pray I am the next to go.

I stare across the gravesite.

The mother of this child stands on the other side of the rabbi. She has brought the *nebish*, the one called Jack. She wears a short black dress. Too short. I can see the skin of her arms and her chest through the lace on this dress. This is a dress for a party. The mother of this child dressed like a *kurve* for her child's funeral. I feel no surprise. I have no anger. I am through being angry with this woman. I have no feeling for her left in me. I have given up on feeling where she is concerned.

I remember a time, long ago, when she brought joy. She was as young then as this child in the ground before us.

———

I treated her as my daughter. She is the child I helped to raise, first in my parents' apartment, then with Yetta. She is the child her mother named Wendy, after the Wendy of *Peter Pan.* This was Wendy's mother's favorite book.

She is the brilliant child, the prodigy, who taught herself to read English by asking the vendors who came to my parents' apartment to translate words. "How do you say?" is the first English phrase she spoke.

"Ice. Not ayz." She corrected the family when we made errors.

I wanted her to become fluent in English to improve her life. I didn't realize she planned to ignore her heritage, marry a Catholic, and denounce our religion once she could abandon the language we spoke. My parents said that by the age of five she read the entire dictionary from cover to cover and refused to speak anything but English with the family. They indulged her. Yes, it was *fehler* to indulge a child, and we knew. We all knew. We could see her *iberfim zikh* before our eyes, like an overripe fruit, but we all wanted to give her all we had been denied. She became our light and our reason.

She grew to be a plump and pretty child. A healthy girl. My mother, a wonderful cook, fed her well. Then, Yetta.

This woman who was that child has never resembled me. She is more like the woman who bore her. She does not know this. She does not know the woman and never will. We never spoke of it. It is done.

She came to live with us when she turned ten. We didn't understand that ten is old enough to understand the world, and we treated her like a child. A brilliant child, yet still a child.

She realized she'd been adopted by my parents when she turned seventeen and applied for her driver's license. We forgot she would need her birth certificate for this and at first refused to allow her to have it. I told her we didn't want her to drive a car to keep her from suspecting our motive.

Rose convinced me to tell her the truth. "Samuel, are you going to forbid her from getting married too? She needs the certificate for this."

We thought she would never have to know. We were unprepared for her questions and the hostility that followed when we refused to provide the information she wanted about her true parentage. This was the first time in her life she did not receive what she wanted from us. We realized we hadn't prepared her for this disappointment. It was never the same with us after that.

Now, she visits to collect money. There is no love in our meeting. There is disappointment for us both.

—

Standing here over the grave of her youngest child, I have no sorrow for her. I grieve for the child, the one who reminded me of Idel. I also grieve for the other children, who will be left with Wendy.

The children who are not here.

The father decided it would be wrong for them to see their brother in the ground.

"It would give them nightmares," he said when I asked why they wouldn't be honoring their brother at the funeral.

He is a fool. I suffered these losses at their ages. There is no avoiding the suffering. There is no avoiding the pain. The children now know a sorrow unlike any other. It will shape them in ways that will affect the rest of their lives. It is the phantom pain in the heart where a muscle should be beating but is gone. Even now, the pain is present.

I think about the suffering my family and I have endured.

First, the devastation of losing my elder brother, Gershon, to typhus, in the same year our beloved *Bubbe* Chava passed. Then the murder of Idel and Berl by the Russian soldiers. And a different kind of murder with the loss of Sura and Ruchel. The camps, the Mefkura murders, the separations.

Now this, the loss of this child, Moses.

Where is Idel's angel for all of them?

Perhaps Idel's angel is a vengeful angel?

This new rabbi from our synagogue teaches that there are *no* angels. Angels are modern-day pagan idols, he says. He says it is time for us to recognize what we create here in our life on earth, that it is our own creation and not the work of an otherworld. When we take responsibility for our misdeeds we will create a better world.

I like this rabbi. I like his new ideas and that he speaks about the *Torah* in a way which takes us out of the Middle Ages and into modern times.

I know I am alone in my age group in these thoughts. I have heard the grumblings of the community sitting with me on the left side of the synagogue, up at the front, where the learned sit. I smile to think I am included in this group of learned men. I never studied the *Talmud*. I never went to college. I attended school at my father's table back at the farm. These men accepted me into their group knowing nothing about me. I am Mocher's brother-in-law, and this is good enough.

———

Yetta. Poor Yetta. It seems I have only recently finished saying the *Kaddish* for her. She died of pneumonia after a long illness and hospitalization. I hated all the visits. The smell reminding me of the time after the Mefkura when I spent months recovering in a Turkish hospital.

Yetta and I found a quiet peace between us those years after Wendy left and started her own family. It became as it always should have been.

She was a great money saver. I discovered this after she passed. She kept her money in a shoebox stuffed away in the back of our closet. Until her death I had no idea how much she managed to save. When I found the box with all the cash rubber-banded and stacked neatly into fives, tens, fifties, hundreds . . . I am astonished to learn she had saved over ten thousand dollars.

I gave her such a small amount each month. I always expected she would ask for more, but she found a way to maintain the same budget for twenty years, even as prices for everything spiked up. She began saving market stamps toward the end of her life. The markets worked out ways to entice their customers' loyalties, and she found a way by collecting these stamps to cut the grocery bills in half. She walked miles to save a few pennies on a loaf of bread or a dozen eggs.

How she managed to save such a great amount could be explained by her behavior, but the thing I wondered about, the biggest mystery of Yetta and her hidden treasure, is why? What was she saving for?

I will never know.

There were no one-dollar bills. Yetta knew I never liked the American one-dollar bills. The eagles on them remind me of the sculpture at the entry to Majdanek—the insane, mocking sculpture with the three eagles imprisoned in concrete.

——

Yetta's body lies here. Her headstone, which was installed and unveiled recently, is to the left of this gravesite. I purchased plots for the rest of the family this week. We would be together in the earth, if not on it. Wendy told me she planned to be cremated when I told her of the purchase today.

"This is a *shanda*, to be burned. You want to bring a horrible shame in your death?" I asked her.

"I don't give a shit. If you buy me a plot I'm gonna sell it and keep the money." If only.

There. The truth of how I feel about this girl, this woman Wendy has become. Why did I agree to take the girl?

I cannot remember all of the reasons my family gave for why I should take this responsibility. She has always been a burden. Like her mother. Anna.

I have not thought about my sister Anna for many years. I never met her. She is born after my parents came to live in America and died seven years before I came to live with them. Her passing a tragedy the family did not discuss.

Wendy, her child, was born in the mental institution Bellevue Hospital. When the infant was released to live with my parents after the birth, Anna remained at Bellevue. My parents trusted the nurses would take care of her. They thought she might be safer there. She passed a few years later from heart disease, a complication of her disorder. We never spoke of her again.

The child, Wendy, lived with my parents in Brooklyn for ten years believing herself to be their daughter.

Wendy's father is a man we never knew. We only knew he was a monster. A man who fled after he forced himself into the apartment when no one was around and raped Anna, a woman with a mental disorder. Down's syndrome.

The guilt my parents suffered. They were still working and sometimes left her alone in the apartment. She was twenty at the time and independent.

When I came to America and lived with my parents, Wendy was a youngster. I marveled at her intelligence and thought she would become the scholar my father had wanted each of us to become.

In the year I spent with them in the Brooklyn apartment, Wendy and I found a quiet appreciation for each other. Later came a time when she couldn't stay with my *mater*. My *foter* passed and my *mater*, now sick and elderly, was barely able to take care of herself without assistance from the family. No one knew what to do with the girl. Oizer offered to take her, but he had five children and four grandchildren already. He already took so much on himself. None of the others could take care of the child. Rose and Mocher were too old.

I almost laugh out loud to think of it. I thought *I* was old. I was forty and Yetta . . . well, now I know Yetta was fifty-two years old when we adopted Wendy.

She kept this secret, like others, with her until after she died. Her youngest sister grudgingly gave me Yetta's correct age when I needed it for the headstone recently. Yetta was the eldest, not the middle, sister. Not what the *shadchen* led us to believe many years ago.

In the end, I agreed to take Wendy. It was my responsibility to care for this child. Yetta and Rose arranged a quick adoption with Oizer's lawyer.

We signed the papers. Yetta wanted her. Wendy was the child she could not, would not, conceive with me. I had never had a want, a need, for a child. Only work. But Yetta believed a child was the natural progression of a marriage, even at her age, and longed for someone to wrap her arms around and care for.

Those were the biggest stones that fell and created the wall between us all those years ago. She became absorbed by the child and gave all the love, all the kindness and gentle caring she possessed, to her. Spoiled her with attention.

I felt left out. I resented the child's presence.

Yetta and I didn't know that by behaving as we did toward each other, we shaped her understanding of what a marriage should be. All she saw was frustrated anger and silence. If we had battled like my TV wrestlers it might have relieved the tension.

I behaved like another spoiled child during those years. I shut them out. Work became my focus and my single goal the accumulation of wealth.

For what? For Wendy and her men? For the children? One now lying in the ground? All those years of work and saving.

I should have followed Rose and Mocher down to Florida long ago and re-tired. I had no need to work any longer and yet I still made the walk to the trolley, to the store. I still spent my days bent over a sewing machine, my shoulders hunched and stiff with arthritis. Every bone in my body aches now in the warm weather as well as the cold. The older, broken ones and the ones I tortured with my work.

I have more help now. The Chinese women who spend their time gossiping while they work. They are good workers. I have learned Chinese over the years and I secretly enjoy the chatter, although it annoyed me before Yetta's passing.

These days this is the sole conversation I have besides the ones with customers, who come with less and less frequency. People don't repair their clothing anymore. They buy new, cheap clothing and throw the old away.

Wasteful.

It is time. Time to close the shops and retire.

To what? What do I have to look forward to with a retirement? Long days with a TV and monthly visits from this one and the two remaining grandchildren?

Who will comfort those children?

When I went to the home to sit with the children before the funeral, I knew I would find it difficult to see their faces. I saw the same loss in their eyes I had seen in Reizel and Oizer's all those years ago.

Who will comfort the children?

———

As the rabbi's voice floats over us, I find the face of the young *shomeret*. I am think-ing again, this face is familiar. How do I know this face?

Yet it is not her I remember. It is someone else.

I glanced down to the copy of the Bible she holds in her hands. Her hands.

A memory floods back to me.

A girl on a train.

A girl whose face I saw briefly in moonlight filtering through a forest on a train to Hell. A girl whose hand I held all night.

Rinna.

Rinna.

I force my mind away from the memory of that moment, of that place. Dwell-ing there is not allowed. That is the place I lived as another.

The rabbi finishes and gestures to me to pick up the shovel. I do, carefully keeping the blade held pointing downwards because this use of the shovel is dif-ferent from all other uses. I put three shovelfuls into the grave and stick the blade back in the earth. To pass it to someone would be to pass my grief.

I watch as the father, the hated man, goes to take the shovel. I am in front of him in two steps. "No," I hiss at him. "You don't deserve this *mitzvah*. You are the reason the child is in this grave. If you had been where you were supposed to be he would not be dead. You're a good-for-nothing."

I watch as my words, like blows, reflect on his face. He is shocked. Throughout his marriage to my daughter I never said to him what I thought of him. For years I felt he was better than nothing for her. Better married than divorced. When he stole the money I gave and spent it like a fool, gambling, I said nothing. I said nothing to the man who left my daughter, left my grandchildren, and moved away without making sure they were cared for.

He is not a man. He is a selfish boy.

I knew this when Wendy brought him home one day to introduce us to him. I knew this all along. There is no reason to deny this now. I could kill him. I could lift this shovel and smash it against his head. I could watch him fall into this hole in the earth with his child. I could do it easily.

I notice the man in the grave next to my grandson's coffin. I recognize the uniform.

I will protect him now, Pieter says in a woman's voice.

I close my eyes to shut away the vision.

The rabbi's hand is on my arm, leading me back to where I was standing before. I peer back to see the father turning away from the shovel.

I won't go back to the home with the father. I won't see him. I will go to my own apartment to sit *shiva*.

My daughter walks forward in the disgraceful black dress. I see she is broken. She weeps as she shovels the dirt.

I want to go to her, embrace her, try to take her pain. I know this will be impossible. Nothing will take her pain. This is the day she will remember as the day her pain took up residence and charged *her* rent for the trouble.

This is good. She will know and understand what pain is. She will suffer for her sins. She will know suffering.

It hits me. Moses has drowned on the same day I lost Idel. September 19th. Idel and Berl both gone on that same day. What can this mean? How can this be?

Moses and Idel.

And I realize it is also my sin I am angry with. I am remembering my failure.

I remember my granddaughter, who pleaded with me to let them come and live with us. To take the children so they could be safe from the monsters in their home. It is as much my fault, the death of my sweet grandson, as the parents'. I knew and I failed to protect them.

This is *my* failure.

Time for the Kaddish. The rabbi begins.

"Exalted and hallowed be His great Name."

"Amen," we answer.

"Throughout the world which He has created according to His will, may His Kingship reign and His redemption come forth and hasten the coming of His Redeemer. In your life and in your days and in the lifetime of the entire House of Israel, speedily and quickly say, Amen."

"Amen."

"May His great Name be blessed in this world and in all worlds. Blessed and praised exalted and extolled, honored, adored and lauded be the Name of the Holy One blessed be. Way beyond all the blessings, hymns, praises and consolations uttered in the world; and say, Amen."

"Amen."

"May there be abundant peace from heaven, and a good life for us and for all and say, Amen."

Amen.

"He who makes peace in His heaven, may he make peace for us and for all Israel; and say, Amen."

Amen.

The service is over. The father has already gone. Wendy and the *nebish* walk away. No words. No kindness. No acknowledgement to anyone, not even the rabbi.

Her rudeness, usually an annoyance, becomes a murderer's stab in this moment. Every ounce of blood in my body turns cold as I watch her step into the sedan without a glance back. I go to the rabbi and thank him. I greet and thank the members of my synagogue who have come to mourn.

The *shomeret,* the girl, nods at me now. Her eyes are kind. She walks to my side and takes my arm to walk with me to the limousine. She is quiet and courteous with me. At the car she turns and faces me.

"My mother is here. We would like to come and sit *shiva* with you, if you would allow it?"

"Of course," I assure her. "It would be an honor to have you and your family in my home."

Such a good girl, this one. Why couldn't Wendy be so good? The *shomeret* introduces me to her mother, who has followed us in the procession to the cars and now steps forward. The girl's mother takes my hand. I look into her eyes and in one second the heart left beating in a ditch bursts in my chest again.

Szaja's heart. A miracle.

The blank world is colored in this instant. We stand in a verdant meadow, not a cemetery. I understand why the *shomeret* appeared familiar. Here in her mother is the face burned into Szaja's fractured mind.

The girl on the train.

Rinna.

How strange. Unimaginable. I spent many years wondering if she escaped or lived to work with the women somewhere in the camp. Or the worst.

"I'm sorry Szaja," she says, and I know she knows, has known, who I am.

I cannot take in air. My throat is dry. A deep sob strains against my throat and I fight to keep it from escaping in a wild-sounding noise. I grasp her hand, her *hant,* and let my breathing come again.

Later, much later, after the joy of this moment and the ones that follow, I realize I have come to believe in angels again, in this moment, despite the new rabbi's teachings. Only an angel could bring me a woman who could ease a life's pain in the midst of a funeral.

Sixteen

AWAKE AND ASLEEP

Open.

I walk in the direction of my neighborhood from the elementary school I used to attend. Stillton. It's sort of like waking up in the middle of a dream, but I don't think I'm dreaming. I can't gather any sense of the time, but it seems late in the day. I know this because of where the sun sits in the sky. There's no traffic and there are no kids out playing. I think it might be dinnertime.

When I step into the yard at our house everything sounds quiet. I see a different car in the driveway. Someone must be visiting. Usually this means a party and loud music, but I don't see Wendy's car.

This is the part where I wake up and realize my brother didn't drown.

As I walk up the porch steps I see schoolbooks stacked on the first step. They seem vaguely familiar. I pick up the one on top, an English textbook. My name is written, in what I recognize as my writing, on the inside of the cover. I pick up the rest of the books and notebooks that lay stacked underneath and bring them in. I can hear the sound of the TV in the den and I walk in that direction.

It still seems like I've been sleeping, but now I've begun to wake up in my mind and body.

I glance up at the clock when I pass through the kitchen and I can see it's almost six o'clock. The ending theme song for *Lost in Space* plays on the TV in the den. David's hair, longer than I ever remember seeing it, curls around his head. He looks like an overgrown cherub.

David catches me peeking and asks me what's for dinner. I walk back into the kitchen and open the refrigerator, which contains a plate of broiled chicken and sliced carrots in a saucepan dropped directly into the refrigerator from the stove. I have no idea how it got there, who made it, or where it came from.

I decide to see if Wendy's upstairs. As I climb, I wonder why, if I'm stuck in a dream, I still feel all of my body and the railing on the stairs?

There are colors. I read that in dreams most people only see black and white. I remember a few where I saw spots of color, but not so many like this. I feel wide awake and everything seems particularly clear now.

At the top of the stairs I knock on Wendy's closed door.

"What?" Wendy says.

"Can I come in?"

"Yeah."

From inside the doorway her room looks the same, but it seems different. There's no cigarette or pot stink embedded in the fabric of the room. It smells like sandalwood and roses. She lies on the bed reading. Her hair, cut shorter, poufs out in curls all around her head, exactly like David's. They could be brother and sister.

I can't think what to say.

"I didn't know if you were here. Where's Jack?"

Wendy stares at me and pauses before she responds.

"He's still in California," she says, like I should know already.

"Right," I say, after a beat. I add, "I wanted to know, where in California?"

"He's in Big Sur."

"Where's that?" I ask, like I want to know.

"It's northern California. Almost San Francisco."

That's where Rice-A-Roni comes from.

"I'm gonna make the chicken and vegetables in the refrigerator for us for dinner, if it's all right?"

Wendy stares at me again.

"Yeah, go ahead. I figured we would have the leftovers from last night. You've got to quit making so much food when you cook dinner, Jules. It's three until Jack comes back. You keep making too much food."

"Okay," I say, and I leave.

I stand at the top of the stairs. I can't remember making dinner last night, or waking up this morning, or even where I was before I walked up onto our front porch a few minutes ago.

This keeps happening to me since Moses drowned.

Mostly I lose time for a few hours, which used to happen when I fall into my drawing and painting. This time it seems like it's been much longer. I can't remember anything that's happened in the past few days. I start shaking.

I try to recall the last thing I remember.

Liver Lips.

The teacher I have a big crush on, who I called Liver Lips Louie, called me out into the school hallway to talk to me. Liver Lips just started his first year teaching contract at Withensea Middle School. His lips are the fullest, most sensuous lips I've ever seen on a man. When he moved them to speak I became instantly distracted until the content of his words drew me back to reality.

He wanted to talk because Wendy had called the school principal complaining that I'd asked her to purchase notebook paper for homework assignments. She was high, I'm certain, and yelled at the principal, saying we were "too poor to purchase school materials." The principal instructed Liver Lips to provide writing paper for our homework.

It was all mortifying: the lie, the fact she was probably high, and that my favorite teacher got messed up with her ridiculousness. I'm nervous enough in the presence of his lips. To explain Wendy's weirdness to this guy was more than I could take. I burst into tears and told him my mother acted "zany" sometimes, which I hoped sufficed as an explanation. He acted nice about it and told me to take as much paper as I needed for homework.

I can't remember what happened the rest of the day or during the days following my Liver Lips encounter. I don't remember Jack leaving for Big Sur. I can't even remember what today is.

It's a school day, I know, because my schoolbooks were on the porch and Lost in Space, which plays in weekday re-runs now, was on TV when I came in.

The calendar on my wall says April and the last day I've crossed is the fifteenth. This means it has only been a few days since it happened. As I stare out the window at the lilac bush, I see there are full blooms on the branches. Which means it's not April. It's close to my birthday. That's when the lilacs bloom.

Terrified, I start trembling again. I can't understand what's happening to me.

I decide to go to the kitchen and check that calendar. I run down the stairs. The word May blares out at me from the top of the calendar on the kitchen cabinet wall.

I think for a minute before I poke my head around the corner to the den and ask David, "What day is it?"

David doesn't look up from the TV. I ask again, "Hey, what day is it?"

"Friday."

"No, what's the date?"

David speaks like a robot. "May the tenth, nineteen seventy-four."

"Duh," I say in response, although I'm glad he added the year.

I walk back into the kitchen and start heating the food from the refrigerator. It's like my head will explode, but it's also like something else, something calming, as if I've stumbled on a big secret. If no one else knows I've been gone a long time, maybe I can time travel? Maybe this is what culture shock is?

I bring Wendy her plate in her room and leave. I tell David his dinner is ready and he walks up the stairs. I realize he's enormous. About six feet tall. I stare. He gives me a mean stare back. I turn back to the stove and dish him out a plate. Then I sit with him and eat dinner.

The space between us at the kitchen bar used to be Moses's seat. I'm aware of the space between us. I'm aware of everything. I notice all the details. The crumbs on the place mat. The stain on the kitchen wall in front of my stool. The scrubby texture of my wool sweater. The sounds David makes as he chews and drinks his milk. I taste my food and think I haven't really tasted anything in a long time.

David asks, "Are you still mad at me?"

I don't know what he means.

"I'm not mad at you. Why do you think that?"

He stops eating.

"Because you never talk to me anymore."

David never acts like he cares about what I think. I wonder if I really haven't talked to him or anyone for a month. How could this happen? I mean, how could I go for such a long time and not talk, or not talk much, or whatever I've been doing?

I'm also wild with curiosity and want to know exactly what's been going on. I'm afraid of what might have happened while I've been checked out. Does everyone else know what happened to me? What have I been doing all this time? Did they put me in the loony bin? I can't even remember how my schoolbooks got on the front porch or what I was doing wandering around up at Stillton. I'm in Withensea Middle School now, aren't I? I haven't gone backwards, right?

I try to breathe normally.

"Come on, I've talked to you a bit, right?" I ask.

"Yeah, a bit, but not much, and you've been acting . . . I don't know . . ."

I wait for him to finish the sentence, but he doesn't.

We continue eating dinner and not saying anything.

"Well, I'm not mad at you, and I think I've just been sad about Moses," I finally say.

"Me too," David says, and we finish our meal in silence.

After dinner I go straight to my room to think about everything. I decide I've gone off my rocker or something since Moses drowned. Maybe this is what people do when someone they love dies. They go away for a while. Still, I'm freaked out.

I wonder if Wendy slipped me another hit of LSD or something that makes you lose time.

They don't make drugs that last that long, silly.

But maybe my brain got fried like that egg on the TV?

I scan the room. On my dresser, perfumes and knickknacks neatly line up exactly the way I remember them, but they're covered with dust. Piles of papers are stacked against the walls. School papers, old drawings, and books. It seems as though I simply dumped things in piles. The walls are exactly the same. The same poems, paintings, and drawings I taped on them a long time ago.

Same crappy, soiled-white chenille bedspread on the bed.

Same old Persian rug on the floor.

In the corner I find a huge stack of library books. They're stamped with return dates for May 20th, next week. So I know I've gone to the library recently since you can only check out books for two weeks.

I jump up and run to the bathroom, stand in front of the mirror, and study myself. Same pale face, same freckles, same everything else on my face, but my cheeks are hollow. My whole body seems thinner and longer than the last time I saw it.

I got even skinnier. Jeez. This is totally depressing.

Maybe I was abducted and returned by aliens? I make a plan to go to the library and check out books on aliens the next morning.

Wendy calls out from the landing that she's going out to a friend's. She needs to use the bathroom. I inhale a deep breath, step out, and slide by Wendy and into my room, where I wait.

When I hear her go downstairs I run to the stair landing window and watch as she climbs into the van parked in the driveway.

Her new car?

It resembles a big, brown, rectangular railroad car. Orange, red, and yellow paint accent a brown base, and the top has an accordion part that's popped out. It definitely looks like it belongs next to the hearse. The psychedelic colors match. I wait until she drives away before going downstairs and finishing clearing the plates and cleaning up the kitchen.

David is back in the den, lounging, and I sit with him and watch TV. Everything is shaky and the TV programs help me calm down even though he wants to watch *The Brady Bunch*, which I hate. Luckily it isn't one of the boring episodes. I go to sleep early.

When I wake up Wendy's car isn't in the driveway. I figure she slept over at her friend's. I dress to go to the library.

I open my closet and see it still holds all of the same clothes I remember, but when I try them on most of them don't fit anymore. Too big. The things still fitting are a few pairs of jeans and a few blouses. Lining the floor—my same shoes. I put on a pair of sneakers, but pull them off immediately because they hurt my toes. They're all too small. The only pair of shoes that fit are the open-toed earth shoes I wore yesterday. Also, there isn't any underwear in my drawer.

Maybe it's all downstairs in the laundry room. Maybe I haven't been wearing underwear for a while.

I pick up one of the library books from the pile on the floor. *Postern of Fate* by Agatha Christie. I can't remember borrowing it, but pieces of my memory are coming back now. I remember walks to the library, down the hill, near where Leigh lives.

Leigh. I can't remember talking with Leigh or hanging out with her lately. I go back to the memory of going to the library to see if I can remember her there. I remember talking with the librarian about the books I checked out, but I don't remember Leigh being there. I remember carrying big stacks of books home from the library, but I can't remember reading them.

This is scary.

I run downstairs. David sits in the den eating a huge bowl of Wheaties and watching cartoons. My stomach rumbles and I realize I'm really hungry. I pour myself an enormous bowl of Raisin Bran and sit in the kitchen by myself to eat.

David comes into the kitchen and asks, "Is Mom back yet?"

I stare at David, amazed at how much he's grown.

"Nope, I don't think so. I think she stayed out all night?"

"Probably." He sounds annoyed.

David grabs more Wheaties and milk from the refrigerator. As he opens the refrigerator door a rancid smell wafts out I didn't notice before. Something has turned. I'll have to check that out later.

David sits down at the counter to eat with me.

I decide to pump him for information, but I know I need to be tricky so he doesn't figure out anything.

"So, how long do you think Jack will be in Big Sur?"

"I don't know. I hope forever."

David's never liked Jack, though Jack doesn't bother me. I decide to agree with David so he'll tell me more about what's been happening.

"Yeah," I say. "He's a pain."

"I don't think it's fair she buys him a big CB antenna. She bought him all that stuff—the van, the camera stuff, and a whole darkroom full of things downstairs. Meantime, we have nothing. She won't even buy me a new tennis racket."

David plays tennis now.

"She likes him better than us. I don't even think she cares what we do or if we die." He's quiet again.

I don't know what to say to him. I agree with what he's saying, but I think it will make him more depressed if I tell him so, like agreeing will make it seem truer in a way or something.

"I wish they had let us go to the funeral," I finally say.

David doesn't answer. He pours out more Wheaties and examines the back of the box on the counter.

I remember Moses's funeral—or rather, the day of Moses's funeral.

I remember that day clearly.

David and I begged to be able to go. We didn't want to stay with a babysitter and miss going to the funeral, but Howard insisted it wouldn't be good for us and Wendy agreed.

My grandfather wanted us to go. I remember he took David and me aside and told us he thought we should go, but he couldn't convince Howard.

It was the first time my grandfather's talked to us like we were grown-ups. I don't know much about my grandfather's life, but he seemed lonely. This was not the first funeral in the last few years we weren't allowed to attend. First my Great-Uncle Mosher, then my Grandmother Yetta. My Great-Aunt Rose, a few months before Moses.

As bad as it got for me with Moses being gone, I knew my grandfather must feel even worse, even more alone. But he never shared this with us.

On the day of Moses's funeral I felt closer to him than I ever have before. He sat with David and me and held our hands for a long time before they left for the funeral. Mostly we sat without saying anything.

I kissed him and told him I loved him and planned to try to persuade Wendy to bring us to visit more often. We'd been visiting less and less.

"I know you must be sad about Moses and there is nothing I can say to take away your sorrow," he said to David and me.

We nodded.

"It's important you remember him. Remember his goodness and the gift of time you shared with him. Remember how much you love him. He is still a part of your family. He will always be a part of you. You have a bit of him inside of you.

Remember this and he will never be gone. Now you must take good care of each other. This is most important."

I remembered Hemingway and said, "You expect to be sad in the fall. But the cold rain has kept on and killed the spring and a young person has died for no reason."

"Weird," David said.

My grandfather hugged me hard.

Howard came up the stairs to my room where we were sitting. He told David he needed to go to his room if he chose to keep crying and he could come out when he finished. He said men don't cry. My grandfather got angry at Howard and called him a fool, but David got sent to his room anyway. I guess crying is okay for girls, though, because he didn't say anything to me. Or maybe I wasn't crying? I can't remember that part.

Howard made me stand behind the bar and mix cocktails for everyone after they came back from the funeral. I didn't care. I still had the old mixology book from the Little Corporal and it gave me something to do.

The drunker everyone got, the more they talked to each other about the whole thing, which was great because no one would tell us anything directly. David didn't come out of his room all day. I took him plates of food. He was still crying every time I went into his room.

Wendy told us my grandfather went to his apartment after the funeral to sit *shiva*. I didn't know anything about the custom, but I remember wishing David and I had been allowed to go home with him.

Howard left that night after the funeral party. I remember this. I remember being relieved because he bossed everyone around all day and Wendy was angry with him for not calling to let us know he wasn't going to show up the morning Moses went off fishing by himself. He hadn't even gotten on the plane from California to fly into Boston that day.

Who knows if that would have changed anything? Who knows what would have happened if I hadn't stayed at Leigh's that morning? I know I should have made sure Moses waited for me to go fishing. Or I shouldn't have told him I would go fishing with him so he didn't get the idea in his head.

I should have been at the house. I knew he'd still be alive if I'd been there. I think I won't ever be considered a good person ever again, even if I try hard to be one for the rest of my life. The rest of my life will be lived in a story about a girl whose brother died. I still can't believe the girl in the story is me. I should have come back earlier and checked to see if Howard came. I would have gone with Moses. It wouldn't have happened like it did. He wouldn't have drowned.

I know it was my fault. Wendy told me it was my fault the day it happened.

That night, when David and I got back from the yacht club, we called around to find Wendy. She called the police and the Coast Guard. She screamed at me and told me it was my fault if something happened to him. I should have come back and waited with him for Howard. She told me I was rotten.

She was right. The biggest thing I was supposed to do was take care of my brothers. Even my grandfather told me this when I was younger. It was my job because I knew Wendy wouldn't do it. Howard is gone. Jack is catatonic. David lives in a television set. My grandfather doesn't know what's going on. Moses died because I didn't do the one most important thing I was supposed to do.

We waited up all night while everybody searched for him, but they didn't find the boat until the next morning, and they didn't find Moses until later that day.

The boat turned up about a mile out from the yacht club. Both life jackets were still in the boat. Moses hadn't put his on. He couldn't swim well. He should have been wearing it. Those were the rules.

His body washed up on the bay side of the island where the tides run.

We never saw him. They wouldn't let us see him. They wouldn't even talk to us about it. Everything we knew we overheard when they thought we weren't listening, mostly at the funeral reception.

Howard treated us like little kids. He doesn't know us anymore.

—⁌—

I wonder about Howard and what he's been up to.

"So, what about Dad?" I ask David while I crunch my Raisin Bran.

"What about him?"

I'm not sure how I'm going to ask this now. "Are you mad at *him?*"

I know it's a stupid question, but I figure it might give me information about where he lived and what's going on with his situation.

"I don't know. Aunt Doreen says he's gonna stay in California this summer. I don't think we're gonna see him . . ."

His voice trails off and he seems maybe mad or sad or something, he doesn't show much on his face.

"Good. It's better when he's gone. You know what I mean?"

David nods. I can tell he isn't going to say either way.

A breeze blows through the kitchen window over the sink and its smell fills the space with the scent of lilacs. "So, I'm going to the library today. What are you gonna do?"

David stares at me funny.

"I don't know, hang around with Joseph. Maybe go play tennis. Why?"

"Oh, I don't know. I might bring a friend over later and I wanted to know if you were going to be here bothering us."

"Who?" he asks. Now I've made him curious and he seems interested to know who it might be.

"Leigh."

David has an odd look on his face. "So, you made up with her?" he asks. "I thought you guys were still in a fight."

You had a fight with Leigh.

I scramble to come up with something as I rinse my bowl and spoon and put them in the dishwasher. "Yeah, but you know," I say, and hope he doesn't ask me any more about it.

David walks over and hands me his spoon and bowl to rinse. He stares hard at me, but he changes the subject.

"Hey Jules, we're gonna be in the same school next year. It'll be freaky-deaky, huh? We haven't been in the same school since elementary. Oh, by the way," he adds, "I saw that guy, Timothy Zand, drop your books off on the porch yesterday. He left before I could talk to him. How did he end up with your books?"

"I must have left them up at Stillton."

Timothy. Who the heck is Timothy?

"You know, Timothy? The new kid who moved into one of the aluminum siding houses? He's a freshman in high school and sometimes he takes the bus with me? Is he your new boyfriend?"

I'm flustered. Avoiding his eyes, I fill the dishwasher soap well and play with the machine's buttons.

"What? No, I don't even know him. No," I say.

I wonder if I have a boyfriend now and I don't even know it. Now that would be big news. A boyfriend.

"Then why did he have your books?"

"I don't know. I forget." The steam from the dishwasher starts to filter out the vents.

David doesn't seem like he buys my story. I blush, even though I'm telling him the truth. I can't remember. I decide to hightail it out of there.

"I gotta go. I'll see you later. If Wendy calls will you tell her there's no food in the freezer and if she can bring back dinner or go shopping, it'd be great?"

"Yeah, Burger King," David says.

I smile at him. He smiles back.

"Are you gonna be nice now?"

"Have I really been a jerk?"

David hesitates and thinks about what to say. "Yup, you've been a real jerk. You've been ignoring everyone and going around slamming doors."

"Sorry," I say. "I'll try not to be one from now on."

"We'll see," he says and laughs.

I laugh too, and I slam the door hard when I leave.

———

Maybe I can trace my steps backwards from the library to remember everything that's happened.

At the library I bring my books in and leave them on the table. I recognize the librarian, and the room smells familiar. Dust and Lemon Pledge. I've connected my past to the present. I remember everything about the library. I remember being there not long ago. I remember walking in and I remember walking out.

I can't remember the librarians name though.

She seems happy to see me, and I realize we're friends now. I mean, she's as much of a friend as an adult can be. I can recall several conversations we've shared recently.

She asks me if I liked the books I borrowed and I tell her I did. I pause at the desk and wonder if I should ask her for books about memory loss, time travel, or even alien abductions. Maybe I should try and find them on my own.

Several other people whisper and mill around and I don't want to be embarrassed. I walk to the young adult section and pretend to pick out books. When I hear the others shuffle away on the wood floors, I go back out to the desk.

"Can I help you find something?" she asks.

"Ummm, actually, I wondered if you have books on the subject of alien abductions?"

She smiles and says, "I think so. Let's see."

She leads me up the windy staircase to the adult section, a huge room I've never been in before. The shelves are lined closely and reach all the way up to the ceilings in here. The light filters dusty beams in through the tall, wavy-paned windows. She shows me bookcases stacked with books about psychic phenomena, witchcraft, and UFOs and lets me sort through them on my own.

I have a blast in there. One of the books tells a story about a guy being abducted and losing his memory. The guy in the story is sure about the aliens though. He can remember the UFO that picked him up and what it looked like from his car. He describes the aliens, too, but can't remember what happened during the surgery they performed on him—except feeling lots of pain before he passed out—or how he got back in his car, which is where he woke up.

I can't remember any spaceships or aliens. Only Moses disappearing that day.

Maybe Moses got taken by aliens. Maybe he didn't drown like everybody thinks. Maybe he got abducted by aliens and they made it seem like a drowning. I don't like the theory, but I'm not ruling anything out.

After I skim the book about UFOs I also leaf through a book about hypnotism. I wonder if someone put me into a trance.

Up at the main library desk I trace the edge of the desk with my index finger where it's carved like a rose vine. I ask the librarian about hypnosis, if it can affect memory. She says it can and that she has another book for me to read I might find interesting.

When she leaves I look across the desk at the paperback she's left open on her desk. I can hear her soft-soled shoes on the wooden floors above me. Flipping the book over to look at the cover, I can see it's one of those books about the women who like men to rip their clothes off and "take them," which has me worried about the choice she's going to bring back for me.

She comes back with a book called *On Death and Dying*, by Elisabeth Kübler-Ross.

I check out the book with my other choices and spend the rest of the weekend reading it. I learn how most people react when someone they know dies. The part about depression makes sense to me and I figure this must be what happened to me. It's a relief to find a logical reason for my memory loss because, to be honest, the alien abduction and the hypnosis thing were too crazy to believe. I like logic. I resolve to figure out a logical way to make my brain stop losing time. I decide the next time I go to the library I will find more books like this one.

———

I'm in the dinghy with Moses and we're fishing. It's an overcast day. The flounder bite like mad and we're laughing and reeling in lots off our hooks and dropping them into the metal bucket on the boat. The bucket overflows and the fish flop out of it and onto the bottom of the boat, but we're having so much fun we ignore it.

Moses gets a huge tug on his line. It's definitely not a flounder because it bends his line more than I've ever seen a fish around here do. All at once the fish lunges out of the water about ten feet from us. It's a swordfish! It's magnificent. Full of silver scales like armor, with golden glints. It's huge! As big as our dinghy, easily six or seven feet. It dives under again with the line attached.

I try to scoot over to where Moses sits on the boat to help him reel it in, but I slip on the flounder in the bottom of the boat and crash into him. The pole goes flying out of his hand and he goes flying over the edge of the dinghy. He's got his life jacket on. I'm not worried. I lean over the edge of the boat to give him my hand, but the swordfish swims up to the side of the boat. It's all black now beneath the water. It stops moving inches away from the boat. It's lying there. It seems like it's sleeping. It lies on its side, just under the water, gills barely moving, a black monster. It's still got the hook line coming out of its mouth, streaming back behind it, the pole floating out about twenty feet from the boat. Moses treads water about two feet away from it, behind the swordfish. We are entranced by it.

Moses swims up to the hull of the boat. He lifts one leg up and I reach over a hand to help him. I grab the ties on his life jacket and pull to lift him. As I do, the swordfish seems to wake up and leaps out of the water between us, sword waving. It catches the inside of Moses's jacket ties. I watch as the fish spears the jacket and then pulls Moses off the boat.

Moses goes into the water with the force of the fish's motion pushing him, and I watch as first the line, then the fishing pole goes snaking after them. He's being pulled farther out by the fish and being bobbled by the waves. Then the fish takes him and the jacket under. It happens fast, in the space of a blink, and my mind tries to register the image but I have to push it away. I'm telling my body to react, but it's a dream and everything goes in slow motion.

This is the part of the dream where I know I'm dreaming.

My mouth opens, vocal cords tighten, air moves in and then out with screams, but I can't hear my screams. The muscles in my mouth stretch. They try to form a word.

Moses!

My heart pounds painfully and races in my chest and my body is weightless at first, arms and legs numb and useless.

You've got to move, got to reach him.

I see Moses surface. He's about thirty yards away and gasping.

You've got to get to him.

I try to force my arms to work—to make my thoughts enervate the muscles.

Shoulders rotate, elbow out, wrist turn, fingers clasp.

Finally, I manage to rip off my vest so I can dive in to swim and grab him. Puppet master thoughts propel my legs, making them kick.

Thigh up, knee up, down, stretch, calf down, push, ankle snap, foot flap, and repeat. Arms cartwheel over me, shoulder rotate, elbow up, bicep up, forearm lift, wrists snap, hand carve, stretch, pull, repeat.

All of these motions, thought manifested. I cannot feel myself in the water, but Moses moves farther out as I head toward him. I have to swim faster.

I'm within a few feet and I can see the black monster's sword tangled in the life jacket ties. I will my hand to reach out for the tie to release it, but he's moving away, pulling Moses under the waves again. The swordfish's massive body plows through the water, away from me.

I can see Moses a few feet under the waves, still captive in the jacket and struggling. The fish moves more slowly with the buoyancy of the jacket pulling against him. Moses is swallowing water. I know I've got to move fast. I dive under and swim toward him. My lungs threaten to burst. I'm about ten feet away when I have to grab air. I come up and dive back down again, but he's not there anymore. I can't see him anywhere. Turning in every direction, I strain to find him. He's completely disappeared. He's completely disappeared. The water is murky and dark now and I can barely see my hand in front of me. The water is murky and dark now and I can barely see my hand in front of me.

Got to find him. Got to save him.

Lungs on fire. Dizzy and weak. Fish clicking. Sonar calls and whistles—electrical and secret. A bit of orange below me.

Neon orange.

Moses's life jacket.

I need air, but I don't want to lose him. I swim down instead. When I'm down there, I see it's a part of a buoy, painted orange.

I'm far from the surface and I know I'm going to swallow water before I make it back up. I swim for it with all my might, but I only make it halfway up and now I'm choking on seawater. It's in my nose, my mouth, my lungs.

Water floods through my head and my body, filling me.

I can't breathe through the water in my throat and lungs and I'm struggling as hard as I can. My thoughts can't make my body move anymore. It's as though my brain—electrical—has been shorted by the water flooding in.

Don't want to die.

The fish clicks. The electrical currents I've been listening to dim until I can't hear anything. The ocean around me—a vast, soundless, dark entity.

I see Moses floating at the top of the water. His legs kicking. He's alive. He's alive.

In the next second, I see *myself* from a few feet away.

Watching myself under the water now.

My eyes closed, mouth slack, arms and legs dangling. I'm spiraling down like a line sinker.

I'm dying. The last conscious thought I have is an aching, strong sadness.

I wake up panicked, sweating, and gasping for air.

You can drown in a dream.

Seventeen

Jules, 12 years | *May 13th, 1974*

UNLOCKING THE DOOR

I DREAMED THE dream again last night. As I dress for school I decide it's probably normal for me to dream about drowning and I'm not going to worry about it. Instead, I worry about how I'm going to pull off going to school and being awake after being a zombie for who knows how long. Did anyone notice or care what's been happening to me? I'm prepared for surprise and humiliation.

Last night I spent time tearing through all the papers in the books and piles on the floor. I need to find my homework papers because I can't remember what's been going on in my classes. It's creepy. Somehow I've managed to prepare for and go to school every day. Apparently, I've been functioning in a seemingly normal fashion, because no one threw me in the loony bin. I must have remembered things from day to day—but, now, awakened out of zombie-land, I'm afraid I won't do as well.

Fortunately, I find some recent homework in one of the piles. So, I sort of know where I am in my studies. I tried to figure out what chapter we were studying using the notes in my books last night, but I've been bad about note-taking and the only clues to what we're studying are the doodles I made in the book margins. I found a few quizzes and tests for the semester that help me orient. As soon as I arrive at school I see a few kids I know standing in the hallway. I nod and say hello, but they just stare and whisper. It's been like this since Moses drowned.

Homeroom comes first. First period messes me up though. My first period is study hall, so I go to the cafeteria where study hall is held. But when I sit down the room fills and someone asks me why I'm not in my "regular" class, I notice there's no one my age in study hall. I'm embarrassed, but my other option, to go to the school office and ask for a copy of my schedule, sounds like a worse plan than what I'm doing.

My other choices for first period, which rotate daily, are gym, art, and music. I decide to troll the hallway and see if I can figure it out.

First, I go to the gym, around the corner from the cafeteria. I peek through the small window in the door and see that the kids aren't in my grade. Next, I head to the music room, which sits one floor up and by the auditorium. Classes have started now, and I have no hall pass. I move quickly, hoping no one will stop me. The tiny window to the music room sits too high for me to see through. I suck in a deep breath and walk in. About twenty people stare up at me when I open the door, but they aren't kids in my grade either. My face burns.

It's got to be art class. At least art is my favorite class, and I love my teacher, Ms. Wheaton. In class, I tell Ms. Wheaton that I've been out talking to a teacher in the hallway. She tells me to grab my seat and start working on my project.

My project? I have no idea what it might be. I slide into an empty seat next to a kid I like and try to gather what I can about what we're working on. When I get up to start looking through my cubby I remember we share spaces with two or three other people. What if I can't recognize my own work?

Luckily, I do. I have begun drawing in charcoal, pen, and ink. According to Ms. Wheaton, I have "developing talent." About a year ago I did a drawing that won a school-wide art contest. I'm not sure if they were trying to be nice to a kid with a dead brother, but this encouraged me to keep drawing.

As I bend over the paper the scent of the charcoal is familiar. I can taste it as I inhale the particles. I am lulled into a state of peacefulness. The paper has a tooth like velvet. I've no idea what sort of work I've been doing, but I sit through class completely immersed in the drawing I'm working on. It's a portrait of a girl I don't recognize.

Math comes next. I stand by a desk, inhaling the scent of chalk dust and sweat in the room. I'm pretending to search for a paper in my book while the class fills up because another kid is sitting in my seat. Apparently, our seats have been changed. Nobody is sitting where I remember they were. When everyone takes their seats, I sit down in one of two empty ones. I must have guessed correctly because no one kicks me out of the seat or acts like I shouldn't be there.

Math has never been my best subject. I try to pay attention to the teacher and catch up. I'm lost. He tells us we're going to have a pop quiz. I panic. My face feels hot and sweaty. I shoot a look over at the girl sitting next to me and give her my "scared eyeball" face. She smiles and turns her paper to the side. I can see her answers easily as she writes her responses to the problems he puts on the board. Fortunately, he never turns around to see what we're doing behind him.

When class ends I smile and thank her for helping me out. She tells me I can "cheat off" her anytime. I take off for my next class after double-checking the room number.

After English I go to my locker to put books away. I'm hoping for clues to what's been happening to me, but there's nothing much inside the locker but empty notebooks, a broken pencil and old homework assignment. The buzzer rings harshly for the next class. It's the last class before my lunch period. History.

As I'm hanging around outside the classroom waiting for the seats to fill just in case there's been another seat rearrangement, I see Leigh walk by and head in. I smile at her, but she ignores me and keeps walking. I think about following her in and starting up a conversation, but I lose my nerve and continue standing outside the class. The next thing I know she comes out and walks up to me.

"What's going on, Jules?"

I try to figure out how to behave since David told me we've been fighting.

I decide to apologize.

"I wanted to tell you I'm sorry."

"What for?"

"I don't know?" I answer honestly. "But I want us to be friends again."

Leigh looks down at her sneakers. "You know, I never understood why you stopped talking to me. I figured it might be because you were sad about Moses, but still . . ."

I can't figure out how to respond. Too many things crowd my mind—regret, confusion, embarrassment, and even anger that Leigh, my best friend, hasn't noticed that I've been checked out for almost a month. I mean, how can you miss the fact something is wrong—like, she can't remember what she had for breakfast or what day it is—with your best friend?

"Can we meet after school?" I begin. "I'd like to hang out and talk."

Can I trust her with my memory loss secret?

"Yeah, we can meet after school . . . or . . ."

She checks around us for teachers, then grabs my arm and drags me to the stairs. "We could cut class."

I'm torn. I've made it halfway through my day trying to figure out my schedule and my life at school. I did a good job covering, I think. The temptation of simply leaving, not having to pretend to remember anymore, proves too great to resist.

We wait until the hallway clears and head for the exit on the stairway landing. We step into a sparkling, sunny spring day and run toward a small street next to the school. The excitement of skipping class combined with the smell of damp earth and the ever-present ocean intoxicates me.

I feel light and careless, even happy. I wonder how long it's been since I've felt this happy.

I've become Jules, the class cutter. Something I've never done before. For years I've been following rules at school, making rules for our chaotic family. It's time to break some.

"I love this smell," I say.

"Filamentous bacteria," Leigh answers.

Who knows what this means? I love that she knows the science of the smell.

We head to the bay, where we shelter in a small, rocky cove and inhale the brine from the tide pools. A starfish clings to a seaweed-covered rock in the tiny pool below us. I pick round, green-colored pebbles out of the water and dry them beside me on the rock. Leigh talks about her sister, who's been in trouble because she keeps staying out late with her boyfriend having sex. Leigh says her mom and sister, Annie, argue all the time and that home life is shitty. I understand how Leigh has missed what's been going on with me. She has her own problems.

We look out at the boats moored on the bay. "I have something to tell you," Leigh says. She pauses, a dramatic pause, and her face is serious.

"What?"

"I don't know if I should tell you this," she says.

"I've got something to tell you too. You go first," I say. I figure I will probably give her a bigger shock.

"Look, you can't tell anyone because I'm supposed to keep it a secret, but my sister's pregnant. My mom is going to kill her when she finds out. Which is gonna be soon. She's been wearing big jackets and stuff to hide her belly, but soon she's going to start to show. The shit is going to hit the fan."

"What's she going to do?" I ask.

"She's not sure yet. She thinks this guy might bail on her if she tells him about the baby. But she's gonna have to decide soon. It's so messed up, and my mom thinks Annie's going to college next year. She keeps shoving college catalogs down her throat."

"Maybe she could have the baby and still go to college?"

Leigh looks at me like I'm crazy. "Yeah, I don't think that's gonna happen. She's probably gonna have the baby and mooch off of my mom."

I'm thinking how sometimes girls in Withensea get pregnant in their senior year, like Annie, and never make it out of Withensea. They marry their high school boyfriends and get stuck here.

"You know the new kid Timothy Zand who lives in your neighborhood? The one with the gorgeous eyes?"

"No." The first time I heard his name was the other day when David told me he'd brought my books to our porch. I don't know him. I don't even know what he looks like. I have a feeling there are lots of peripheral things that have been going on all around me that I can't remember.

"He lives right around the corner from you. He's in high school, a freshman. He walks to school sometimes. I've watched him walk by my bus stop on his way."

"What about him?" I smile at her to continue.

"Well, I have a huge crush on him. There's something different about him. It's almost like he comes from another country. We should try to meet him."

I almost laugh. Leigh is totally boy crazy. This crush counts as one in fifty she's developed since I became her friend. She's gone on dates with lots of boys in the past—dates to school dances, dates at the bowling lanes. Her mother makes strict rules about dating, however. Leigh's not supposed to be dating boys her mom hasn't met. So she invents a cover for most of her dates. That was always *me* in the past. I wonder who has been covering for her in the last few weeks. "What have you been doing since we stopped talking?" I ask.

"Nothing much. I hang out with the chess club guys and my sister, but I only see her once in a while, after school and on the weekends she doesn't spend with her boyfriend." She squints down at the rocks on the beach. "Yesterday I joined the Methodist church down the street from the library."

"Church?"

"Yeah, they have a teen group. Methodist Youth Friendship. I made some new friends there. I might date a guy there too, Edgar . . . ."

I decide I will see how much Leigh has noticed about what happened to me before telling her about my memory loss. "So, when we stopped talking, do you remember what happened? I mean, why do you think we haven't been hanging out?"

Leigh seems thoughtful. She's making a decision about what and how much she will say. "Please don't think you're going to hurt me. I want you to be honest. What happened?"

"I don't think any one thing happened. I mean, we would hang out and everything, but you never wanted to do anything or go anywhere. You only wanted to go to the library and read. I got sick of reading. I felt like I had to talk you into doing stuff all the time. Every time I asked you to go somewhere, like to Quincy or something, you didn't want to. You started acting weird. We would finally make a plan to do something, like go to the park or to a movie, and you wouldn't show— or you'd show up an hour late and act like you were on time or something . . . I don't know. And there was other weird stuff."

"Like what weird stuff?" I ask.

"I don't know . . . like the time with locking the door?"

Locking the door?

I don't know what she means, but I think I should pretend I know, that not knowing might be even more bizarre-sounding.

"Yeah, I guess it seemed weird."

I hope she will tell me more. I wait.

"Yeah." Leigh avoids my eyes.

I stay quiet.

Leigh speaks softly. "Can you explain why you did it?"

I suck in a deep breath. I know this is the moment to tell her, to try and explain that I can't remember what happened. But I'm terribly afraid of what she might think. I'm afraid of the complexities of my own secretive mind, which has become a maze that hides its entrance and its exit in a spot I can't find. "I have something to tell you. It's hard to talk about. I think you need to know something about me if you want to be my friend again."

I take another big breath while Leigh waits. "On Friday, walking back to my house, I realized I didn't know where I'd been. It seemed like I was waking up from a dream. When I got to school today I wouldn't have known what we were study-ing if I hadn't found some homework or a recent quiz. I can't remember last week. I can't even remember the weeks before." I add.

I realize as the words hang in the air how completely scary it is and how freaky it must sound to someone else. Leigh doesn't say anything for a while. I can tell she can't decide whether to believe me or not. I think she's waiting for me to tell her I've been teasing or tricking her.

"When's the last day you remember?" she asks.

I start to cry. I can't stop. I heave and choke and my body shakes violently. I bend over to try to catch my breath.

Leigh puts her hand on my back. "Oh God, are you gonna be okay?"

I try to tell her I'll be fine, but I can only shake my head from side to side.

"N-n-noo," I stammer.

I'm not okay. My brain's been hijacked. Nothing is okay. Leigh sits still with me while I cry. We sit like that for a long time. She lets me cry and puts an arm around me when the shaking gets more intense. After a while, my body feels weak and I'm tired. I lie across one of the flat rocks. After a while I start to drift into sleep in the warmth of the sun.

I must have slept for a few hours, because the sun has shifted over the horizon. I squint up to see where the sunlight bends over the sky. Finding the northern point on the horizon, I look behind me for my shadow and see it reads about two o'clock. I search for Leigh. The tide has gone out and the rocky sand stretches far out beyond the boat launch. At first I can't find her, but then I see her down at the water's edge, her head a small sunlit pale-reddish speck against the black rocks.

She's crabbing. The bay side of Withensea is the best for crabbing because there are tons of small tide pools. The crabs cling to the sides of the rocks and slide inside pools loaded with seaweed and snails. Leigh found a bucket somewhere. She drags it beside her.

"Hey," I shout out to her.

Leigh turns around. "Hey!" She yells back and waves at me join her. It takes me a while to walk out to her.

"I fell asleep."

"Yeah, I figured I should let you sleep a bit, but I didn't want to leave you out here alone. I saw a crab and found this bucket. I've got lots. See?"

Leigh's bucket swims with crabs.

"Let's go to your place and boil these. Do you think your mom's home?" she asks.

"I have no idea if she's there today or not. Jack's in California. It's hard to say. But let's go anyway. If there's a party, we can go down to your place, right?"

"Okay, but if we go to mine we'll have to wait until later, when school is out, or my mom will know we skipped. Oh, and we don't have a big enough pot for the crabs. Remember?"

I do remember this. Ms. Westerfield doesn't like shellfish and never cooks it. David and I practically live on the stuff we dig out of the sand when the weather allows. Crabs, clams, snails.

Leigh and I take turns carrying the bucket of crabs and walk along the bay beach so no one can see us and catch us out of school. We have one section of Withensea Avenue to cross that lies out in the open, and we run as fast as we can when we get there. I hold the bucket this time. As we make it over to the ocean-side beach we hear a car cross the land bridge. We duck behind tall beach grass and watch as Ms. Westerfield drives by.

"That's so weird. What are the chances? Do you think she saw us?" Leigh asks.

"No. But it freaked me out."

We crack up with laughter until our sides hurt.

"How lucky that I caught you outside class today. I'm sorry we went this long without talking, Jules. Let's never do it again." She squeezes my hand tightly.

"I know," I say. "It was serendipitous."

Leigh giggles. "*Serendipitous*," she mimics me playfully.

She turns serious. "I've missed you so much. I'm sorry. I thought you didn't want to be my friend anymore, like maybe I asked you too many questions about Moses. I even thought you blamed me because I kept you late that morning and maybe you would have made it back to go fishing with him or something."

"Oh, no. I don't blame you. I never blamed you. It's my fault I stayed. It's my . . ." My throat catches. "It was *all* my fault."

"It wasn't your fault Moses drowned," Leigh says angrily.

At first, I can't meet her eyes. I have wanted someone to say those words to me for a long time, but she sounds angry and I can't figure out why.

She goes on.

"I wish we could have adopted you after it happened. I asked my mom if maybe you could come to live with us. I think she considered it, but decided you should stay with your family. I think she knows how much you take care of everything, and she said . . ." Leigh stops.

I can tell she's leaving things out. Things she thinks she shouldn't say, because I haven't said them to her, but that we know are true.

"She said you needed to stay put and take care of David." Leigh shakes her head and says, "I wonder if your memory is having trouble because you feel so badly about Moses. Maybe you just want to forget everything so you don't have to remember the one really sad thing?"

———

No one is home when we get to my house. We cook the crabs, but of course there's no butter or lemon in our refrigerator to flavor them. Still, they're a sweet and salty treat. We play a killer chess game. Leigh teaches me all the new sequences and openings she's been learning from her new friends on the chess team. Later, Wendy waltzes in and asks us how school went. I don't answer. Leigh speaks up. "It was boring."

Wendy smiles and chats with Leigh a bit. She acts like a normal mother even though she's wearing platform shoes, a blouse made of crochet flowers, and a miniskirt that shows the bottom of her butt when she bends over.

I'm annoyed with how Wendy acts all fakey nice around other people, and I'm relieved when she walks upstairs and leaves us alone until it's time for Leigh to go home.

"I'll meet you in front of school tomorrow and we can figure out your schedule together, okay?" Leigh says.

"That would chase all my mimsy away," I answer.

"Serendipitous!" Leigh shouts as she rounds the corner.

She's teasing me. It's wonderful.

Two days later it's my thirteenth birthday. Leigh throws me a surprise party after school at her house. She's invited the chess guys, a few kids she knows from school, and her new church buddies, which is weird, since I don't hang out with them, but Leigh is friends with everyone and they're all nice to me anyway. It's probably the best birthday party I've ever had.

I manage to stumble through the next few weeks at school until the summer break, recovering my reality as I go.

But I dream the drowning dream almost every night.

Eighteen

Jules, 13 years | Late June, 1974

A GRAPE-SIZED SPACE

LEIGH CALLS ME on a Wednesday morning. We've been out of school for a week, spending most of our time down at the jetty swimming. The song sparrows chirp like crazy. There's no breeze and I can already smell muggy seaweed in the air. It's going to be a hot day. I'm thinking we should head down to the beach early to find a good spot, but Leigh calls to ask if I want to go into Boston on the bus and go shopping.

I know she's already been this week. She went with her sister and got lots of really cool new clothes. Since Annie decided to have an abortion and not to go to college, Ms. Westerfield's been trying to help her get a decent job somewhere. According to Ms. Westerfield, Annie needs a more professional wardrobe, so Leigh's helping out with that since Annie and her mom are still not talking.

Leigh tells me she wants to show me something.

Later that day we're in Gilchrist's, shopping, and Leigh pulls me aside to show me a shirt stuffed under her blouse. I am so blown away I blurt out, "What are you doing?" She shushes me and then drags my arm and pushes me out of the store. She steals the shirt.

Leigh tells me how easy it is and when we walk into another store she dares me to stuff a bra she wants inside my shirt. I grab a handful of bras and consider whether to do it or not. My heart beats a mile a minute and I think I might throw up with nervousness. I do it. I'm exhilarated.

I've broken another rule. The day we skipped classes was the first time I did something delinquent, even though I've been brought up by criminals. Now I've stolen something. I feel like a real kid and not somebody's mother.

We spend the rest of the day shoplifting from different department stores. It's a total blast.

———

That night, I have my nightmare again. I've started keeping a log of it. The dream doesn't come every night, but it comes often. I also write down the events of the day before I fall asleep every night. I want to see if they contain a pattern I might be able to interrupt. I keep a count.

I think there might be a magic number? Maybe if I dream the dream fifty times, or a hundred times, it might go away forever. It seems crazy to me that I keep having the same one over and over. I'm certain most people don't do this. Trying to sort out a pattern might be a good way to track my craziness in case I'm ever sent to the loony bin. I'm sure that can happen at any time.

———

The next few weeks are roughly the same. Leigh and I go into Boston every weekend and shoplift from stores. The trip to Boston is quick if we take the ferry—just an hour. But if we want to travel in by bus, we have to catch three buses, and that takes hours.

A couple of times I talk Leigh into visiting my grandfather's apartment with me since we aren't far from where he lives, off Commonwealth Avenue. We take the T after the buses. Those visits are sad, though, because he acts sweet and gives me money, which makes me feel guilty for shoplifting.

After Moses died, my grandfather met and married a woman named Ruth from his synagogue. He seems happier than I've ever known him to be before. Ruth is younger than him and he perks up around her, almost like a teenager. Ruth speaks perfect English and is nice to us. I've grown to love her as much as I loved Grandmother Yetta. The best thing is the way the two of them act so *in love*. I never saw my grandfather kiss Grandmother Yetta, but he kisses Ruth all the time.

When Leigh and I visit, Ruth makes us lunch.

It's the same lunch Grandmother Yetta used to make: chopped liver and chicken soup with rice. Ruth even gives me the *poopach*. They treat Leigh and I like we're kids, but I don't mind. I know if my grandfather had any idea about what I've been doing he would be horrified. His life seems pure and innocent compared to mine. He doesn't seem to understand what *my* life is like. The one time I tried to explain what a horrible mother Wendy is he got angry with me for being disrespectful and ungrateful. I gave up trying to make him understand. David and I pretend everything is normal when we see him and he seems to want it that way.

Maybe he feels like he can't change it.

One day in Boston, a few weeks after we've started becoming delinquents, I'm having a smoke outside of Bloomingdales and Leigh walks out of the store with one of those lighted makeup mirrors right on her head. "If you put it somewhere obvious, no one questions you," she says.

I'm completely freaked out. "That's it! I'm not stealing anything anymore. We're probably one eye shadow away from juvenile hall."

"Nobody's paying attention to us. Don't worry!"

"Listen, if I get in trouble, they could send me away. If I go, who's gonna take care of David?"

"Okay. Okay. Nobody's getting sent away. Probably best if we quit while we're ahead, anyway."

I don't feel like I'm ahead. I feel like I'm right in the path of punishment.

That punishment comes swiftly.

Back at the house, Wendy drives up with a Burger King dinner for David and me. As we start eating in the kitchen, Wendy announces that David and I will be spending the rest of the summer at camp. David's been to summer camp a few times since Moses died. Wendy gets him into a free program at a two-week camp every year. This time we're both going for the whole summer and my grandfather's paying. David loves it, so he's thrilled. But I've never been to camp. The prospect of being away from Wendy and the madness is intriguing, but I've been looking forward to a summer with Leigh and our normal, *non*-shoplifting summer activities—swimming, reading, riding bikes, and making trips to the library and the beach. Wendy has apparently arranged for me to go to a YMCA girl's summer camp in Cape Cod with the daughter of a friend of hers, a girl named Smith. I do not like this girl.

Smith is a summer dude. Her family owns a bungalow in Withensea and they come to live on the island every summer. Her parents have tons of money and send her to a private girl's school in Cambridge. She acts spoiled, stuck up and childish even though she's a year older than I am. She's always bragging about something she can do better than everyone else. She thinks all the "townies" are poverty-level ingrates with no sense of culture or sophistication. I have no desire to change her mind about this and even encourage her perception so she won't try to be my friend.

It's true that Withensea is more a place to leave than a place where people arrive.

I've been to the suburb she lives in outside of Boston. It has prettier houses, but practically no natural beauty. Withensea has that in spades.

Also, and this is a big also, I've seen her parents naked and having sex with Wendy on one of those orgy nights. The connection grosses me out. However, Wendy and Smith's mother, Betty, have decided we should become friends. They are unaware, as parents usually are, of the fact that we are mutually repelled by each other.

———

The next day I'm coerced by Wendy into spending the morning with Smith at her house so that we can "make plans about camp." She promises we'll go and visit my grandfather afterwards. Smith gamely plays the hostess and makes an effort to entertain me by showing me her bedroom, which includes her extensive collection of small crystal animal figurines. This lasts about an hour, as all the animals have names and individual "personalities" that Smith describes in detail. It's like she's trying to be Laura in the *Glass Menagerie*. Smith is a huge phony.

I sit on her pink ruffled bedspread in her very pink room, and she prattles on as I try to conjure a reason to force Wendy to drive me back to the house or make an excuse to jump on the next bus. Miraculously, my body responds with its own answer to my dilemma. I begin to have wicked bad stomach cramps.

Smith moves on with the display of her belongings, showing me every item in her wardrobe, and the cramps begin to intensify. All my life I've been pretty stoic about handling pain, but it begins to feel uncomfortable enough for me to lie back on the pink froth of her bedspread. When I do this she screams and points to my crotch, which has become saturated with blood.

"Get up! Get up!" she shouts at me.

I am bleeding onto her pink bedspread. Smith runs out to tell our mother's about my predicament—not the way I planned to announce the beginning of my menstruation.

Soon Wendy and this girl's mother, Betty, stand in the room while I writhe on the bed. Wendy smirks in the doorway and makes the same pronouncement over and over—"She's a woman!"—while Betty makes consoling noises and instructs me to take off my pants in the bathroom. She wants to wash everything.

"How come she gets her period first?" Smith pouts. "I'm a year older. It's not fair!"

Really? This idiot chick is going to freak out on me because I got my period first?

Smith whines about the blood on the bedspread. Betty, who turns out to be decent about the whole thing, tells her to pipe down. She'll buy her another one.

I'm freaked out and embarrassed. More by the attention than the physical mess I've created. Betty pulls me into the hallway bathroom to show me the Kotex pads to put on. She takes me in the bathroom and shuts the door, leaving Wendy standing in the hallway. She gives me the Kotex pad, but Wendy, standing outside the bathroom, insists that I try using a tampon. Betty reluctantly gives me a box of tampons. I have never seen what a tampon's unwrapped interior holds. She argues with Wendy that the tampons are too large for me, but Wendy shouts to me through the bathroom door that I should try it first before using the pad.

I wrap myself in a towel and take off my pants for Betty to launder. Betty hands me a pair of Smith's underwear. Pink, of course. She leaves and I lock the bathroom door.

This is the part where I get my period and Wendy tries to teach me how to use a humungous tampon while she stands outside the door shouting instructions.

I ignore Wendy's voice barreling through the closed bathroom door as I read the directions on the paper inside of the tampon box. I've never been interested enough in my own anatomy to explore what the inside of a vagina might look like, and the diagram is a revelation.

How could I have that much space inside me? I envisioned a much smaller space, more like a grape than a small, deformed banana.

In the hallway Wendy argues with Betty about the benefits of using tampons vs. pads. Wendy wants me to try using a tampon, but Betty says she plans to start Smith on pads for a year or two before she buys her tampons—until she's "developed." I don't quite understand the relevance of the word until I start trying to fit the plus-sized tampon inside of me. I become convinced I have tried the wrong orifice. Perhaps I am horribly disfigured and I am grape-sized?

I decide I've tried the wrong angle. I begin to explore the various angles of insertion based on the diagram in the directions. Nothing works. I've been inside the bathroom for about an hour. Wendy finally gives up her shouted instructions from outside because I yell at her to go away.

Betty, however, hovers somewhere outside and asks at intervals, "Okay in there?" to which I repeatedly respond, "Yeah . . ."

Finally, I give up on trying to use the tampons; I've massacred about four of them in my attempts. I use the small pins I've been given to pin the pad into place in Smith's borrowed underwear.

When I come out, Betty, who's been standing in the hallway, hands me a pair of cutoffs to wear, and tells me she put my pants into the laundry and she'll give them to Wendy the next time she sees her. She tells me she can't find my underwear.

"I don't wear underwear," I explain while I pull the cutoffs on. I figure this won't be shocking for her, since she thinks orgies are okay.

She smiles. "I don't wear underwear either."

I smile back although I don't want to hear this.

"My God, you're thin! Those shorts fit Smith when she was ten. Does your stomach still hurt?" she asks.

"Yeah."

"Let me find you a Midol."

"Oh, no. I don't take any drugs." I'm afraid it might be one of Wendy's types of pharmaceutical fixes.

Betty laughs, "No, it's not . . . it's okay, these come from the drugstore."

This doesn't appease my fears, since I know most of what Wendy keeps in her *special pharmaceutical drawer* has been prescribed to her or someone else by a doctor.

"I don't take any drugs."

"But this will make your stomachache go away."

"I don't care. I'd rather take the pain. I don't do drugs."

Since I know she does, I also know I risk offending her, but I don't care. I know enough about the way Wendy and her friends abuse the legal meds they obtain to know any drug is capable of making people behave oddly. I'm odd enough without the help of a pill.

Wendy's annoyed when I tell her I need to go, but Betty tells Wendy she should let me rest at home. In the car, Wendy yells at me about ruining her day and says we can't go to my grandfather's apartment. I pretend to fall asleep. At the house she pulls up and drops me off before she goes out again to grab a book from the library for a psychology class she's taking.

Wendy's started insisting that we lock the front door ever since she caught a kid from the neighborhood trying on her bras one day. I pull the key out from under the milk box and let myself in.

I call my grandfather to tell him we can't make it because I don't feel well. He sounds sad and tells me my Grandmother Ruth made a nice dinner for us. I apologize. He asks me if Wendy plans to come and visit without me.

"No, she decided not to come."

My grandfather is quiet at first. But I can tell by the way he's breathing that he's mad about it. He's sort of snorting into the phone. "Good. It's better this way," he suddenly says.

I'm shocked. It's been worse between my grandfather and Wendy lately. I noticed it got especially bad after his wedding to his new wife, Ruth, but he's never said anything unkind about her to me before. I think he must realize how he sounds because he says, "Never mind. We'll miss you, Chavalah."

I promise I'll visit him before I leave for camp. After I hang up I call Leigh to tell her about the arrival of my period and my trouble with the tampons.

"That's wicked pissa!" Leigh reserves this exclamation for the best news. She laughs and continues, "You have to use the junior-sized tampons though."

"No wonder," I say.

I laugh. I'm happy Leigh and I are friends again.

"I can't believe you got your period. You don't even have boobs yet. Mine are practically bigger than my sister's and I still don't have my period."

I had no idea boob size was supposed to correlate with the start of your period.

"Don't you remember the film they showed us after Christmas break?"

"Um, no. I don't remember much about last semester."

"Oh, right," Leigh says. "Sorry, I forgot . . ."

"No, it's all right. It's weird, I know. I still don't totally understand it myself."

"It's trauma," Leigh says matter-of-factly. "You suffered a major trauma and your brain compensated by giving your memory a rest for a while."

Leigh sounds like one of the articles Wendy reads in Psychology Today. I'm surprised to hear Leigh using psychology terms. She talks with the authority I hear adults use.

"Have you read Elizabeth Kübler-Ross?" I ask.

"Who?"

"Never mind. I can't believe she's making me go to camp next week. I wish I could stay here for the summer. "

"You're gonna have a great time," Leigh says gamely. "I asked my mom if I could go too, but she says we don't have enough money."

I know she's as sad as I am, but she's trying to make me feel better.

"Write and tell me how you're doing and I'll write back," she says.

Nineteen

Jules, 13 years | July, 1974

TWIRLING

I DO WRITE to her. I use the tiny boxes of Raisin Bran I eat for breakfast at camp every morning as stationary. I take the box apart and write on the inside, then I fold it back into a square, put masking tape over the sides, add a piece on top for an address label and a stamp on the corner, and mail it to her. I do this a few times a week. I wonder in the beginning if she's getting them, but then I start receiving her responses on her own cereal carton creations. This becomes our communication mode all summer. I send them to David at his camp too, but he never writes me back. I figure he's having fun.

Camp turns out to be a good thing for my nightmares. I don't dream a single one while I stay here.

My days are busy and I never have a moment to journal. I spend my time water skiing, boating, and canoeing in the cold lake. At the camp festival I win first place for archery, which I've never even tried before. We have arts and crafts activities every day, which is, of course, my favorite. Every mealtime we sing camp songs like "Black socks they never get dirty, the longer you wear them the stronger they get. Sometimes they long for the laundry but something inside you says, 'Don't send them yet.'" I even have a new camp name. We all give each other camp names. I'm called Dusty.

The best part of the summer is that I'm making new friends and I hardly ever see Smith. She hangs out with some other snotty girls who spend all day rehearsing a play we're going to be forced to watch at the end of camp.

The summer flies by. I thought I'd be able to read through the old, leather-bound Shakespeare canon I brought from our library, but I've only made it through a couple of comedies. I've been checking off days on a small calendar I brought and hung on the wall of the small cabin I share with my camp friends. In the beginning of the summer I checked off how many days until I *got* to go back to Withensea; now that it's the end of the summer, I check off how many days before I *have* to go.

———

When I get back to Withensea it's two weeks before the start of school. Leigh and I spend every day hanging out by the seawall at the high school. We're excited to start Withensea High, but feel nervous about being freshmen. Timothy Zand, the neighborhood guy she has a crush on, has started training with the football team, and Leigh's always trying to find reasons to hang around and talk to him. They started to get to know each other when I went to camp.

We decide to try out for the majorette squad. Leigh insists. It probably has something to do with the football games where we would be performing, and, of course, Timothy. Becoming a majorette isn't exactly something I've longed to do, but Leigh has her heart set on it and I know if she plans to spend every afternoon practicing with the majorette squad I should do it too, or I'll be totally bored.

We start practicing like mad with big silver batons we buy at the hardware store in Withensea. They're clunky and old-fashioned, but they're all we can find. I feel sure they'll pick Leigh. The way she swings her baton around seems professional. She's been practicing all summer. Even with a few of the easy moves she teaches me I'm still bad. I can't learn the knack of catching the baton on the throws. I've never been particularly athletic. I can run fast, but my hand/eye coordination rots. Also, the majorettes are the pretty, popular girls at school and Leigh will fit right in. The majorettes usually go on to become the Homecoming Court and Queen, then the Prom Court and Queen. There's a lot of dressing up and pretending to be royalty in high school. I think it seems dippy, but I don't tell Leigh. I figure if she wants to be part of it she must like that stuff. I pretend to like it too.

The tryouts are the first week of school. I ramp up my own practice to include a session every night in my backyard. I stay out there, sometimes in the near dark with the porch light on, and twirl my baton for hours.

There are multiple days of tryouts. On the first day we're all taught a choreographed dance routine that incorporates several different twirling patterns. All the ballet and dance classes I've taken as a kid make the choreographed dance part of the routines easier for me.

We have to learn all the new twirling patterns in few days. We carry our batons constantly, twirling every spare minute of the day. Over the next few days we meet in the gym to learn new routines and practice. I walk rather than ride the bus all week so I can twirl all the way to and from school. I twirl between classes and I twirl right up until I go to sleep every night. Even in bed.

On the day of the final tryouts Leigh and I walk to the gym. Leigh seems confident, but I feel nervous. Leigh studied gymnastics and dance and her baton skills are great. She goes first and performs perfectly. Even the majorette captain comments that she's given a great performance. The majorette captain leads the selection committee. Sometimes you can tell a lot about a girl based on what type of earrings she wears. The majorette captain wears big, white, plastic hoops. Definitely not trustworthy, I decide. But at least she was honest about Leigh's performance being good.

The committee includes the band teacher, who also teaches math, an English teacher, one of the gym teachers, the home economics instructor, and the school nurse. So altogether there are six of them including the majorette squad captain. I don't know any of the teachers well yet and want to make a good impression.

When it's my turn, I stand in front of all the teachers and wait for the music to play for my routine. The next thing I know, I'm sitting on the bleachers next to Leigh and the other girls.

I don't remember my routine. I don't remember sitting down. It's freaking me out. I'm having the memory loss thing again and I thought I was done with it.

"I think I'm in trauma mode," I whisper to Leigh. "I don't remember doing my routine."

"I got scared too," she says. "It happens when you're scared. You did great!"

I'm not convinced about memory loss being related to fear, and I'm not convinced I did great.

I force a smile. "You were amazing!" I say.

Leigh and I are both chosen, which feels like skyrockets.

Afterwards, we walk along the seawall by the high school.

"I'm glad we got picked," Leigh confesses. "I worried one of us might not and we'd never see each other because of practice and the games and all that."

"Yeah, I know what you mean. I didn't think I'd be picked either."

Leigh laughs. "No, that's not what I meant. I don't think they picked based on our twirling abilities. I think they want to give certain girls a chance to belong to a club. Like a step-up or something."

I nod, not understanding what she means.

She sees that I don't get it. "I think they're trying to end the popularity contest it's been and turn it into more of an equal opportunity for everyone," she explains.

I think about what she said. They told us at the beginning of tryouts that there were three slots open for the majorette squad. There were already two seniors, two juniors, and one sophomore on the squad. This left three extra spaces to complete an eight-person squad. They picked four of us. This means the squad is now an uneven nine.

"Do you think they picked me because of Moses or something?"

Something about Leigh's lack of immediate reassurance tells me I may be right, but she says, "No, I think they picked Leslie Simon because they felt badly for her because of the acne. I think they picked Gracia Cassivetes because she's shy. This will be a good thing for both of them, socially. I think they picked you because you performed the dance moves well. You did a good job."

Then Leigh says, "You were the best, you know that? You caught all your throws and you were the best dancer that tried out."

Although I don't remember, I'm sure I haven't done particularly well. I feel relieved it's over, but I'm sure my spins weren't as fast or practiced as the other girls'.

"You were absolutely perfect," Leigh insists.

"Why, thank you, ma'am," I say.

She beams at me and even though I know I wasn't really perfect, I smile back.

———

It's clear that Withensea High will be tougher than middle school was. I'll have to try harder in class and find a way to do more homework in my room rather than on the school bus. I've been placed in advanced classes, which will mean having to study for tests instead of doing quick memorizations of material before class.

Between this summer at summer camp, becoming a majorette, and settling into high school, this is the first time in my life I've felt like a normal kid. David's presence, as a senior, has helped pave the way for me academically, too. He's a great student and his teachers adore him. Sometimes I feel like I make better grades because the teachers we share like him so much.

David's on the football, basketball, and tennis teams, so he knows lots of kids at school and has also always been popular. It's like he has a separate personality with us from the one he has at school. But I suppose I do too. Now, though, we've become friends. The majorettes perform at all the football games he plays in and at school rallies. We often show up at the same school parties. He ushers me out when it gets rowdy. I think he's enjoying being the "big brother." The only thing we still don't talk about much is Moses. I've tried bringing it up. He just changes the subject or says, "Drugs kill kids!" or "Call Freddy."

High school is making me wish I had a big sister, however, to help me navigate the social scene. I've been too worried about Wendy's potential for arrest to bother about things like popularity and pity votes in the past, but now I see these are the things girls my age are supposed to worry about. I become afraid if I don't start I might end up isolated and alone.

Wendy continues to divide her time between school classes and partying. The partying intensifies when Jack returns from Big Sur.

Mostly, I fear losing Leigh's friendship. She is my only anchor.

Twenty

Jules, 16 years | September 19th, 1977

HIGH

I RUN-WALK to the bus stop because I woke up late as usual and I'll miss my bus unless I hoof it up the hill. It doesn't matter how early I'm up or how much I try to prepare in the morning, I often run late. It's my junior year in high school and time is still a puzzle for me. It goes by excruciatingly slow sometimes and other times slides by as though I'm in a time warp. I don't experience the amnesiac episodes I did years ago anymore, but I still have trouble keeping track of time. My internal clock has a dead battery.

I awoke this morning after having the nightmare. Today is the anniversary of Moses's death.

Because one of Wendy's Psychology Today articles suggested it, I decided to try behavior modification for my nightmares. Behavior modification appeals to me because it advocates personal responsibility. When I wake up from a nightmare, instead of lying in the dark with dread, I switch on the light and start reading. I keep encyclopedia volumes by my bed and use them to sedate me so I can fall back asleep again, which I usually do.

Last night, however, I didn't fall back asleep for a long time. Not even reading my encyclopedia article. I have no idea what I read. I woke up with the light on, the book on my chest, and an indentation on my chin where the book corner had dug in.

My first thought was about David. I wanted to call him. He's now in his second year of college at the School of Business at University of Massachusetts at

Amherst, which everybody calls Zoo Mass. This was my grandfather's request, but David enjoys his classes.

My clock read 7:50 when I finally rolled out of bed. I figured he was still sleeping. I didn't call.

I wondered if the date registers with him. We never discuss it. I wanted to ask him this or call to tell him I love and miss him. I decided to call later and raced to dress and catch the bus.

On my way to the bus stop, I pass the raised ranch homes built along the border of the land Howard sold to the developers. Timothy lives here. I think about the first day I heard about him, the day I left my schoolbooks up at the elementary school and he returned them to my porch.

Leigh was in love with Timothy for a while, and she made sure we met him. "Timothy is a boy with secrets," she used to say repeatedly and cryptically.

After a while, she lost her romantic interest in Timothy and found another crush, but they stayed friends. Now we all hang out nearly every day. Leigh and Timothy are both science nerds and while I don't always understand the stuff they talk about, it's always interesting.

Timothy calls to me as I run by his house.

"Hey, Jules, stop. The bus already went by. Walk with me."

I stop and turn around. I'm surprised to see him because he normally walks to school and leaves a half-hour earlier. I never walk because it means giving up a half-hour of sleep, and I don't like the trade.

"Did it just go by?"

"It came five minutes early. I'm late because Crikey ran out when I left before." Crikey is Timothy's German Shepherd.

Timothy almost always smiles a great, big, lopsided smile that turns the corner of the left side of his mouth up and crinkles his left eye shut. He doesn't seem bothered by much. He's the most peaceful person I've met and I'm a bit in awe of him. I know not everything in his world is good. His mother died when he was seven. He and his older brother are taken care of by his father, a Harvard professor who teaches neuroscience, and his grandmother. He rarely talks about his mother and then usually only within the context of a family story.

We walk along Withensea Avenue. The avenue is lined with oak and maple trees. Beyond them sits the Boston ferry landing pier with its tiny parking lot, a high seawall, and a few small, tied-up harbor boats.

I'm thinking what a perfect fall day it is. The crisp air smells like wet grass and turned soil. The sun shines and it makes the maple leaves glimmer in their colors, deep rich velvet reds, vibrant beach ball oranges, and squash blossom yellows.

I pull a leaf off and study it while Timothy and I chat and walk.

"Look at this leaf. There are cities in this leaf."

"What?" Timothy laughs. He stops and examines the leaf closely to see what I'm talking about. I love this about him. He jumps into my world with me.

"Yup . . . looks like Chicago."

Ms. Wheaton, who now teaches at the high school, pulls up to us in her car. It's a tomato red Eldorado. She rolls down her window.

"Hey you two, get in. Jules, I've got something to tell you." We jump in, Timothy in back, me in front.

"What is it?" I ask.

She's smiling as wide as piano keys, and I'm smiling now even though I have no idea why.

"You got accepted into the Boston Museum of Fine Arts student exhibition."

"What? H-how?" I stammer.

"Well, remember I told you last spring they had a student exhibition every winter? I asked you if you would be interested and you said you would, so I submitted for you. I'm your sponsor. They sent me the letter yesterday. Here." She hands me a thick envelope.

I open the envelope, which holds a packet of letters. "What? You did? What did you submit?"

"I sent the one of the boy with the eyes."

I can't remember the project she's talking about, but I don't care. I read my acceptance letter, which includes information about the art jury and the competition at the exhibition.

"It's unfair they judge you and you compete based on your artwork. I mean, it's so subjective," I say. Ms. Wheaton and Timothy laugh.

Timothy says, "Spoken like a true artist. Hey, congratulations."

"Don't forget to sign the contract and mail it back. It gives them permission to display the artwork."

Ms. Wheaton takes the Eldorado out of park with a grinding noise and continues driving toward the high school as I stare at the contract, the next set of papers in the envelope. I know I should be excited but I'm numb. I've never won anything before. Until this moment I believed Ms. Wheaton encouraged me to give me an emotional boost because she felt sorry for me. I don't really know if my work is any good or not.

This, a professional notice, is what I've yearned for. I love drawing and painting and sculpture and doing all kinds of art, and even though I dream about a career in art I've never thought I might actually achieve that dream.

"I won't forget," I say as Timothy and I step out of the Eldorado.

Sitting in homeroom about fifteen minutes later, I finally feel excited. I feel like I won a million dollars.

This is the part where I get accepted by an art show.

The principal comes on over the loudspeaker with the morning announcements.

I'm not paying attention until I hear my name and the announcement that I've won a spot at the museum exhibition. The principal finishes this announcement by saying how proud we should all be for this achievement. I'm completely embarrassed. I can't believe Ms. Wheaton would share this—but maybe she thought it was the right, *teacherly* thing to do. I'm sitting in the front seat of my row. When the principal finishes I nod my head and say, "I paid him to say that." Luckily, a bunch of kids laugh and the bell rings. I slink out after homeroom and on my way to class I pop my head into the art room, where Ms. Wheaton sits.

"I might have to kill you," I say, leaning in.

She laughs and shakes her head. "You're a nice person. You won't kill me. You should feel proud of yourself. You're talented."

My insides feel tingly. Everybody is smiling at me in the halls, though it isn't until I go into the girl's restroom, and see my reflection in the mirror over the long sink that I realize I'm smiling too. When I go into the bathroom stall someone whispers, "That's the girl who won the art contest."

I can't remember feeling this happy—ever.

It's September 19th and a pretty good day after all.

This isn't the first time major events have fallen on the same day in my life. My head injury on the playground and Wendy's motorcycle accident happened on the same day. Howard's father died on my birthday two years ago.

I figure the older you are the more this stuff happens. Soon your life is filled with experiences that are bound to fall on days with other major life events.

This is also the day where the gossip about me, behind bathroom stalls, can become about *the girl who won the art contest* rather than *the girl whose brother drowned.*

— —

The bad part of the year comes in December when our cat, Felix, gets run over by a car in our driveway. Jack's friend, some druggie, was pulling into our driveway too fast. Felix loved to lie in the middle of the asphalt, where the snow would melt away first, in the sun. We were all used to pulling in slow to warn her. She didn't have a chance to run. She died right away. When David came back from college for the holidays he hung a sign on the refrigerator that says DRUGS KILL CATS.

No one's taken it down so I guess Wendy and Jack agree.

I win first place in my age group at the exhibition in January. It's astounding to me still that I got chosen at all. Winning an art award feels unreal and overwhelming. Dessert after dessert!

My grandfather, Grandmother Ruth, and her daughter Bethyl arrive early and congratulate me when they see the ribbon. Wendy and Jack show up and behave themselves for once. Leigh and Timothy stand by me all evening. It's definitely the best moment in my life so far.

Ms. Wheaton introduces me to a woman she calls "her partner." I don't understand it then, but later when Leigh and Timothy and I scarf *real* desserts at Brighams, Leigh says, matter-of-factly, "Ms. Wheaton is a lesbian."

Then she takes another bite of her Chocolate Mocha ice-cream.

I am practically inhaling my Butter Crunch sundae, but I put down my spoon and stare at her. Timothy keeps eating his sundae.

"So?" he says through a full mouth of Pistachio.

"Huh," I say, but I'm thinking a million things.

Ms. Wheaton is now much more interesting. The only lesbians I have knowingly met are friends of Wendy's who go to college at Northeastern with her. They live near Leigh.

I know they're brave to live in Withensea and be open about their lives. Withensea is small-town-minded and scary because of this sometimes. I like them a lot, but they make me nervous because being a lesbian, or even being a friend of a lesbian, is totally uncool in Withensea. Here, everybody acts uptight about everything. Being different in any way makes other people nervous. It's basically a rubber stamp for social failure.

As far as our own difference, David and I have managed to create a bubble of homogenous existence at school and with our friends although life at the house continues to challenge the boundaries of normalcy. Since David went away to college I feel compelled to try extra hard to blend in with my peers and identify myself independently from my family. I still feel nervous about Social Services showing up, even though Wendy no longer uses this threat to her advantage.

Leigh says, "I think it's pretty fab."

Timothy and I finish our ice cream and say nothing else.

Twenty-one

IT'S BEEN A long time and yet each year, on this day more than others, the sorrow of loss strikes my heart in its deepest chamber.

The clock that sits on the nightstand tells me the date and the time. This is the clock that Yetta traded for her grocery stamps at the A&P. Ruth would prefer we buy another, more modern one. But I can't bear to part with the things I shared with Yetta in my first marriage. Ruth understands.

In the year of Moses's death, this woman, Ruth, became my wife. She is the woman I finally find my passion with. She is my *bashert*. It seems strange, people don't talk about such things, I know—things like old men finding passion—but it is my truth.

Ruth kindles something ancient in me. Fire. The fire that grows out of embers buried under trampled ash. Fire that grows big but doesn't swallow all the air. Splendid, multicolored fire that is strong but doesn't destroy. Fire that doesn't smell like flesh or bones but like fine wood and earth and flowers.

It breathes, this fire. It extinguished the worst of the anguish I felt after the loss of my sweet grandson.

Ruth and her daughter, Bethyl, came back to sit *shiva* with me after Moses's funeral.

They prepared the meal of condolence. The rabbi and other men from the congregation visited every day to make a *minyan* and sing the blessing for Moses while Ruth and Bethyl prepared our meals, cleaned the apartment, and sat on my living room couch while I sat on the low stool.

Over the course of those seven days of mourning, sitting in my apartment with shrouded mirrors, Ruth reflected all the history of my life, and out of the history I found small miracles. In astonishment, I understood that all those small miracles had led me to my small apartment, sitting in a room with shrouded mirrors with my true mirror, Ruth.

After I had shared my stories of my young grandson we began to share our own stories with one another. We waited for Bethyl's absence to talk of other things. Those things were the horrors we had witnessed and withstood. The memories that survivors can only share with other survivors. The things we keep behind our eyes like lidded vaults.

There were things I shared in those seven days that unburdened my soul simply because of Ruth's finely tuned acceptance. Her unblinking eyes released my fears. Her tears released my own. Her touch made my skin—like a dried old leaf—crumble. Underneath, there were bright new limbs that grew stronger with each embrace.

There were things I learned in those seven days of *shiva* that changed my life forever.

Ruth taught me how to take my guilt and move it into a space where it has no power over my own survival. I hadn't realized how much the pain of surviving the people I loved had shaped every interaction I'd had with every person I knew.

Ruth was on the same train I am put on after being arrested as a conspirator for the Polish Home Army, the resistance movement during the war. She told me she had watched the murder of her family—her precious mother and father, her two brothers, and her younger sister. She never volunteered details regarding their deaths at the hands of the Nazis. I never shared the details about my own family's violent tragedy. We shared that particular sorrow, but it was also our own.

After being transported to the camp at Majdanek, Ruth—then Rinna—was selected to become a servant for the camp commandant. He lived outside the camp, in the town of Lublin. She was pulled from a line of women at the camp within an hour of her arrival. This line, she later learned, had led directly to the gas chamber, as they were murdering Jews immediately after they came inside the camps in those last months.

This death camp, Majdanek, is different from the other Nazi death camps. The others were hidden in forests or in places where there were no witnesses. Majdanek is in plain sight of the city of Lublin. The camp is separated from the city by just a farm field. The smokestacks with the acrid, sour smell of burning flesh were clearly visible from the nearby homes. The entire city of Lublin witnessed the crimes at Majdanek.

Ruth shared her horror at looking from the windows of the officer's home to see the billowing gray smokestacks of human ash and at hearing the machine guns in those final days, murdering the last of the Jews.

She said this man and his wife were kind to her. I find this hard to believe, that a monster would have compassion for a Polish Jew, but she insists they treated her well. She said they kept her safe even as they packed and fled the city before the liberation of the camp. The officer told her to stay on in the home, a home that had formerly belonged to a Polish Jew who was killed at the camp. The officer and his wife never returned, of course. Later he was tried and executed like the rest of the criminals they caught.

Eventually Ruth married a man, another Polish Jew who had been a part of the Polish Home Army, the resistance. He had returned to Lublin after the war. It was this man, her husband, who convinced her to move to Boston, where his brothers had come before him.

The man, Bethyl's father, had died young in a factory accident, leaving Ruth to raise her daughter alone.

Ruth and her daughter were active in their synagogue, more orthodox in its practice than our current synagogue. They left that congregation as a result of its old traditions and ideas and joined ours mere months before we met again.

Our rabbi encouraged Bethyl when she shared her wish to study theology and someday become a rabbi herself. He agreed with her that it is simply custom and not law that stood between her and her goals. Now she is a *cantor* for the congregation, and while she loves her work she is also studying and organizing other women to petition the Jewish Theological Seminary in New York to admit female students. Bethyl is the daughter who will make me proud.

Wendy, in comparison, has only become more of a disappointment. Now her behavior seems intolerable, although nothing has changed. My open heart has opened my eyes to my own daughter's cruelty.

Soon after Moses's funeral, Ruth and I made plans to marry. We waited a year until after our synagogue's *Yahrzeit* observance of Moses's death to have our celebration. But then we did celebrate.

Ruth made a small wedding with her first husband and my own, with Yetta, was remarkably simple, although Rose campaigned for a more elaborate affair. This time, we agreed, it was time for a proper wedding ceremony. My one regret was the absence of my closest family members. Rose, Mocher, Oizer, my parents—all were gone. The other surviving members of the family, Oizer's children and my youngest siblings, who came to America with *Foter* and *Mater* so long ago, have families of their own now, children whom I have never met.

It was best not to invite them. Too much bad memories for everyone.

Wendy and the children, David and Jules, were included, of course, although I worry about Wendy and her behavior towards Ruth and Bethyl. Something about my new happiness seems to make her angry and she makes every interaction a battle. In the beginning I believed the sorrow of Moses's death caused her to resent my joy. As time goes on, I see that it is Wendy's manner to destroy what is good in the world and perceive it as her enemy.

The wedding reception took place in the synagogue basement, which is lavishly decorated for the occasion. Wendy dressed like a meshugener in something fit for maybe a circus. Her nebish boyfriend drank too much wine and had to be put to bed, like a child, in the car outside the synagogue. Wendy and I loaded him in through the side door of her van like a potato sack after he fell from the chair he sat on in the reception hall.

"You obviously spent a lot of money on a wedding to this woman. How did she talk you into that?" Wendy says as she catches her breath with me on the parking lot sidewalk.

"Ruth is a wonderful woman and I wanted to please her with a good wedding. This is a nice way to start a marriage, no?"

"It's not like you to spend money on anything, never mind a frivolous thing like a party. I'm starting to worry about you . . . about this woman, and her control over your finances. Will she be writing my checks now?"

"After all this time I take such good care of you and the children and the *nebish* here, and your good-for-nothing husband before him, now you complain I spend a little money on myself to make a good wedding?"

"I'm just saying—"

"You're worried that you won't be inheriting all the money when I die, that I spent too much on the wedding, no? Maybe you counted on a better inheritance and now that there's another woman, another family I care for, you think there will be less for you?"

A light drizzle of rain has begun and the hot asphalt gives off steam that rises like a hot shower. The rain mingles with the dirty street. This smell always reminds me of Paris, where it seemed to rain constantly. Wendy's voice draws me back to the moment.

"You say *family*. You're not supporting her daughter as well, are you?"

"And what if I am? It's my money to do with as I wish. Bethyl is a good girl.

I will take care of her as long as she likes. She's a scholar. She wants to be a rabbi. Imagine that, a female rabbi?"

"She's highly unattractive, nearly as old as I am, and I don't see a guy around. It's good you don't mind taking care of her; you'll be doing it for the rest of her life. Speaking of taking care of, the dishwasher broke. I need a couple hundred to replace it."

I am wondering how long it would take for her to bring up something she needed me to pay for.

"Yes. Why don't you bring Jules and David for dinner sometime this week and I can settle it then." I don't argue that washing the dishes without the machine won't kill her. It's not like she doesn't have time for these things. Today I will let her think I believe she really needs this machine to wash the dishes.

———

On that day, five years ago, I am mostly joyous. Wendy and the *nebish* were there making fools of themselves, of course. But the one true dark spot that day was my deep worry for my granddaughter. For you, Jules. Do you have a memory for that day? I wonder.

We stood at the buffet table. The table held an enormous selection of foods. Steaming roast chicken with aromatic spiced carrots. Ruth had insisted we offer fish with the meat and we also had fresh lox, bagels, whitefish, and capers. There is Ruth's homemade noodle *kugel*, the cinnamon smells mingled with the fresh challah from our favorite bakery. The same bakery had supplied our grand wedding cake and the sugary *rugelach*, *halva*, and specially ordered *hamantashen* pastries. My mouth watered at the luscious smells and succulent sights.

Noticing you didn't have a plate in your hands, I passed one to you. You hadn't seen me beside you, even as I called your name, and you startled when the dish appeared in front of you. You turned your eyes to me. It is then that I notice the pain. I saw the familiar torment in you, that same shadow I carried for many years.

———

"You'd better eat something, Chavalah. You're so little I think you might blow away in a big wind."

"I'm not hungry."

I am thinking of a time when food had no taste for me.

"Sometimes it is good to eat even when our minds don't remind us to do it. Look at all this good food. Surely those desserts tempt you?" I lean in closer to her ear. "I won't tell your mother if you eat only desserts today."

"Edgar Allen Poe said 'death is but a painful metamorphosis and our present incarnation is temporary.' Do you believe that?"

The answer I want to give is not an answer for an eleven-year-old child. My true answer will have to wait. And so I kneel and say, "In the afterlife there is no *hamentash* or *noodle kugel*, so I think while we are temporarily here, we should avoid this painful death and eat to stay healthy."

———

I waited for a smile that did not come. Instead, a solemn nod and a half-hearted placement of a single *rugelach* on your plate. My heart, which had only recently been replaced, burst with pain at your suffering. After this day, your happiness became the thing I prayed for at *shul*.

Every prayer from my lips is this prayer, until this day, September 19th, 1977. This is the day my prayer is answered. I receive a phone call from you, late in the day, after school.

———

"It's in January at the Boston Museum of Fine Arts. A student exhibition. I found out today. I had to sign a real artist contract and everything! I hope you and Ruth and Bethyl can come."

"This is extraordinary, Chavalah. Congratulations. We will come to the Boston Museum to see the dedicated artist's creation. We will celebrate with a fine dinner in your honor."

———

The pure elation in your little voice erased my worries. I heard the sound of a happy young girl. This is a new sound that I will cherish. This is the sound of a young girl without a shadow.

Twenty-two

HELLO AND GOOD-BYE

THIS YEAR HAS become my favorite year in high school and not because of the museum exhibition.

Leigh and Timothy and I have become great friends. Somehow the balance of Timothy in our lives creates a perfect triad of fun. Last fall we started sneaking out in the middle of the night to ride our bikes. I climb down the trellis from the widow's walk. I could probably go out the front unnoticed, but I do it to avoid the horror of potentially waking Wendy. She becomes a witch when we wake her up, and it embarrasses me when she screams in front of my friends.

I think I also do it to be like Leigh and Timothy. They have to sneak out at night. Timothy sneaks out through his back sliding door. Leigh escapes by tiptoe-ing down her creaky stairs.

David and I have never had a curfew. Wendy brags to her friends that she never has to make curfews because the kids we hang out with have parents who do, and who are we going to hang out with when they go home?

My classmates voted me Class Secretary in this, my junior year, because Leigh wrote me a funny, sarcastic speech to read that talked about all the ridiculous things I would do if I won. It had nothing to do with anything because being a class officer has nothing to do with anything. Leigh wrote it as a big joke. I read it like it was a joke, and the class voted me in like it was a joke, I'm sure. Still, I feel surprised. I've never been one of the popular kids in my class. I keep to myself. I don't like attention, and when it I get it, besides making me feel embarrassed, it scares me, because I worry it might bring attention to Wendy and Jack and the illegal activities going on and that we could get busted or something worse.

I feel like a social misfit, because other than Leigh and Timothy I don't understand most of the kids in my school. The things they talk about, sports and TV for instance, don't interest me.

I also don't understand high school humor—dunking kids in toilets, throwing them in lockers, pinning things to the back of their shirts, making up nasty nicknames—it all seems ridiculous to me. I'm often the target of a joke I don't understand right away, and when I get it, if I get it, it never seems funny to me.

I spend more time trying to figure out what someone has *really* meant, or why they've *really* said it, than is ever necessary. Leigh constantly tells me I "think too much." I can't control it. Anyway, student government is wicked pissa because I'm allowed to skip math class once a month for meetings. We never work on anything at the meetings except making decisions about the prom.

We decided the junior and senior class will celebrate their proms together this year. Since I have absolutely no interest in the prom and don't plan to go, it doesn't interest me to sit and listen to my classmates debate the life-changing matters of prom themes and decorations.

Timothy got voted Senior Class Vice President, so he attends the meetings with me. He brings powdered donuts from the bakery table in the cafeteria and I bring chocolate milk cartons I swipe from the lunch counter. We sit in the back row of the classroom during the meetings and shoot the shit about our days.

Today we've already scarfed the donuts and the chocolate milk.

—

"Are you even gonna go to this thing?" Timothy asks me.

"Prom? I . . . don't . . . I don't know."

I don't have a date and I don't want to be a third wheel with Leigh and her Boy-Du-Jour. I'm certain the guy she currently calls her boyfriend isn't the guy she'll be dating in May. She goes through boys like socks.

"Are you?"

He smiles. "If you're my date."

I'm shocked and—curiously—embarrassed. Timothy never suggested anything remotely resembling a date before. I've never even considered the possibility of something more than a friendship with him. My face burns, I'm starting to sweat, and I'm sure I'm a deep shade of scarlet. He kindly glances away and softly says, "We could go hang out like we're going to any dance. I didn't mean to suggest anything . . . I mean . . . Jules, it doesn't have to be . . ."

He's fumbling, and I realize I've misread an invitation he meant to be light-hearted and now he's trying not to offend me. "Oh, totally. That sounds perfect."

Timothy picks up my tone and says, "Yeah it would be lots of fun."

Now he's serious again. "But if there's a better offer, you have to promise me you'll tell me. I don't want you feel like you can't renege on this."

I'm laughing now. "Timothy . . . I'm practically socially retarded. No one is going to ask me and I'm not interested enough in anyone to ask them. But the same goes for you."

I lift my eyebrow at him and he's laughing now.

"Deal," he says.

We're quiet, thinking our own thoughts and pretending to listen to our classmates debating how to raise money for the night.

After the meeting ends I walk back to our neighborhood with him. Leigh joins us until her turnoff. Being with the two of them, I realize how lucky I am to have them in my life. I feel a sense of happiness and *collectedness.*

"I love you guys."

Leigh hugs me and says, "I love you too, Jules."

Timothy and I say good-bye to Leigh and start to walk away. Leigh calls to us, "Hey, did they come up with a prom theme yet?"

"No," I say, and I realize we haven't told her. "But Timothy and I decided we're going."

Leigh doesn't respond at first.

"You mean together?"

"Yeah," I say. I'm smiling like, *Isn't it funny?*

She nods and turns away. She calls over her shoulder, "Talk to you later, you guys."

Timothy and I wait there for a second, then turn to walk up the hill to our neighborhood. "Is it me," he says, "or did that seem to shake her up a bit?"

"I think, well, maybe she's . . . wondering what we meant. I mean, I felt surprised and confused at first, maybe she's feeling . . . you know, the same."

I'm lost and wondering if maybe Leigh still has a crush on Timothy and I missed it. I don't want to say any of this to him, though, because if it's true I don't want to betray Leigh's feelings.

I have the idea he might like teasing Leigh a bit. They dated for a minute when Leigh and I were freshmen and he was a sophomore, but it fizzled. Leigh said it burned out because she wasn't attracted to him after all. Timothy never talked about it. I wonder what happened, but I never want to butt in and be nosy about it.

"Do you want to go to prom for real?" I ask.

"Yeah. Do you?"

"Yeah. I guess . . . yeah. It's just that I didn't see myself going and I talked myself out of it, you know?"

I wonder if he regrets his decision to ask me.

"Let's go and see what it's like," he says. "I wanna be able to say I went and enjoyed it. Or if I don't . . . I can move on."

"Hey, that's me you're including in your good time or you're moving on," I protest.

"I didn't mean it like that." He chuckles.

I laugh back. We say good-bye at his house and I walk on around the corner.

I'm surprised to see Wendy's car in the driveway. She rarely comes back to the house during the day. She's been taking a full semester of classes at Northeastern to finish her degree and usually goes to her friends' houses after class. She decided to focus on psychology. It makes sense, since she's nuts, that she wants to immerse herself in crazy.

Jack's been gone for about a month, sailing someone's boat around the Panama Canal to California. When I walk in I find her sitting on the couch reading *The Feminine Mystique* by Betty Friedan, which I know is old because I took it off our shelves when I was little and read it.

"Did you have majorette practice?"

"Um, no . . . I haven't had a practice since Homecoming—you know, last November? There are no more football games until next September. We'll march with the band for the Memorial Day parade, but that's it for the year. You don't pay attention to anything in my life, do you?"

I know I'm being a bit dramatic about it, but she never fails to totally push my buttons when she reveals how little she cares about me. My good mood is sinking, as it usually does when I'm dealing with Wendy.

She shuts her book with a snap. "Don't be rude. I'm trying to talk to you and find out what's going on with you."

"Why?" I challenge. "What do you want?" I'm suspicious now.

Wendy pats the spot on the couch next to her. "Sit with me."

I hesitate and sit in the white, fur-upholstered, double chaise.

"Talk," I say roughly.

I'm not sure when I started talking to Wendy like this, but it's become our normal pattern of communication. I never give an inch with her. Of course, she never gives an inch with me, either. We've just fallen into this awful pattern of bitchiness with each other.

"Tell me what's going on in your world. I want to know. I want to know what you're studying in class, what kind of artwork you're doing now, if you have a boyfriend?"

At this question, a burst of air escapes from my mouth in an annoyed "Pfffftt."

"No boyfriend? Do you like anyone?"

"Why the sudden interest? Is this a therapeutic practice theory you're testing out on me?"

It's weird that she's asking this question today of all days, but I'm sure it's co-incidence. For the past few months, she's been trying to slide psychology weirdness into our interactions. One day she'll tell me my behavior displays an "adolescent Electra complex" and the next day she'll tell me I was "self-actualized" at the age of eight.

"You never share anything going on in your life with me. I have no idea what you're thinking or how you're doing," Wendy says as her volume rises.

"Do you care?"

"What do you mean, do I care?" she practically screams.

I stand to leave then turn to face her. "I can't talk to you. All you do is yell. If you cared about me, you'd pay attention to me and my life. You'd have a clue what I've been doing—like I haven't been carrying around a baton, so how could I be at majorette practice? All you do is party, get high, and slide in around here once in a while. I cook my own meals. I keep the house clean. I do all the laundry and the dishes. I take out the garbage and I shovel the snow. What do you do around here besides sleep, read books, and polish your nails?"

Wendy sits on the couch saying nothing. I turn to go upstairs.

"I don't do drugs."

I turn back to her.

"You don't do drugs?" I repeat incredulously.

"No. I don't do drugs and I don't want you to tell other people I do. And . . . if I'm such a good-for-nothing mother, then you won't miss me if I go away for a while."

Ah, this is what it's all about.

"I leave on Monday for the Virgin Islands. I'm going to meet Jack and sail with him for a while."

"What do you mean 'a while'?"

"What do you mean, what do I mean? You just said you take care of every-thing around here, and you obviously don't need me. So I'm going away for *a while*. You'll be fine," she says matter-of-factly.

"You're right," I say and turn quickly to walk up the stairs. Although it infuri-ates me, I burst into tears when I'm inside my room.

How typical. She wants to cozy up so she can go on a vacation with Jack and not feel guilty about taking off.

I hate that I still want her to express genuine interest in my life after all that she's done to hurt me.

I decide to avoid her until after she leaves. The sole thing I have to work out is how I will cash the checks my grandfather sends every month for living expenses. I figure I can write checks off her account to send for bills, I've done that many times, but I don't know how I'll use checks to shop for food and things I need. I don't have my own bank account.

Also, I don't have my car license yet, although I've been driving with and without her permission for a few years. It started a few years ago during a snowstorm when she got stuck in Boston and David and I ran out of milk. I got David to swear he wouldn't tell Wendy if I drove the car to the market down Withensea Avenue. Afterwards, he did the same, on occasion, when he needed to.

But I don't want to take the chance of being arrested without a license if Wendy is going to be gone for a long time. So I need to ask her to stock up the cabinets with canned foods and fill the freezer with frozen stuff before she leaves.

I write a letter with instructions for her and leave it on the kitchen table when I go to school in the morning. In the afternoon, when I'm back from school, the cabinets and the fridge are absolutely stuffed with food.

This is the fastest response to a food request I've ever gotten from Wendy. This evening, when she comes back, I find out why.

"There's supposed to be a storm coming in a few days. I'm flying out tomorrow so I'm not stuck here," Wendy says as I walk by her bedroom.

"Tomorrow? Fine. Have a good time. Thanks for the groceries."

"You're welcome," is all she says. She flicks on the TV and starts watching a show called *Dallas*. She becomes transfixed whenever it comes on. In my room I start a school report due on Monday.

I study more at the house lately because without Jack and the constant party there are actually more nights that it stays quiet and I can focus. The truth is, even though I yelled at Wendy about the parties and stuff, it's been fairly normal around here lately. Wendy still smokes dope on a regular basis, but she's slowed down on the drinking. I'm glad for this, but I'm not convinced it won't change back to the way it's been before. I hate Wendy. I hate the way she treats me. I hate the way she treated David before he left for college. I hate that she was such a rotten mother when Moses was alive, and even though she didn't do anything directly to cause his death, I'm angry at her for leaving me in charge of him all the time.

I've been studying for about two hours when Wendy knocks.

"What?"

"Can I come in?" she asks.

"Yeah."

"You won't be up when I leave in the morning. I want to say goodnight and good-bye for a while."

I realize I don't know how long she plans to be gone. I assume it will be a few weeks, but now I'm curious. "How long are you going for?"

"At least a month, maybe longer."

A month? At most she's left for a couple of weeks in the past. All at once I'm shocked, angry, resigned, rejected—and, in the midst of this, almost giddy with a sense of adventure. I have no idea what will happen if I don't have to worry about her and Jack. I know I'll be able to do exactly what I want, when I want, but I've had this freedom for years. Still, this will be different; thirty days (or more) of previews of coming attractions for my solitary adult life. In a month, I can construct a new life.

"Give me a hug?" She steps toward me and awkwardly opens her arms.

"You're kidding me, right?" I don't move. We never hug.

"Give me a hug?" she says more insistently.

"I'm not going to hug you. I'm pissed at you. It sucks you're leaving me alone here." I say this not fully believing it, but I want to punish her anyway.

"Fine," Wendy says. "You'll be fine, and I'll call and check in with you from time to time to see how you're doing."

She walks through the doorway and I call out, "Shut it, please."

She turns around and smiles. "Okay, I'm shutting the door."

She opens it again.

"By the way, I'm taking the car into Boston and Dorothy's gonna give me a ride to the airport. I got the food, and I'm leaving you a hundred dollars. You can take the bus if you need to go somewhere. It's not legal for you to drive without a license."

"You do lots of illegal things," I shoot back.

"And you can do them too, when you're old enough to make those choices," she says.

I think she feels as happy to be leaving me as I am to see her go.

Twenty-three

Jules, 16 years | February, 1978

THE BLIZZARD OF '78

WHEN I WAKE up Wendy is gone.

The fog hangs thick and wafts up from the ocean as I make my way around the corner to Timothy's. My nostrils fill with brine, the scent sticks to the insides of my nose. The fog rolls off the ocean quickly and the weather has grown colder than it's been in a while. I wonder if the storm will come in more quickly than Wendy thought.

By the end of the day, long after I've come home and Wendy's plane has left, the rain starts. It rains off and on all night as the temperature continues to fall.

In the morning it's still raining. Leigh and Timothy and I decide to cancel our plans to meet at my house—we'll wait until after the storm. We're excited that we're going to have a parentless place at our disposal for an entire month.

I spend the day in a blissful daze, drawing. I realize it's the first time I've done an art project in the house since Moses drowned.

———

It was still raining this morning when I was on my way to the bus stop, but now the rain has turned to snow. When the buses come early to pick us up from school, everybody buzzes with the news that a major storm is howling toward us. School will probably be cancelled tomorrow, and we'll have a snow day.

I feel elated. I usually hate snow days because they mean long days stuck with Wendy, who inevitably grows irritated and screamy. But now I have time to myself, and I feel like celebrating.

By the time the bus drops us off, Timothy and I are so excited we practically blow down the road. When he says good-bye and heads in the direction of his place, he tells me he'll call me that night to check on me. As I turn the corner and change my direction, straight into the wind, I'm hit full force with the power of the storm. I swing my body forward into it, but I'm still blown back. My face stings with the sleety snow. I didn't bother with a scarf this morning, so I'm especially glad for my warm hat and gloves. I curse my hastiness as my face becomes an icy mask.

The snow has already begun to pile up along the road, and the sky has grown so clotted with it I can't see the ocean over the cliff. I can barely see ten feet in front of me. I walk in the middle of Alethea Road until I hear a car approaching from behind me. As I move to the side, the car pulls up next to me and Mrs. O'Connell rolls her car window down. "Would ya be wantin' a ride?"

"Oh, no thanks, I'm almost there now."

"Jump in anyway, dearie. Ya don't want to be walking around in this mess."

I slide into the passenger seat and almost instantly feel sorry I did.

"I seen your mother leave the other day with a big suitcase. Are you on your own through this storm?"

Before I can answer she continues.

"If you need anything, dearie, come over. Anytime, you hear, sweetheart? Come over and we can see about it."

She passes her own driveway across the road and pulls into our driveway to drop me off. The electric blue of our house paint stands out like neon in the snow.

"No chance getting lost in a snowstorm with a paint job like this," I joke.

"Well, we wondered at it when your mother chose the color, but to each their own, they say, right?" Mrs. O'Connell smiles and winks at me.

I smile back. "Thanks a lot. For everything. I appreciate the offer. I might take you up on it." I pile out of the car and onto the snowy street. As I walk up the steps, hunting for the key in my pocket, I turn to wave her good-bye and slip a bit on the stoop, which is already layered with ice and snow. I can't see her face through the snowy windshield anymore, but I smile and wave anyway as I let myself in.

Once inside, I peel away my coat, hat, and gloves, which are frozen stiff. I walk over to the thermostat and crank the heater up. I head up and savor a long, steamy shower.

———

The storm has become a blizzard by the time I wake up. The wind howls and rages all morning. Alone on the cliff, our house has become a target. With no development around it to buffer the gales, the roof groans and branches from our trees scrape across the wooden shingles, making unearthly noises. The power has gone out, the telephone lines are down, and the heavens still dump snow. I decide to start a fire in the fireplace. We still have quite a bit of wood left in the backyard, and the cupboards are full. But I have a new problem—a refrigerator and freezer full of food. I know it all won't last more than a day with the power out.

It takes the better part of an hour to dig a hole in the snow in the backyard where I can store the food. The snow still pounds down, and the wind howls at huge speeds. Once I finish digging, I transfer the food outside. I have no idea if everything will be fine, but I figure it's probably my best bet, and with the phone lines down I have no way of contacting anyone to ask. I know if I need assistance I can ask the O'Connells, or another neighbor, or even walk around the corner to grab Timothy. I feel glad to find a solution myself, though, and when I finish and sit in front of the fireplace, warming back up, I feel industrious.

Someone knocks. Mr. O'Connell cowers on the stoop. I'm surprised because neither he nor Mrs. O'Connell has ever come over. I unlock the door and try to brace it as the wind blows it open. "Hello there. Come in."

He steps inside and we push the door closed against the wind. "Hello Jules. The Missus sent me over to check and make sure you were all right here. I understand you're roughing it on your own for a few. It's a nasty storm and a full tide. I expect we'll see enormous damage when we're through here. I heard there's another going to move through tonight and the tides will be high again."

"I'm fine, but thank you," I say.

"I see you've got a fire going. Keep the grate up and be careful of the downdrafts, they'll blow the fire right back in on ya. Did you need anything? Food or a flashlight for tonight? It'll be awhile before they pull the power up again. You can join us for dinner if you like?"

"No, thanks. I've got a flashlight and lots of batteries. I put the food in a snow bank out back to keep it cold. How long do you think it'll keep that way?"

"Oh I expect as long as it's freezing out there it'll keep, as long as an animal doesn't route it out. That was smart thinking, young lady. Remember to keep the faucet running a bit in the sink so's the pipes don't freeze."

I hadn't thought of this. "I'll keep the fences locked and the faucet running."

Mr. O'Connell moves to go. "You do that. I'll be checking back. You come over if you'll need anything. All right?"

"All right. I will, and thank you for stopping over."

"It's no problem, Jules. You come over if you need anything. Anything at all."

I'm overcome with his kindness and don't know how to express my gratitude. "Thank you," I manage to say as I push and he pulls the door closed. I watch him make his way gingerly down the slippery walkway, the snow now almost knee high, although I shoveled it away just this morning.

I have another visit later that day from Timothy, who comes carrying a basket of goodies from his grandmother. I have more than enough food, so I invite him in to share it with me. We eat canned oysters, water crackers, and homemade canned peaches. Afterwards, we play backgammon and he teaches me how to play Blackjack and Gin Rummy.

Before the sky darkens again he helps me carry several loads of wood in to stack by the fireplace. He bundles up and makes his way back home after I assure him I'm fine. I have several good books and my flashlight. I make up my sleeping bag in front of the fireplace and settle in for the night.

In the middle of the night I wake up to what sounds like a freight train roaring outside. I've never heard the wind so strong and loud and scary-sounding.

I hear a long, loud, groaning and cracking sound.

The old willow tree in the backyard.

It comes down with a giant thud that makes the foundation tremble, and when I look outside I can see it lying perfectly perpendicular to the back stairs. A few more feet and the branches would have taken out all the windows on the back side of the house. I clutch the flashlight and make a round of taping all the big windows on the north side of the house. The panes rattle in the sills, and I worry the wind might blow them in.

I think about calling Timothy. He has a private phone and I know I won't wake up his family. Then I remember the phone lines are down.

———

The blizzard continues for another full day.

After perusing our library wall, I find one of the largest books I haven't read yet, Tolstoy's *War and Peace*. The power is still off. I bundle up in my sweatshirt and coat in front of the fireplace. I don't sleep at all, but the book keeps my mind off the storm.

When I take a break early the next day and check, the power and phones are still down. The storm has stopped, but the sky is still draped in a deep, pearl-gray shroud.

I settle back in with my book, but a knock at the door soon breaks my concentration. Timothy poses in the doorway with a huge grin on his face. He lifts a pail up. "Grab your boots. I wanna show you something."

"What's going on? Where are you taking me?"

"Down to the beach."

"Are we going clamming?"

By the time we've gotten halfway down the cliff, I see something I've never seen before.

The beach swarms with lobsters. I've never seen so many crawly things except in a horror film.

"Oh my gosh! We are going to have a lobster feast!"

The craggy rocks that line the jetty are covered in icy snow, and the lobsters must have slid over them, falling back onto the beach. The high tides have created a strange dividing line between the rocky sand and the mounds of snow that blanket the seawall down below. The lobsters dot the snow mounds like slow-moving bites of red licorice.

As we scramble down the beach path I ask, "Why is this happening?"

Timothy calls over his shoulder. "The high tides, the changes in water salinity and temperature . . . so many things can cause their movement."

"Will they find their way back to the water?"

"Most of them will, but let's move the ones by the seawall back towards the water. They won't live more than a day out of the water."

First we fill our pail with the lobsters that were moving in the wrong direction, toward the cliffs, and we dump them back at the water's edge. We do this until we can't find any more stragglers. Then we fill our pail with lobsters and seaweed to bring back with us. I figure I can cook them all and store what we don't eat out in the igloo refrigerator I've built in our backyard.

Back at my place, we drop the pail of lobsters on the porch. After throwing off our wet boots and coats inside, we grab newspaper from the fireplace and lay it out on the kitchen floor and around the sink. Lobster makes a mess. Timothy brings the pail inside and helps me stuff them all in the sink while we get everything else ready. They drip all over everything.

I put our lobster pot—a beat-up big old silver-colored thing—in the sink, covering the bottom of the pan with water. After transferring the pot to the grate in the fireplace, I boil the water with salt and white vinegar. Timothy helps me grab the backs of the lobsters, lift them, and throw them into the pot headfirst to stun them. I throw the lid on and wait for it to boil again. They're small lobsters, so they'll be tasty. I set the timer on the stove for ten minutes. The lobsters knock against the pot like they're doing a sabre dance. Without opening my mouth I make a high-pitched sound in the back of my throat to make Timothy think they're screaming.

"Stop that!" he laughs. "It makes me sad to think they have to die so we can eat them."

After a while the sabre dancing stops inside the pot. I have a smaller pot on the grate. I run outside to my snow igloo of food, and I bring back a stick of butter to melt in the pot.

When the timer goes off, the lobsters are carnelian red, my favorite red. I use a long-handled wooden spoon to test the tails and make sure they're all curled tight.

I move the pot into the kitchen sink and let it cool down with the lid off. I can smell the salty cooked lobsters and start to taste it in my mouth. By this time the butter smell is mingling with the salt, and I can feel my stomach grumbling.

"Plates are in that cabinet," I remind Timothy. We hardly ever eat here, so he doesn't know my kitchen very well.

We are moments away from savoring cracked lobster. I grab the tiny tined forks from the drawer, and then remember I need more newspaper for under our plates on the counter.

By the time I'm back from the living room Timothy's already put the lobsters on our plates and soaked the floors and counter with the briny water.

"This floor is a Slip 'N Slide," I exclaim.

"Whoops." Timothy grins.

After mopping up what I can with the newspaper, I grab the hammer from the tool drawer we keep in the kitchen and we go to work—first twisting the claws off, then bending back the claws to expose the soft, pinky-white flesh inside, then trading off with the hammer to open the hard shells. We pull at the meat with our tiny forks and dip it into the small saucepan set on countertop. I worry that it might burn the Formica, so I grab a couple of potholders to put underneath. I figure they'll catch any unruly butter drips.

The lobster is tender and sweet. We're quickly creating a pile of lobster carcasses, passing the hammer back and forth. We grab spoons from the drawer to drizzle butter over the midsections before we suck the juicy meat out of the small, sharp-edged holes. I almost lick the buttery spoon, but remember my manners. The meat is moist, sweet, and salty. Lobster heaven! We eat every single one.

Outside the kitchen windows the sun is finally shining, and the sky is a deep cobalt blue. It's still snowing, but now the wind is light and the snow falls like dust on everything. It looks like someone in the sky is sifting flour onto the landscape.

After we clean up the kitchen we play multiple games of Scrabble. Timothy wins. He always wins.

At two o'clock he says it's his turn to shovel his walk and walk his dog Crikey, and he heads home. We make a plan to do the lobster thing again the next day.

I decide I should probably shovel my own walk, as the snow has piled another foot on top of what we already had this morning. By the time I finish shoveling, the wind has picked up and is whipping the snow into tiny ice pebbles. The sun has disappeared, and the sky has darkened into the color of pale ashes. My gloves, my hat, my scarf, my coat—everything is studded with tiny ice crystal buds.

Inside, I peel off my snow gear and change into dry clothing. As I sit warming up by the fireplace, someone knocks again. I assume it's Timothy and don't bother to check out the window before opening the door.

Howard squats on the stoop.

I'm sure my face must register the shock of seeing him. It's been about two years since any of us have seen him. He's made himself scarce since Moses's funeral, and in the last few years the only contact we've had with him has been an occasional call.

He pushes the door open as he steps inside. He's collected a keg-sized beer gut and he resembles a Wishnik Troll with his rusty orange hair sticking up everywhere. I can see he's starting to go gray where his hair is thinning at the temples. He smells musty, like a dirty, wet dog.

"Aren't you going to give me a kiss?" he asks as he sticks his tongue into the side of his face and pushes it out for me to kiss.

"Wow. I'm surprised to see you," I say, giving his protruded cheek a kiss. "What are you doing here?"

"That's no way to greet your father after you haven't seen him in a long time. I came to make sure you were all doing all right. The car got stuck down by the yacht club. It's like a lake at the bottom of the hill right now. So I hiked the rest of the way over on the seawall. The top of the seawall's the only dry ground to walk on right now."

I'm interested to hear that the storm has divided the island into two islands. I'm also happy, because this will surely lead to more school cancellations. But I'm angry to hear he's been staying in Withensea for who knows how long and, as usual, hasn't bothered to let us know or to visit.

"Oh, well, we're doing as well as we can here. We still don't have any power or phones, but we've got food and lots of firewood. We should be fine for a long time."

I try to be upbeat and friendly with him, but I'm nervous since I'm uncertain why he's bothered to show up. He probably assumes Wendy and Jack are also here. I don't know how he might react to Wendy's leaving me alone.

"Well, Aunt Doreen's has no more firewood. I can't stay there anymore. I can barely sleep at night. I've gone through most of the food already, and what was left went bad in the freezer before I got to it. Where's your mother?" he asks, almost as an afterthought.

"I buried ours in the backyard in a snow cooler I built," I say proudly. He stares at me like I might be an idiot, but doesn't comment.

"Do you have any canned foods?" He heads toward the kitchen and starts pulling open the cabinets and hunting through everything.

"Where's your mother?"

I have to tell him.

"She's on a vacation in the Virgin Islands with Jack."

He turns. "You're here alone?" Now he stares at me and my face is feeling hot.

"For now. At, at least u . . . u . . . until they get back." I'm hoping he isn't going to ask the next question.

You have to tell him.

"When's that?"

"Huh?"

Now he acts like a dog on a scent. He sticks his face in mine and holds my chin between his fingers.

He speaks the question slowly. I can smell Chivas Regal on his breath. The smell of it brings an instant knot to my gut. I realize he's likely drunk. "When are they getting back?"

"We . . . well. She left a few days ago to go meet up with him and she wa-wasn't real spe-specific about whe-when she might come back."

I hate this. I hate the stutter he brings out in my speech and the way I cower around him.

I step backwards and out of his grip and he turns away from me and starts pulling the canned food onto the counter.

"Your mother shouldn't have left you here by yourself. Anything could happen to you. Didn't she know about the storm coming? I'll be here to take care of you now. You don't have to worry about being alone."

I speak before I can stop myself. "Oh, I'm fine here by myself. I don't need you to stay with me."

He ignores me and starts banging the cans on the counter. "All this shit needs to be heated, and we don't have a stove." He starts to rant and shove all the cans to the back of the counter.

"I can heat something for you over the fire. What do you want?"

"It's too dangerous to stick your hands into an open fire. You can't heat things up without something to hold it into the fire with."

"I've been heating things up with this." I show him a pot I've taped with a long-handled metal serving spoon at the handle. The spoon's cup rests perfectly into the pot's slotted handle and allows me to hold it at a safe distance.

Howard scowls at my pot, but he picks out a can of baked beans and holds it out to me. "Show me how it works."

I heat up the beans and put them in a bowl for him while he hunts around. I can hear him up in Wendy's room stomping around, and I wonder what he's doing up there.

"Your beans are ready," I call up to him.

He comes down the stairs fast, and judging by how quickly he eats the beans he must be hungry. Without saying thanks, he hands me back the bowl. I put it into the sink knowing I'll be cleaning up after *him* later.

"Yeah. I'm gonna stay here until your mother's back and make sure you're all right. You shouldn't stay here by yourself."

I nod. I decide not to argue with him, but something inside me starts a slow boil. I know he probably thinks Wendy is gone for a week or so, and I don't want to tell him otherwise. I'm positive he'll settle in the entire time she's gone.

I want him out of there as quickly as possible, but I have absolutely no idea how I can do it. Something tells me a nighttime fish delivery isn't going to work twice in a lifetime.

Howard tells me he'd like to lie down for a while and sleep and before I can even offer him another sleeping bag or pillow, he lays down on the one I have in front of the fireplace and falls asleep. I sit on the chaise and watch him for a while until he starts to snore. I walk into the kitchen and gather all the liquor bottles out of the cabinet and pour every drop of alcohol down the drain.

Wendy has quite the collection, and I don't want to contribute to Howard's habit. He doesn't do drugs, so I know the pharmacy in her bedroom won't pose a problem.

I put on my coat, leave using the back exit, and drop the empties into the trash before I make my way over to Timothy's. Leigh has stopped over there. They tell me they were planning to come over and spend the night. I'm glad to see Leigh and relieved she seems comfortable with us. Her response the other day to our "prom decision" had me worried. I decide she was simply surprised by the idea and isn't offended in any way. There are bigger issues at hand now anyway.

"Let's stay here. It's not a good idea to go to my place. My father's there."

Later, Timothy, Leigh, Crikey and I settle upstairs in the privacy of his room, coats on against the chill. His room always makes me feel warm despite the weather. It smells like him. Ivory soap and cedar. The walls are painted a moss green and his bedspread is a tropical jungle with brightly colored parrots. I think his grand-mother must have decorated. He's applied glow-in-the-dark stars to his ceiling, and Leigh and I spend lots of time resting back on his parrot pillows in the dark and letting Timothy teach us the galaxy. When someone has a passion for something, anything in the world can become the most fascinating topic in the world. Stacked in every corner of his room are books about biology, chemistry, and conservation. He plans to study environmental design in college.

I sit in a red bean bag chair. Crikey plops himself next to me and lays his head across my knee. I tell them about my unwelcome guest.

"Yeah. He showed up pretending he was concerned about me. He ran out of firewood at my Aunt Doreen's, and I think he doesn't have anywhere else to go. I didn't tell him how long Wendy's going to be gone. He probably thinks it's going to be a week or something. Maybe he'll go before he thinks she'll show up. I could pretend she's coming back early or something."

"What if he waits until she comes home?" Leigh asks.

I don't think he'll wait around, considering how much they fight, but I'm not sure.

"I don't know. I'll have to think of something. Any ideas?"

"Is it bad with him there?" Timothy asks.

Crikey looks up at me. I scratch his head and stall Timothy off.

I'm sure he thinks I'm being a jerk about my father. His father is kind and thoughtful. It's hard for a person like Timothy to understand how mean a person like Howard can be to their own kids.

As much as I don't want to, I know I'll have to introduce Howard for him to understand. The idea frightens me, in a way. I've spent considerable effort trying to isolate my invitations to times when Wendy isn't there, and Howard is a whole other story. His behavior is embarrassing on a completely different level. Drunken rants, coarse language, generally hostile behavior . . .

"Why don't I stay with you? With me there and my family here, around the corner, he can't use the excuse that you're alone, and maybe he won't want to stick around if he knows your friends are going to be around too."

Leigh thinks it's a great idea, and they convince me it will work. We decide to put the plan into action. First, Timothy has to ask his family if it will be all right. They're totally supportive, and his grandmother tells me it makes her feel a lot better about things to know I'm not alone. I'm relieved, since I know Howard might call here to check on our story.

"I wish we had room for you here, Jules," Timothy's grandmother says.

"It's fine. It's better somebody's in the house to make sure pipes don't burst and stuff."

We walk back through the snowdrifts on Withensea Avenue. By this time the grayness of the late afternoon has gradually darkened into dusk. The snow reflects a smoky purple-gray that turns our skin the same shade. We are purple-gray shadows moving through the landscape.

Snow covers everything. Cars, trees, homes, roads, street signs. The exposed rocky cliffs are the only spots of landscape sticking out in their own deeper, coal-gray-shadowed silhouettes. Their darker colors create an ominous backdrop to the neon blue shock of our Victorian peeking through the ice and snow cover. I stop on the stoop and draw a breath before I turn the key. As I turn it, the door opens.

Howard waits inside. He glowers. "Where've you been?" he demands.

"We were over at my friend's. Thi . . . this is Timothy," I say, gesturing to him. "This is Leigh."

I force a calm voice and attitude, hoping it will work to tame his temper a bit. We all step into the entryway.

"Who told you it was okay to leave?" he shouts.

I'm stunned. It's been a very, very long time since someone has placed any rule or restriction on me for coming or going from my own house. I answer calmly and honestly. "I don't have any rules about leaving. I mean, we haven't had those kinds of rules here. We were hanging out at Timothy's . . ." I stop, unsure what to say next to him.

"Well, guess what? Those days are over. You've got rules now. I'm here, and your mother's not. You're going have to play by *my* rules now. Do you understand that?"

His mouth actually froths.

Timothy and Leigh stand beside me. Timothy's face holds a restrained but palpable anger. I know I have to find a way to end the conversation quickly and without more irritation for everyone.

"Yes," I say. "I understand. I'll let you know where I'm going from n . . . now on."

"Yeah you will, and you'll *ask* me before you go anywhere. This isn't going to be the wild animal farm your mother runs. You're going to learn discipline and respect for your elders . . . for your father."

He walks toward the kitchen. Then he turns around. "Your friends," he says with a scowl at Timothy and in a tone that tells me he has doubts about the nature of our friendship, "need to go home now. You've got work to do and it's late for visitors." He stomps away.

I turn to Timothy and Leigh. The shock of his anger has worn off. The rough way he acts is unfamiliar and unsettling at first, but then my memory places it and an old anger resurfaces in me. I'm certain Howard's rules are going to be broken. I'm equally certain I'll have to play along a bit longer in order to gain my freedom.

"You guys better go," I say, realizing after the words are out how wooden they sound. I brighten my tone to reassure them. They look stricken by Howard's words and actions. "I'll be fine."

"Will we see you tomorrow?" Timothy asks.

"We could hang out at my place tomorrow, Jules," Leigh offers.

"That sounds good. I'll see what my father says."

They stand glued in the doorway with worried faces.

"I'll be fine," I say again.

"See what he says about what we decided earlier," Timothy says.

"I'll let you know what happens."

"Okay. See you," Leigh says and grabs Timothy's arm. He moves away reluctantly.

"See you," he says, and they're gone into the night, which has turned from slate blue into a thick black curtain.

Twenty-four

INSIDE OUT IN THE COLD

HOWARD APPEARS BESIDE me as soon as I close the door behind Timothy and Leigh.

"That kid your boyfriend? What did he mean, 'What you decided'? What did you decide?" He doesn't wait for an answer. "You've got rules now, and they include asking permission to go out, to bring your boyfriend here, or to go see him. Well?"

"Well," I begin. I debate whether to be completely honest with him or to give him the idea in doses. "Timothy is a friend. I don't have a boyfriend."

He smiles suspiciously. I realize our idea won't fly in a million years with the level of paranoia Howard has about our relationship. I decide to try a different tack.

"We were thinking Leigh could stay here with me. Her mom is close, and that way I wouldn't have to be alone here. I mean, you wouldn't have stay here for my sake. I can take care of myself, and if something comes up, we can ask Ms. Westerfield to help out."

I hold my breath and wait for him to reply.

He grows quiet and actually seems like he might consider my suggestion. I become hopeful. Then I hear the answer I expected.

"Do you think you can get rid of me that easily? You think you can set up the place as a party zone for you and your friends and your *boyfriend*? Don't tell me he's not your boyfriend. Girls your age don't have male *friends*."

"Are you two having sex?" he asks me, his face about two inches from mine.

I stare back at him, not entirely containing my anger, which erases my fear. "Timothy is a friend, not a boyfriend. We're not having sex. I'm not having sex with anyone, not that it's any of your business," I add. "And I have no intention of having parties here. If I'd wanted to have parties, don't you think I would have before you showed up? I've been on my own for a few days now. Look, no parties!" At this I gesture around at the house. There is no stutter in my speech, which I hope convinces him I'm telling the truth.

He blinks, digesting my words.

"Well, you're either a good liar, or . . ."

Good liar, it appears, marks the boundary of his imagination.

I wait for him to finish, and maintain eye contact while he continues making his assessment of my sexual status, or whatever he's doing.

"Well, whatever the kid is—boyfriend, friend—he's not allowed over here unless I'm here. That goes for anyone. No visitors unless I'm here. No visits to your friends, either, unless their parents are home. You're gonna have to start learning discipline. This place is a mess. Starting tomorrow I want you to do a thorough cleaning of each and every room. Everything clean, floor to ceiling. There are cobwebs on the cobwebs in this place. How can you live in this filth?"

He's exaggerating, for sure, but it's true that the house, with the exception of my room, is not what I would call truly clean. Wendy never cleans, and I try to avoid doing what I can most of the time. I do keep it tidy, however.

"All right. I'll clean up tomorrow. I'm gonna head upstairs and study now."

The temperature hovers somewhere around freezing in my room, but I decide it's better to be cold than have to deal with him.

"Not so fast. First, you need to whip up another one of those fireplace meals for dinner. Do you know where your mother keeps the booze around here? I couldn't find anything in the cupboard."

"Yeah, there isn't any in the house," I answer, perhaps a bit too definitively.

"What? I'm gonna have to go to the packie. There's no way I'm stuck in a blizzard without something to drink. Is the market down the hill still open?"

"I don't know. I haven't been out until today and I didn't make it too far."

"Well, I'm gonna walk down and check it out. Start dinner. I'll be back in half an hour."

He puts on his old, ripped peacoat and leaves. I'm not surprised he's battling the snow and cold for a bottle of whiskey. His absence is a relief.

I go digging into the food stock in the backyard snow pile and produce a frozen chicken, which I pull out for tomorrow, and frozen vegetables for both evenings. I also find stuffed clams I think I might be able to slow-thaw for dinner, as well as some French-fried potatoes. I pull these out, scheming how I can rig the frying pan over the fire to cook them.

Shivering from the cold, I go back inside and sit by the fire to warm up. Howard built a huge fire, using more wood than necessary. With the fireplace tongs I pull the unburned pieces away from the others and set them on the hearth for later.

I flatten the pile, pull one of the racks from the oven, and place it over the logs . . . and I have an instant grill! I set the stuffed clams in a metal pan on the front of the rack to start them thawing and put the waxed green beans I pulled out into a small iron saucepan. I set it aside to wait for my father's return.

———

Howard is back, and I finish preparing my fireplace dinner, as he calls it, as he watches.

When I think everything's ready, I load up our plates and we begin eating. The clams, are, however, still slightly frozen in the middle.

"Cook 'em again!" Howard's eyes blink separately at me. He had quite a bit of the whiskey as he hiked back up the hill. I can smell his drunken breath and the stale sweat from his clothing wafting across the coffee table as we sit in front of the fireplace.

I pull our plates away and slide the clams back on the metal tray on the fireplace rack. After a while I spoon them all back onto his plate.

"I don't want yours. I didn't ask for yours."

"I know. I don't want them anymore. Have them," I say.

"I don't want 'em," he says insistently and forks them back onto my plate. "You've taken bites out of 'em already. I'm not gonna eat your food."

This time, I guess, his clams are cooked enough for him, and he eats them noisily, as though he's starving. I wait for him to finish his meal, and then I take the dishes to the sink, where I wash and dry them. Our dishwasher has been broken for months.

When I go back out, I see he's crawled into my sleeping bag. I grab the flashlight and go downstairs to the basement, which creeps me out, and find David's old camp sleeping bag. I bring it upstairs and unroll it under the piano.

Howard snores.

I wish I'd thought of grabbing the sleeping bag earlier in the daytime. I could have checked it for spiders and bugs. I'm too tired now. I crawl inside, dreading what the next day might bring with Howard.

I wake up in the middle of the night to a crashing sound by the fireplace. Howard swears profusely as he tries to rekindle the fire. He's trying to do it the same way he did earlier, by laying the logs upon each other and trying to light the ends. It's funny to me that he's somehow managed to live this long without learning how to build a proper fire.

"I can help you with it if you like?" I offer as gently as I can.

"What the fuck do you think you can do that I can't?"

I pull the sleeping bag back over my head and lie down again. If he isn't going to be nice, screw him.

His swearing and stumbling goes on for a while. I pretend to sleep. Eventually he gives up and settles back into a fitful sleep.

"It's fucking cold!" he calls out occasionally.

At sunrise, I rise and walk around his body, which lays perpendicular to the hearth. I build a fire, which takes me about two minutes, and warm up a bit.

"Where'd you learn to do that?" Howard startles me, and I jump away from the fireplace.

"Th . . . the heating goes o . . . off about two or three times a year. I learned a long time ago." I want to ask him how he *doesn't* know. Instead, I head toward the kitchen.

The phone rings. At first I can't tell where the ringing is coming from. It's been days since the lines went down and the surprising sound adds to my heightened sense of anxiety. Once I register that it's the phone, I walk over to the piano, where it sits, and pick it up from its cradle.

"Hello?"

"Oh my God! Why weren't you picking up the phone for three days? What's going on?" Wendy's strident voice rings out from the phone.

"The phones have been down. We've had a blizzard."

"I know, for Chrissakes, it's why I'm calling. It's all over the news down here. Are you all right? How's the house?"

"Yeah, the house and I are all right. We don't have heat yet, and I'm sure the phone lines have been back up only recently."

"Are you using the fireplace? You've got plenty of wood, you'll be fine. You've got food. How are the pipes?"

"The pipes are fine. I've got water running. I put the food out in the snow. It should keep until the temperature starts to rise again. Hopefully by that time the power will be back on. I can go over to the Zands' if things get hairy."

"Tell her I'm here," Howard demands.

Silence echoes on Wendy's end of the phone. I didn't want to test her reaction to this news, but since he's been the one to offer it . . .

"Is that bastard there?" her voice rings out, filling the room.

"Yeah, I'm here. Whaddya gonna do about it from the Virgin Islands? Who's gonna take care of your kid you left by herself?" He jumps up and grabs the phone from me and begins a rant.

"It's a fucking nightmare here. There's no fucking power, there were no fucking phone lines until now, and the streets aren't even passable. I had to leave my car down by the yacht club and walk in the middle of a blizzard to make it here."

"If there were no phones how did you know Jules was on her own?"

Wendy knows I'd never call him, and I think she smells a rat.

"You were at Doreen's and ran out of wood, didn't you? Probably ran out of food and had nowhere to go. You thought you'd sponge off us for a while?"

Twenty-five

LITTLE PIECES

"SHUT YOUR FUCKING mouth, you bitch. If you were here I'd tear your head off and shove it up your ass! Don't you give a shit about your daughter here alone in the middle of a blizzard? What kind of a mother leaves a kid alone and goes off on a vacation? I should report you!"

"Go right ahead, asshole, and I'll be sure to slap a lawsuit right on you for back pay on alimony and child support that'll leave you so broke you'll be paying me until the day you fucking die!" Wendy screams.

I back up to the edge of the couch, about ten feet away from where Howard now holds the phone receiver away from his ear, hanging from his hand. He drops the phone on the floor.

"Say good-bye to your mother."

I walk over and pick up the phone off the floor. We can hear Wendy,

"Hello? Hello? Are you still there? Hello?"

I'm experiencing a myriad of emotions—shock, fright, spiking anxiety at a flood of parental fight memories, bitterness, disgust at my parents' hypocrisy and behavior. There's also a righteous anger and vindictive glee at Howard's parental neglect allegations toward Wendy.

This emotion drives the next thing I say.

"You know, I was fine before he got here, and I'll be fine when he leaves. So, don't think you have to rush back here on my account. I've got everything I need."

Wendy is silent. After a while, she speaks in a calm voice. I can tell she's trying to gain her composure. "Good. I *will* stay. Maybe your father should stay with you for a while. I'll feel better you're not alone there. Make sure he doesn't go in my room. I don't want him nosing around. Where is he sleeping?'

"We're sleeping in front of the living room fireplace. It's the only warm spot. There's no heat."

"Fine. Let him sleep in the living room. I'll call you in a few days and check in. Stay warm."

I'm breathing slowly to calm my voice but now a rushed plea escapes. "Wait. I don't need anyone here. He doesn't have to stay here. I'm fine."

"Yes, you do! You're not staying here by yourself. You're sixteen years old. You're not an adult," Howard shouts over me.

"Let him stay!" Wendy says. "I don't need to rush back."

"What about your classes?" I ask. I'm panicky now.

"I'll drop my classes and start again next semester."

She raises her voice again. "He's gonna make a big scene about how I left you alone after abandoning his children for the last ten years. Big man. Let him show what a great father he is and let him stay there. I'll be here in the sunshine while he steps up for a change. Be a man, Howard."

"Go fuck yourself, Wendy." Howards walks over, grabs the phone out of my hands, and slams it into the receiver.

"Make me coffee."

I go into the kitchen to fill the teakettle for a fireplace boil. The rest of the day is tedious, but relatively uneventful. I spend the day cleaning and cooking while Howard grabs an ax from our shed and chops up tree branches from the fallen willow in our back yard. He plans to haul the logs down to his stranded car and load the car up with firewood to take back to Doreen's when he leaves.

He's at least made an exit plan, and I'm ecstatic he isn't going to take a part of the cord we have stacked in the backyard. I think about how lucky it turns out to be that the willow fell.

About midway through the day I receive calls from Leigh and Timothy, who want to see if I can come out for a bit. I tell them what I'm doing, and that I'll check back with them the next day.

———

But the next day there's another long list of things on Howard's agenda. My first task: polishing the goldware, an old wedding present relic from Wendy's parents, which stays stored in an antique wooden case. I wonder if Howard plans to take it with him when he leaves.

He makes one trip to his car with the wood while I set to work on the utensils, and on his return pronounces his decision that I should help him carry the wood to the car. So I load a backpack with as much wood as I can carry, and stack a few more pieces in my arms. He carries a few under his arm, and we hike down the snow-filled avenue to where his car is abandoned.

The sun reflects blindingly off the mountains of snow. I have to squint my eyes nearly shut to see anything. I wish I'd brought sunglasses. Howard wears the pair of Wayfarers from the stuffed deer in the den.

When we reach the parking lot at the yacht club, there are cars strewn everywhere. Snow stacks nearly thigh high on me in the lot, and except for the places that have already been packed down a bit by snowshoes and skis, my legs sink into the snowdrifts. I'm soaked. We can hear snowplows working their way across the land bridges, but the parking lot and all the cars, still stuck frozen like huge popsicles, sit draped in icy snow. It will probably be at least another day before the cars are cleared to move. Nothing can melt in the cold that remains.

"We should wait until the ice melts, and then you can drive the car up to the house and load it there," I say.

I really don't want him to stay at the house any longer, but it makes no sense to carry all this wood down here if the car can't move anyway.

"This part of the road will be cleared long before the others, and I wanna leave as soon as I can."

This response is thrilling.

We pile the wood in the trunk of Howard's car and trudge back up Withensea Avenue. Back at the house, soaked and freezing, I build another fire and warm up in front of it. Howard goes out back to continue chopping wood.

Timothy calls while he's gone and we speak for a while, until I hear Howard come in. "I gotta go," I tell him, and hang up.

"Who was that?" Howard asks.

Lying would be easy, but I've decided to be straightforward. "Timothy. He's just checking in."

Howard informs me I will be making the next round of trips to load the firewood into the car while he continues to chop wood. I don't argue. I put on my ski suit and bundle up against the cold. It's much better this time.

I spend the rest of the day hauling wood down to Howard's car. After the last load it's so full I have to lean against the doors to close them. By the end of the day a snowplow finishes the last clearing of Withensea Avenue. Because there's been flooding with the blizzard, the plow pushes seawater off the avenue as well. Several city workers and residents line the seawall with sandbags to try and keep the roads clear. My last walk back becomes a slushy trek. The water sloshes through my boots to my socks, and my feet are frozen.

Howard gives me about ten minutes in front of the fire before he demands his dinner. I make the chicken and vegetables I've defrosted and kept chilled in an ice bucket in the refrigerator. I split the chicken breasts and season them before I grill them on the fire.

As I'm bending over the grill, Howard says, "You've got your mother's figure, I see."

His tone is not complimentary. I decide to ignore the comment. Somewhere in there is his acknowledgment of my physical maturity. Somewhere in there is my dread at the belief that he hates women and now counts me as "one of them."

———

"This is good," Howard says between large bites a bit later. "I know you didn't learn to cook from your mother. She's a lousy cook. Who taught you?"

"No one. I read cookbooks and follow recipes. It's not rocket science."

He laughs. "You would think a genius could figure it out, but everything your mother made ended up burnt or not fit for humans."

"She never gave us salad with grub garnishes." I'm instantly sorry for the crack, but fortunately Howard takes it lightly.

"Christ! I forgot about her cooking. The woman was such an idiot. At least your mother could hold a conversation."

I decide to change the subject and see if his happiness with my cooking might buy me a bit of freedom. "So, do you think it would be all right if I went over to Leigh's tomorrow? We have a project we're working on."

He considers it.

"I'll tell you what? If you clean out all the shit in the cabinets and wipe them down, you can go when you finish."

It's pointless busywork, since we rarely have food in the cabinets and our glassware, dish, and pan collections are measly, but I know it won't take me long to finish the chore. I agree.

———

In the morning he sleeps in while I work in the kitchen. By eleven o'clock I've fed him breakfast and finished the dishes. I start to bundle up to go out.

"Be back by four. I don't want you walking around in the dark."

It didn't bother him the day before when I hauled wood for him, but I'm glad to be getting away from him and I don't argue. I practically run out. It's already been too many days of Howard Hell, and I'm stir-crazy.

I stop at Timothy's, stepping inside for lunch with his family, before we leave for Leigh's. I haven't mentioned that Timothy will join us or that Ms. Westerfield will be leaving for work later. We will be, *gasp*, un-chaperoned, but I don't think I owe Howard an explanation. His demands are ridiculous. I'm a sixteen-year-old girl with a social life.

After lunch, Timothy and I walk down the hill to Leigh's. When we arrive we're invited to go into Boston with Ms. Westerfield while she works for a bit in her travel agency office. She says she'll drop us at the Boston Commons—one of our favorite places to hang out. I think it will be fun to make snowmen on the Commons. It also sounds great to bust out of Withensea.

I try calling Howard to let him know I'm going, but he isn't there. By the time we make it into Boston, an hour later, it's starting to snow again.

Two hours after we've been hanging out in the Commons in the light snow, it starts to snow harder. Ms. Westerfield picks us up and tells us she's booked a room for us in a hotel. Her treat. We'll have to spend the night because it isn't safe to drive in the weather.

———

When we check in at about four o'clock and Ms. Westerfield goes to her room, I call Howard to let him know where I am and what our plans are. He answers on the first ring.

"Hello," he growls into the phone.

"Hi. It's Jules."

"Where the hell are you? Come home. There's gonna be another blizzard!"

"I know. I heard it on the radio. Hey, I'm in Boston."

I keep my voice light and try to ignore the menace I hear in his.

"Get your ass back here. What the hell are you doing in Boston?"

"I tried to call you earlier to let you know that Leigh's mom had to come in for work. She works here. She . . . she's a travel agent." I start to ramble with nervousness.

"I don't care what the fuck she is. Haul your ass back home."

"I-I can't . . . the snow . . . she can't drive us back in this. We . . . we're going to stay at a hotel. Leigh . . . Leigh's mom, Ms. Westerfield, can . . ."

Howard interrupts, "I don't give a shit. You'd better find a way to take yourself back here right now. You're not staying at a hotel. Are you there with your boyfriend?"

Leigh and Timothy sit on the two beds and can hear every word of what Howard screams into the phone. The heat in my face and body makes me start to sweat. I hesitate for a moment, thinking how easily I can lie and deny that Timothy, my "boyfriend," is there with us, but I decide to be honest and hope that somewhere in Howard's pebble heart he can hear the truth and trust me.

"Yes. He's here with Leigh and me, but he's not my boyfriend. I'm telling you the truth, and we're going to spend the night here and drive back tomorrow."

Big mistake.

"What? Listen to me, you whore! You're nothing but a slut! You're going to stay in a hotel with him? Do you think I'm an idiot? Do you think I'm an *idiot*?"

He's had a *lot* to drink. Howard can handle his liquor to a point, but beyond that, his fury, which typically remains somewhat tempered, becomes a slurry hurricane of screaming swears.

Timothy walks over to me. I'm trembling.

"Do you want me to talk to him?"

I shake my head at him. I know I've made an awful mistake and I don't want him to suffer for it.

Howard goes on. "If you don't get your slutty ass back here tonight, don't bother coming back or I'll take the ax and chop you into little pieces when you do! Do you hear me? Do you *hear me*?"

Timothy leans back on his heels and whips his head back like he's been slapped. Leigh rocks upright on the bed, stunned. Neither of them has probably heard people talk to their kids like this.

"I-I'm so-sorry. I shou-shouldn't have co-come into Boston, I know. Bu-but I'm stuck he-here now, a-and I ca-can't come back. I have to wait for Le-Leigh's mom to drive us back in the morning. Do you want to talk to Ms. Westerfield? I-I can tell her to call you?"

My ears start to have a strange sensation. I hear every word we're saying with crystal clarity, but the blood is pounding in my ears, giving everything an ominous echo.

"You're a fucking liar! Don't fucking lie to me. Who are you gonna put on the phone? Some friend? Listen to me. Come home now"—here he softens his voice and lowers his volume almost instantly, which scares me more—"and you won't be in trouble. But if you stay there, I swear to you, you're going to . . ."

Leigh shoots forward from where she's been frozen on the bed, pries the phone out of my hand, and places it in the cradle. I stand stunned and silent, still trembling.

She holds her hand on the phone. I think she expects it to ring again, and she guards it as though I might try to grab it away from her. She breathes hard, and I realize that she, having never dealt with Howard's fury, probably feels more scared than I do.

"H-he won't call back. He doesn't even know wh-what hotel we're a-at."

The enormity of this fact and the increased rage it will create for him hit me.

Leigh nods and moves her hand away from the phone. She steps closer to put her arms around me. I stand still, my arms by my sides, tolerating the embrace. I don't like to be touched. It's almost painful to experience. Timothy leans forward and puts his hand on my shoulder and gives it a squeeze.

This is the part where my father calls me a slut and a whore.

Leigh says, "I'm so sorry, Jules. We never should have come here. I thought we'd be back early. I didn't mean to make trouble. I guess I shouldn't have hung up on him, either, but I couldn't listen to it anymore. I guess I got you into more trouble though, didn't I?"

I move away from them and go to the other side of the bed, putting it between us.

"No Leigh. You did the right thing," Timothy says. "No one deserves to be talked to the way he talked to you, Jules. No one should have to take that. I don't care if it's your father or Joe Shmoe. That was . . ."—he searches for the right word—"shitty. Is he always like this? I thought maybe the other day he might be upset about the blizzard and all, but . . . is he like this all the time?"

I have never heard Timothy swear. The sound of the word, *shitty*, coming from his mouth sounds wrong, as though he's repeating a line from a school play.

I smile at him, and he immediately grins and blushes. "Yeah, it's shitty. He's a shitty person."

"I'm gonna ask my mom to call him and explain what happened. She'll be able to tell him so he understands it's not your fault." Leigh reaches her hand forward and picks up the phone before I can stop her. She dials the hotel operator.

"Hello. Can you connect me with Bridget Westerfield's room?"

"Don't. I don't think it's a good idea. You heard him. He's gonna think I set it up with a friend of mine posing as your mom. You . . ."

"My mom'll fix it. Don't worry. She'll explain it to him in a way he'll be able to understa . . ." She breaks off. "Hi Mom, it's me. Hey, can you call Jules's Dad? He's real mad about us staying here. He thinks Jules lied to him and we're gonna have a party or something."

"Of course I'll call him," I hear Ms. Westerfield say on the other end. I'm sure Leigh told her about Howard's rough behavior toward us the other day.

"I've got her number in my address book, but give it to me and I won't have to fish it out."

I nod to Leigh and gesture for her to give me the phone. She hands it over.

"Hi, Ms. Westerfield. It's Jules. Hey, my father is strict, and I wasn't supposed to leave Withensea or anything. I . . . I messed up, he's really, really mad at me. He doesn't trust me, and he might think you're a friend of mine calling. So he might be rude to you. You don't have to do this. I'll deal with this when I go back tomorrow.

I'm sure he'll settle down by then."

"Don't worry, Jules. I'll talk to him. I'm sure when we speak he'll recognize the fact I'm another adult and we'll work this out."

I'm skeptical, but I know Ms. Westerfield isn't going to back down.

"I don't know, I'm worried he's going to be a . . . jerk." This is the worst word I can muster for her.

I don't have the right words to prepare her for what I fear he might say.

"I don't want you to worry, Jules. I'll make sure he understands. Are you going to be okay if I call him?"

I think about that.

Leigh grabs the phone away from me.

"Call him, Mom. She's never gonna say she's okay with it. She's afraid of him. He's said lots of awful things to her, Mom, about what he's going to do to her . . . about how he's going to punish her. He's an ogre, Mom."

"Okay, done," Ms. Westerfield says before she hangs up.

At first I stare at the phone in its cradle on the hotel desk. I'm distracted watching small drops of water collect on the felt pad on the desk's surface. The pad, a mint green color, becomes mossy with the liquid, which spreads like ink blots in the porous material. I stand in an almost hypnotic state trying to sort the shapes into something recognizable. My eyes fill with liquid, and I realize I am the source of the watery creation. I turn away, not wanting Leigh or Timothy, who now sit a few feet away on one of the beds, to see me crying.

I'm ashamed, but I'm not clear about the source. My tears? Howard? My rule-breaking behavior? My inability to communicate how trustworthy I am to my own father?

I'm ashamed and experiencing it physically as an almost vise-like constriction in my gut and around my heart, which pumps against it painfully and insistently, as though it's rejecting the emotion.

Leigh leads me to the bed as my tears begin to morph into convulsive sobs.

I try to calm myself.

"I-I'm sorry. I didn't want to pull you guys into this. I shouldn't have come."

"It's not your fault, Jules. His rules are ridiculous," Leigh says.

Timothy adds, "You shouldn't have to deal with this stuff, Jules. You're right, he's a jerk. He comes down crazy hard. It could have been anything. Maybe you shouldn't even go back until your mom comes home. You should call her and tell her to come back. Tell her what's going on and what he said to you."

Leigh glances over at Timothy first. I can tell she's debating whether to educate him as to Wendy's equally "non-parental" personality. Leigh has known me and my family a long time, and in the last two years of my friendship with Timothy I've done a good job at soft-pedaling the stuff that goes on

"Wendy is . . . she's not the kind of mother who would be motivated enough by Howard's behavior to come back. She lived it for years before she decided she was done. I think she thinks I'm old enough to handle it myself."

I remember that Wendy met Howard when she was fifteen. I'm sixteen.

I realize the truth of my statement.

It's stifling living with him, but instead of trying to talk to him, to get to know him and allow him to know me, I've let him bully me into behaving like a child. I've done every ridiculous thing he's asked me to. I've been a spineless wimp instead of standing up to him.

Maybe if I tried to talk to him like an adult, he would realize he can't push me around, that I *am* old enough to make my own decisions. Instead, I've played into whatever fantasy he has about me being a "good girl" and let him control me like a robot.

I've known all along I would eventually have to break it to him that I'm not who he wants me to be. I know if it isn't this showdown, a bad scene will come sooner or later. The realization that I've set myself up makes me break down into a new round of tears. "I did this to myself. I should have stood up to him the minute he showed up. At least he wouldn't have been shocked by it now."

"But you didn't. You didn't stand up to him," Timothy says before he realizes his words might be insulting. I'm sure my expression registers my hurt feelings. He softens his tone. "I mean, you were nice to him. Even though he talked to you so mean . . ."—he pauses—"so roughly . . . you were still polite and respectful. And he still acted like . . . that. Has he always been this way? I mean, from when you were young?"

I imagine how difficult it will be for him to understand my parents' behavior toward me. Timothy's world tilts differently. His father and his grandmother love him and his brother and treat them kindly. Their home is a clean, orderly, and harmonious haven, a place where you can relax and laugh. A place where you have dinners around a table every night with everyone. His family sits around a tiny television set in the living room and passes the popcorn bowl around until the last person to eat a kernel gets up, without a complaint, and makes another bowl to share. There's always more popcorn and space for another person. The love in that family feels expansive, generous. It makes you want to be included and invited. It makes me want to be one of them.

There's no way he can ever understand what my parents are like. They exist outside of his experience of family life. I've never even read about families like mine except in a Dickens story. I've never seen television shows with characters like Wendy and Howard unless they're criminals.

"There's no way you can understand what it's like," is all I say.

"I guess not."

I realize I have somehow insulted him. Before I have a chance to explain it to him he makes a call to his own family. While he's talking to them, Ms. Westerfield knocks on the door. Leigh lets her in. She seems upset, but her words come out calmly.

"Jules, you were on target about your father. He had a hard time believing who I was and an even harder time listening to me. *Listening*." She repeats the word with emphasis. I can tell she's really pissed, but she's trying not to sound angry.

"When I drive you back tomorrow I'm going to go inside with you, and if you don't feel"—here she corrects her statement carefully—"if *I* don't feel like it's safe to leave you there, I'm going to take you back to our place, where you're going to stay until your mother comes back. Okay?"

Ms. Westerfield is probably shocked at what Howard had to say. He probably laid a number on her. I think until now she may have thought Leigh exaggerated the truth about how rude and mean he was. It seems she has the total picture now. I wonder what that means. I worry she might be getting herself into deep water with my messed-up family dynamics, like she has to be responsible for me or something. I can't stand the idea of my family's psycho behavior bleeding onto anyone else. I know I have to handle the situation quickly by myself.

"I know it seems bad right now, but he's probably been drinking and he says stupid things when he drinks. He's gonna be fine tomorrow, despite how he sounds right now. I know . . . you don't believe it. But it's the truth. I do need to start back early, though . . . so he doesn't get worked up again."

I add this because I don't want to have to explain what I know. If we can catch Howard after he wakes up—after his coffee and before his first drink—he'll probably have enough sense to keep it together in front of Ms. Westerfield.

"We can leave early," she says.

After a little light conversation with Leigh and Timothy, who's now off the phone, about dinner, she leaves.

We watch movie after movie on the hotel TV and eat the food from room service. We are actually having fun, even though I know that whatever happens tomorrow might erase the nice memory of this moment.

Stevie Nicks sings "Rhiannon" on a rerun of *The Midnight Special* and spins around in a lacy black dress. Her dress reminds me of a spider costume.

I drift into sleep while both of them stay glued to the set. The last thing I remember hearing is Timothy's voice to Leigh.

"Do you think she's asleep?"

"Yeah. I think so."

Silence.

Then Timothy's soft voice. "Jesus."

I want to open my eyes and say, "Leave him out of it," to make them laugh about it, but I can't stop myself from falling asleep.

———

It's morning.

I check out the hotel windows and see the snow still pounding down thick like pillow batting and no cars moving on the city streets below. I dread the day ahead.

After a while the snowplows come and clear the streets around the hotel. Ms. Westerfield calls Leigh's sister to make sure the roads in Withensea have been plowed again as well. She says it's still snowing but it's lightened up. We have a slow drive through the messy freeways on the way out to Withensea.

I'm sure Ms. Westerfield wanted to avoid driving in this weather but she also wants to keep her word to Howard about delivering me back.

We make it back at about four thirty, as the sky turns into a deep charcoal smudge.

Howard's car sits parked in front. I realize he probably got it when I left for Boston, which was when the avenue opened up. The trunk of the car, its lid tied down with rope, holds the wood he's stacked high inside it. He's done a lot of chopping, and the memory of him swinging the ax makes me shudder.

The lights inside are on. Ms. Westerfield pulls her car up in the driveway next to the Daemler Hearse. She's seen it before, many times, but in the snow the psychedelic colors pop out and we all stare at it for a second.

"I'm going in," Ms. Westerfield says.

I try to talk her into staying in the car, but she's stubborn about it. She makes her voice all friendly and calm. I wonder if she's practicing for Howard, but I can also see how tired she is from the long drive through the snow. We sit in the car for a few more minutes before I step out and she turns off the car. As soon as she does, she turns it back on again. "I'll leave it running," she says to Leigh and Timothy. "You guys stay warm."

"I'm coming," Timothy says

"Me too," Leigh says.

"No," Ms. Westerfield practically shouts, which surprises us all. "I want you to stay in the car." She turns to me now, "Actually, Jules, I'd like you to stay here while I talk to your father."

Twenty-six

Jules, 16 years | *February, 1978*

AS FAR AWAY AS POSSIBLE

"I DON'T THINK it's a good idea. I mean, I better go with you so he knows I'm really here."

She thinks about it and lets me go with her.

We knock.

When Howard answers, he doesn't seem surprised to see Ms. Westerfield standing there with me. I notice he's wearing Jack's leather coat.

"Hello," he says calmly to Ms. Westerfield as he gestures for us to step inside. He acts like we're guests in his house.

"Hello," she answers hesitantly as she steps around him.

He places himself with his back to the door now. Threatening.

"Thank you for bringing Julianne back. I appreciate your driving through this weather. I'm sure it was a difficult drive."

"Yes, well . . ." Ms. Westerfield seems as surprised as I am to experience his manner. Almost charming. Almost.

But Ms. Westerfield is smarter than most of the women he pulls this stuff on. She straightens up, and I can tell she feels nervous as she speaks. Her voice develops the warning tone teachers use in front of kids when we start to goof off in class.

"I'd like your assurance that Jules won't be punished for something that was clearly not her fault. She came with us innocently. I felt certain I would have her back early yesterday. I accept full responsibility for the situation."

"I see. Well, I understand. But Jules knows the rules, and she knows she's not supposed to go anywhere without my permission. She broke the rules, and she knows it."

Howard actually smiles when he says this to Ms. Westerfield, but when he finishes he stares at me and I can see his pupils adjust with a miniscule shift, his anger simmering beneath his façade of control.

"I understand you're angry because she didn't discuss it with you, but she tried. I was present when she tried to call you. When you didn't answer she made the decision to come with us with an assurance that we'd be back shortly. As I've said, I didn't realize we were due for another big snowstorm. Not even the weather forecasters saw this one coming."

It's the simple truth. All the newscasters said it surprised everyone.

Howard nods. "Well it's moot anyway, isn't it? The damage is done. She's safe and sound at home now." He smiles his fake charming smile at Ms. Westerfield, who doesn't seem impressed with it.

I scan back and forth between them and wonder what might happen next.

"As a matter of fact, I'm pretty sure she can do an excellent job taking care of herself until her mother returns. If she needs anything, she can reach me where I'm staying, in town." He glances at me and the same glimmer of menace flicks in his eyes despite his small polite smile. "At your Aunt Doreen's."

He opens the door. "I'll be leaving now. Call me if you need me, Jules."

He leaves before I can even respond. I practically fall backwards as the door closes.

Ms. Westerfield and I stare at each other. "Wow. That's . . . that's . . . mystifying," I say.

Ms. Westerfield stares at the door now, looking as stunned as I am. I wonder what she said to him last night on the phone to make him leave. I can't believe he's come to the decision on his own. Without saying a word, we pull the curtains away from the sidelight window and watch him back his car out and drive away.

Then Ms. Westerfield says something I think I'm going to remember always. "Jules, I know your life hasn't been wonderful so far. Your parents have been . . . less than perfect parents to you. But I promise you, when you go to college, when you grow into your adulthood—it will never be this hard for you again. You'll be able to make your own choices. You'll be able to walk away from people who don't treat you well. You'll be able to create your life the way you imagine it will be."

I don't know what to say. I know she's telling me something important. She's telling me exactly the thing I need to hear. It's like radiant sunshine and I'm standing there basking in it.

"Thank you. I hope . . . I hope what you're telling me is true."

"It's true," she says and smiles.

Leigh and Timothy come inside. Leigh ends up spending the night with me. I think they're all a bit skeptical about Howard's change of heart and Ms. Westerfield doesn't want me to spend the night alone, even though I'm certain Howard won't show up again.

They don't know Howard like I do. The food supply has run low. He's got all the wood he needs for Aunt Doreen's fireplace, even if the power doesn't come back on for the rest of the month, and I'm sure he thinks Wendy will be back in a few days and the jig will be up anyway.

He also walked out wearing Jack's expensive leather jacket, and who knows what else he's already taken? He's a louse who sponges off people and leaves whenever the welcome mat rolls back up. And he knows he's burned the mat this time.

———

Wendy doesn't show up in a few days, or even a few weeks. When she calls, I tell her what has happened and ask her when she plans to come back. She tells me I seem to be doing a great job and I'll be fine.

I've already been writing checks off her checkbook to pay the utility bills for a few years. She's right that I already know how to take care of stuff. But I don't have much more cash left from the hundred she's left me with. I tell her the milkman has expanded the grocery offerings they deliver, and since the storm I've been ordering my food this way. I guess she figures if I have shelter and food and don't need anything else, she can keep partying.

We don't have school for a whole month, but the electric power returns after a week.

Wendy stays gone a total of ten weeks, and by the time she comes back the seasons have changed. She comes back April 15th. Withensea looks ragged from the blizzard damage, but the weather has turned warm and sunny. She returns with Jack, which was her ultimate mission.

———

One day a few weeks after they get back I'm studying when I hear them come tearing up Alethea Road in two cars. Wendy screams out my name when she steps into the front room and says there are groceries in the car and will I please help her carry them in. As I walk out I see the VW parked in the driveway and a new car parked out front: a 1966 cherry red Mustang Coupe—the most radical car I have ever seen!

I wait on the porch and stare at the car. I say to Jack, "Wow. New car?"

"Here," he says, and he throws me the keys.

"It's your car," he says.

I shoot a glare at him. "Funny one."

"No, it's for real. It's your car. Take a spin." I know he wouldn't lie about the car. So I figure it really is for real.

"Why?" I ask.

This time Wendy speaks. "Because you did a great job taking care of everything and you put up with your father. You probably deserve a medal, he's such an asshole, but a car is good, right?"

I smile at her. "Yeah, a car is great."

"Go take it for a ride. You better get your license soon so you can drive it legally."

"Thank you. Thank you so much. This is the most incredible thing you've ever done."

When I jump into the car and start the engine I check the gas meter. I plan to drive as far away as possible.

Twenty-seven

Jules, 17 years | *Summer, 1978*

JAIL TIME

A WEEK LATER, after a quick Driver's Ed class, I get my license. The teacher can tell I already know how to drive. He focuses on parallel parking and passes me on the second drive.

I love driving my Mustang more than almost anything. The paint blazes cherry red with a black hardtop and a black interior. It's freedom in a metal frame. It's wicked great!

I drive it to school every day, and on the weekends I drive it almost all the time. To pay for gas and stuff I get a job working part-time for the town newspaper. I do ad layout and work the copy machine.

When summer starts, I begin working full-time at the newspaper. Leigh and Timothy work down at the old amusement park at the other end of town. Everybody and their brother works there.

After work I head down to the game stands and hang out until they can leave. Timothy usually works a huge game with a bunch of clown heads. You have to shoot water from guns into tabs placed in the open mouths of the clown heads to win prizes. Leigh runs a ride called the Kooky Kastle. We love hiding in there and scaring people.

When we aren't working, Leigh and Timothy and I pile into the Mustang and drive for hours. It doesn't matter where we go. We drive out of Withensea into the nearby towns. Sometimes I drive all the way into Boston to visit my grandfather and Ruth. They love it, and it's nice to be able to visit them more often now that I can do it on my own without having to take three buses and a trolley.

Meantime, Wendy and Jack booze it up and swallow whatever drugs they can't inhale. Wendy earned her bachelor's degree in psychology, and after her graduation in June she threw a huge party that hasn't seemed to end. I wonder if she'll party for the next ten years, which is about how long it took her to earn her degree.

A few of the guests have moved into the basement for a while, including a chick named Seraphina who decided to quit using heroin while she stayed with us, which makes me sure I'm never taking drugs in my entire life. She spent the first three days awake, either sick in the bathroom or shaking on the living room couch. She wouldn't eat or drink much because she said her stomach hurt. Her nose was runny, she cried almost all the time, and she sweated like she was running a fever. Finally, she fell asleep downstairs and slept for three days. Even with Jack's new favorite band, Crosby, Stills, Nash and Young, blaring. The house never quiets down. Jack seems more withdrawn since Wendy's graduation and they fight all the time and are generally unpleasant to be around, even when they're sober.

At the end of July they were arrested on a drunk and disorderly charge outside their favorite dive bar. David and I weren't around for the jail call. They had to ask a friend to bail them out.

David is spending his summer working as a golf instructor in one of the nearby towns. He's taken up golf at college and become quite good. He has a girlfriend and when he isn't working he spends time at her place or out with their friends. We rarely see him unless one of us happens to be up late when he comes in.

Toward the end of the summer I find Jack and David standing in the front yard, in the middle of an argument. I don't even know how it started. It's stupid because neither one of them has ever yelled at or even talked much to the other before.

When I walked into the yard, Jack is goading David, jabbing him with his finger in his chest. "Throw a punch, why dontcha?"

I'm thinking David will laugh it off and tell Jack to go kick a stone, but instead David throws a punch at him that glances off his cheek. When Jack turns back to David his eyes are insane. He turns into a monster and starts punching David hard in the face, in the chest, in the stomach.

I'm stunned. He might kill David. Wendy sits on a porch step, watching all of this impassively.

"Aren't you going to say anything to stop this?" I run up to her and ask.

"Let them punch each other out."

"They're not going to punch each other out . . ." I want to say Jack will kill

David, but I don't want David to hear me and be offended. I scream at her, "Do something!"

She sits there and I run down to where Jack has David on the ground, punching him, and starts screaming at him to stop. He doesn't at first, but finally he seems to come to his senses. I can tell he's high. He staggers and stumbles up the stairs onto the porch and inside.

David's face is all bloody from what I think is a broken nose. I help him up and we hear horrible crashes coming from inside. Jack's tearing the living room apart. We hear the sound of lamps flying, of crunching wood, and of glass shattering—followed by Jack's howling.

We all hesitate—I think because we're all scared about what we'll find—but then we race in. Jack evidently punched the aquarium, shattering it and liberating the fish, which lie squirming around us on the carpet. His hand and wrist literally pump blood.

I run to the linen closet and grab a handful of towels. When I run back, Wendy and David still stand in the same place. I hand David a towel.

"Put this on your face," I say to him.

"Call an ambulance," I tell Wendy. She goes to the phone, screaming something about having to call the "fucking cops," and dials.

I walk over to Jack and help him wrap up his wrist. I can see the monster has disappeared. For some reason, this makes me angrier. "What's up, Jack?" I ask.

"Sorry," he says. "Sorry, David."

David doesn't respond. He stares at the fish I try to scoop up and put into a cup I grabbed off the coffee table. He walks upstairs holding the towel to his nose.

I hold pressure on Jack's wrist until the ambulance arrives. They put him on a stretcher and take him to the hospital. Wendy rides along.

I stay with David although he doesn't come out of his room all night. The next day he has awful bruises around his eyes, a big gash over the bridge of his nose, and scratches on his face.

Wendy sees him and says, "I'll pay for the surgery to fix your nose if you want."

"No thanks," David answers on his way out to the golf course.

Later that night, I catch him staring at his nose in the bathroom mirror. "It looks like it's broken. You should take her up on the offer to have it fixed," I say.

David stares into the mirror. "I think it makes me look like Paul Newman. I don't mind it." He makes a mean face at himself in the mirror and leans over to shut the door.

———

A few days later, when we finally talk about the whole thing, he tells me he plans to stay with a friend until his classes start again. He says he doesn't think he'll come back to stay here because he doesn't ever want to see Jack and Wendy again.

I don't try to talk him out of going. I know he's made the right decision and I don't blame him. I would go, too, but I still have one more year of high school. We make a pact to call each other more often and check in.

As far as I know Wendy has no plans to take another three-month vacation. I'm not certain I can handle living with them for the entire school year, but I don't have a choice. I have to stick it out.

Timothy's been accepted at Harvard and plans to study something called "conservation biology." Part of it concerns saving Komodo dragons and stuff so they don't become extinct.

School starts at Harvard in September. We all drive into Cambridge several times and hang out in the city getting to know the campus with him. I figure we'll be visiting him on the weekends during the school year. Leigh and I go with him and his family for the first of his Opening Days. We see his new dorm room and help him unpack his things.

Leigh and I begin our senior year one week later. That's when everything changes.

Twenty-eight

Jules, 17 years | Fall, 1978

YOU WANT . . . YOU WANT TO BELIEVE

WHEN TIMOTHY LEAVES for college, Leigh and I begin to drift apart.

We rarely see each other during school because we don't share any classes or study halls. Even our lunch times are different. She met a college guy the first week of school, and when she isn't at school or majorette practice she spends most of her time with him. He goes to a community college in a nearby town.

Then Leigh drops out of majorettes because practice interferes with her boyfriend time. I drop out two weeks later. Without Leigh there to hang out with, twirling my baton for the football games holds no appeal.

At first we try to make time to see each other, but eventually we stop trying. I'm angry with Leigh. I can't believe that after everything, all the years we've been inseparable, a guy could make her disappear like she never existed in my life at all.

She's just been waiting for a ride out of Withensea on some guy's white horse. But she pulls up my anchor and drags it along when she rides away. I can't hold it. Eventually the line snaps.

Timothy and I were calling one another occasionally at first, but he's grown busy with college life, classes, and meeting new people. I'm the dull hick from back home he's outgrown. I stopped returning his phone calls to avoid talking to him. Eventually, he stopped trying.

My life has grown unbearably small.

My social life, outside of school, is nonexistent. It seems like there's an emotional chasm between me and most of the kids I know. Over the years I've occasionally found small connections, but no one besides Leigh or Timothy has ever seemed capable of unconditionally accepting my life experience. The truth is, I'm too tired to start unfolding myself again. It's exhausting to think about.

Folding in and guarding what is left feels better, so I spend my time after school either in the art room at school or in my room, painting and drawing. Alone.

High school becomes a dance I watch without hearing the music the dancers move to.

On the weekends I work at the town newspaper. They've promoted me to a position they call Junior Copy Editor. Complete gopher job. When I'm not fetching things I make up inane advertising slogans for the local businesses and try not to lose my mind.

————

In October, Wendy and Jack are arrested again for being drunk and starting a fight at the bar. They're held for the night then released. When they come back to the house they have another fight about a chick Jack slept with. Jack tears the house apart again, grabs his things, and moves out. He takes another job sailing a boat and leaves the state.

Wendy responds by sleeping with so many different men I stop paying attention to their names and faces as they drift in and out. As far as I can tell, they're the same man in different sneakers. I figure she has sex with these guys because Jack's been having affairs on her and she's pissed. I ask her if it makes her feel better to have sex with all these men.

"Absolutely."

"Why? How?" I ask. "Don't you feel used all over again?"

She laughs. "I'm using them!"

Life is just a long series of rationalizations for Wendy.

————

IT'S TUESDAY, THE week of Thanksgiving.

Timothy called last night to say he's coming back from school for the holiday and that he'd like to spend time with me over the weekend. I'm surprised by the call and I'm doubtful if we'll really see one another.

I know I'll be spending our Turkey Day at Pier 4, where my grandfather takes us every year to celebrate this American tradition. We order stuffed lobsters. I wish we celebrated like normal families with turkeys and green bean casseroles and passing out in front of the TV, but we don't. Wendy usually dresses up like she's going to a rock concert.

Jack is in Mexico or the Bahamas or somewhere sailing boats and having affairs.

This year, David isn't going to join us. His Thanksgiving will be with somebody from his fraternity. He's become President of his fraternity, and I know he's having fun. I don't blame him for not wanting to come back.

So the group will be Wendy and me, my grandfather, Ruth, and Bethyl.

My grandfather doesn't go to restaurants often. Maybe twice a year. But there's something about this restaurant, on this day, with a branch of the Kennedy clan celebrating in a private space somewhere in the same restaurant. He's proud to be able to do this once a year and it gives him pleasure.

But today is Tuesday. Two days before Thanksgiving at Pier 4.

I walk into Shakespeare with Ms. Epstein. I love this class like no other, mostly because I love Shakespeare and Ms. Epstein reads it superbly to us.

As class starts, Marcy Drake, a cheerleader, calls me over to her seat. I'm curious and a bit nervous because although Marcy and I were friendly once, back in the days when I twirled my baton for the football team, she treats me like I'm invisible now. She asks me why I didn't go out painting the seawall with the rest of the senior class the night before.

"I had no idea the seniors were painting the seawall last night."

The painting of the seawall is an old Withensea High senior year tradition.

"Well, we were—and your mother was there too."

"My mother?" I'm startled to hear this.

"Yeah, I saw your mother parked at the seawall with a guy. When we were done painting we went back to our cars. I needed a light and I walked over to their car, and . . ." Marcy pauses dramatically and a small, nasty smile spreads across her face.

"Your mother was busy in the guy's lap." She smiles at me like I should know what she means. I don't.

She realizes this and decides to educate me.

"She was, you know . . . busy?"

I still don't understand.

"Your mother was giving the guy a blow job," she says loudly enough for several students nearby to hear.

Marcy starts laughing like a hyena. The other kids laugh as well.

I turn and walk to my seat.

I am embarrassed. Mortified.

And the next thing I remember is standing in front of my locker, staring at my coat, at the end of the day.

Big deal, Wendy gave a guy a blow job in a car down by the seawall. I'm sure it's something lots of girls do. Marcy probably gives her boyfriend blow jobs.

But I know it must have been surprising for Marcy to discover Wendy like that. Wendy's behavior stopped shocking *me* a long time ago. This will become another story in an already long list of bizarre behaviors. I wish, though, she'd chosen a less public place to have sex, like anywhere other than a place where school kids could see her.

But Wendy lives by her credo: "Who cares what the neighbors think?"

———

The next day, our last day of class before Thanksgiving break, I rock back and forth in front of my locker deciding whether to leave my books or take them for the break. I don't have any assignments and I probably won't read anything. I close the locker and this guy Nick, whom I know from peer counseling class, is standing there.

"Hey Jules."

"Hi Nick ."

"What are you doing tonight?"

I haven't spoken directly with him in probably a year, although he lives in my neighborhood. He's a football player, and since I quit the majorettes, kids avoid me. It's like throwing away your popularity ticket in Withensea.

I have no identity beyond the art room.

Anyway, I'm wondering why he's asking me this, and I study him closely. "Why? What's tonight?" I'm thinking there must be a senior activity again.

"Nothing going on. I thought you might want to get together, you know, drive around or something?"

This sounds fishy. I ask, "What's up Nick? What do you want?"

"I wanted to talk to you about something . . ."

He seems uncomfortable and like he's sincerely trying to make a connection, and I don't want to hurt his feelings.

"All right."

"Okay?" He acts like I told him he won the lottery.

"Yeah, all right."

"Okay. I don't have a car. Can you pick me up?"

I like the role reversal. "Yeah, no problem. I'll see you around six."

He's still standing by my locker as I walk away.

———

In retrospect, I suppose I should have known that something was up. During our sophomore year, Nick and I were peer counselors for a local birth control clinic a volunteer school program encouraging responsible teen sex. A few of the kids from the church group Leigh and I were part of had been recruited.

Nick acts like a nice guy, one of those guys who doesn't say much in a crowd but acts decent when you talk one on one with him. He's been on a football team all his life. He's big and built. David played on the team with him before he left for college.

I trusted Nick, even though I hadn't been around him in a while.

This turned out to be a big mistake.

———

From the moment he enters the car, he acts abnormal. He doesn't seem to want to talk. I ask him where we're headed and he gives me a vague answer.

"Let me drive."

"No way. I'll drive my car. No offense, but I don't let anyone else drive my car."

He's sullen. This seems more than abnormal. It's creepy.

"Drive around. It doesn't matter."

"Are you paying for the gas?" I joke.

"Yeah, I'll pay for gas."

"All right, I'll drive around."

I head down to the library. I like the historic, gray stone building and the old homes that surround it. Lots of them have been restored since the big blizzard, and at night they have a particular, eerie beauty.

The first big snow hit a few weeks ago, but bits of shriveled leaves still cling to bare branches. Past dusk, the sky reflects a deep periwinkle blue, lit by the old arcing streetlights.

We drive for a while, up and down the avenues and surrounding streets, not saying much.

"Let's go up to the Forts. I want to talk to you."

"We can park somewhere around here and talk."

"No, I wanna go up there and maybe walk around."

I'm unsure about this. The old Revolutionary War Forts are a great spot to walk around during the day because they have a spectacular view. They sit on one of the highest ocean cliffs in Withensea. But at night, they become a spot for teen-agers to make out or go drinking.

I drive up there anyway.

"I'm not going to make out with you," I tell him when we park up at the Forts. I figure I'll be honest in case this is what he has in mind.

He acts shocked. "I know. I mean . . . it's not why . . . that's not what I asked you up here for."

"What did you want to talk about?"

He glances at me and out the back car window. It's like he's concerned someone else might be there, although no one else is around. I think he might be worried someone might interrupt him or hear what he wants to tell me.

It's scary sitting there in the dark. The Forts are scary at night, and, parked there with Nick, I sense an almost ominous energy.

"I wanted to ask you about prom."

"Prom?"

I'm stunned, then afraid he plans to ask me to the senior prom. I have absolutely no intention of going. I plan to go see my grandparents and go to the Boston Museum of Fine Arts on prom weekend. I already went to prom with Timothy last year and had a blast. I don't need to go again.

"Nick, I—"

"Do you think Leigh would go with me?"

Nick thinks Leigh and I are still close, although we barely speak anymore.

"Nick, I guess you don't know, but Leigh has a boyfriend. She's been seeing a guy who goes to college in Quincy. She's wrapped up. I don't see her often myself."

"Oh, I didn't know, huh."

"But, you never know. She may be single by the time prom comes. You're a nice guy, I'm sure you'll have a shot if she's single."

He doesn't seem disappointed to hear this. I can't tell how he feels.

Then I hear a sound. A loud, rough-sounding gang of boys comes driving up the hill behind us, weaving wildly, their headlights waving. My car windows are up and I can still hear them yelling. They sound drunk, rowdy.

My car lights are out and I'm afraid they won't see us parked by the side of the road. I lean in to turn my lights on, and Nick grabs my shoulders and pulls me down onto his lap. I don't understand why he does this. At first I'm completely terrified. Are they going to attack us?

The other car slows down right next to us and the boys shout at our car. I try to push Nick's hands off my shoulders, to pick my head up and make out what they're shouting about, but Nick has a vise-like grip on me.

I think he might be trying to protect me from something. "What's going on? What are you doing?"

"Stay down."

I'm angry now—I'm not going to let a bunch of kids my own age threaten me. I fight off Nick's hands and turn around to see what they're shouting about. As soon as I do I realize what's happening.

The kids in the car explode with laughter at what they think they've interrupted. Several crude comments about "giving head" are thrown out. I turn to

Nick. "That's what this was all about—you set me up in front of your football buddies to make it look like I gave you a blow job?"

Nick avoids my eyes and doesn't answer.

"Get out of the car," I say quietly.

"No."

I'm pissed. I turn on the car, throw it into drive and peel out so fast Nick doesn't have a chance to catch himself. He's thrown backwards in his seat. My heart is pounding in my chest, hard and hot. My entire body is aching with pain that feels unlike anything I've ever felt before. My blood burns. Every muscle stabs. Even my bones throb.

I am completely present, and every action feels precise and, in a strange way, predestined.

"Hey, slow down."

"Fuck you." I push my foot as far down on the pedal as I can. I fly down the hill toward the cliff across the road from the Forts.

"Hey, cut it out. Stop the car. Stop. I'm sorry!" he yells at the top of his lungs.

I slam on the brakes. Nick's arm shields his head against the dash. The car skids for a long time before it stops sickeningly close to the edge of the cliff.

"Get out!" I scream at him. I watch as he fumbles with the door handle and practically falls out. He's kneeling in the gravelly sand at the edge of the cliff. I throw the car into reverse so fast sand spits up at him. He's still cowering there when I peel off.

I'm trembling with anger and adrenaline from nearly going over the cliff. I drive around and think about what an asshole Nick is. How scared and angry I was when those boys were screaming in the car next to us.

How I hadn't known what was going to happen and how terrifying that was.

I'm certain Marcy's story about Wendy has been spread all over the school. I'm sure it inspired a number of cruel jokes. Nick did this to me because of a dare from a group of bored, low-minded, sexually frustrated young boys.

Nothing happened. I haven't been raped or molested. It was a prank, a joke. A stupid, puerile exercise. I can handle it.

What bothers me most is that I trusted Nick. I went along with him, believing he wanted to talk to me, wanted to share something important with me. I hate that I'm a fool. I'm humiliated.

What also bothers me is that the whole scheme was hatched out of gossip about Wendy and her behavior.

It pisses me off that Wendy's "Who cares what the neighbors think!" mantra was the cause of a horrible experience for me.

I'm angry that I have to be the daughter of a mother who does these things.

I'm tired of having to live in Wendy's mess. Her life reflects on mine, influences the way people think about me.

I'm tired of the whole thing.

I don't want to stop believing my life will somehow transcend this bad part, this bad beginning, but I'm starting to think that maybe this isn't the bad part. Maybe this is just how life goes.

———

I drive back to my house.

Wendy is gone.

I think about calling Leigh, but I'm too angry and too proud to let her know how badly I miss her. Plus, I'm a mess. I don't want her to know how much her leaving me has hurt me. I want her to think I haven't noticed her absence. I figure she must not notice mine.

Timothy will be back tomorrow, but I don't think I'll share what happened. I'm too embarrassed to tell him how stupid I was, and I definitely don't want to tell him the story about Wendy.

On the way to my room I decide to open Moses's bedroom door.

It took about a year after he drowned for any of us to go inside and go through his things. No one wanted to. But now we've all been in there at some point, separately, sifting through his belongings, trying to catch a bit of him.

A year or so after he died, we gave all his clothing and most of his belongings to The Salvation Army. But we kept his collections in boxes, which have sat gathering dust since then. No one could bear throwing them away. We gave away the toys. We gave away all the things that might have had value to other people.

Now all that's left are the feathers and pebbles, the shells and the sea glass.

I drag the afghan my Grandmother Ruth made for me from my bed into Moses's room, wrap it around myself, and curl up on his bed.

I can't sleep. I lie there thinking about Moses when he was a little boy and how he used to smell his food before he ate it.

I think about how carefully he acted and about the meaning of the word careful.

I wonder if Moses collected all our caring, all our goodness. Did we all give Moses permission to store all the things that we were afraid or unable to share with each other?

He's gone, and it's all lost.

Everything bad that's happened to me has been punishment for letting Moses drown. I know I'm never going to be able to make it up, to make it better.

Every action, every word, every day since his death has been tarred with this truth.

Inside of me are tiny silver daggers that cut me with this knowledge every time I draw a breath.

I start to cry, and I can't stop.

Twenty-nine

Jules, 17 years | December 23rd, 1978

WHEN RAIN BENDS DOWN THE BOUGH

I HAVE NO memory of Thanksgiving with my grandfather at Pier 4.

David spent his college break with a fraternity friend and his family.

Timothy called while he was home that weekend, but I pretended I had the flu.

Wendy and Jack are back together. Wendy flew down to Florida to meet him. He's running fishing tours on a charter.

Wendy, without asking me, purchased a plane ticket for me to join them for the holidays in Palm Beach. I think she wants to make sure she has company if Jack flakes out.

David decided to spend Christmas with his new girlfriend. I understand. Our new friendship and occasional phone calls began to falter before Thanksgiving. I didn't share what was happening. I wouldn't have been able to find words to explain, and I know he can't do anything to change my situation. Most of all, it's important to me that he moves into a life without the interference of our family's history. We've stopped calling one another.

I understand his absence—it's the familiar absence of the days before Moses died, the days where the Stooges entertained and Freddy reigned—but I feel the loss of his attention more keenly now, having finally gained it, than I ever did before.

Something inside me started to shift after the night in Moses's room. I've fallen into the same sleepwalking state I was in after he died. Each day is a blur.

I've stopped talking to kids at school and no one talks to me. It frightens me, but I don't know what to do about it.

I quit my job at the newspaper.

I've tried to find a way to stay present, to focus on my schoolwork or an art project, but it's all fragile and contrived. It's too exhausting for me to manifest desire for anything. I don't want to wake up in the morning. I constantly show up late to school. I've lost interest in eating and have lost weight, which I only noticed because one day I put on a pair of pants and they slid right off me and onto the floor. When that happened, I tried on a pair of pants I've had since middle school, and they fit.

I've begun to forget homework assignments and the day of the week.

My teachers sometimes stop me in the hall with small encouragements about a drawing I've done or a paper I've written. Their efforts to connect might be genuine, but I've become embarrassed by the attention and fake a cheeriness to appease them.

I'm numb.

This is the part where I begin to think about checking out.

At first the idea snuck into my brain when I was especially tired. I'd tell myself I needed more sleep. Then it was the same after I slept, and I'd tell myself I needed to make it through another day. After each day was finished, I'd set my clothes out for the next day thinking that if I went through the motions—papers done, clothing selected, one step in front of the other—I'd push myself to the other side of wherever I was.

But I still got lost.

I don't have a specific reason. Nothing truly horrible happened. Not any one thing, anyway.

Each day slides by like the last one.

Most nights I have the old nightmare about drowning.

Sometimes when I wake up struggling to find my breath, I'm afraid to fall into sleep again, and I spend the rest of the night fighting to stay awake. Other times, I fight to keep my place in the nightmare. I try to find a different ending.

I have a stack of college applications sitting on my bureau, but it's pointless to think about next fall when I can barely imagine next week. The applications sit there in their crisp packets, collecting dust and taunting me with all my past hopes.

I've lost my ability to believe in certain things . . . friendship or honesty or happy endings. Collusion is intolerable. I want to find a way to slide out of life in the most painless way possible. The other day I realized that Wendy's pharmacy might provide a perfect escape.

When Wendy told me about the Palm Beach vacation, I took it as my opportunity. I told her I have term finals to take, and I'll meet them down there on Christmas Eve. She changed my departure date and left without me.

It arranged itself so easily it seems fated.

I am on my own.

———

Sitting on my bedroom rug, I stare at the carefully arranged members of Wendy's pharmaceutical family in front of me.

About two hours ago I positioned myself before her famous drawer, examining the labels and trying to find the most toxic-sounding selections. I now have about forty pills of various shapes, colors, and sizes creating a three-dimensional, almost hypnotically enticing, pattern before me. Now all I have to do is choose the right combination of pills to make certain I create a permanent ending and not a brain-damaged nightmare.

It's exhilarating! I can't remember a moment in my life I've felt more in control, and I'm relishing the moment.

I glance at the clock. Close to midnight. I hadn't thought about a time, but midnight seems an appropriate moment. I came into the world at 11:59 p.m., according to Wendy.

I swallow the first three pills—the small white ones. These are from the prescription bottle labeled *Seconal Sodium*, and I know they're barbiturates. There are many of them spread out on the rug. Several others, unfamiliar to me, are from the film canisters full of unlabeled drugs. Many of them are sedatives—at least I'm pretty sure they are, based on the way they affect Wendy when she takes them. I'm ready to take my chances. Besides, I have enough barbiturates to seal the deal even if I choose a few pills that might not have the desired effect.

Next to the rug sits a huge bottle of Orange Fanta, which I purchased yesterday for this purpose. I am going out with my favorite beverage.

I hadn't thought about a last meal except to note that the pills will probably work better if I have an empty stomach. This is not an isolated experience for me, dietarily speaking, anyway. Food hasn't appealed to me much lately.

I usually have trouble swallowing pills, so I place each of the larger pills separately on my tongue. Once I swallow them down, I make my next selections. The design I created with the pills was more about following the pattern on the rug and less about putting them in order of intended intake. I select three more of the small white pills and swallow them with a sip of Fanta.

My bed is carefully made. Two letters and two books sit atop the bedspread. One letter for Wendy, one for David. One book for Leigh, one for Timothy. There are no apologies, no blame, and no explanations beyond one central expression of truth: I have no desire to be alive any longer.

I swallow another of the larger pills. I have no idea if forty pills are going to accomplish anything, but I figure if it doesn't work, I can go back to the source and continue the quest. I decide to quicken the poison. I imagine the pills are candy. I take a few more at a time, and fairly quickly, with the help of the Fanta, I finish.

The rug takes on an almost mystical energy. It was my grandfather's family's rug. I start to believe that its threads hold secrets, their colors worn in a pattern reflecting the lives of which it's been a part. Like a genetic memory.

Where it came from originally, I have no idea. It belonged to my grandfather's *bubbe* and his parents brought it with them when they immigrated to America. Peeling back the corner of the rug, I find a faded tan label sewed to the underside. *Product of Iran.*

Iran? How did this Iranian rug arrive in the Ukraine all those years ago?

I wish I knew this story. I realize I have no knowledge whatsoever of my grandfather's childhood. Wendy never talks about it; she rarely brings up her father at all. I wonder if she has any idea about his family. Once I asked where his family came from and she answered, "the Ukraine," but that was it. She doesn't know anything else, which, I think, is weird. My grandfather never talks about most of his family, except to say they died in World War II. I never saw Rose, his sister, after I was a toddler. She lived in Brookline at one time, near him, but she died in Florida around the time that Moses and my Grandmother Yetta died.

I miss my Grandmother Yetta. I love Ruth, and my grandfather seems happier in many ways than I've ever known him to be, but I've seen him less and less since they got married.

Ruth mails checks to Wendy and me since we aren't visiting often. I think Wendy feels a bit jealous of her new stepmother. She barely speaks to her when she does see her.

I begin to feel dizzy; I lie back against the rug. I wonder if this happens when people lose their minds. In being lost to the world, I seem to have found a more direct link to mine.

I wait for what I hope will be a slow, sleepy descent into death. Instead I find myself becoming even more aware.

I study the carpet design. The wool threads become individually interesting. Each thread holds its own secrets, its own portent. Each detail on the rug, and in the room itself, is strikingly crystalline in its definition.

My skin becomes warm, then prickly, as each pore opens and perspires.

My scalp, first warm, then unbearably itchy.

My eyes at first unfocused, then sharply tuned to each color.

Images pop across my retina with the rapidity of subliminal messages in a commercial ad: The jacquard design of the curtains. The letters with their carefully scripted names on the envelopes that lay across the bed. Timothy's copy of *Illusions*.

A feather from my bedspread floats out and over the bed, landing softly beside me at the edge of the carpet and the wooden floor.

This does not seem peculiar, but merely a pleasant offering.

My hand reaches for the feather, but as I do it becomes a fascinating tool, an entity—its intention unknown and sinister.

I pull my eyes away, terrified.

My bureau with its array of perfume bottles. I can smell each bottled scent individually as I look over them one by one. Lavender. Rose. Cinnamon. Musk.

My drawings and paintings, which cover the walls, come alive. The pop art painting of a Raisin Bran box breathes its purple package like a lung. I smell sugar-coated raisins.

Shutting my eyes, I tell myself *it's not real.*

My hearing becomes highly alert. The brush of my hand against the wool of the rug. My throat clearing, my breathing, the sound of my heart beating against its chamber walls.

I begin to have odd, floaty feelings, although they aren't the feelings I hoped for. This is not a peaceful drift into sleeping death.

The pattern in the rug. I trail my fingers through the wool threads, admiring the colors, which have become quite vibrant and glorious. I can see the paisley, the complexity of the pattern, in ways I've never noticed before. The design takes on a remarkable richness and artistry. I never noticed how the midnight blue paisley is dotted with black lines and surrounded by magenta shadows. Even the beige background is not truly beige, but dabs of chestnut brown speckled with grass green, glinty gold, and magenta, spoke-like circular flowers on a creamy canvas. As I run my fingers over them, the colors each feel different. The blue paisleys are velvety and soft. The reds are coarse. The gold is silky like stockings. The multicolored flower spokes have three-dimensional textures.

I have a sudden vision of the time Wendy drugged me with acid and I climbed the backyard willow tree. I remember the boy who came into the backyard and tried to stop me from jumping from the branch limb. The boy I thought was Moses. I wonder who he was.

The phone rings. I glare at it disbelievingly, then I speak to it.

"What?"

The phone responds with another set of rings.

I let the phone continue until whoever is calling hangs up.

I sit up, my heart beating fast. So fast I worry.

What if I accidentally took hits of acid with the sleeping pills? I realize this could easily be what the unlabeled film canister drugs were.

What if I end up living with a completely scrambled brain?

What if the call was Wendy in trouble?

What if it was David in trouble?

What if someone needs something, and because I'm unavailable—and so useless— something terrible is happening right now?

It occurs to me my last human act toward another person might be ignoring his or her phone call, and in doing so providing an opportunity for chaos for that person.

I am, of course, filled with guilt.

I thought I'd carefully calculated guilt out of the act I'm about to complete. Now here it is anyway, in what I know are my last moments.

The telephone rings again. I glare at it and roll over to where it sits by my bedside and lift the receiver out of its cradle.

"What?"

Timothy's calm voice says, "What are you doing?"

I laugh. I'm thinking his question imitates the phrasing in the seductive tones of a crank caller, "What are you wearing?" Knowing him, he has no clue he's come off like that.

I feel sure the effects of the drugs are hitting me, because I can't stop laughing.

Timothy's voice breaks through. "Why are you laughing?"

"I thought your question might be followed by 'Talk dirty to me,'" I choke out through my laughter.

"Talk dirty to me," he says, joking.

I answer without hesitation: "Slime, mud, piles of rubbish, moldy carpets, red tides . . ."

"Stop," he says. "I couldn't sleep, and I had this feeling you might be up too. What are you doing?"

I can't answer. I didn't count on anyone sensing what I might be doing. I was as casual as ever when I said good-bye for the semester to my teachers.

I wonder if he suspected what I was up to or if he truly wants to connect and figured I'd forgive him if I'd been sleeping soundly and his call woke me.

"Are you all right? I had this feeling you might not be all right."

I try to unwind our conversation. What did I say? What have I done to alert him? I have trouble finding words. I have trouble thinking words.

I find a few.

"I'm fine. What are you doing calling?"

I hoped my lack of response would be interpreted as sleepiness, but he persists.

"You were awake, weren't you?"

I can't lie to him. "Yeah, I'm up."

"Are you okay?"

I can't lie to him about this either. He sounds concerned, and I know that if I do lie it will leave him with absolutely the wrong idea about his last interaction with me.

I feel frustrated and trapped. If I say I feel fine, he'll think he missed it.

His chance to save me from my death.

He will have the same legacy I've been trying to escape. I can see the recrimination, the guilt, the remorse, the endless questioning.

If I tell the truth, though, my plan will be shattered. The instant I think this, I'm realizing that it's true already; my plan is shattered.

I haven't responded for quite a while. I lie there, trying to form an answer. To give word forms to my scattered feelings. I'm not sure how much time has gone by. I become acutely aware of the beating of my heart.

"Why are you calling me?" I ask.

"I'm coming over," he says.

"How will you? Are you going to fly from Cambridge?"

I imagine I can see my heart beating out of the T-shirt I'm wearing. It's faint, but I can definitely see movement toward the center of my chest. I remember it must be my lungs moving with my breath. But it's such a small area; shouldn't the rise be on both sides?

I can see a small beat, very definitely the beat of my heart,

Off-center left.

I feel faint, lying back against the rug again with the phone in my hand.

Thirty

Jules, 17 years | December 23rd, 1978

THINK OF ME AS AN ANGEL

TIMOTHY'S VOICE SHOUTS at me, and I notice my hand, which is holding the phone an arm's length away. His distant, tinny yells bring me back to focus.

I pull the phone over to my ear. This is a slow, laborious process of joint enervation. I am acutely aware of each part of my arm's pull and the muscle mechanism taken to achieve the task.

When the phone is against my ear I hear Timothy's voice clearly shouting: "Jules, Jules, are you there? Can you hear me? I'm home, and I'm coming over."

"No!" I shout.

I am deeply ashamed. I'm ashamed for shouting: I have released the demon I save for my fights with Wendy. I feel ashamed for my anger.

This is the part where I share the side of me I have never wanted anyone else to know.

I also feel ashamed at my actions this night. The pills, this pathetic suicide drama.

I'm still thinking these thoughts when I see Timothy standing above me. I had no idea he he'd hung up the phone. I thought he might still be deciding whether to respond.

"How did you get here so fast?"

"It took me the usual amount of time."

I locate the phone by my ear and roll over on my side to put it into its cradle.

I notice how slowly I'm moving. I try to cover it by getting up quickly, but as I'm kneeling to stand, a blanket of dizziness hits me, and I'm falling backwards.

In the next moment he's holding me, he's under me and we're falling, him backwards, onto my bed. The movement is unbearably slow, and I can barely feel my body. But I know he's holding me. I can see his arms surrounding me.

I experience something like wind around me, covering him, pushing him with its force, blowing us where we land, him thudding on top of the letters and books, me without substance. I cannot feel my body any longer. I have become a sail.

Timothy talks in my ear, arms still around me. His voice is soft and deep, and I can taste it. It tastes like chocolate pudding. His voice has a cedar and ivory soap smell.

"What's going on Jules? Have you been drinking? What's all this?"

He's pulling the cards to Wendy and David, the books I left for him and Leigh, out from underneath us.

Timothy is almost six feet tall, and his body is contorted with the effort of pulling these things from underneath us, but I can see his focus is complete.

He's unaware my body still covers him. In any other circumstance, we might find this extremely uncomfortable. But now, in this moment, while I'm highly aware of his body, the fabric of his green wool sweater and his jeans, I cannot feel myself, and he is distracted, and it's comfortable.

I'm realizing I've never touched Timothy. We've only gotten to know one another in the past few years, during what has been a physically awkward time for both of us.

"Oh." I cannot find words to cover what I now know he will know.

Now he lifts me off of him and swings his legs over the bed, opening up the copy of Richard Bach's *Illusions* I've given him. He has dropped everything else. He finds the letter I've written inside.

I panic. "No." I am trying to grab the letter, but I am still dizzy and I find myself falling off the edge of the bed. Timothy reaches out an arm to catch my fall, but it's not enough to stop my trajectory forward. I am rolling onto the rug when a wave of nausea hits me.

I manage to moan through my teeth. He pulls me up and drags me into the hallway toward the bath. If I could stand, walk, feel my legs at all . . . I might be able to make it to the bathroom. Instead I vomit Orange Fanta all over the wooden floors of the hallway. Instead of the shame I know I should be feeling, I am admiring the blending of colors—the orange of the bile against the wood grain.

"Resplendent."

"Huh? Yeah . . . real pretty." He starts to laugh. I am laughing too.

Shame comes later, much later, during a long night in the bathroom, my head stuck down in the toilet bowl, where Orange Fanta-colored particles swim, while Timothy alternately holds a washcloth against my neck and reads the letter I've written to him.

"So, this is what you left me? A schlocky book and a reassurance that nothing I could have done would have stopped you?" He pauses, but doesn't wait for an answer. He is angry now. "Did you think this would keep me from losing my mind over this? Over losing you?"

I lift my head miserably, and I realize what he's saying is true.

"It's a great book. One of my favorites."

He smiles.

"This isn't the way I thought it would go. My plan had no drama or pain."

"What about your family? What about your friends? Did you think we weren't going to be incredibly sad? Or pissed off? What did you take, anyway? Pills?"

He grimaces at the toilet, wrinkling his nose.

He's right. How embarrassing. How selfish.

I've been so self-absorbed, so caught up in my thoughts about leaving, that I haven't considered the effects of my actions. I haven't cared.

I took all the responsibility for my actions in my letters, and I convinced myself I wouldn't be causing chaos for anyone because I was absolving them.

This thought brings another wave of nausea, and while I try to bring up something to satisfy my stomach's urges, I wave Timothy out.

"I'm fine. Wait for me outside."

He obeys and walks out. After what seems like a long time, I can tell I have nothing left in me. I need sleep. I pull myself up and catch myself in the mirror above the sink as I'm brushing my teeth and gargling with the Listerine from the cabinet. My eyes seem sunken in my face, my pupils wide and staring. I wonder at the chemical mix I made with the meds I chose. At least the psychedelic effects are finally starting to wear off.

I have no idea what time it is, but as I open the door to the bath I can see the sun slinking its way across the hallway floors.

I find Timothy in my room. He's sitting on the bed reading *Illusions*. As I make my way across the floor he moves against the wall and makes space for me, opening the covers for me first.

"This book is weird."

"I know, but read it anyway. Turn away."

"Okay, I'm not looking." He turns his head, and I peel off my jeans and T-shirt and crawl under the sheets. I'm relieved and sleepy, and I'm smiling now as I think about Timothy actually reading *Illusions*.

——

When I wake up he's gone. I'm shocked to see it's already eleven thirty. I'm supposed to be dead or on an airplane to Miami right now.

I'm showering when I'm startled by Timothy's voice. "Hey, do you want Raisin Bran or pancakes for breakfast? I can't find any butter or syrup in the fridge, but I could run over to my place and grab some. I called home and they haven't figured out I didn't sleep there last night. My grandmother thought I went to play basketball this morning."

"Jeez, you scared me." I turn off the shower and grab the towel hanging by the stall, wrapping it around me as I step out. I'm hit with embarrassment as I remember the details of last night.

"Sorry. I got hungry and you've been sleeping all morning. You must be hungry too—there can't be anything left in your stomach. I found the empty bottle of soda. You put down a lot of Orange Fanta."

God, did I drink it all? No wonder I got sick.

I'm embarrassed again.

"Oh my God." I sit down on the edge of the bathtub, holding the towel around me.

"What?"

"Can't we forget last night happened?"

He's quiet in the doorway. Then he answers, "Well, it might be possible for you, but for me it's going to be impossible. I nearly lost my best friend last night, and it's not the first time I've known someone who wanted to check out."

I look up, puzzled.

"My mother killed herself. I know I should have told you this a long, long time ago, but it never felt like the right time. I wanted, badly, to tell you last night, but I figured I would wait. I want you to hear this with a clear head: No matter how bad it is, it's never going to be bad enough to make killing yourself a viable option. In my book the only people who get to check out are the ones who are on their way out anyway and want to avoid unnecessary pain."

I'm nervous. "Well, that would be all of us," I laugh. "We're all on our way out . . ."

"Listen to me," he says, not smiling at my joke. "This is hard enough." He takes a long breath. "When my mother decided to end things, I thought it was because she was angry with me. Now I know she did feel angry, but not with me. She got pissed off at the world. She got pissed off she'd been sold a lie. She felt stuck in our family, stuck with a husband and two kids and a suburban nightmare she never wanted in the first place. But she left me, my brother, my father, and her mother, everyone in her life, totally holding this angry bag of shit. She didn't clear anything. She left us holding a shit bag while she split out the back door."

I'm overwhelmed with his story. "The back door?" I ask.

"Yeah, she took the back door out. It's always there for us to take, but it's a shitty exit."

"I'm sorry."

"The first day I saw you it felt like I was watching myself. You were up at the elementary school. You were sitting on the swings. You weren't even swinging. You were sitting and staring at the ground. You didn't see me at all, but I sat on the baseball field watching you.

"I knew you were David's sister. I even knew your story—I mean, about Moses and everything.

"I watched you push up off the swing, leave your books, and walk away. I knew you were kind of sleepwalking, like I'd been for years, and I wondered if you thought it might be your fault your brother drowned, like I thought it was my fault my mother offed herself. But then I realized how crazy that thinking is. It wasn't your fault. It wasn't my fault. People do stupid things. Selfish things. They do things because they can't see any other way to handle things. Or they make bad choices. And there's not much we can do to stop them most of the time. Ultimately, bad choices are the responsibility of the person who makes those bad choices.

"So I put down the angry bag of shit I'd been carrying since I was seven, and I left it in the field at the elementary school. I picked up your books, ran here, and put them on your steps so you wouldn't see me. I wanted you to believe someone might be out there watching over you. I think I wanted you to believe in something magical . . . something transcendent. You know? Like the belief in angels? People don't know, don't really know, if things like angels exist, but they believe and hope and the hope keeps them going."

He takes a breath. "I care about you, and it would have sucked if you'd managed to kill yourself last night. I would be wicked, wicked pissed at you for doing that—but I wouldn't feel guilty about it, or like I should have done something to stop you. It would have been your bad choice."

"Thanks."

"Listen, I'm not saying I'm not glad I called and came over . . . I think you would have barfed up all the pills eventually on your own, though. What the hell did you take, anyway?"

"I don't know. I think I may have taken a mix of sleeping pills and acid."

Timothy's eyes are huge, and I worry he might think I'm an idiot.

"Promise me you won't ever do it again."

I'm hesitant to answer. Promises are important to me.

"I promise I won't ever try that again."

It's the truth. It's my right to end my life if I want to, but I know I'll never try to do it *that way* again. If I need to check out I'm not ever going to do it like that. I'll do it much more mysteriously. No one will ever know that's what I had in mind. No one will ever have to hold my shit bag.

He stares at me like he can tell what I'm thinking. He seems like he knows I've only told part of the truth. Like he realizes he can't ask a person to make that promise.

"My brother saw you drop the books," I say.

"Oh."

I laugh. "I used to believe in angels. I'm not sure anymore. But something told you to call and bother me in the middle of the night, right? Maybe *you're* an angel, and you saved me from my death." I smile at him.

I remember the ship masthead from the Little Corporal. The wooden woman. This crystal memory pops in my head about the time I thought she spoke to me.

Think of me as an angel. Everything will be all right.

You are loved and I'll always be with you.

Icy prickles shudder through me. Then sudden, calming warmth.

"When you stopped returning my calls I thought you were busy with school and new friends. I missed you so much, but I felt stupid bugging you," he says. "I thought maybe you had a boyfriend. I almost called Leigh to ask her what was up, but Leigh and I haven't talked since the day you guys brought me up to start school."

I smile at him sadly. "No, no boyfriends. No new friends. Leigh and I don't even talk. I'm not sure why anymore. I didn't take your calls because you sounded so lighthearted, and I didn't want you to know how depressed I've been. I didn't want you to worry about me when you should be focusing on your own stuff."

"You are part of my stuff," he says quietly. "You're my best friend, and I love you." He's practically whispering this.

I'm frozen.

Before I can answer, he says, "So, do you want syrup and butter on your pancakes?"

I go over to him and give him a huge hug. I press my head against his chest and speak my words into his green, ivory soap-scented sweater: "I love you, too."

I feel like crying, but my tears are frozen, so I keep hugging him until he pulls away.

"I'll be right back," he says. He smiles and turns to walk downstairs. Then he calls over his shoulder, "Your towel is falling off."

My towel has fallen down to my waist.

Much later—long after the pancakes and Wendy's angry call from the Palm Beach airport and my excuse about oversleeping and deciding to stay in Withensea over the holidays with Timothy and his family—when I think about it, the moment in the bathroom with Timothy, I think how, in a movie, we might have kissed and made out and maybe had sex. But we didn't. I didn't even think about the possibility. I mean, it never crossed my mind. I had absolutely no physical urge to kiss him. It felt nice hugging him, but that's all I wanted or needed from him.

I figure he probably felt the same, but part of me wonders if maybe he took off for the maple syrup right then because he got a stiffy when I hugged him half-naked. Maybe he didn't feel like he should have sex with me after my suicide attempt because that might be behavior modification in a bad way. Or something.

But I know the experience held more importance than sex, even though I haven't had it so I can't really compare.

I feel like after this, Timothy has become a person who'll be a part of my story whether he stays involved in my life later or not. He lives in my skin now.

Something else happened to me because of this too.

A hole in my chest opened, and all the tiny silver daggers spilled out.

Part 3 | The Raveling

Thirty-one

TRUTHS AND LIES

IT'S SPRING BREAK. Graduation comes in a few months.

I've been accepted by two of the three colleges where I applied, and I've made up my mind to attend the Boston School of the Arts if they accept me. Ms. Wheaton helped me with my submissions portfolio. I've already been there to do my entrance interview, and I've practically grown an ulcer waiting to hear about my acceptance status.

Sarah Lawrence accepted me two weeks after my interview. I told them I wanted to study English Lit, but as soon as I got my acceptance I knew I could never go there. The Caucasian population accounts for about 95 percent of the students, and after living in diversity-void Withensea my whole life, I've had enough of homogenous living. I applied because I thought I would receive an original education there, but it just didn't feel right.

My safety school is Boston University. I've been accepted as a liberal arts major. I figure I can study art and earn a decent BA degree there as well.

My grandfather has been putting David through college. He's offered to do the same for me. The sole caveat is that I have to spend spring break week, my last free week before graduation, with him and my Grandmother Ruth. He says he wants to go over the details of my college plans.

I'm delighted to oblige. Wendy hasn't displayed an interest in my college plans and progress. She never offered to help with any of the applications and seems barely interested.

"I knew you'd be accepted wherever you applied," she says.

Sometimes you need a person not to know everything so they can be excited with you.

I haven't had a chance to really talk with Ruth during our brief visits to Boston. Wendy doesn't like her or her daughter Bethyl much. I've been going on my own to see them, but only occasionally.

Wendy says they don't like her because they consider her a sinner. The Jews have at least four Hebrew words for the different kinds of sins you can commit. I'm sure Wendy has earned every word. But I also know the Jews believe sin is an act and not a state of being. Maybe she'll be forgiven.

My car needs new brakes and a service so Wendy offers to drive me into Boston to their apartment. I'm shocked at first, but then I figure she needs to pick up a check from him and that's why she's volunteering.

—⁀—

After dropping my car at the home of our mechanic, a guy Wendy dated last summer, I climb into Wendy's new car, a green 1973 Gremlin. She and Jack call it the "Green Goblin" because it gobbles so much money with repairs to the ignition system.

The glove box won't shut and I'm trying to fix the locking mechanism. It's stuck.

"So, I wanted to congratulate you again on your acceptance to your colleges. I'm proud of you," Wendy says, gesturing wildly with both hands as she drives.

"I'm still waiting to hear from the Boston School of the Arts."

She keeps talking like she hasn't heard me.

"I also wanted to tell you I'm proud you're going to pursue your artistic passions. You're talented and I'm sure you're going to succeed. You can do anything you put your mind to. You're smart, you know?"

The car seat upholstery looks like Levi's jeans, but it's cheap nylon—frayed at the seams. I pick at it and pretend I'm distracted by the cars we pass on the highway.

"I want you to understand that your grandfather loves you a lot, but he comes from a different era. He believes it's wasteful to study artistic endeavors. He thinks you should study education. Actually, I think he wants you to go to college so you can find and marry a doctor."

"I told Grandpa my plans and he said he'd support me through college."

"I know what he told you. I'm telling you now, he plans to change your mind about your major and he won't take no for an answer. He's a stubborn man, believe me. He's not going to change his mind about this. The best thing for you to do is go and study whatever you want, but tell him you're going to study education, or law, or medicine . . . or tell him you're studying to be a teacher. He'll accept that."

I can't understand why my grandfather wouldn't tell me this himself and why Wendy is telling me now. But I can't think of any reason she might have to lie to me.

"Why are you telling me this?" I ask.

"Because. I know you think your grandfather is a nice man, but you don't know how he acts when you cross him. He's a bull. All my life he's been trying to control what I do, how I behave, how I live. I used to pray to God I would be the daughter he wanted, that he would see me and love me for the girl I truly was and not the girl he wanted me to be."

I'm surprised to hear Wendy talking about her childhood. I realize I know little about her years living with my grandparents. She never talks about it.

"What kind of a girl were you, and what kind of girl did he want you to be?"

"Good question. What kind . . . ?" She falls silent. I can tell she's trying to answer thoughtfully, and I wonder what nerve I've touched.

"I was a quiet kid."

I laugh. "Quiet?"

She laughs.

"Yeah, I was quiet. I started to gain more confidence as a teenager, but I was exceptionally withdrawn. I never felt like I could talk. I certainly wasn't encouraged to share my opinions. Your grandfather kept a tight rein on every aspect of my life. I wasn't allowed to have friends from school over or to play outside. I had one friend, a young boy who lived in the next apartment. His mother was the daughter of some family friends, and the boy and I played in the hallway between our apartments. We rode our bikes around the hallway like it was a racetrack, and we played together in one or the other of our apartments after school."

Wendy is weaving in and out of lanes as she talks. I'm nervous about responding, about distracting her further, but curiosity wins.

"What happened to him?"

"When I turned twelve, he moved away. It wasn't until high school I was allowed to go places after school with my friends."

"That must have been hard."

"Well, everything changed. As soon as I had freedom things went haywire with your grandfather. He lost control. I lost my will to please him. We started fighting about everything, and we've never stopped. After I met your father it got even worse. He hated the idea of me dating a *goyem*. He told me I'd sinned and I'd shamed the entire family

"When they told me the truth about my adoption, I was devastated. I was seventeen. I'd gone to live with your grandfather when I turned ten. Until then, I'd been living with his parents, who I thought were my real parents. But they'd been lying to me all those years. I felt like I couldn't trust anything or anyone. If I hadn't needed my birth certificate for my driver's license, they wouldn't have ever told me. They would have continued to lie about everything."

This is stunning. I had no idea they waited that long to tell her.

The driver behind us honks loudly as she cuts him off, crossing two lanes to get to our exit ramp. "Fuck you, asshole!" Wendy screams at the man as he passes her on the left.

"So, who do you think he wanted you to be?" I ask.

"He wanted me to be someone impossible. He wanted me to be a great scholar—something no one in his family had been able to achieve. He never wanted me to marry or be a wife. He wanted me to achieve greatness as a woman in a man's world. He wanted me to deny that I was female, or even human."

"What do you mean?"

"When I left for college I started dating a man in one of my classes. I got pregnant."

Another driver honks at us when Wendy pulls a U-y in a no-turn lane without using her signal. She grows quiet again and concentrates on her driving.

"What happened?"

"I went home. The guy I'd been dating didn't want to have a kid, but I wasn't going to have an abortion. I wanted the baby. Your grandfather said he wouldn't help me. He told me I'd ruined my life and he didn't want anything to do with me. He called me the same names your father called you."

"Oh my God. How awful. You must have felt so scared."

"Yes it was awful. I was frightened and all alone. I had no idea what to do. I had no job; he wouldn't pay for school now that I'd gotten pregnant. I had no way of returning to finish the semester or continue my schooling after the baby came. I couldn't abort that baby. I wanted my own flesh and blood. I wanted my own family."

I got confused.

"So, what happened to the baby?"

She grows quiet for a long time, and I can see she's having difficulty telling me the rest of the story.

"I married your father. I convinced him the baby was his. His family made him marry me because they didn't want the dishonor of having a bastard, or a baby they believed might be his bastard, running around. I'd never told your grandfather who had fathered the baby. He assumed it was Howard's."

"Oh my God. This means David isn't—isn't Dad's kid."

She seems surprised I haven't figured this out instantly. Like I'm an idiot.

"Yeah, that's right." She does a double take and looks almost angry for a moment. "If you ever repeat this, I'll deny it. Your father would kill me, do you understand? He would kill me."

"Fine. But don't you think David would like to know who his real father is? I mean, think how you felt learning about the lie your parents told you."

"No. I don't think it would do David any good, and it's not like the lie my parents told me. The people who raised him were his parents. I am his mother. David's not going to hear about it, right? Don't make me sorry I told you. I don't want him to have to feel badly, like I did."

She slams her hands into the wheel of the car. "I shouldn't have told you. I thought you were old enough to be trusted."

I'm worried we're going to have an accident. When she gets agitated Wendy drives more erratically than usual, a pattern that has caused me great anxiety over the years.

"I won't. I won't tell him. But I'm not going to stop wanting you to tell him. I still think he should know."

She doesn't answer. Instead, as we pass it, she points to the Rainbow Swash on the Boston Gas storage tank. "Did I tell you Jack met the artist who designed that? Do you see Ho Chi Minh?"

"Like a million times! So, is Howard *my* father? Is he Moses's father?"

I figure if she could lie about one kid, she could definitely be lying about others.

"Yeah, yeah, he's your father. As much as you may not want him to be your dad, he's still your biological father. Sorry."

I laugh. I'm not sure exactly why I'm laughing, but I find it funny. It's incredible to be hearing this story, and I can't believe she's told me.

"Why are you telling me all this now?"

"I don't know, maybe because you're at an important point in your life. I can see how much you want to achieve your dreams of pursuing your art. I don't want you to make the same mistakes I made. I want you to follow your dreams and do what you want."

"Don't you think you did what you wanted? You had the baby. You had David. It's what you said you wanted."

She grows quiet, and then says, "I wanted your brother, and I wanted a career. I enrolled at Columbia as a sociology major. I wasn't sure what I would do with a sociology degree—your grandfather wanted me to teach, but I didn't feel sure about that idea—but regardless, I wanted more than what I settled for."

"Why have more babies?"

"I didn't want David to be an only child. In my experience it felt lonely. I wanted David to have a sister. I wanted a girl. That was you."

"Okay, I guess I understand. But why have another one . . . why have Moses?"

"My birth control method consisted of douching after sex."

I have no idea what this means. I've never heard the word "douche"before. I ignore that, though, so she'll tell me the rest of the story.

"So what happened? Did you decide you wanted another baby?"

"No. I found out your father had had another affair, this time with a friend of mine. I told him I was divorcing him. He flipped out. He told me he'd never agree to a divorce, then he beat me and raped me. I went back to your grandfather's house. I don't know why, I guess I thought he would protect me. It was the second time I could remember really needing him to do something for me. I told him what had happened and that I wanted to divorce your father. He said, 'You made your bed, go lie in it.' So, I went home. I realized pretty quickly that he'd gotten me pregnant again. I didn't want another baby, and I tried everything I could to abort it this time. I carried boxes across the living room all day for a week to try and lose the baby. It didn't work. I told your father I would name the baby Spite."

I want to throw up, but she won't stop talking. I'm having trouble accepting her story about Howard raping her, I'm sure she's exaggerating. I reach over to punch another radio station on the dashboard and dial up the volume.

"You were actually the one planned pregnancy I had. I decided one night not to douche after your father and I had sex," Wendy says, turning the volume back down.

I can tell she isn't going to stop telling these stories, and while they hold a curious fascination for me, I realize I've had more information than I want to process for one day.

"Can we stop talking now? I don't want to hear any more." I'm scanning the buildings out my car window. Everything is wavy.

"Jules, I know you don't want to hear any of this shit. I know you're angry with me and you think I ruined your life with the way I raised you, and I'm sorry about all that. One day you're going to understand that I raised you the way I did because of the things I went through. I wanted to be sure you didn't have to suffer like I did. I wanted you to be an independent person. I didn't want you to feel like you had to rely on a man, or anyone, to take care of you. I wanted you to be prepared for the world, not sheltered and coddled the way I'd been. The real world shocked me. It sent me straight into a rotten marriage and left me financially dependent on your grandfather the rest of my life."

"You don't have to depend on anyone anymore. That's an excuse to be lazy."

"Sometimes depression looks like lazy."

We don't talk at all for the rest of the ride.

When we pull up to my grandfather's brownstone, the sunset has turned the dusty brown stone into crimson. I jump out at the curb and slam my door shut before Wendy turns off the car.

Her voice catches me as I start to walk toward the building.

"Give me a break. I did the best I could! What can I say to you? I'm sorry. I'm sorry for every lousy thing that's happened. I'm sorry I wasn't the mother you wanted or felt like you deserved. I'm sorry I pick losers for husbands and boyfriends. I don't know what else I can say, but I'm sorry!" Wendy is screaming now.

"Sorry works. Sorry is a good start. You never say you're sorry about anything. You act like I'm the one out of line for asking you to be different and behave like a person who cares about her kids. You've done terrible things to us. You made me feel . . ." I can't finish what I wanted to say.

"I made you feel what?"

I start to cry. "You told me it was my fault Moses died."

"I . . . what? I never said that!" She seems mystified by my statement.

"You did!"

"When?"

"After . . . after it happened."

"No, I didn't. Or I didn't mean it if I did say it. I can't remember what I said. I remember that I was out of my fucking mind that Moses died. It wasn't your fault. My God! It wasn't your fault."

Wendy starts crying. I've never seen her cry. Not once. Not even when Howard beat her. Not even when she found Jack with the girl down in Key West. Not even the day of Moses's funeral. It freaks me out.

"Why are you both shouting in the street like criminals?" my grandfather calls down from his apartment window.

Crap. We're standing there crying and screaming like morons. I'm mortified and hope my grandfather hasn't heard what we've been fighting about. Wendy and I stare at each other. I start to laugh. At first she crosses her eyes at me like I'm crazy, then she starts to laugh as well.

We go into the brownstone, climbing the steep stairs to my grandfather's apartment together.

Wendy stays for dinner and her check, as usual. I plan to stay for a week and take the T and the buses back. I walk her out to the hallway at the end of the evening and say good-bye.

"Remember, you're old enough to make your own choices. Don't let him bully you into doing what he wants. Don't let him buy your will."

I think about her warning. Will he try to *buy my will?* I'm certain I'm not going to let that happen. I've already secured financial aid if I need it, I won a National Merit Scholarship and I've been offered a small grant if I'm accepted as an art student. My plan, if I'm accepted to the Boston School of the Arts, is to stay in the dorms the first year and then rent a room from David's high school friend who has a place in the city. I'm also planning to get a work study job.

There's nothing my Grandfather Samuel can do to change my mind.

Thirty-two

Jules, 17 years | March, 1979

a little sorrow

AT FIRST, MY grandparents and I hang out together.

In the morning, when I wake up, my Grandmother Ruth offers me Frosted Flakes. The same box my grandfather has kept in the cupboard since Moses spent the night ten years ago. I ask her if she'll make me fried matzoh instead. I love fried matzoh.

Later, we go shopping for groceries and my grandfather goes to work. He's sixty-nine years old and he's still working four or five days a week at his tailor shops. Ruth walks everywhere to do errands. She walks miles out of the way to save five cents for a particular item. I had no idea how much exercise she manages on a daily basis.

After we bring the groceries home and put them away we go to the movies. We watch *Harold and Maude*. I love it. Ruth hates it. When we're home, I help her make dinner, and then we go to visit friends of theirs in the next apartment building over.

I sleep in the dining room, which doubles as their guest quarters, on a cot.

After three days of more or less the same activities, I wake up one morning to find my grandfather sitting in one of the chairs at the dining table. I have the feeling he's been sitting here for a while, waiting for me to wake up.

"Morning," I mumble.

"Good morning," he says with his thick accent. "I want to talk with you while your grandmother shops."

I sit up and pull the covers around me, self-consciously trying to tidy my hair, which sticks out everywhere in its morning mess. I figure this must be the *college conversation*, but it starts out differently than I expect.

"You don't look like your mother or the father. You look like my twin sisters, Ruchel and Sura."

I've wondered most of my life why I don't resemble anyone in my family. Wendy's revelations a few days ago have certainly made me wonder about my true paternity—despite her assurances that Howard is my father. But I don't understand how, if Wendy is adopted, I could resemble my grandfather's sisters.

I go from sleepy to completely alert in a few seconds.

"Tell me about them. You never talk about your family. What were they like? Are they still alive in the Ukraine?"

My grandfather turns his gaze to the wall, and we remain there, silent, for a while as he removes his glasses and begins to clean them with the handkerchief he always keeps in his pocket. Then he speaks slowly and quietly. I can barely understand him.

"No. They are *toyt. Meysim.*" He pauses, realizing he isn't speaking English anymore. "They are gone. They are all gone now. I have family still in New York who I don't know . . . but the brothers and sisters who stayed behind . . . are gone."

He sounds sad. I'm afraid to ask more questions, but if I don't, I may never have another chance.

I ask softly, "What happened to everyone? What happened to Ruchel and Sura?"

He's quiet so long I don't think he'll answer me at all.

Then my grandfather stares straight into my eyes and says, "They were killed by the Russian soldiers. They were murdered. They killed Berl, my sister Rose's first husband. They killed my brother Idel."

When he says his brother's name, his voice breaks and he makes a sound like a gull's cry. The pain of it makes my own heart ache.

"My parents, they had come here, to America, with the young ones. Rose, my brother Oizer and I, and the others . . . we were the ones left. After the camps, Rose and Oizer came to America to be with the family. I sailed for Palestine. I am thinking I am going to start my life there."

Again, he grows quiet. I have many questions, but I can see how upset he's become and I'm afraid to ask them. I've never seen my grandfather like this. His emotions scare me.

"You see, there is a little of sorrow in everyone's life," he says.

"But in the end, I come here . . . to America, to start my life, instead of Palestine. I stay with my *foter* and *mater* in New York for a short time. Then Rose and her new husband, Mocher, they take me here to Boston to work with them. I never see the rest of my family much after this. Over the years, I went back to New York twice, once for my *foter's* funeral, then for the *kind*."

He stares out the long casement window of the brownstone.

"This is the last time I see my *mater* before she goes. When I take the *kind*."

"What *kind*?" I ask.

"The child. The child. She couldn't stay with my *mater* anymore. My *mater* is dying. Yetta and I, we brought her here to live."

I realize he's talking about Wendy.

They went to get Wendy in New York because she was staying with his mother. Wendy told me she was ten when this happened.

"Why did she live with your parents? Was the orphanage in New York? How come they adopted her?"

"*Tsu vos* orphanage? There is no orphanage."

"My mother wasn't adopted?"

Now I'm mystified. I wonder if Wendy made up the story about her adoption. My grandfather continues, "*Dayn mother* is *mayn* family."

He says this last thing with anger. I'm not sure what I said to upset him.

"I don't understand."

"Your mother is *mayn* family. She is *mayn* sister's daughter."

I think about what he just said. Wendy is his niece? His sister's daughter? What sister? He told me Ruchel and Sura were murdered in the Ukraine.

"Do you mean Rose? Is my mother Rose's daughter?"

"No, not Rose. Anna."

Anna? Who is Anna?

This question triggers more questions in my mind. Also, the knowledge that my grandfather truly is my blood relative fills me with so many emotions I can't sort them.

"Anna is my youngest sister. She is born here in America. She died alone in a hospital. She . . ." His voice is breaking, but he continues. "There are stories I have not shared with your mother. There are stories it is best we don't tell, Chavalah. For what good would it do to tell these things?"

"I want to know you, Grandpa. I want to know my family."

With these words, my grandfather sighs, his body sagging against his chair. The lines in his face sink somehow deeper. He raises his handkerchief to his face and begins to weep. I move to his side and wind my arms around his shoulders, leaning in to nest my head against his neck. My stomach is in knots and my throat is choked, but I don't let go.

"The world is full of terrible things, terrible people. I have witnessed more horror than you can dream."

At his words my body grows cold. Something in his manner terrifies me. It's my Grandfather Samuel's body, but it's as though he's gone away and someone else is speaking.

Then, as quickly as I have this thought, my grandfather pushes me away and puts his glasses back on. He shoves the handkerchief back in his pocket and looks directly at me. His face is alarmingly composed and serious.

"I want to talk with you about college."

"Yes," I answer, shaking my head to try and clear away my questions.

"I want to talk with you about your studies. What, what are you going to study?"

"I'm going to study art, Grandpa."

"What do you mean art? Nobody studies art. You should study teaching. This is what you must do."

I start to feel uncomfortable, but I tell myself I need to be honest and patient and clear with my grandfather. He'll understand why I want to pursue art as my major.

"Grandpa, I know that when you were young, the idea of studying art probably sounded decadent, but now it's an accepted area of college study."

"I am not accepting. This is foolish thinking. You must think of your future and the life you will have when you graduate. You're not a *kind* anymore and you must think of a steady career. This will not make money. A degree for an artist. This means nothing. This is foolishness."

I suck in a breath. I can see this is going to be difficult.

"Grandpa, there are lots of things I can do with my art degree. These days, if I want my art to be taken seriously, if I want to work in the field of art, I need a degree to compete in the art world."

"You don't need to compete in this world. You should take a degree in education and teach. This is what you should do. Forget this dream of being an artist."

"Grandpa, I can't forget this dream. I understand you're worried for me that I won't succeed as an artist. I can't assure you I will, but I can assure you I'll never be happy unless I try."

"What is this happiness? We don't go to college to be happy. We go to be educated. Enough with this happiness. You should study teaching. That's enough."

He waves his hand dismissively. I think he might end the conversation here, with a standoff.

"I will give you money. You will have money to study teaching. No money to study foolishness."

"I don't want money from you. I don't expect you to pay for my college if you don't want to. I've got a grant, student loans and scholarships lined up for school."

He seems surprised to hear this. I'm relieved. I think maybe he was worried or even offended by the idea that I would expect him to support me. Maybe he'll support my plan now that he knows I've secured the funding?

"They give you scholarships for this foolishness? This is foolishness!" he shouts.

He's even angrier now. I'm trying to understand why.

"No. You should use the scholarship for education studies. Write to them and thank them, then tell them you want to use the scholarship for this instead."

"It doesn't work like that. I got an arts grant. A visual design grant. I can't use the money for an education major. They don't teach anything but art education at the school I want to attend."

"What school this is where they don't teach anything but dreams? This is a *meshugener* school."

He laughs. Then I laugh. I'm relieved we're laughing now.

But he stops laughing and says, "If you go to this *meshugener* school, I will not give you anything. I will give you no money. I will die and you will have none. No money."

He's shouting again. He's never spoken to me like this.

Wendy warned me.

I don't want to disappoint him, but can see he might never accept my decision.

I consider my options. I know I can take Wendy's suggestion and lie to him about my intention. I can let him think he's changed my mind. I can accept his offer to support me through college and never tell him what I'm really studying. I don't think he'll continue to ask to see my report cards each semester, as he has throughout high school.

But I can't. I can't lie to him about something important to each of us. I want to try and build a relationship with him based on honesty and openness, not like what he and Wendy have. I want to help bring him into the end of the twentieth century. I come up with a compromise I think he'll be happier with.

"I promise you, if I don't make it as an artist, I can use this degree to teach."

He considers this.

"Why not study to be a teacher? You can teach what you want. This is good. A teacher. This is a good idea."

"I'll think about it. I don't want you to be angry with me, Grandpa. I want you to be proud of me."

I'm hurt. I try to separate my own feelings of sadness and hurt from his intention to protect me.

"Do you want to end up alone and penniless? Don't you want to find a husband? Who will marry a woman who studies to be an artist? Men don't want women who dream. They want strong women who can work and raise children."

"I don't care if I marry. I don't need a man to keep me safe or to take care of me. I don't even want children. Do you think my mother felt safe in her marriage?"

"Your mother married a *beyz* man. He is a bad *foter* and bad husband. You will marry a good man. A strong man. A doctor. Marry a doctor. He will be rich and take good care of you and your *kinder*."

Wendy's right. My grandfather has a huge fantasy about me and a doctor. I realize I don't want to ruin this fantasy for him.

"Grandpa, if I do marry, I'll try to marry a doctor. Would this make *you* happy?"

If he's catching my attempt at humor, he's ignoring it.

"Yes. That would make me happy. Remember, it's as simple to love a rich man as a poor man." He doesn't smile when he says this, but he hands me a butterscotch candy from his pocket.

"I would be contented if you behaved like a good girl and not like your wild *mater*."

"I won't behave like my wild mother. I'll be a good girl." I'm certain I know what he's worried about. I look him in the eye. "I won't get in trouble like my mother."

He finally smiles. "You're still on your own if you study to be artist."

"Fine. I'd rather do it on my own anyway."

"You are like your mother. Stubborn and proud."

"No, Grandpa. I have more pride than my mother. I don't expect anyone to take care of me. I want to take care of myself. I'm ready to take care of myself."

"Good. That's what you receive. Nothing."

He stands up abruptly and stalks out of the room. I hear the door open and close as he leaves the apartment. I sit there reeling until my grandmother comes home.

When she asks me where my grandfather is, I say he's gone out for a walk.

He comes back about an hour later and acts like nothing's happened between us. We spend the day doing puzzles. Later we go out for ice cream.

I'm starting to understand why Wendy went nuts.

———

I have the nightmare that night. It's the same as always, except the person in my dream who is drowning, who I swim to save, is my grandfather.

I don't understand why he appeared in the dream or what it means. I know it means something, though.

Thirty-three

ENDING WITH A BEGINNING

LAST NIGHT I dreamed Moses and I were rowing underwater. We could breathe and talk to one another. We rowed past schools of fish and sea anemones and Moses named them for me.

In two weeks I'm driving the Mustang into Boston to start college at the School of the Arts.

Things here in Withensea seem to be changing. Last year's blizzard turned out to be the worst in Massachusetts's history, and the town was declared a national disaster area. The full tides literally swept homes into the ocean and left most others with severe damage.

The relief money people received to rebuild homes and businesses has gone a long way toward giving the town the facelift it needs. Insurance claims were made—a few were sketchy, but many allowed people to tear down termite-hollowed, weather-beaten homes that would otherwise have fallen down.

My grandfather has never mentioned the conversation we had about Wendy and college again. I'm curious about what he said to me that day, especially the statement regarding Wendy being his sister's daughter, but I know I can't ask more questions for a while—even though I have so many it makes me feel crazy.

A few days after I left his and Ruth's apartment, I called and asked him if he'd write all the family history down so I can read it someday. I especially want to know what his boyhood was like and how he and his family decided to come to America. He said he would try.

I'm certain he communicated what he intended to about college. We have reached what feels like détente. I've managed to escape his permanent wrath by vowing to marry a doctor if I can and teaching if I fail as an independent artist. These ideas feel like fairy tales to me, but they make him feel good. I wonder if he knows they're fairy tales.

I'm leaving with the knowledge that I'm on my own financially, which isn't what I'd expected, but is, ultimately, I think, exactly what I want.

Timothy and I hang out on all our days off. I'm working through the summer at my new job at the library. He has a research job working in the marshes around Withensea studying the phytoplankton. I'm impressed with how much time he actually spends studying the stuff. He tells me if we don't make sure the phytoplankton algae stays healthy, then basically all the marsh plants will die off, and if that happens all the fish and shellfish will die. I have no idea what he means when he goes off about the nitrogen exchange and things, but he makes me care about it and want to be involved. I spend my free days hanging out at the salt marshes with him and Crikey, cleaning up trash and examining algae samples.

We've had a blast all summer and plan to see each other on the weekends when I go to school.

Oh, and . . .

This is the part where Timothy and I camped out in the marsh one night and watched the Perseid meteor shower and had sex.

It was the first time for both of us. We laugh when we talk about it because we know later, when we're old, we can say we saw stars.

Leigh lives with her boyfriend in Duxbury now, and she came back to visit her family for a few days this summer. We got together one night and hung out at the bar Howard used to own. It's called McGillicuddy's now, and the brother of a guy we graduated with owns it. We sat at the old, oak bar underneath the gold-leaf mirror. The spot above the mirror, where the wooden woman had once been, was empty. We drank Shirley Temples because Massachusetts raised the legal drinking age to twenty a month before my eighteenth birthday. I don't care. I don't care if I never drink a beer my whole life.

All Leigh talked about when we hung out was her wedding in December. She has no plans to go to college. She's always been so smart, but now it's like all she wants is to marry this guy and have babies. It feels hopeless to me. She got out of Withensea, though, and for that I'm happy for her. Not a lot of people leave this place. If it doesn't suck you in, like an undertow, you're lucky. We've grown so far apart. We didn't make any plans to see each other before the wedding, and I wonder if I'll even go. Still, I'll miss her. Her leaving feels like another death I can't understand.

———

I've been thinking about what my grandfather said about every life having a little sorrow. I picture my grandfather's life. I imagine what it must have felt like for him to lose members of his family when he was young and be separated from the rest for such a long time. Being an immigrant and having no money and no real prospects.

Comparatively, I've had a decent life. But still, we share sorrow.

I wonder if my grandfather feels like I do—like outliving his brother and sisters deserves punishment. Like somehow we'd caused our own sorrow. I wonder if our sorrow is an inheritance, like the blue eyes I know Moses got from him. Can it somehow be genetic?

Or how about survival? Have we been born with a gene that makes us stronger than the other members of our family? Like a spiritual power gene?

Maybe there are angels. Maybe my Grandfather Samuel and I have an angel. Maybe the same angel protects us because she wants us to keep living for a specific reason. Like writing a great book or curing cancer.

But why us? Why not Moses? Why not my grandfather's family members who died young? Where were their angels? Maybe angels can fail too. Maybe angels are human after all.

So I'm not complaining, but I'm having difficulty processing everything that's happened in my life so far. And sometimes I believe in angels more than I believe in all the bad stuff I've experienced.

Withensea is beautiful, but my life here has been mostly ugly. I'm not counting on an angel to rescue me. I'm lifting myself out of here, and I'm not coming back. I don't have to. I'm taking it with me. Every bit of skin and hair, every pore, every cell in my body is built of Withensea matter.

Wendy can visit me in my new life if she wants. I'm still angry she didn't tell David about his real father, and she forbids me from telling the truth. I've decided not to say anything to her about *her* real mother . . . yet, because of my promise to my grandfather, but I'm going to find a way to make sure all this family's secrets are eventually told. They have to if we're ever going to build a different legacy. I need more time to figure out how to make this possible. I believe it's possible.

Time.

My story will push on from here. I have an ending in mind now, but I'm not sure I'll want the same ending in sixty years, or ten years, or even next year.

I'm hopeful my grandfather will understand my choices someday, but I can understand why he might not. He's a man with a brain from a different country. From a different century, even. And he's a man with many secrets. Most of them I will never know.

Secrets drive people crazy, though. I think secrets add up to more secrets that keep truths stuffed deep inside them.

Secrets helped make Wendy nuts. She's had a rough go of it, and I'm willing to cut her some slack. Actually I'm *going* to cut her some slack, but only because I want to give myself room to escape without feeling a tug.

I'm going to try to forgive Howard for the things he's done, but I'm not going to cut him any slack. I'm going to cut the tether entirely. I'm certain it's the best way for me to go forward into a new life. I don't think he's going to change. I don't want to have to be tied to him in any way that might make me remember him except in the ways I want to. I want to remember birthday parades with paper hats. I want to remember piggyback rides and trips to the zoo. I want to look at old photos of all of us smiling and imagine we smiled because we were happy, or at least untroubled, in those moments.

I wish things had been different for us growing up. I know it sounds like a simplistic statement about my circumstances, but it's countered with an acceptance, maybe also simplistic, that things go as they go.

Still, I wish David and I had become friends sooner than we did. Sooner than his last year of high school. I hope we'll become better friends in the years ahead. I'm glad he's my brother. I don't think I would have survived without a witness, even if my witness was a person who turned up the volume on the television set while the house caved in.

Moses witnessed everything while he remained on earth, and he's become a witness to the chaos even now that he's left. Every time I dream the drowning dream. Every time I think about him.

His death is evidence of the things that went missing in my life.

I wish Moses were alive. I wish Moses were alive so much it hurts. I understand why all the descriptions of lost loved ones are physically descriptive. Lovesick, heart-broken, grief-stricken. I can feel the loss of Moses in my marrow, my joints, my tissues. It aches inside-out when I think of him. I miss him every day. Sometimes it's all I can think about. It's a good thing I miss him, though, because it means I'm feeling things, and I think feeling things is a good way to stay present. Much of the time I feel guilt. I wonder what I can possibly do in my life to somehow make up for the fact that we didn't protect him better. At times it feels like a test of resilience. Other times I feel incredibly small and insignificant and I marvel how anything survives within a world of such seemingly random chaos.

Sometimes my feelings are so strong they terrify me. But I'm grateful for the terrifying feelings as well. I've found a kind of beauty in them.

And I can live with these feelings.

I've decided I can live with this.

Epilogue

Szaja Trautman, 34 years | August 5th, 1944

THE BLACK SEA

A few moments before 1:00 a.m., twenty-five miles northeast of Igneada, Turkey
I CARRIED PIETER'S body from the hospital like a stick and piled it in a ditch with a thousand other sticks. This became my job in those last days. We piled them precisely, like railroad ties alongside a track bed.

My mind had already split so many times I knew nothing remained inside my head but tiny bits. I lay down there in the ditch, in the dusk, with the dead Russian soldier Pieter, praying for my own death. I expected the guards to discover and kill me, but the guards had gone on. They had failed to notice my presence in the pile. There is no surprise in this, only an empty acceptance. They wouldn't notice. The guards' eyes crawled away from what is left of our faces—our bones. Without fat and muscle we all looked so similar.

Most of the Jews and other prisoners had been killed or marched away to other camps months before.

There in the ditch, the smell of rotting flesh filled my nostrils. The frozen, muddy earth chilled my body to a numb weightlessness. Time opened and I became lost, but Pieter's voice pulled me back to awareness.

Here, he said.

Pieter's mind remained whole, even after the typhoid delirium, even in death. He could conceive and grow an idea.

He shared his thoughts—at first whispers, then fully-sounded words.

The voice of a man who still craved life.

He spoke directly to me. He knew my name. He knew my family. He knew everything I had forgotten.

We made our deal. In exchange for my body, I let him gather and sort the bits of my mind that remained. He told me he would invent the pieces that had been lost. He would direct my thoughts.

My body is a coffin for my soul, Pieter informed me.

It is his idea to hide his naked body under another's after I had clothed my body in his uniform. He directed me to take off the bandage on his foot and wrap my own. The Russians had butchered Pieter's foot when he defected.

I climbed, with Pieter's whole mind, out of the ditch.

At any second, I expected, I would be shouted at, found out—killed on my way back to the camp hospital in Field II. I waited for the bullets as I found my way, as I entered the hospital door. No bullets came. No one noticed that Pieter's hospital uniform had returned from the pile of sticks.

Then I lay in a moldy hospital bed, listening as the machine guns kill the last of the Jews. Hundreds of starving Jews are shot in those last days. These are the same Jews who had piled the dead bodies of other Jews, the Russian prisoners who are dying of typhus, and the German guards, who started to turn on each other in those last days.

I should have been one of them.

I found Pieter Aleksandrov's name on the papers in his hospital uniform. But I know he may have been another man. Most of the Russian soldiers there in the camp hospital are defectors like me.

War changes a man's name.

It changes like blood congealing, Pieter thought.

Names change, just as allegiances change, during war.

Iberkumen—survival. My father's word. A word from another lifetime. Another past.

But I have no past. Only one goal. Survival.

—•—

I stand on the deck of the Mefkura. On this ship are Jewish refugees, most of them camp survivors and war orphans. I have been free a few weeks.

The Mefkura set off from Constanta. We are headed to Palestine by way of Istanbul.

By way of any means now.

It is past midnight. We are fourteen miles off the coast of Turkey.

I still call myself Pieter.

I am an officer on this ship.

I wear another uniform and hold a position. I have become a Romanian crew-member.

I am fluid as the water we are floating on.

I am thinking what must be done now to survive.

We have mere minutes to save ourselves from the attack.

To my right several officers lower the boat.

The lifeboat.

To the left . . . the stairs lead down to the hold, to the sleeping ones who won't have lifeboats, who don't know what we are about to do.

The ones who don't know what is about to happen.

The boat is life.

I am choosing life, Pieter thinks as I step down the ladder rung by rung.

I help to row now. I am rowing away from death.

I wonder how many strokes to safety.

My heart—no, the place where my heart should be—has phantom pains. My heart lies in a ditch with a thousand sticks. It is beating there still. It could be rescued at another time by another person, but not by me.

This thought makes me want to retch. I do, quietly and swiftly, over the edge of the lifeboat. The officer next to me leans in. "Seasick, eh?"

Isaak. I think the man's name is Isaak.

Is this a Jewish name? Or German?

Save yourself. Save yourself.

Then another voice. A woman's voice.

Save the part of yourself you need to stay alive.

The Mefkura floats on the horizon, a ghostly gray silhouette shimmering in the light of a full moon. How beautiful the ship looks floating there.

There are two more schooner ships somewhere out there, traveling with us on our voyage to the Promised Land.

Two ships also filled with survivors.

I taste bile on my tongue again.

Then it happens.

A flare illuminates the boat beneath the moon. The quiet of the oars' in . . . out . . . shatters.

First the scream.

A piercing scream flies by us and crashes out against the ship with a huge booming and splintering.

The sound of a thousand sticks breaking.

The sight is terrifying. The explosion lights up the shards of boat that are their own missiles now, shooting out in every direction. Firelit and flying, sending arcs of death shooting out into the sea.

The sudden movement of the rowboat.

Geferlekh—too close.

The boat hurtles backward from the blast and blows apart.

Slamming into the back of the rowboat, I feel bones breaking.

In this moment of shattering pain Pieter abandons me. He is, after all, a defector.

I feel the life painfully ripping out of me and imagine I see other, smaller boats around us.

I imagine I see soldiers in them, with their guns.

Then I see nothing.

I hear sounds of machine guns and people screaming.

The SS. They have found me again. I died in the blast. I am back in the camp.

After the confinement of my soul, the bargain made with Pieter, all my survivals through the murders, the pogroms, the work camps, the trains, my imprisonment in Majdanek, and the escape, I am back in the blackness with the SS.

I knew I would be punished for living through those horrors, but this? This is my punishment? My Hell?

Ah, so it is.

Then, I hear nothing.

———

September, 1944, Constanta, Turkey

The smell of something astringent.

Like the tonic my *foter* used to shave many years ago.

Foter.

Maybe I have gone to one of the heavens after all and the SS are the Hell I left.

Idel is my next thought. Where is Idel in this heaven? I am aching to see him.

Idel. I've not thought about you for many years, and the thought of you now breaks my mind apart.

Berl, Ruchel, Sura.

———

Breathe.

I cannot breathe.

You have no need for breath here.

———

Hants.

Soft hands almost touching me. Touching the air above what would be my skin if I am alive. Smoothing the air above my hair.

Whispering.

Whispering what? I cannot hear the words, merely the soft whispering around me.

Ahhhhh. Idel's angel. You finally come. Interesting moment you have picked for my rescue.

I cannot feel my body. Cannot feel the physical. I am experiencing everything in my mind now. Everything that has been stopped, cut, consumed, bottled, bled, stomped, gutted, kicked, pressed upon, slashed.

Foter, you said this slash and burn is important for the survival of the crop. For the good of the inheritors. Slash and burn and there can be new.

I am screaming with the pain without my voice.

Please let me not feel this. It will kill me.

I remember I am already dead.

This is my Hell. To feel again.

———

The smell. The same smell and the whispers.

And the hants.

This time touching more on my body. I can feel these hands on my body and it cannot be an angel touching me there, on my *mi'leh.*

I am in Hell and *sotn* will do what he wants with my privates. Like the boy, Stanoff, with the guards at Majdanek.

No, not that poor boy.

I witnessed the rape of a prisoner and his execution after. I never talked of it to anyone, of course. I had not known men could do this to other men. Would want to do this to another man.

You will not think of this now. You will not think of this again. I am still a virgin. I am thirty-four, but I have never kissed a girl. Simply held a hand.

Eyn hant.

The *hant* of the girl on the train to Lublin.

To the dark place.

They threw me on the cattle train after dark. I'd been beaten and given nothing to eat or drink for days. The only reason I remained standing is the number of people pressing at my shoulders, keeping me from falling to the ground.

She found my hand in the dark on the awful train, and I grasped hers and realized in the midst of a train ride to a place I knew meant death that I had already begun to die.

Perhaps I would be dead when we arrived. Starved or dead of thirst.

Don't think of the thirst.

I kept my mind busy by thinking of the softness of her *hant*.

I stole glances at her face in the moonlight. The curve of her brow, her cheek, her lips. I tried not to stare for fear she might take her *hant* away.

We exchanged names and not much more.

Rinna.

In the morning we arrived in the city of Lublin.

We are separated, the men and women. The women are put into trucks and taken away while the men are marched about a half-mile in orderly rows.

Then I stepped into Hell.

I have not forgotten her face or her *hant*—they gave me a reason to reinvent myself again in the midst of that place, they saved me as surely as the Russian soldier whose life I borrowed in the last days.

The soldier Pieter. The defector. The typhoid-carrying Russian whose clothing is stripped from him in the ditch full of sticks. The soldier whose uniform I traded for my tattered clothing.

Why hadn't I thought to do it sooner? It doesn't work to think these things now. Now I am here in a Hell that smells like my *foter's* hair tonic.

———

The sounds and smells go away again.

I am losing time.

This is what happens when you die. You lose time.

———

I learned when you have lost time, your understanding of time, time finds you, and time tells the truth. Time will find you and give you your truth if you want it.

Time found me in the hair tonic hospital with the angels in white dresses who cared for me as my broken limbs healed. Both hands and arms are in casts and slings. My left leg in traction.

The nurse who spoke Russian told me many bones in my body had been shattered by the blast of the torpedo. My lung collapsed. My eardrums punctured.

I had been in a coma for weeks.

Six surviving crew members and five surviving passengers. Five Jews.

Am I counted as a Jew or an officer? In Turkey, who is it safe to be now? I know I will become whoever it is safe to be.

The angels with white dresses call me Pieter, and so I am named. They found his papers in the shreds of my uniform. The Romanian uniform. They also found the address for my parents in America, which I kept folded in the bottom of my boot.

I am called Pieter. So it is.

There are others in the large hospital room. We sometimes talk to one another. We mutter occasional words between suspicious glances.

We are all hiding from death.

I don't recognize anyone from the Mefkura.

Through the pain medication I receive, the conversation is foreign and fragmented. I hear them say the Russians torpedoed the Mefkura and shot the survivors in the waves with machine guns.

But I know those are German soldiers with machine guns around us in the water, not the Russians. I heard German voices.

———

The captain gave the order to ignore the warning flare and continue sailing.

Why?

He ordered the crew members in the pilothouse to lower a lifeboat and evacuate. No one argued, although we all knew it meant death for the others.

Pieter is present in the pilothouse because of a shift switch with another officer. There is no time to notify anyone else.

The captain's order: "Save yourself." He said this as we loaded into the lifeboat.

If I am not for myself, who will be for me? Hillel's teaching.

It is mere minutes before the Mefkura is illuminated again, then torpedoed.

———

I am told by the nurses that the Jewish survivors have gone. They are taken up by the other ships traveling with us. The Bulbul and the Morina sailed on. They are home now.

Where are we headed? Palestine. The Promised Land.

Yes. This is where Pieter, now a Romanian crewmember, journeyed.

My intention—killing Pieter when I arrived.

I knew no one in Palestine. I could become anyone. I could become a Jew again.

A survivor.

I thought I could become a person with no past.

But now I don't know if I have the strength.

Can I be a person with only a future? What is the future?
It is a man who walks out of a ditch and rescues himself.
How can I be this man?

    Assemble. Assemble.

———

Deep in the middle of a dark night, a night spent fighting German murderers who wear Russian uniforms, a new nurse comes to my hospital bed.

I whisper to her, "My name is Szaja Trautman, but he died in the camp."

    Maybe now he is alive again.

"How can a man live without a heart?" I ask.

    She whispers back, *Iberkumen.*

"But I don't remember what I am surviving for."

At first she is silent; then she leans in close.

    Survive for your family who pray they will see you again;
    survive for all who could not.

Reader's Guide

1. Discuss the relationship between Jules and her grandfather. Do you think he made the best decisions for Wendy and his grandchildren? Have you experienced or known grandparents and grandchildren who are closer to one another than to their children and parents?

2. Are you the child or grandchild of someone like Samuel/Szaja (Jules's grandfather)—someone who has lived through horrible violence? How has that affected your relationship with them? How does the presence of this history affect generations within a family in relation to their ability to connect with one another and form loving relationships within the family and with others?

3. *The Belief in Angels* contains vivid scenes of murder, domestic abuse, drug abuse, and alcoholism. Has reading it altered your perspective on any of these issues?

4. What is the impact of keeping secrets for Samuel/Szaja, Wendy, David, and Jules? How could the revelation of these secrets change their lives? Is there good reason to keep some family secrets?

5. The narrative of *The Belief in Angels* spans a fifty-year time period, from the '20s through the '70s. Discuss the cultural changes that happened in those eras. What are the historical and cultural forces at play in Samuel's refusal to allow Wendy to move back home when she reveals that Howard is abusing her? How about his inability to view art studies as an acceptable college major for Jules?

6. How did you respond to Jules's struggle to take care of her family? How did that influence the way you responded to Wendy? Did your opinion

of Wendy change as you learned more about her? What about the other family members? Who did you relate with most at the beginning? Did your empathy build for another character as the story progressed?

7. Jules has two drug-induced episodes. What happens and what does she take away from each experience?

8. Both Samuel/Szaja and Jules have episodes of dissociative fugues. Describe the way they are triggered and the way it manifests in each of them, keeping in mind the science of mental disorders and the role genetics vs. environment plays in the disorder process.

9. Throughout the story, Jules describes herself as an alien or outsider. In what ways? How does this shift over time? Does her friendship with Leigh and Timothy influence these feelings? What are your experiences of feeling like an outsider?

10. Jules experiences a recurring nightmare. What is the symbolic meaning of the swordfish within the dream? How does the dream shift in relation to Jules's experiences throughout the book? What do you think the shifts within the dreams symbolize?

11. Both Jules and Samuel/Szaja experience moments of profound sadness and isolation. How do they resolve their personal doubts with their spiritual beliefs?

12. Both Jules and Samuel/Szaja experience many moments of angel-like intervention. Where in the novel did you find evidence of this possibility? Have you had experiences that support your belief in divine intervention?

13. If the character Moses were a metaphor, what do you think he would represent in the context of this book?

Acknowledgments

THANK YOU TO Mr. Viden, whose encouragement meant more to me than he could probably imagine. I've kept your words.

Thank you to the late Professor Nadeau for not kicking me out of playwriting class for my bad behavior, for your sage words, and, most of all, for your droll humor.

Thank you to Jane Shepard for telling me not to "give up the sheep" so many years ago. I am passing that encouragement back to you.

Thank you to Delia Taylor, who read the awful beginning things and still loved me.

Thank you to the talented Writers of the Clear Moon: Dan Amato for all his sweetness in the midst of the most gruesome moments of artistic futility and for reminding me about the way a story unfolds; Brian Joyner, who consistently comes to our meetings with structure and purpose, and whose motivation is contagious and inspiring; Stacy Magic, who redirected our intent from finishing to publication; and Phyllis Olins, for your kind support and tenacious notes as a beta reader. You reminded me that I am a storyteller, and you connected me to truth and authenticity, which is the curve I continually crave.

Thank you to Alexis Masters, one of my angels, for choosing me amidst a sea of writers to acknowledge with her scholarship. You inspired me in a terrifically uninspired time and gave me the courage to continue writing.

Thanks to Jan Graham and Robin Wright, who offered me their lovely home to dream and write. Additionally, I would like to express my appreciation for the deliciously unique creations at Eclipse Chocolate Bar and Bistro that I enjoyed during WOTCM meetings and while escaping the heat of our A/C-less bungalow. Many early chapters were also written with the buttery smell of pancakes wafting upwards toward the writer's loft at Claire De Lune while sipping chai lattes and savoring too many freshly baked pastries.

My grateful thanks to San Diego Writers, Ink, which is the ultimate place to create. Thanks to my SDWI teachers, Tammy Greenwood, Drucilla Campbell, and especially Judy Reeves, whose magical muse inspirations are woven into passages of this novel. Judy's book, *A Writer's Book of Days*, has inspired a legion of artists I am proud to join.

Thanks to the incredibly well-connected Liz Morrison, who got me tuned to the Writers, Ink station at the beginning of this book's journey to completion.

My gratitude and thanks to Laurel Corona, whose captivating writing and generous mentoring inspired me to finish . . . and finish . . . and finish again!

Thanks to my fellow writer and superb editorial consultant, Ellen Orleans, for sharing your talents, time, wise suggestions, and encouragement.

Thank you to Holli Berman, Cantorial Soloist in Boulder, Colorado's Congregation Har HaShem, for her kind "rabbinical" help, and for sharing the manuscript with Nanette Mannheimer, whose wisdom and suggestions as a Holocaust survivor and Yiddish speaker were invaluable.

Thank you to my initial editor, Lesley Kellas Payne, who whipped the novel into shape in record time.

Deepest thanks to the She Writes Press team of talented women. Special thanks to Krissa Lagos, my editor, whose kind enthusiasm buoyed me and whose sharp eyes pulled this novel to polished. Thanks to Brooke Warner, my publisher, for her continued, generous, masterful guidance and for being the best coach and cheering squad a writer could ask for. Also, thanks to the Ingram team for your fortunate timing in partnership and support.

Thank you to Kara, my dear friend, who continues to get me there and bring me back, like a soldier.

Thank you to my talented son, Jaime, and my dear family and amazing friends, old and new. Your support has been my reason. I love you.

Most of all, thank you to Jo-El, the sweet love of my life and my chief patron.

About the Author

RAISED ON A tiny, New England peninsula, J. Dylan Yates pursued her BA from the University of Colorado at Boulder.

The Belief in Angels, Dylan's debut novel, was written over the course of many years while she attempted a number of BA-related jobs, including: teaching, corporate training, real estate, nursing, interior design, parenting, and reluctant housewifery.

Dylan's next novel, *Szaja's Story*, focused on the character created in *The Belief in Angels*, invites the reader back to the Ukranian orchards of Szaja Trautman's tragic childhood, tracing his ultimate journey to America via the desperate Ukranian refugee work camps of the '20s, his amazing survival of both the Majdanek death camp and the torpedoing of refugees aboard the Mefkura, and his fascinating experiences in the post-war Parisian couture houses.

Prior to publication, *The Belief in Angels* won the Alexis Masters Scholarship Award at the February 2012 San Francisco Writers Conference.

Dylan worked with Boulder County's Voices for Children program as a CASA volunteer for 15 years and now volunteers with the Big Sister program in San Diego. She lives in San Diego with her partner and a talking cat. Her son, Jaime, is a professional musician.

To arrange a speaking engagement for J. Dylan Yates, please contact jdylanyates @aol.com

Stay in touch: **www.jdylanyates.com.**

SELECTED TITLES FROM SHE WRITES PRESS

She Writes Press is an independent publishing company founded to serve women writers everywhere. Visit us at www.shewritespress.com.

Letting Go into Perfect Love: Discovering the Extraordinary After Abuse by Gwendolyn M. Plano. $16.95, 978-1-938314-74-2. After staying in an abusive marriage for twenty-five years, Gwen Plano finally broke free—and started down the long road toward healing.

Seeing Red: A Woman's Quest for Truth, Power, and the Sacred by Lone Morch. $16.95, 978-1-938314-12-4. One woman's journey over inner and outer mountains—a quest that takes her to the holy Mt. Kailas in Tibet, through a seven-year marriage, and into the arms of the fierce goddess Kali, where she discovers her powerful, feminine self.

Splitting the Difference: A Heart-Shaped Memoir by Tré Miller-Rodríguez. $19.95, 978-1-938314-20-9. When 34-year-old Tré Miller-Rodríguez's husband dies suddenly from a heart attack, her grief sends her on an unexpected journey that culminates in a reunion with the biological daughter she gave up at 18.

Don't Call Me Mother: A Daughter's Journey from Abandonment to Forgiveness by Linda Joy Myers. $16.95, 978-1-938314-02 -5. Linda Joy Myers's story of how she transcended the prisons of her childhood by seeking—and offering—forgiveness for her family's sins.

Americashire: A Field Guide to a Marriage by Jennifer Richardson. $15.95, 978-1-938314-30-8. A couple's decision about whether or not to have a child plays out against the backdrop of their new home in the English countryside.

Warrior Mother: A Memoir of Fierce Love, Unbearable Loss, and Rituals that Heal by Sheila K. Collins, PhD. $16.95, 978-1-938314-46-9. The story of the lengths one mother goes to when two of her three adult children are diagnosed with potentially terminal diseases.

You can help J. Dylan Yates and other authors by spreading the word about a good book on www.Goodreads.com and Amazon.com by signing up and reviewing their books.